MURDER AT LEISURE DREAMS– GALAPAGOS

A GIOVANNA ROGERS MYSTERY

SHARON MARCHISELLO

MILFORD HOUSE

an imprint of Sunbury Press, Inc.
Mechanicsburg, PA USA

MILFORD HOUSE

an imprint of Sunbury Press, Inc.
Mechanicsburg, PA USA

NOTE: This is a work of fiction. Names, characters, places, and incidents either are the product of the author's imagination or are used fictitiously. While, as in all fiction, the literary perceptions and insights are shaped by experiences, any resemblance to actual persons, living or dead, events, or locales is entirely coincidental.

For information about special discounts for bulk purchases, please contact Sunbury Press Orders Dept. at (855) 338-8359 or orders@sunburypress.com.

To request one of our authors for speaking engagements or book signings, please contact Sunbury Press Publicity Dept. at publicity@sunburypress.com.

FIRST MILFORD HOUSE PRESS EDITION: June 2025

Set in Adobe Garamond Pro | Interior design by Crystal Devine | Cover by Angeleen Hill | Edited by Gabrielle Kirk.

Publisher's Cataloging-in-Publication Data
Names: Marchisello, Sharon, author.
Title: Murder at Leisure Dreams – Galapagos / Sharon Marchisello.
Description: First trade paperback edition. | Mechanicsburg, PA : Milford House Press, 2025.
Summary: Giovanna Rogers manages a new resort in the Galapagos. When renowned documentary producer Claire Costello and her film crew arrive for the grand opening, Giovanna welcomes Claire with a bottle of champagne. The next morning, the VIP guest is found dead of poisoning. Giovanna and her police detective boyfriend, Victor, must solve the case while juggling details of the opening. But things keep getting worse.
Identifiers: ISBN : 979-8-88819-301-3 (paperback).
Subjects: FICTION / Crime | FICTION / Mystery & Detective / General | FICTION / Mystery & Detective / International Crime & Mystery.

Designed in the USA
0 1 1 2 3 5 8 13 21 34 55

For the Love of Books!

To my loving husband, Michael,
who puts up with my writing addiction
and is still waiting for the money
to start rolling in.

ACKNOWLEDGMENTS

Thank you to Luci Zahray, "the poison lady," who answered my numerous questions about physostigmine, the poison found in the manzanillo tree, the only toxic plant in the Galapagos. Any errors or flawed assumptions are my own.

I'm also grateful to my many critique groups who read this manuscript from its inception, chapter by chapter, and offered valuable feedback: the Atlanta Writers Club Renegades, the Peachtree City Writers Circle, the Hometown Novel Writers group, and my morning Sisters in Crime Zoom writing buddies: Angela Costa, Linda Sands, and Liz Tully. And of course, my beta readers: Donna Black, Ann Michelle Harris, Paul Lentz, Brett Nichols, and Darija Pichanick.

I'd also like to thank the team at Sunbury Press—Gabrielle Kirk, Crystal Devine, and Angeleen Hill—for their great work on editing, formatting, and cover design in order to bring this book to life.

I never could have written a story set in the Galapagos without having visited this fascinating archipelago. I hope we will preserve its unique wildlife and habitat for future generations to appreciate. And I apologize to the people of Ecuador and the Galapagos for any facts I may have gotten wrong.

Chapter One

Early Wednesday morning, Leisure Dreams Resort,
Santa Cruz Island, Galapagos

Breathless, Giovanna Rogers collapsed against her king-size down pillow. She smiled into Victor Zuniga's chocolate-brown eyes as he hovered above her, also breathing heavily.

When he returned her smile, a dimple formed on one smooth cheek, highlighting the small, dark mole that might be called a beauty mark on a woman. She never tired of gazing at his camera-worthy face. Gently, he pushed a long strand of brown hair off her forehead and lowered his face to kiss her. His lips were tender and hungry at the same time.

She freed her arm from the twisted Egyptian cotton sheet and wrapped her slim legs around his again, running her fingers through his thick black hair, unable to get enough of him.

The phone on her bedside nightstand rang. Giovanna groaned.

Victor pulled back to prop himself on an elbow and raised an eyebrow.

The ringing continued.

With a sigh, she reached for the phone. As manager of the new Leisure Dreams—Galapagos resort, she could never be truly off duty. She'd moved 2500 miles from her home in Georgia for a fresh start, and there was no way she could shirk her responsibilities. After her devastating business failure last year, she now had a chance to redeem herself in the corporate world.

On the third ring, she picked up. "*Hola.*"

"Señora Rogers!" The panicked voice belonged to her assistant, twenty-three-year-old Belinda Chavez, newly promoted from a front-desk job at the Quito property. Perky little Belinda tried hard to please, but sometimes she needed more direction than Giovanna normally provided.

"What?" Giovanna tried not to sound like she'd been roused from a passionate embrace. "Is something wrong?"

"It's . . . it's . . ." A sob swallowed the rest of the caller's words.

"Belinda, what is it?" Giovanna threw Victor a grimace as he nuzzled her neck and then extricated himself from the rumpled bedding. She admired his muscular, bronze body as he climbed out of bed and scooped up scattered items of clothing.

Belinda's voice quavered. "Señora Costello. In the Tio Armando suite."

Giovanna rose to a sitting position, one hand on the phone and the other splayed across her naked chest. "Did you deliver the bottle of champagne to her room last night? With the welcome package?" Claire Costello, a world-renowned documentary producer, had chosen the hotel as her base while shooting a nature film in the Galapagos, and the CEO had asked the team to roll out the VIP treatment.

More sobs.

"Belinda, what's wrong? Jim Roberts and all the corporate bigwigs will be here tomorrow for our grand opening." At age twenty-six, Giovanna was one of the youngest managers in the Leisure Dreams international resort chain, and she had a lot to prove. Everything must be perfect. A disgruntled celebrity guest was the last thing she needed.

"Señora Costello, she's—" Another sob drowned the rest of Belinda's sentence.

"Belinda, please don't cry. Tell me what happened with señora Costello. Whatever it is, we can fix it." Giovanna cast her eyes helplessly at Victor, wishing they could crawl back under the covers together, but knowing the mood had been shattered.

"*Señora Rogers, Claire Costello está muerta.*"

Giovanna almost dropped the phone. Restoring her grip on the receiver, she pressed it closer to her ear. "Claire Costello is dead?"

Victor froze, a sock dangling from his hand. He stared at Giovanna, brow creased, and mouthed the word, *dead.*

"*Dios mío,* she's ice cold." Switching to her native Spanish, Belinda bantered on.

Giovanna was slowly learning Spanish, thanks to Victor and several language apps, but she couldn't make out anything else her assistant was saying. "Slow down, Belinda. Are you sure? Have you called an ambulance?" She glanced at Victor, who was making urgent gestures. "*La policia?*"

"No, señora, I called you first. I will call the police now."

Giovanna eyed Victor. "I'll call the police."

An awkward silence ensued. "Señora Rogers, is Detective Zuniga with you?"

Giovanna had never made an effort to hide from her staff her budding relationship with Detective Victor Zuniga—her glowing face probably gave her away—but she saw no need to broadcast his comings and goings. "I'll notify him. In the meantime, make sure no one else goes into that room. Do you understand?" She glanced at Victor, and he nodded.

"*Claro, señora*. No one goes in."

Giovanna hung up the phone and scooted back against the padded headboard, drawing her knees to her chest. Some of the color had drained from her olive face. She stared at Victor. "You heard? My first VIP guest is dead."

Fully dressed, he crossed the room to sit beside her. "Tell me what happened."

She shook her head. "Belinda found her. That's about all I could understand."

He stroked her thigh. "You must be in shock."

Nodding, she covered his hand with hers.

"I have to go check this out." He tucked a strand of hair behind her ear and stood.

She rose from the bed, and he held out her lace-covered bra. "*Mi reinita*."

Smiling at his pet name for her, "my little queen," she slipped her arms into the bra, turned, and let him fasten it for her, his gentle hands warm against her bare back. "I'm coming with you."

CHAPTER TWO

Wednesday morning, Leisure Dreams Hotel

Giovanna resisted the urge to cling to Victor while they hurried down the marble-tiled hallway. She finished buttoning her blouse, tucked the tails into her loose khaki pants, and clipped her long, brown hair into a messy ponytail. The smell of fresh paint from the peach-tinted plaster walls tickled her nose.

They reached Claire's Tio Armando suite, the best guest room in the new hotel. All on a single floor, the suites were named after key locations or iconic animals found on the islands. Tio Armando, once thought to be the last surviving member of the Floreana subspecies, was one of the most famous of the Galapagos giant tortoises.

Giovanna had expected to find Belinda guarding the door, but her young assistant was nowhere to be found. At least the room was locked, and the *Do Not Disturb* sign hung on the handle.

With her master keycard, Giovanna opened the heavy mahogany door.

Victor inspected the wooden jamb and the floor around the entrance. "No sign of forced entry," he murmured. He took a few photos with his cellphone, and she started inside.

He held up his hand. "Better stay back here. We don't know what we're walking into, and if there's been a crime, we can't contaminate the scene."

Giovanna waited by the door as Victor entered the suite, eyes roving, absorbing every detail. The living room resembled a photograph in the upscale design magazine, *Architectural Digest*. Aluminum-framed paintings of seascapes by local artists decorated the walls, subtly complementing the pastel colors in the upholstered furniture.

On the glass coffee table, an open bottle of champagne rested in a stainless-steel ice bucket surrounded by an expanding ring of water dripping onto the marble floor. Two crystal flutes, one partially filled, stood upright. Next to the champagne sat a bowl of fresh fruit. A banana peel had been folded across the rim of the bowl, and a partially peeled orange, with several sections missing, perched on top of the pile.

As Giovanna moved closer to the coffee table, Victor wagged his finger. "Don't touch anything."

"One of the glasses has lipstick on it." The vivid coral shade caught her eye.

He leaned closer to the table and narrowed his gaze. "You're right." Centering the viewfinder and zooming in, he shot another photo.

He headed toward the bedroom, and Giovanna followed. A sickly sweet-and-sour stench of alcohol-tinged vomit permeated the air, growing stronger as they neared the chamber.

"Stop." Victor held out his hand to keep Giovanna back.

She froze, suppressing a scream that escaped as a whimper.

The middle-aged woman Giovanna presumed was Claire Costello lay sprawled across the teal sheets, her mouth fixed in an expression of anguish, partially covered by a lock of bright auburn hair. Now dried and crusted, a white fluid had leaked down her chin. Her glassy eyes stared blankly from a blue-gray face.

Victor touched Giovanna's shoulder to steady her. With his other hand, he snapped a photo with his cellphone and then punched a speed-dial button.

Giovanna clung to Victor's arm and pressed her face against his shoulder.

Phone still in hand, he pulled her head to his chest as he spoke into the mouthpiece in rapid Spanish.

Giovanna couldn't make out most of the words, but she figured he was calling for the forensic team.

The door to the suite opened.

Giovanna lifted her head from Victor's shoulder and took a step toward the bedroom entrance.

Belinda, dressed in a neatly pressed beige business suit, her dark hair pinned into a tight bun, carried a tray and a rag.

Giovanna opened her mouth, but before she could emit a word, Belinda picked up the two champagne glasses, set them on the tray, and then reached for the bucket.

"No!" shouted Victor as he ended his call and rushed out of the bedroom.

Startled, Belinda dropped the tray. The glasses crashed to the floor, shattering against the marble tile. The bottle tumbled from the bucket, spilling champagne and melted ice into a puddle at her feet.

"Belinda!" Giovanna held her tongue to squelch the unkind words forming in her thoughts. *So much for lifting any fingerprints.*

Belinda clasped her hand to her mouth. "I'm sorry!"

Victor tightened his lips and waved his arms at the two women. "*Vamanos.*"

CHAPTER THREE

Wednesday morning, Leisure Dreams Hotel

"*Pues . . .*" Belinda's brown eyes watered, still wide with fear. "*Dios mío*," she murmured, making the sign of the cross.

"That might have been evidence." Giovanna stared at her assistant. "What else did you clean up?"

"Nothing else, señora." Belinda trembled.

"It's done." Victor touched Giovanna's shoulder as they proceeded down the hall. "Our team will figure out what happened."

The three descended the wide marble and glass staircase that wound in a gentle curve from the floor of guest rooms to the spacious lobby. The chandeliers sparkled in the morning's brilliant sunshine filtering through the tall windows, starkly contrasting the gloom Giovanna felt from the death in her hotel.

"I need coffee." She looked at Victor and Belinda. "Anyone else?"

Both nodded, and Giovanna signaled a waitress en route to the Isabela restaurant. Although the hotel was not officially open, its restaurant had been doing a booming business with the locals for several months.

She held up three fingers, made a circle in the air to include herself and her companions, and pointed toward a secluded seating area in the lobby. "*Por favor, señorita, tres cafés.*" She smiled at Victor for approval. "*Con lait . . .lech . . .*"

Victor grinned. "*Con leche.*"

Belinda suppressed an amused smile and told the woman. "*Café solo para mí. Sin leche.*"

Giovanna abandoned her attempt to practice Spanish in front of Belinda and turned to the waitress. "Just bring us three black coffees and a little pitcher of milk for me." The Leisure Dreams chain catered to an English-speaking clientele, and the staff had been trained to communicate proficiently. Nevertheless, her lack of fluency in the local language made her self-conscious. Revealing this flaw sparked speculation that she had obtained her position through a family relationship with the CEO. Or perhaps because of what had happened to her here last year, while the hotel was still under construction.

With few guests, the lobby was deserted. The three seated themselves on the soft leather furniture; Victor took an armchair, leaving the women the nearby couch. Giovanna wished she'd had time to shower. If only she could stand in a stream of hot water and let it wash away that alcoholic vomit smell, let it wake her from the nightmare of seeing a guest dead in her hotel. But there was no time. Once the police team arrived, the staff would be buzzing, and she'd have to do damage control.

"Belinda," Victor began. "Tell me about finding señora Costello. What made you go to her room?"

Belinda burst into another round of tears.

Giovanna studied her young assistant, who was not usually so emotional. *Why the waterworks?*

Victor cast a commiserating glance at Giovanna while they waited for the sobs to subside.

The server brought the coffee. Giovanna doctored hers with a generous portion of milk. The others used sugar.

Belinda took a drink and looked up. Victor's eyes lingered on her face. She cleared her throat and set down her cup. With the back of her hand, she wiped her eyes. "Señora Costello asked for a wake-up call at five-thirty this morning. I phoned several times, but there was no answer. So, I went to her suite." Belinda's eyes flitted from the detective to her boss. "I knocked on the door. No answer. I listened for the shower. When there was no sound of movement, I used my master keycard. And then . . ." She looked down. "I found her."

Giovanna frowned. She wasn't pleased that her assistant had let herself into a guest's room, but obviously, something had been wrong.

Belinda buried her face in her hands.

"What did you do then?" asked Victor. "Did you touch anything?"

Belinda shook her head and looked at Giovanna. "I called you."

"And then what?" Victor asked.

"I went back to work. Señora Rogers told me she'd call the police." Despite her distress, the hint of a smirk crept over Belinda's face, a look that insinuated she knew there was a police detective already on the premises, in her manager's bed.

Giovanna caught the smirk but chose to ignore it. "You were supposed to make sure no one went into that room."

"The door was locked."

"But you came back to the Tio Armando suite," Victor said. "Why?"

Belinda bit her lip. "I thought I should clean up."

"Don't you ever watch those crime shows on TV?" Giovanna exploded. "You're not supposed to touch anything! You certainly don't 'clean up' unless you have something to hide."

Victor shot Giovanna a sharp look and turned back to Belinda. "Why did you pick up the champagne glasses?"

Belinda's eyes watered again. "I knew not to disturb the b . . . body. But I didn't think tidying up the living room would make a difference. People would be coming in, investigating her death. I wanted the place to be neat, worthy of the Leisure Dreams brand."

Her borderline mocking emphasis on "Leisure Dreams brand" was not lost on Giovanna. Most of the communications they received from the corporate office preached the importance of maintaining their *brand*, and Giovanna had instilled those values in her staff.

"Can you check if Claire had any visitors last night?" Victor glanced at the photo on his phone. "It looks like she shared a glass of champagne with someone."

"No visitors that I know of." Belinda sounded almost too certain.

"Were you here when she checked in?" he asked. "I assume she wasn't traveling alone."

Belinda nodded. "She arrived with several people, but I don't know if she met with any of them after everyone got their keycards."

"Who delivered the champagne?" asked Victor. "They could tell us if Claire was in the room at the time, and if anyone was with her."

"I delivered it myself." Belinda straightened her shoulders. "And the only fingerprints I destroyed on those glasses were my own."

CHAPTER FOUR

Wednesday morning, Leisure Dreams Lobby

Victor tapped his chipped front tooth with his thumbnail and scrutinized Belinda. "What do you mean? Were you the one who shared a glass of champagne with Claire Costello?"

Tucking her neck into her shoulders like a frightened tortoise, Belinda nodded.

"You were on duty last night as well as this morning?" His eyes shifted from Belinda to Giovanna.

"Belinda's been staying at the hotel all week to help me get ready for the grand opening," Giovanna explained, taking another sip of her coffee.

"Did you know señora Costello before she arrived at Leisure Dreams?" Victor eyed the assistant manager.

"No. I've seen some of her documentaries, and I wanted to meet her." With a glance at Giovanna, Belinda defended herself. "When I brought the champagne, Claire . . . uh, señora Costello insisted I come in and chat. I only had a few sips, I swear. To be polite. To please our guest." She looked at her boss. "I don't even like champagne. It tasted awful, and I felt nauseated later."

Victor's brow furrowed. "You think something was wrong with the champagne?"

"Oh, no, that's not what I'm saying. Señora Costello seemed to enjoy it. She even poured herself a second glass."

And now she's dead, thought Giovanna, fighting her own wave of nausea. *What if there was something wrong with our champagne?*

"Did you open the champagne?" asked Victor.

Belinda shook her head. "They opened it in the kitchen before I brought it up."

"The bottle was already open?" Giovanna curled her lip. "Why?"

"When I called señora Costello to tell her we had a welcome package for her, she asked if someone could open the champagne."

"But she probably meant for someone to open it in the room," said Giovanna. "People like to hear the cork pop." Her pitch rose, and she forced herself to bring her voice under control. "What if she wasn't ready to drink the champagne right then? And with the bottle already open, anyone could have tampered with it."

"I was afraid the cork would fly across the room if I opened it myself. I didn't want to make a poor impression in front of señora Costello." Belinda hung her head. "And she said she was ready to drink it. I asked Pedro to open the bottle for me."

"Pedro?" said Victor.

"Pedro Lopez is our sous chef," Giovanna explained.

"Did you watch him open the bottle?" asked Victor. When Belinda nodded, he continued, "Did you see any indication of tampering?"

Belinda touched her chest. "I wouldn't have served it if there had been."

"Where's the cork?" asked Victor.

Belinda moved her hand to her mouth. "Pedro threw it away."

"Did señora Costello ask for two glasses?"

"No need. There are already glasses in all of the suites," replied Belinda.

Victor located the photo on his phone and showed her the champagne set-up. "Which glass was yours?"

She bent toward the screen and pointed to the almost-full flute. The one without lipstick.

Victor thanked her and put his phone away. "What was señora Costello's mood like? Did she seem worried about anything?"

"Not really. She said she had an important interview today." Belinda sucked her lip. "Oh, and she received a phone call while I was in her room."

"A phone call?" Victor nodded at Giovanna, and she made a mental note to check the hotel's record of incoming calls. "What time?"

"A little after nine."

"On the hotel phone, or her cellphone?" Giovanna asked.

"Her cellphone."

So much for a clue from the hotel's phone records, thought Giovanna. *But the police can get the number from her cellphone.*

"Who called?" asked Victor.

"She didn't tell me, but I heard an angry male voice through the line. I couldn't make out what he said, but he upset her. She chugged the rest of her champagne and poured herself another glass."

"Was she speaking English or Spanish to this caller?" Victor asked.

"Spanish. Quite good, too."

He frowned. "Probably someone local then. Do you think this person threatened her?"

Belinda shrugged again. "I don't know, but her mood changed. I never thought she'd kill herself, though."

Giovanna set her coffee cup onto the glass table harder than she'd intended. "Kill herself?"

"Well, yes. Didn't señora Costello commit suicide? I thought it was obvious."

Victor eyed Belinda. "What do you mean? How would you know?"

"I guess it could have been an accident. Looked like an overdose to me," Belinda said. "I've seen that before."

Flinching, Giovanna studied her young assistant, surprised at her knowledge of overdoses. There was a lot she didn't know about Belinda, but now wasn't the time to probe.

"It's too soon to say what caused her death," Victor cautioned.

Belinda's eyes grew wide. "You mean someone might have killed her?"

Victor nodded. "We can't rule out homicide."

Belinda crossed herself. "*Dios mío.*"

Giovanna turned to Belinda. "What will señor Roberts say about the death of our VIP guest? He and his family are arriving tomorrow for the grand opening on Friday."

"Señor Roberts," Belinda began. She stared past Giovanna. "Señor Roberts arrived last night."

As if on cue, CEO Jim Roberts came down the grand staircase and sauntered into the lobby.

CHAPTER FIVE

Wednesday morning, Leisure Dreams Hotel

Jim Roberts, CEO of Leisure Dreams, was also the face of the resort chain's advertising. Late-forties, ruggedly handsome, with a full head of salt-and-pepper hair, he exuded confidence. He could turn his public relations smile on and off like a flashlight. When Giovanna first met him and his family, she'd thought he might be a dentist because of his perfect set of pearly whites. Everyone in the Roberts family had beautiful teeth.

Giovanna stood when she saw him. She hoped her friendship with the CEO was not too obvious to the staff, lest they think she hadn't earned her position strictly on merit.

Belinda and Victor followed her lead.

"Giovanna, how goes it?" Jim pumped her hand, flashing that toothy smile.

"Sir, we have a problem."

Before Giovanna could explain further, police officers and crime scene investigators swarmed the lobby.

"Excuse me." Victor strode toward his colleagues.

Jim's smile faded and his eyes followed the detective. "What are the police doing here?"

Giovanna gestured toward the officers. "We had a death—"

Before she could complete her sentence, Jim had joined Victor and inserted himself into the group of officers and technicians.

Sitting back down to finish her coffee, Giovanna looked at Belinda. "When did señor Roberts get here?"

"Last night, while you were out for dinner." She tilted her head toward Victor.

"Why didn't you call me? You knew I wasn't expecting the CEO until tomorrow."

Belinda eyed the spot Victor had just vacated. "You were busy."

Giovanna felt her cheeks grow hot, uncomfortable that her love life was under scrutiny by her staff. Had someone seen their passionate kiss in the hallway? Had Belinda or the maids been listening at the door? "You could have sent me a text or left a message that the boss had arrived." *Is she trying to sabotage me? So she can be promoted into my position?*

"I'm sorry, señora." Belinda's eyes shifted downward.

"Did señor Roberts talk to Claire last night?"

Belinda shrugged. "I thought he was going to. He knew she was here."

Giovanna watched the investigators tromp up the grand staircase toward the guest suites. Victor led; Jim trailed behind the group. The few employees in the area stopped their work to stare after them.

The women sipped their coffee in silence.

"Señora?"

Giovanna raised her eyebrows.

"Could señor Roberts have—?" Belinda's lip trembled.

"No way." Giovanna shook her head vigorously.

The lobby's revolving glass door began to move, ejecting a tall, dark-haired woman in knee-length khaki shorts accentuating her long, tanned legs. Laurel Pardo, an independently wealthy Ecuadorian-American tortoise researcher, worked at the Charles Darwin Research Station in nearby Puerto Ayora. Laurel was Giovanna's closest friend on the island. The two had met on a cruise of the Galapagos archipelago the previous year, the same one where she'd met the Roberts family, which ultimately led to her position at Leisure Dreams.

"Laurel," Giovanna called, waving her over.

Laurel crossed the lobby. Giovanna rose, and they shared the customary cheek kiss. At first, she'd found air-kissing female acquaintances awkward, but now she accepted the ritual as part of being a gracious hostess and friend, part of fitting in. Belinda likewise rose and exchanged cheek kisses with Laurel.

"What's with the cop cars outside?" Laurel gestured toward the front door. "One officer didn't want to let me through."

"Let's go into my office where it's quiet." Giovanna led Laurel toward a corridor behind the main lobby. "Belinda, please draft a statement we can send to the rest of the staff. After I approve the English version, I'll need you to translate it into Spanish."

"Statement?" Laurel followed Giovanna into her office. The room projected comfort and professionalism, with modern furnishings and a view of sunshine sparkling invitingly in the pool's sky-blue water.

Giovanna rounded her mahogany desk and pulled out her leather swivel chair. "I didn't know you were coming by."

"I'm a little early for my interview with one of your guests. Claire Costello."

Giovanna almost missed the seat. "Claire—"

"She's doing a documentary about giant tortoises, featuring Tio Armando." Laurel sat down in one of the cushioned side chairs. "I met her when she worked with my father on a film project. Claire can be a royal pain in the ass, but she does good work."

"Laurel—"

Her friend consulted her watch. "I don't know why I expected Claire to be on time. She can be such a diva."

"Laurel." Giovanna wriggled in her chair. "Claire Costello is dead."

CHAPTER SIX

Wednesday morning, Leisure Dreams Hotel

Giovanna watched Laurel's expression change from mild irritation to absolute shock.

"Claire's dead?" Laurel gripped the arm of her chair. Her eyes flitted around the brightly painted walls of Giovanna's office as if tracing the path of a moth. "But she can't be. I just talked to her last night. What happened?"

"How did you talk to her last night?" asked Giovanna. "In person, or over the phone?"

"She called me. To set our meeting for this morning. I told her the afternoon would be better, but she said it couldn't wait. So, I rearranged my schedule."

"Did she say why it couldn't wait until afternoon?"

"You don't know Claire. Everything has to be her way, on her time. Excuse me, *had*." Laurel kneaded her forehead. "Wow, I can't believe this."

"How did Claire sound?" Giovanna's eyes strayed to her computer, which was already on. Belinda must have been working in here earlier.

"Do you mean was Claire depressed? No way." Laurel leaned forward. "Do they suspect suicide?"

"Did she have any enemies?" An email notification popped up on Giovanna's computer, and she resisted the urge to open it.

Laurel shook her head. "Wait. Someone killed her?"

Giovanna watched another message enter her inbox. More details about the upcoming grand opening were screaming to be handled. "The police haven't ruled out anything."

Laurel fingered the ends of her long, thick braid. "Claire asked me not to discuss our interview with Jim Roberts."

"Why not?"

"You know how controlling he is." Laurel grimaced. "She was probably worried he'd want to edit everything, to make sure he and the company appear in the best possible light. Make it more about the resort's grand opening than my research."

Giovanna nodded. "Turn a documentary into an advertisement?"

"Exactly." Laurel peered at her watch again. "I should go. We have a new volunteer starting today, and I'm in charge of training him." She rose and opened the door, then turned back to her friend. "Gosh, what's this going to mean for your opening ceremonies? Will you have to postpone?"

Giovanna thought about all the construction delays, staffing issues, and corporate pressure she'd faced over the past several months. All the regulations involved with building a hotel in a remote region comprised of 97% protected parklands. A UNESCO heritage site, the Galapagos contained thousands of unique animal and plant species, some of them endangered. And now there had been a mysterious death on her watch. Her stomach churned. "The police are here now, investigating the scene, so we'll see what they say. But I think you should stay; they'll want to ask about your conversation with Claire last night." Her desk phone rang; with a glance at the caller I.D., she let the call go to voicemail.

Laurel sat back down. "Guess I'm not going anywhere. I'm sure Victor's looking forward to talking with me."

Giovanna gave a tight-lipped smile.

Last year, she'd reported her friend missing after a snorkeling excursion. Laurel's hasty "disappearance" from their cruise ship had created panic and a search for a potential drowning victim, all because she hadn't told Giovanna she was leaving. Victor blamed Laurel for the wasted resources.

* * *

Jim Roberts hovered at the entrance to the Tio Armando suite while the crime scene investigators inspected the body and gathered evidence. "What's the cause of death?"

"Please, señor Roberts, let us do our jobs." Extending both arms, Victor struggled to keep the taller man from coming in and contaminating the scene. "We'll tell you what we find as soon as possible."

"Well, did she leave a note?" Jim craned his neck toward the bedroom where Claire's body lay. "This makes no sense." He cast his eyes down the empty hallway. "Guests will arrive soon. What are they going to think?"

Captain Juan Estevez, Victor's boss, stomped over. The stocky, middle-aged officer with thinning hair directed an onslaught of Spanish at Victor. He turned to Jim, forcefully pointing at the door. "Out! *Señor.*"

Victor touched Jim's arm. "Señor Roberts, let's leave the investigators to finish their work. Can we go to the manager's office and talk?"

With a grunt, Jim followed Victor into the hallway. "My grand opening is in two days. This needs to go away."

Victor's dark eyes blazed. "Señor, a woman is dead on your property, under puzzling circumstances. This will go away when the case is resolved."

Jim was silent on the walk downstairs to Giovanna's office. They passed through the lobby and entered a side hallway.

Giovanna's door was open, and she was talking to . . . *Who's that? Laurel Pardo?* Victor groaned. He hoped Laurel was not involved in this situation, but he had a feeling she was connected. *Of course.*

"I don't want to disturb Giovanna; she has too much going on," said Jim as they passed her office. The CEO ushered the detective into an empty office, closed the door, and took a seat behind the desk. Victor moved a chair to position himself directly across, not intimidated by the CEO's power move.

Jim leaned back in the swivel chair. "How can I help you, Detective?"

"Do you mind if I record this?" Victor took Jim's nonresponse as a *yes* and pressed the record button on his phone. As a backup, he retrieved a notepad from his pocket. "Let's start with last night. What time did you arrive at the hotel?"

"You'll have to ask my driver; I don't remember. Jet lag and all that. There's a time difference, you know."

"Between Puerto Ayora and Dallas? I think they're in the same time zone."

Jim waved his arms. "I was in Honolulu and Los Angeles earlier in the week, and Europe the week before that. Can't keep track. But it was almost dark when we arrived."

"Who was your driver?"

"Miguel Ruiz, my head groundskeeper."

Victor jotted the name on his notepad. "Is Miguel on duty today?"

"You'll have to ask the staff."

Victor continued to write. "Was Claire Costello already at the hotel when you arrived?"

"I assume so, but you'll have to ask the staff what time she checked in." Jim shifted in his seat and rolled closer to the desk.

"Did you see señora Costello last night? Or speak to her?"

"No," said Jim. "I ordered a sandwich and a scotch from room service, handled a few emails, and then went to bed. I told Belinda I didn't want to be disturbed."

Victor took more notes. "Giovanna wasn't expecting you until tomorrow. Why did you decide to come earlier?"

"I wrapped up my meetings at headquarters sooner than planned, which gave me more time to devote to the grand opening here."

"You arranged for a driver from the hotel to pick you up, but you didn't tell Giovanna, the hotel manager, you were arriving early?" Victor knew Giovanna to be a detail-oriented person, and she would have wanted to prepare for the CEO's change in plans. He'd only been able to persuade her to take yesterday off because everything seemed under control.

"I called the hotel, and her assistant said Giovanna was out all day." Jim eyed Victor. "With *you*. There was no need for her to come back on my account, which I suspect she would have done." He rocked forward in the chair. "Listen, Detective, I know the two of you are dating, and it's fine with me. You'll give Giovanna an incentive to stay here for a while. She's doing a great job, and I want her happy, not homesick for the States. That happens too often with my expatriate managers."

Victor figured Jim had intended a compliment, but he'd also made him feel like a gigolo, which left a bad taste in his mouth. He rose. "Thank you for your cooperation, señor Roberts. We'll try to conduct our investigation as discreetly as possible." He put his hand on the doorknob. "I'll need a list of everyone who was on duty last night, as we'll have to interview them. I trust you're okay with that?"

"Of course. I'll help in any way I can." Jim flashed his public relations smile.

Victor showed himself out of the office. Giovanna looked up from her conversation with Laurel and beamed as he walked by. Gazing at his girlfriend's smiling face instead of looking straight ahead, he almost collided with Belinda.

"*Permiso*," they said simultaneously.

Recovering, he asked Belinda, "Can I trouble you for a list of everyone who was working here last night?"

"Certainly, Detective." She turned back toward the lobby.

"Wait, Belinda." Victor held up his hand. "What about the other hotel guests? Did anyone check out this morning?"

"No. The ones who are here now are staying for the opening."

"Can you get me the names of the people who were traveling with Claire Costello? I'll need to speak with them too."

"Sure, Detective."

"One more thing," said Victor before she could walk away. "When Claire and her team checked in, did you notice any tension or animosity among them?"

Belinda puckered her lower lip. "None that I can remember. Señora Costello spoke sharply to them, but they acted like they were used to it."

"Has anyone told them about señora Costello's death?" Victor asked.

"They probably don't know, unless one of them walked by the Tio Armando suite this morning and saw the police activity."

"Did anyone besides Claire Costello get a keycard to that room?"

Belinda narrowed her eyes in thought. "Her assistant, Susie Southworth."

Victor jotted down the name and then leaned into Giovanna's office. He could tell she'd been listening to his conversation with Belinda. "Will one of you gather Claire Costello's people for a meeting?" He looked at Giovanna. "Can we use the conference room?"

"We're on it," said Belinda, still in the hallway. "I'll go open it now."

As soon as Belinda had gone, Victor eyed Laurel, who'd been staring at her phone during the entire exchange. "Laurel Pardo," he said. "Imagine finding you here."

"Laurel was supposed to meet with Claire this morning." Giovanna gestured toward her friend. "About the documentary she was making."

Victor raised an eyebrow. "So, you knew Claire Costello?"

"I didn't realize that was a crime, Detective."

"I have a few questions." He nodded at Giovanna and motioned Laurel toward the door. "Shall we?"

Laurel rose to her full five-foot-ten, towering over Victor by an inch, and followed him to the conference room.

CHAPTER SEVEN

Wednesday morning, Leisure Dreams Hotel

Laurel sat at the opposite end of the long conference table from Victor.

He set his pocket notebook and cellphone on the polished granite surface. "I can't hear you from way down there." He hated that his status as a police detective made people uneasy. This woman had been particularly evasive in the past, and it appeared he could expect more of the same with this investigation.

She shrugged. "I'm comfortable here."

He held up his phone. "By the way, I'm recording our conversation."

"I'll speak up." Laurel raised her voice several decibels.

"Very well." Victor adjusted his chair and moved closer to the table. Into his phone, he stated the date, time, location, and names of the participants. "Now, Laurel Pardo, you stated you were supposed to meet with Claire Costello this morning. Have you seen her since she arrived in the Galapagos?"

"I'm a suspect? Should I hire a lawyer?"

His finger hovered over the Record button. "Of course, you're entitled to a lawyer, but do you think you need one?"

"Do I?"

Victor sighed. "Just answer the question. Or call your lawyer if you think it's necessary."

"I didn't see Claire, but she and I talked last night. Over the phone. That's when we arranged to meet today."

Victor moved his finger away from the Record button. "Did you call her?"

"She called *me* while I was having dinner with some friends in town. Bahia Mar, in case you want to check." Laurel tilted her chin upward in a passive-aggressive manner.

Victor jotted the name of the restaurant, which he knew well; he'd taken Giovanna there on their first date. Verifying Laurel's story would be easy. "Was Claire at the hotel when you spoke?"

"I believe so. While we were talking, someone came to the door. She excused herself to answer."

"Did she say who it was?"

"Room service. A bottle of champagne and a fruit basket, compliments of the resort. Claire seemed impressed." Laurel flashed a smile that Victor suspected was fake.

"What time was that?"

"Around nine."

Victor made more notes. "What happened after the champagne arrived?"

"I got the feeling someone else was in the room. Claire said she had something important to tell me, but we'd discuss it during our interview." Laurel pushed her long bangs away from her eyes. "Now she's gone, and we'll never know."

"When you spoke, how did she seem?"

"Giovanna asked me that too. I don't think Claire killed herself."

"That's not what I asked."

"Claire didn't seem depressed." Laurel leaned forward. "Do *you* think it was suicide?"

"We haven't ruled out anything yet." Victor scrutinized Laurel's face from down the length of the conference table.

"Like I told Giovanna, I can't see it. But you never know what's going on inside a person's head." She pounded the table with her fist, winced after striking the hard granite surface, then flexed her hand. "Claire was excited about this documentary. It makes no sense if she was going to off herself."

Victor tapped his front tooth with his pencil. "Tell me more about this meeting you were supposed to have with Claire today."

"She wanted to interview me about the Darwin Research Station's tortoise breeding program. Especially concerning Tio Armando." Laurel leaned toward the microphone and spoke more distinctly, as if he'd broached subject matter she cared about. "You know, the giant tortoise formerly thought to be the last survivor of the Floreana subspecies."

"Until *you* found his relatives last year on Isla Isabela." Victor remembered that, initially, the tourist industry had not embraced news that the celebrity tortoise wasn't unique after all. In fact, Laurel had feared for her safety after sharing her discovery.

"Finding other tortoises from the same subspecies was a big part of the story, which I'm always happy to tell." Laurel's eyes lit up as she talked about her work. "But Claire said there was more. And Jim Roberts wouldn't have liked it."

"Why not?"

"I have a feeling he and his company would not have been presented in the most positive light."

"What do you know that would hurt Roberts if it came out in the documentary?"

"Besides the typical corporate greed and political palm-greasing?" Laurel scoffed. "Claire was going to tell me."

CHAPTER EIGHT

Wednesday morning, Leisure Dreams Hotel

By the time Victor finished his interview with Laurel, Belinda had printed a list of the employees who'd been on duty the night before, complete with their schedules for the week. Giovanna had asked the guests traveling with Claire Costello to gather in the conference room at ten.

An ambulance had arrived to take away Claire's body, which would be flown to the mainland for an autopsy. At the CEO's insistence, the vehicle had parked under a tree behind the building, and the gurney carriers used the back entrance.

Victor returned to the Tio Armando suite, where his colleagues worked on the scene. Despite Jim's protests, they had blocked off the entrance with yellow tape. Victor ducked under it.

A gloved officer looked up from gathering shards of glass. "Might have been a struggle here."

"No," said Victor. "The champagne glasses were intact when señora Rogers and I came in. An employee attempted to clean up and dropped the tray with the glasses when we startled her." He pulled out his phone and showed the officer the photo he had taken.

"That's unfortunate. It will be hard to lift any usable fingerprints now." The officer bagged the champagne bottle. "Good thing there are a few drops of liquid left in the bottle."

"I trust that's going to the mainland, too, to be tested for toxins?"

"You bet." He pointed to the fruit bowl on the coffee table, which still contained the banana peel and partially eaten orange. "The fruit too. Looks like she ate some of it."

Victor walked toward the bedroom, where officers were taking pictures and collecting evidence. Seeing a person's death turned into a science project always made him sad. "Did anyone find a note?"

One of the officers held up a crumpled piece of resort stationery. "Found this under the bed, but it looks more like a to-do list than a suicide note. And here's a business card for a boat rental company." He pointed to the desk where a loose-leaf notebook lay open. "Lots of handwritten material in there to go through. And we have her phone. No computer, though."

Captain Estevez came out of the bathroom holding several bottles of pills. "These look like new prescriptions." He turned to Victor. "How did it go with Roberts?"

"Said he got in last night and went straight to his room. Didn't talk to the victim." Victor and his boss exchanged skeptical glances.

"Of course not. And let me guess, no one can vouch for his whereabouts?"

"He left instructions that he not be disturbed." Victor gave Estevez a wry smile. This was not Jim Roberts's first involvement in one of their investigations.

"Wonder what other 'instructions' he gave. I don't trust that man," said Estevez.

"We have to be careful with him," Victor warned. Not only did Jim have powerful, far-reaching connections, he was Giovanna's boss.

* * *

The three people who had traveled to the Galapagos with Claire Costello assembled in the conference room with Giovanna and Victor. The two tall men appeared to be in their late thirties; the petite woman in her early twenties. As they entered, each gazed appreciatively at the framed wildlife photos adorning the walls: a breaching humpback whale, a frigatebird in mid-dive, a marine iguana perched on a rock.

Once they were seated, Giovanna introduced herself and Victor, who broke the news about Claire's death. While he was speaking, she surveyed the audience, gauging everyone's reactions.

Susie Southworth, Claire's perky assistant with white-blond hair and ivory skin, looked too delicate to be traipsing around in the wild on a nature documentary. Her sky-blue eyes watered almost before Victor finished delivering the message.

The surreptitious look that passed between Susie and Claire's sound technician/editor, the preppy, bespectacled Colin Ashton, was not lost on Giovanna. It was the same kind of secret, tender look she found herself exchanging with Victor these past few weeks, ever since they had become intimate. The smile that said, *I see inside your soul.*

Colin shifted his gaze from Susie, wiped his horn-rimmed glasses on the tail of his blue Oxford shirt, and focused on Victor's face as he spoke. His solemn expression did not change at the news of his leader's demise.

Cameraman Tyler Thompson looked like he'd slept in his wrinkled, earth-tone clothes. He ran his fingers through his mop-like brown hair and let out a moan. His dark eyes darted wildly around the room, taking in the reactions of his colleagues.

"I'm so sorry this happened," Giovanna said. "I never got a chance to meet Claire, and I can't imagine what you're going through right now." She studied Claire's colleagues. No one had touched the coffee and pastries she'd provided. Giovanna had no appetite either, and she hadn't even known the victim. "Please let me know if there's anything I can do." She gestured toward the buffet table. "Maybe you don't feel like eating . . ."

Tyler leaned toward the buffet and grabbed a Danish. He ripped it apart and stuffed large chunks into his mouth, shedding crumbs all over the carpeted floor and granite conference table.

Susie rose and poured two cups of coffee. One she flavored with cream and a packet of artificial sweetener, the other with four large tablespoons of sugar. After stirring them both, she handed Colin the coffee syrup and sat back down to sip her beverage.

Cringing at the thought of drinking that sugary concoction, Giovanna nodded toward Victor. "Detective Zuniga needs to ask everyone a few questions." Again, her eyes scanned the room, assessing reactions. "He needs to understand Claire's last movements and state of mind. Also, if any of you know how to reach her family, please tell the detective. She didn't leave an emergency contact when she checked in."

Susie stole another glance at Colin. His eyes met hers, although his expression remained stony. She turned to Giovanna. "I can get you that information."

Victor crooked a finger at Tyler. "Will you please come with me, señor?"

Tyler finished chewing his pastry and rose to follow Victor outside the conference room.

Giovanna smiled at Susie and Colin. "He wants to talk to each person individually, so he'll take you to my office one at a time when he's ready for you."

"We're happy to help," said Colin. With a hint of a southern drawl, he uttered the right words, but his body language projected annoyance.

An awkward silence ensued.

Giovanna felt the need to fill it. And she wanted to learn more about the people who'd been close to her VIP guest. "You must be in shock."

Susie blinked. Her eyes no longer watered.

Giovanna made another attempt at conversation. "How long have you worked with Claire Costello?"

The two looked at each other as if deciding who would speak.

"This is my first overseas project," said Susie. "I've never been outside the U.S. before." She smiled at Colin, a bit too brightly. "Brand new passport."

"Claire and I have been together for about four years." Colin gazed at the wall.

Susie cast her eyes downward. Her smile lost some of its luster.

The way Colin pronounced "together" made Giovanna wonder if his relationship with his boss might have been more than professional. *But what about the intimate vibes with Susie?* "What was Claire like?"

"Demanding." A trace of melancholy seeped into Colin's voice, but his description did not sound negative.

"What will happen to your documentary now? Will you stay and finish it?"

"I don't know," replied Colin. "I can't think that far ahead. I'm still processing the fact that she's gone."

Of course. I'm making things worse for them. Giovanna studied her short fingernails, in need of a manicure before the opening ceremonies.

After an excruciating twenty minutes of chit-chat, Giovanna was relieved to see Victor return with Tyler. The cameraman took another pastry, and Victor beckoned to Susie.

Giovanna smiled at Tyler. "I was just asking these guys how long they'd worked with Claire. And what she was like."

Tyler kept chewing. Just when he'd slowed down and Giovanna thought he would answer, he took another bite.

Colin responded for his colleague. "Tyler was already working with Claire when I joined the team. What's it been now, Big Guy? Ten years?"

The cameraman nodded, his jaws still moving.

Giovanna still felt like she was trying too hard to fill the silence. "Have you ever done a project in the Galapagos before?"

"A few years ago," replied Colin. "We made a documentary about Lonesome George, Tio Armando's predecessor." With a slightly condescending look, he added, "George was the last survivor of the Pinta Island tortoises, and while he was at the Darwin Research Station, he was one of the archipelago's most popular tourist attractions until his death in 2012." When Giovanna acknowledged her awareness of the icon, Colin continued, "That was before Susie joined our team."

Tyler swallowed and gave Colin a deadpan look. "Claire knew about you and Susie."

Giovanna's eyes widened.

CHAPTER NINE

Wednesday morning, Leisure Dreams Hotel

Giovanna and Victor lingered in the conference room after Claire's colleagues had left. They exchanged a companionable smile before he closed his notebook.

"What do you think?" Giovanna asked.

"They weren't much help." He glanced at his watch. "I need to go home and shower, mull over the facts so far."

Giovanna needed to get to her office to finalize last-minute details for the opening events. "Are you coming back later to talk to the night shift? Most of the people on Belinda's list won't be here until after five."

Victor gave her a kiss on the forehead. "Want to have dinner together before I start the interviews?"

She touched his hand, which felt warm and comforting, despite the horror of the morning. "Sounds great. Here in the Isabela restaurant would be easiest. Or we could order room service if you prefer more privacy . . . to talk about the case."

His response was a devilish smile.

"Colin and Susie are having an affair." She spoke in a stage whisper, unnecessary since they were alone in the conference room.

Halfway to the door, Victor stopped. He raised an eyebrow. "How do you know?"

"I can tell by the way they look at each other. The way they act."

"Ah, woman's intuition?" His brown eyes sparkled playfully.

"More than that." She flared her nostrils. "Tyler said Claire knew."

"What does that mean? An off-limits office romance? A love triangle?"

"Maybe there's a company policy against fraternizing at work, and she would have fired them," Giovanna suggested. "Although it doesn't seem like a strong enough motive to kill someone."

"Maybe their affair has nothing to do with Claire's death," Victor said. "But it might explain why they both had shaky alibis."

Giovanna tapped her forehead like a soothsayer. "Let me guess: they each went to bed early? Didn't leave the room all night?"

Victor grinned and resumed walking toward the door. "I'll see you this evening."

After he left, Giovanna picked up the coffee cups and set them on a tray on the credenza for housekeeping. She adjusted the clip on her ponytail and headed toward her office, hoping to restore some normalcy to her day.

Seated at her desk, she logged back into her computer. Emails about the event on Friday required responses, but curiosity trumped her good intentions. She googled Claire Costello.

Giovanna found a website, a Facebook page, a LinkedIn page, even a Wikipedia page, all of which she examined closely. From the pictures, Claire appeared to be a beautiful woman, not surprising for someone who spent much of her career in front of the camera. Her bright auburn hair, creamy peach skin, and unusual chartreuse eyes peering from the screen made a stunning combination. Giovanna shuddered at the contrast with the ghastly corpse she'd seen this morning.

Claire spent her childhood in upstate New York, earned a degree in film and television from NYU, and produced numerous documentaries. Unlike many documentary producers, she often appeared in her films as well as working behind the scenes. According to the birth date in Wikipedia, Claire was almost forty.

Many of her films were listed in IMDb, the movie database. Laurel's father, José Pardo, had produced several nature documentaries with Claire. Laurel received credit as technical adviser and co-writer on one, which had aired on PBS two years earlier.

Giovanna leaned back in her chair. Yes, Laurel and Claire had been well acquainted.

Online gossip magazines published more personal details than Giovanna could find in Claire's professional social media. Rumors linked her romantically with several high-profile celebrities. A brief marriage in her twenties produced a daughter, Lindsey, who had stayed with her father after the divorce.

Giovanna calculated the child's age; she must be a teenager by now. Had Claire kept in contact? She wondered why Claire's husband had been awarded custody and whether there was any resentment. Had Claire's career been too demanding for family life? Giovanna stared past the screen. She knew what it was like to grow up without a mother.

Her eyes strayed to the photo on her desk, taken when she was ten years old, not long before her mother went away. The blue-green eye color she'd inherited from the father she never knew, the heart-shaped face and light olive skin tone from a mother now gone too. She wished she'd been more forgiving, reached out, but she'd been so angry during her teen years. And then it was too late.

With a wistful sigh, Giovanna continued her online search. Newspaper articles covered premieres of films, with pictures of Claire among the guests, always looking regal, polished, and pleased with herself, wearing broad-brimmed hats, surrounded by admiring fans. Her glamourous lifestyle seemed more like a movie star's than that of a typical documentary producer.

An article written about her latest film included a photo of a beaming Claire on the arm of a handsome young man in a tuxedo. Giovanna studied the image more closely. She almost didn't recognize him without his glasses, but the young man in the photo was Colin.

Giovanna skimmed the article, which contained hype about the talented soundman/editor from Alabama, a graduate of Auburn, who had recently won an award for his work on another film. There were complimentary quotes about his abilities from Claire, and the prediction that theirs would be "a long and fruitful relationship."

In addition to a personal Facebook account, there was a professional page, "Claire Costello, documentary producer." It displayed news and postings from Claire's professional life. With Colin on her arm. A lot.

Colin and Claire. No wonder Tyler thought it was a big deal that Claire knew about Colin's affair with Susie.

Giovanna drummed her fingers on the keyboard, so deep in thought she didn't hear Jim Roberts enter her office.

He cleared his throat. "Is everything set for the opening?"

Giovanna quickly navigated to her project management file and retrieved the master schedule. She looked up and smiled. "Coming right along."

"Any issues with the catering?"

She shook her head. "Our restaurant staff is handling it. Everything on your menu has been ordered." Before he could ask, she added, "The music is confirmed. I've booked a great local band. Belinda's taking care of the flowers and decorations."

"Good. And the rooms will be ready?"

"They already are." She made a solemn face. "Except the Tio Armando suite."

He grimaced. Neither needed to say more. "What about—"

"The champagne arrived the day before yesterday. The sommelier inspected the boxes, and everything's in good shape."

"Excellent." Jim's eyes swept the office, which Giovanna had customized with family photos and a watercolor landscape of snow-covered mountains painted by her great-grandmother. "What about the guests' travel arrangements?"

"The corporate travel department made the airline reservations for all the U.S. guests. Belinda worked with Quito to book the Ecuadorian officials." Giovanna looked up from her computer screen. "What about your family? Are Janice and the twins coming?"

"Janice has another doctor's appointment today, and he'll let her know if she's strong enough to travel. Jessy stayed to help her on the flight. Jenny will be here tomorrow."

"Things are looking hopeful, then?" Jim's wife, Janice, had spent the last year recovering from a life-threatening stab wound that had damaged several organs.

Jim's eyes watered. "As well as can be expected. I'm a little worried that coming here will stir up those horrific memories." While the Leisure Dreams hotel was still under construction, Janice and Giovanna had been attacked by Jerome Haddad, a conman from their mutual pasts, whose primary source of income was ripping off charities. When Giovanna exposed his latest scheme, he turned unexpectedly violent, stabbing Janice and kidnapping Giovanna.

Fortunately, Giovanna's physical injuries had only been superficial, and, to do her job, she'd put the trauma behind her. She often wondered if Jim had offered her the position as manager of his new hotel to make up for that tragic experience. She feared seeing Janice again would trigger the nightmare—Jerome's rough hands seizing her body, the knife at her throat, the stuffy trunk of the car—and she half-hoped Janice would decide to stay in Dallas.

"Is your grandmother coming?" Jim asked.

Giovanna brightened. Michelle DePalma, her paternal grandmother, had been a surrogate mother to Giovanna since her pre-teen years. Michelle, as Giovanna had always called her, had taken her on the Galapagos cruise last year where they'd met the Roberts family. "Michelle wouldn't miss it. She loves the Galapagos. And she's bringing Roberto this time."

"Great. I'm looking forward to meeting her husband." Jim walked closer to the desk, to a vantage point where he could peer at the open project plan on Giovanna's computer. "What else?"

"The press."

"Oh, yeah." Jim glanced at the document, but Giovanna had a feeling he wasn't really reading her notes. "We want them here to cover the opening but downplay the . . . unfortunate . . . you know."

"Won't work." Giovanna shook her head. "It's going to be big news, whether we like it or not, so we need to get in front of it." She consulted her watch. "Laurel is friends with Maria Vasquez at the local newspaper. She's probably already told Maria about Claire's death."

Someone knocked on the office door amid the sound of a scuffle.

"Señora, you can't—" protested a female voice.

"Señor Roberts?" Pushing aside the receptionist who had followed her, a stout, dark-haired thirty-something woman, teetering on spike heels and carrying an iPad, barged into Giovanna's office.

"I'm sorry, señor," murmured the retreating receptionist.

The reporter gave a satisfied smile and turned to the CEO. "Señor Roberts? I'm Maria Vasquez from the *Ayora Times,* and I'd like a word with you."

CHAPTER TEN

Wednesday, Leisure Dreams Hotel

Giovanna and her boss exchanged glances. Maria hovered at the office door.

"How can we help you, señora Vasquez?" Giovanna forced a smile.

"What can you tell me about the death here last night?" Maria consulted her tablet. "Claire Costello? An American documentary producer."

Giovanna put on a somber face. "Unfortunately, señora Costello was found dead in her suite early this morning."

Maria typed into her tablet. "Cause of death?"

"Yet to be determined."

"Do they think it was a homicide?"

Giovanna watched the reporter type. "You'll have to ask the police."

"Was there a struggle? Any sign of forced entry?" Maria fired questions leaving little time in between for answers.

"No forced entry that we're aware of. Our hotel is very safe."

Maria raised an eyebrow. "How long had Claire Costello been staying at the resort?"

"She arrived yesterday." Giovanna glanced at the CEO, whose lips remained clamped shut.

"Is it true she flew here to make a promotional video for the grand opening of Leisure Dreams?"

"I'm not—" Giovanna began.

"Claire came to make a nature documentary," Jim interjected. "But I asked her to shoot some promotional footage while the team was here."

When did they have that discussion? Giovanna wondered.

Maria jotted some notes. "She's traveling with a team?"

"Yes," Giovanna replied.

"Who are they?"

"I can't disclose personal information about our guests." Giovanna smiled sweetly.

Maria gave her the side-eye. "Do the police have any suspects in her murder?"

Murder! We don't need the press spreading that kind of rumor. Giovanna narrowed her eyes. "I told you, they've yet to determine the manner of death. You'll have to direct those questions to the police."

"But isn't it true they questioned your staff?"

"They're questioning everyone who might have helpful information. Other guests, her crew, anyone who had contact with señora Costello." Giovanna pressed her lips together. "I'm sure the police will fill you in when they have more answers."

Maria sighed and put away her tablet. "Thank you for your time."

Giovanna pegged her tone as insincere.

After Maria left, Jim turned to Giovanna. "You handled that brilliantly. Just enough information so she can't accuse us of stonewalling her. I made the right choice hiring you."

It felt good to receive a compliment, even though her boss probably had an ulterior motive. Before she could bask in the glow of praise, the intercom on her desk phone buzzed. "*Si, señorita?*"

"Is señor Roberts still in there?"

Jim leaned over the desk to pick up the receiver. He listened, then replied, "I'll meet you in the conference room in five minutes," before turning to Giovanna. "Why don't you join us? I'm going to talk with the film crew about the video and the areas where they'll need access."

"But—" Giovanna's mouth hung open. "Claire just—"

"The show must go on," said Jim.

CHAPTER ELEVEN

Wednesday, Leisure Dreams Hotel

Back in the conference room with Claire's team, Giovanna felt a sense of *déjà vu*. Except instead of Detective Victor Zuniga, CEO Jim Roberts sat at the head of the table and addressed the group. *What's Victor doing now?* she wondered.

"You're still planning to shoot your documentary with Laurel Pardo at the Darwin, aren't you?" Jim was saying.

The film crew exchanged glances, and Susie leaned forward. "We have enough notes for a partial script, and we're prepared to move ahead." The others nodded their agreement, although less emphatically. "It's awful about Claire, really," Susie continued. "Obviously, we're all shocked. Devastated. But we've come this far; Claire would have wanted us to carry on."

Tyler and Colin gave lukewarm nods of support.

Giovanna scanned their faces. *No one appears devastated. Or even shocked.*

"Glad to hear it," said Jim. "Can you insert some of that Galapagos nature footage into our video? A few blue-footed boobies and an iguana or two? And a tortoise, of course. This commercial will run worldwide, and I want to show potential guests what an iconic location they're getting when they book a stay here."

Giovanna detected a hint of amusement on Tyler's face. Not unlike the semi-smirks she'd learned to suppress when listening to corporate propaganda.

"You got it," said Colin. "We'll be shooting plenty of natural flora and fauna while we're on the islands. Even if we don't get everything we need on this trip, we can insert footage from our last visit. We have lots of giant tortoise pictures, and those are timeless."

"This is a beautiful setting," agreed Susie. "We'll showcase your resort in the best light possible."

"Did Claire share the shot list with you yet?" asked Jim. "I want to make sure my vision comes across."

"The cops took her papers, but we talked on the flight down," said Colin. "What did you have in mind?"

Jim's cellphone vibrated, and he glimpsed the caller ID. "Excuse me, I have to take this." Cupping the phone to his ear, he hastened out of the room.

Giovanna turned to the film crew, her eyes roving from face to face. Business as usual; no trace of a tear in sight. *How did they really feel about their boss?* "So . . . are your rooms comfortable?"

Slightly more enthusiastic nods all around.

"I'm sorry I didn't get a chance to meet Claire. I've been reading about her work, and how passionate she was about bringing her subjects to life. It's great that you want to continue this project." Giovanna knew she was rambling, repeating platitudes she'd uttered earlier.

"Claire was difficult, but she made great films," said Tyler. "She insisted on quality, perfection even."

Colin sighed. "She put a lot of pressure on us. But we did good work together."

Susie's lips tightened. "She taught me everything I know."

Tyler snorted. "More than she realized." His dark eyes narrowed as they flitted between Colin and Susie.

"Do you know when the police will return her notebooks?" Colin asked Giovanna. "Certainly, they need to go through them, but she's compiled a lot of information that would make our work easier."

"Don't you have everything on a shared drive?" Giovanna asked. "Like a script? A shot list?"

Colin shook his head. "Not much. Claire kept so many of her ideas to herself, and sometimes she didn't articulate her vision until we were on the set. And she made lots of last-minute, spur-of-the-moment changes to capture the unexpected."

"What do they want with Claire's notes anyway?" Susie's lower lip protruded in a pout. "I'd be surprised if they can even read them."

Tyler gave her a condescending look. "Don't you watch TV? There could be all kinds of clues in those papers. Suicide notes, threatening letters, a diary. Maybe her thoughts about being betrayed by her boyfriend and her assistant—"

"Enough," Colin snapped.

Susie's face turned bright crimson.

Giovanna smiled to herself. *I was right about the affair.* But was it a motive for murder? Or suicide? She turned to Claire's colleagues. "Look, it's none of my business what you do with your personal lives. I didn't know Claire, but she died in my hotel, on my watch, and I'd like to find out what happened."

The three stopped glaring at each other and focused on Giovanna.

"So would I," said Tyler.

"Of course," said Colin.

Susie swallowed and gave a faint nod. Her color slowly returned to its ivory hue.

"Did Claire ever seem depressed?" asked Giovanna. "The police haven't ruled out suicide." Even though Claire's death was most likely murder, a ruling of suicide would be better news for the hotel. And God forbid the killer was someone who worked at Leisure Dreams . . .

"Never," said Colin.

"After her divorce," said Tyler.

"But that was a long time ago, wasn't it?" Giovanna said.

"She always regretted losing custody of her daughter," Tyler said. "The last time Claire tried to visit, Lindsey didn't even want to see her."

Giovanna flashed back to the online research she'd done on Claire, and how the tabloids had speculated about why Claire lost her only child. *Poor Claire. Even if she didn't fight hard enough for custody, she must have had some maternal instincts.*

"She doesn't talk about it," Colin insisted. "*Didn't* talk about it."

"She kept a lot inside," said Tyler. "Maybe a sign of depression. Holding in your feelings too much is unhealthy."

"Expressing them would be a sign of weakness," snickered Susie. "Claire doesn't . . . *didn't* do weak."

The conference room door opened, and Jim re-entered. His face had lost the public relations smile. "I'm sorry, folks, but I'm going to have to cut this short. Giovanna, can you show the crew around the property and let them know what we want included in the project?" With a salute, he was off again.

Giovanna stared after her boss. *Great. No notes, no direction. I have no idea what Jim and Claire planned for this video. And neither does her crew.*

CHAPTER TWELVE

Wednesday, Leisure Dreams Hotel

Giovanna led the film crew around the two-story lobby, calling their attention to the way the massive, multi-faceted Waterford chandelier caught sunlight from various angles. They marveled at the wide, curved staircase that gently wound from the reception area to the first floor, where all the guest rooms were located.

They entered the Isabela restaurant with its floor-to-ceiling windows overlooking the azure waters of the bay. The hostess handed them menus, and they perused the mouth-watering Ecuadorian and seafood specialties.

"We were here last night," said Susie. "I tried the *llapingachos*. Isn't that a traditional Ecuadorian dish? I'm not a fan of potatoes, but it tasted . . . how do you say . . . *mucho bien*."

Tyler looked down his nose at his colleague. "*Muy bueno*."

Bristling, Susie turned away.

Colin gazed out the picture window. "Look at how the birds swarm around those boats. The fishermen must have had a good haul."

"Our chef is at the fish market now." Giovanna followed his gaze. "Picking out the freshest selections for tonight's menu."

"I presume everything is sustainably harvested?" Colin pursed his lips as if he expected her to falter.

Giovanna raised her chin. "Overfishing has been a problem, and the government strictly regulates it around the islands. We only purchase our seafood from trusted sources."

They moved to the elegant Floreana ballroom, with polished marble floors, cathedral ceilings, faux columns, and recessed lighting. Giovanna gave them a preview of the decorations for the grand opening reception—the banners, the balloons, the native flowers. "Feel free to ask me any questions," she said.

Appreciative nods, but no questions.

They proceeded outside, and she pointed to the paved driveway winding to the lobby entrance from the end of the road, which had been constructed as an access route to the resort. "Here's where the shuttle bus will pick up and drop off guests."

"You have a shuttle?" asked Tyler. "We didn't know that when we arrived yesterday."

"Not to and from the airport," explained Giovanna. "To the Charles Darwin Research Station in Puerto Ayora. We'll make several trips a day to accommodate guests who come for the grand opening."

"We have to shoot at the Darwin for our documentary," said Colin. "We plan to use your shuttle, since it's been a challenge arranging transportation around here."

"I'll have Belinda give you the schedule."

Giovanna led them to the rear of the hotel, where the sweet scent of yellow Cordia permeated the air. The swimming pool beckoned, flanked by a tower of gray indigenous rocks, wet from the recycled waterfall cascading over them into the deep end. The songs of Darwin's finches and Galapagos mockingbirds in the nearby mangroves competed with the tinkling of running water.

"I love this postcard view." Giovanna gestured toward Academy Bay. "It's even better than the one from the dining room." White and gray fishing boats dotted the blue water of the harbor where flocks of pelicans and frigatebirds hovered, squawking for handouts.

"Wow," said Susie. "Y'all picked a beautiful site."

Giovanna beamed, even though the resort's location had been established long before she came on board. She glanced back at the hotel she managed—a crescent-shaped, two-story, peach stucco edifice curving along the shoreline so every guest room had a spectacular view.

She pointed to a wooden door that appeared to blend into the landscape like a Hobbit hole. "Over there against the hillside is our wine cellar."

"Aha," said Colin. "Can we tour that?"

"Not much to see. It's smaller than a cellar at a vineyard." Before she could elaborate on the Leisure Dreams wine collection, Giovanna spied a fat sea lion undulating out of the brush toward the pool. She clapped her hands. "Shoo, Harvey. Don't even think about it."

The beast barked but retreated.

Susie grinned. "That's so cool! A seal."

"Sea lion," corrected Tyler, aiming his camera at the massive, brownish-gray pinniped as it slinked back into the bushes.

"It is pretty cool," said Giovanna. "But this animal is annoying. He's always trying to swim in our pool." She wrinkled her nose. "And no one wants to go in after he's done."

Satisfied the sea lion had left, she pointed to a trail winding down a gentle slope. "There's a dock by the water for people who arrive by boat."

"You've thought of everything," said Colin.

Susie turned to Giovanna. "Where was Tio Armando kept when he was here?"

Giovanna blinked. *How do they know Tio Armando was here? Was that Claire's angle for the film?* She cleared her throat and recited her standard answer. "No one knows how that giant tortoise got here last year from the Beagle Galapaguera on San Cristóbal, the reserve where he'd been housed since he was discovered. The park service moved him to the Darwin Research Station shortly after we found him roaming the hotel grounds."

"Did Jim Roberts have him stolen?" asked Susie, a conspiratorial twinkle in her eye.

"He wasn't *stolen*. We don't know how he ended up here." To convince herself as much as Susie, Giovanna added, "Mr. Roberts was as surprised as everyone else to see Tio Armando wandering on the resort property, and he cooperated fully with the authorities during their investigation." She pivoted. "Would you like to see the docks?"

As they walked toward a stand of native trees en route to the water's edge, Tyler stopped in front of a large evergreen covered in gray bark, glossy green leaves with pointed tips, and yellow-green fruit. "Is that a manzanillo?"

Glancing at the tree, Giovanna shrugged. "I don't know plants very well. You'll have to ask Miguel Ruiz, our groundskeeper."

Susie inspected the branches. "Looks like it produces apples. Green apples." She moved closer.

Tyler yanked her back. "Don't get too close. If it's a manzanillo, or manchineel as it's called in English, the sap can burn your skin."

Giovanna shuddered. "Really?"

Tyler nodded. "Everything about the manchineel is toxic."

"I had no idea." Giovanna stared at the offending plant. "I'll ask Miguel to put a fence around it. We don't want anyone to get injured." *Lawsuit waiting to happen. And no one got rid of that tree during construction?*

A stifled cough punctuated some rustling in the bushes. Giovanna's head jerked in the direction of the sound. "Who's there?" When no one answered, she took a step toward the hedge. "Come out, whoever you are."

Sheepishly, Maria Vasquez stood up, computer tablet in hand.

"Really? Hiding in the shrubbery like the paparazzi?" Giovanna glared. "I thought you left."

"I'm sticking around for the tour. The *Ayora Times* is covering your grand opening."

"I thought you'd already toured the site with Belinda." Giovanna studied the reporter, wondering what she expected to learn.

"I may have missed something. Surely, you'll want the most extensive coverage possible. Especially now that—"

"Maria, I'll be happy to give you another tour later. Right now, I'm busy."

Maria trotted after the group. "I understand you're making a video featuring the property." She addressed the film crew rather than Giovanna.

"Please don't pester my guests," said Giovanna.

"It's okay," said Susie. "Claire would have wanted us to face the media. I'm Susie Southworth, Claire's right hand." She extended her own right hand to shake Maria's.

Maria threw Giovanna a triumphant look. "Maria Vasquez, from the *Ayora Times*."

Giovanna shifted her gaze from face to face among Claire's entourage. "The *Ayora Times* is our local newspaper. Maria, this is the crew making the nature documentary." The men followed Susie's lead and introduced themselves.

"Can we go down by the dock now?" asked Susie.

"Of course," Giovanna replied. "Let's take the stone steps over there. It's easier and shorter than the trail, and the surrounding vegetation has been trimmed. We've also added a handrail and lights for guests who arrive by boat after dark."

Maria turned to Susie. "I'm sorry about what happened to Claire Costello. Do you mind telling me a little more about her?"

"Is this on the record?" Tyler groused.

"Is there something you want to tell me that should be off the record?" Maria gave him a sidelong glance.

"Maria," warned Giovanna.

"I understand Claire tended to get sick whenever she started a new project." Maria's eyes darted from Tyler to Susie. "How did that affect her performance? Her state of mind?"

Tyler tightened his jaw. "She was a consummate professional."

"Your relationship was purely business, then?" Maria shifted her scrutiny to Colin.

"Maria," chided Giovanna. *If she did her homework, which Maria does, she most likely read all about the personal relationship between Colin and Claire. Just like I did.*

Maria tried again. "Did Claire Costello have enemies? Anyone who might want her dead?"

"Did the police tell you her death was a homicide?" Tyler challenged.

"Not yet. But what do you think?" The reporter poised her finger over her tablet. "You knew her best."

Tyler relented. "She was a successful producer who undoubtedly stepped on some toes on her way up the ladder. But no one wanted her dead."

"Certainly not the three of us," Colin assured her. "We're still in shock."

"Well, I'm glad you'll be able to continue the project," said Maria. "It would be a shame to come all this way and then go right back because you lost your producer."

She doesn't believe they're in shock, either, thought Giovanna.

"Claire would have wanted us to stay and make the documentary. We're prepared to carry on." Susie straightened her shoulders as if ready to be pinned with a badge of courage.

They'd reached the water's edge. Inhaling the salty sea air, Giovanna led them onto the pier. Two large brown pelicans perched on opposite pilings like sentries guarding the harbor, and they made no effort to flee the approaching humans. "Here are the slips for the boats."

"Are you expecting people to arrive at the opening banquet by boat?" Maria peered at one of the slips.

Giovanna replied, "Yes, some from town and other parts of the island."

"Do you have the guest list?"

"Belinda can get it for you when we go back inside."

Susie gave a little squeal and pointed at the water. "What's that?"

"A sea turtle." Giovanna turned toward the area where Susie was pointing. "There are quite a few around here."

The others gazed at the large green turtle swimming just below the surface. Its flippers barely made a ripple as they transported its massive carapace through the water.

"Maybe he's one of Tio Armando's cousins," said Susie as she watched the turtle's graceful glide.

Tyler rolled his eyes. "Tio Armando is a tortoise, not a turtle. Tortoises live on land."

Blushing, Susie stared at the bay.

"How hard would it be for someone to sneak into the hotel undetected?" Maria asked.

"What are you trying to say, Maria?" Giovanna placed a hand on her hip.

"I'm just saying someone could have arrived by boat and—"

Splash! A surprised shriek accompanied the spray of water.

The sea turtle they had been observing slid away, and the two pelicans startled to life, flapping their six-foot wings as they flew off.

Giovanna turned her attention to the group, which had shrunk from four to three. Maria floundered in the bay, waving her tablet in the air to protect it from the lapping waves.

"Help! I can't swim!" she sputtered.

Giovanna tossed Maria a life preserver attached to a rope. The reporter grabbed hold, and slowly, the hotel manager dragged her to shore.

Shaking her curls like a wet dog, Maria clutched her tablet to her chest and glared at Tyler.

Tyler didn't look at her. The corners of his mouth twitched with traces of a diabolic grin.

"Careful." Giovanna stifled an amused smile. "It gets slippery out here sometimes."

Chapter Thirteen

Wednesday evening, Leisure Dreams Hotel

Victor arrived in the lobby at seven that evening, freshly showered and dabbed with the aftershave that made Giovanna wish they could spend the entire evening alone in her suite. If only he didn't have hours ahead interviewing witnesses.

She took his arm and nudged her head against his strong shoulder. "Shall we eat in the restaurant, or do you want to go upstairs and order room service?"

The lopsided smile revealed his rakish chipped tooth. "Much as I'd prefer room service, *mi reinita*, eating in the dining room will allow me to observe some of the witnesses before I start my interviews."

Touching her elbow gently, he propelled her past the hostess station toward a white-clothed table for four by the window, now covered by filmy drapes that had been drawn to block the blinding afternoon sun. They sat next to each other instead of across so they could view the entire room.

Gabriela, Giovanna's favorite server, came to take their order. The twenty-year-old black-haired beauty looked more suited to competing in a Miss Ecuador pageant than waiting tables.

"What's the catch of the day?" Victor looked up from the menu.

"Char-grilled tuna served with a side of steamed vegetables." A tiny dimple appeared when she smiled. "I tried it earlier. It's the best fish I've had in a long time."

"Sold." Victor closed his menu and looked at Giovanna. "And a ceviche appetizer."

"Me, too." She handed their menus back to Gabriela.

As the server wrote down their orders, Victor asked, "Señorita, were you working here last night?"

"Yes, why?" Her dark eyes shifted to the door, where Colin, Susie, and Tyler had just entered.

"Can we talk later?" Victor asked. "When you get a break."

Gabriela dropped her order pad. She stooped to retrieve it, but Victor picked it up first and handed it to her. "Thank you." Straightening, she eyed him. "I know you're here to find out what happened to señora Costello, but I don't know what I could tell you that would help. I never saw the woman."

He smiled, his brown eyes kind. "You'd be surprised what details might be important."

"I'll have some time after nine." She glanced toward the table where Claire's colleagues had settled. Susie craned her neck as if impatiently scanning the room for service. "Will you please excuse me?" Gabriela strode across the floor to the trio.

Giovanna eyed the film crew. "Can't get away from those people. I spent the entire afternoon with them."

Victor took a sip of his water. "Did you learn anything?"

"You're not going to tell me to stay out of your investigation?" she teased.

He arched an eyebrow. "I always appreciate usable information."

She leaned toward him conspiratorially. "From what I gather, Claire was a tough boss. A perfectionist. Sounds like a pain in the ass. As you know, her assistant, Susie, and Claire's supposed boyfriend, Colin, are having an affair."

"Wait." He held up a hand. "Claire's 'supposed boyfriend'?"

Giovanna nodded. "I did some internet research on Claire. She and Colin were an item. You didn't know?"

Victor leaned back in his chair and gave Giovanna a bemused look. Gabriela arrived with their ceviche.

Giovanna picked up her fork when the server had gone. "Tyler seems the most loyal of the three. He disapproves of the affair between Susie and Colin, the disrespect they showed their boss. I guess they were trying to be discreet, but Claire figured it out."

"Yes, you told me about their affair. What else?"

"They're moving forward with the documentary as well as the commercial for the hotel that Jim Roberts talked Claire into making. Not sure when she and Jim had that conversation. They might have been on the same flight from the States, but Jim didn't arrive at the hotel with them, so maybe they connected by phone or email before the trip."

"They're going ahead with the film project?" Victor did the arched eyebrow thing again, which Giovanna found charming.

"Susie says it's what Claire would want."

"I imagine they'll have to change the original plan."

"I got the impression Susie thinks she's ready to step into Claire's shoes. She's already taken over her boss's boyfriend." Giovanna let out a small chuckle. "Claire's career may be the next target."

"Doesn't Claire own the company?"

"A bigger role, then. Or maybe this is a stepping stone to something more." Giovanna shrugged. "Susie seems to care more about fitting the image of an important documentary producer than about actually making quality films."

"Another glint of woman's intuition?" His lips curved into an impish grin.

Giovanna gave his arm a playful squeeze. "Oh, and they want Claire's notes back as soon as possible."

Victor shook his head. "Not happening right away. There's a lot to go through. It was a diary of sorts. Personal observations mixed with the professional stuff."

"A diary? Did she write about her colleagues?"

"Some."

"Does she mention the affair? Someone she didn't trust?"

"We're still analyzing the contents." He sipped his water.

"Do you have someone on the force who reads English well? Besides yourself?" Victor had an American stepmother, and, as a teenager, he'd spent summers in California with her and his father. Most of the other officers in their precinct were not as proficient in English.

"Are you volunteering?" His brown eyes twinkled. "I thought you had your hands full with managing the hotel and preparing for the opening."

"I'm happy to help." She lowered her lashes. "Unless I'm also a person of interest."

He flashed that devilish grin and patted Giovanna's knee under the table. "A person of interest, yes. But not a suspect. You have a rock-solid alibi."

Susie sashayed over to their table. "Good evening, Ms. Rogers. I want to thank you again for our tour this afternoon. You gave us some great ideas for our shot list for the commercial." She turned to Victor. "Detective, may I have a word with you when you're free?"

Gabriela approached, carrying plates of sizzling fish on her arm.

Susie stepped aside to allow the server to set the plates in front of Giovanna and Victor. She held up her hand. "I'll talk to you later."

"*Buen provecho*," said Gabriela. "Can I bring you anything else? More water?"

Giovanna lifted her half-empty glass. "Please. When you get a chance." She eyed Susie, who had returned to her table with the men. "I wonder what she wants."

"Claire's notes, I suspect," said Victor. "Man's intuition." He winked.

"Then I guess you'll disappoint her."

Victor picked up his knife and fork. "I'm used to disappointing people of interest."

"How can I help you tonight?" Giovanna cut off a bite of seared tuna and savored the flavors of citrus marinade and herbs. The texture was melt-in-your-mouth tender. "I asked Belinda to set up the conference room for the interviews. There'll be water, notepaper, tissues."

"Thanks."

"You have the staff list. Do you have a preferred order?"

He shook his head. "This is disruptive enough. I'll work around their schedules, try to talk to the employees when they have a break or slow time."

"Okay. Everyone on duty yesterday afternoon or last night is here except for Miguel Ruiz. He called in sick today."

Victor raised an eyebrow. "He seemed fine yesterday. Remember? We talked to him before we left for our hike."

Giovanna sighed. "Belinda's the one who took Miguel's call this morning. Thinks it's one of those twenty-four-hour bugs. I hope he'll be back tomorrow; I need to talk to him about a tree near the trailhead."

"Miguel drove your CEO here from the airport. And neglected to tell you he'd been asked to do it. I wonder if he also drove Claire and her team."

Staring at her plate, Giovanna contemplated the arrival logistics. "I don't think so. Tyler asked about our shuttle service today; he didn't know we had one. Sounds like they arranged their own transportation."

Victor cut another piece of fish. "You weren't expecting Jim until tomorrow, but he changed his flight. Why?"

"Jim's anxious about the opening," said Giovanna. "I know you're working as quickly as you can, but he's pushing to have this investigation wrapped up before then."

"I'm sure." Victor curled his lip. "He's also eager to get started on the video, but if that's the case, I don't buy his story about not talking to Claire last night."

Giovanna's eyes strayed to the door, and she almost dropped her fork. "Oh, no! Not her again."

CHAPTER FOURTEEN

Wednesday evening, Leisure Dreams Hotel

Victor's eyes followed Giovanna's to the new arrival in the restaurant: Maria Vasquez, reporter for the *Ayora Times*. She'd dried off and changed clothes after her impromptu swim in the bay.

"I don't want to talk to her right now," Giovanna muttered, fiddling with her linen napkin.

Maria had spotted them, and she made a beeline toward their table.

Giovanna pursed her lips. Victor reached into her lap and squeezed her hand. She squeezed back.

"Good evening, Ms. Rogers. So nice to see you again." Maria's syrupy tone was as fake as her smile. She turned to Victor. "Detective, you're just the person I need to speak with."

Giovanna blew out an exasperated puff of air. "Will you please let the man finish his dinner?"

Maria acted oblivious to the fact she'd interrupted. "Of course. I'll be right over there when you're ready." She headed to a table for two in the corner.

Victor sighed. "This is a big story for her. As you know, we rarely get this much excitement in the Galapagos."

"I bet she's going over to bother Claire's crew." Giovanna watched Maria cross the floor and pretend to have just noticed the group. "I knew it. I should make her quit harassing my customers." When she yanked the napkin off her lap and started to get up, Victor placed his hand on her arm.

"They can handle her themselves, *mi reinita.*"

Although out of earshot, Giovanna and Victor observed the body language during the interaction between Maria and the film crew. Tyler's seemed downright hostile; Colin appeared amused. Susie feigned interest in the reporter's questions.

Maria hovered over them until Gabriela arrived with their food. The server nudged the reporter aside and pointed to the table where she had been sitting as if banishing an unruly child to the corner of the classroom.

Creeping back to her table, Maria took out her phone, with one eye trained on the entrance to the restaurant. Gabriela brought her a glass of wine. After only a small sip, Maria set the glass down hard and popped up again like the jester inside a jack-in-the-box.

Before Giovanna could run interference, Maria headed toward the entrance. Jim Roberts had arrived.

He caught Giovanna's eye and strode toward her table.

"Señor Roberts." Maria jogged across the restaurant floor after the CEO.

"Good evening, Jim." Giovanna ignored Maria at his heels. "Did you get some rest this afternoon?"

"Not really. I've been making phone calls and sending emails." He sat down across from Giovanna.

"Señor Roberts." Maria stood beside their table. Giovanna was afraid she'd have enough gall to plop into the empty chair beside the CEO. "May I have a word with you?"

He waved her off. "Give me a minute. I'll come to you. Where are you sitting?"

She gestured toward the corner table. Before withdrawing, she muttered, "If you want fair coverage, I need your version of events for my story."

Jim turned to Giovanna and Victor. "Janice had a setback. She's not going to make it for the opening."

Giovanna hid her relief. "Oh, Jim, I'm so sorry. Please tell your wife we'll miss her. But she should listen to the doctors so she can get strong again."

"I'll tell her." Although his smile was warm, his reddened eyes betrayed worry.

Gabriela returned and set Jim's usual scotch-on-the-rocks in front of him. He nodded his thanks and picked up the glass. "Jessy's with Janice, so now she won't get to come either, and the twins are disappointed. You might have to help cheer up Jenny when she arrives tomorrow."

Giovanna forced a smile. "I'm sure we can find plenty to keep your daughter busy."

"How's the fish tonight?" Jim eyed their almost-finished plates.

"Divine," said Victor. "Your chef uses precisely the right combination of spices, and the tuna was cooked perfectly. Moist and flaky."

Jim took a sip of scotch. "I suppose you'll want to question him tonight?"

"I'm questioning everyone. You know the drill. Nothing personal."

"Jim," said Giovanna. "When I was giving the film crew a tour of the grounds this afternoon, the cameraman pointed out a manzanillo tree near the beach path. He said the sap can burn your skin. I had no idea. I'll have Miguel build a fence around it. What if kids try to climb it? We don't want anyone to get hurt."

Jim furrowed his brow. "Maybe we should just take it out? Have a nice bonfire."

"I thought about that, too," said Giovanna.

"You don't want to do that," said Victor. "The sap could spatter, and if the smoke gets in your eyes, it can cause blindness. Some teenagers found that out last year when they built a fire on the beach. One of them ended up in the hospital."

"I didn't know we had such a hazard on the property." Giovanna touched her cheek.

"The manzanillo is the only indigenous toxic plant in the Galapagos," said Victor. "We sometimes call it 'the poison apple tree' because eating the fruit can be lethal to humans."

Giovanna gasped.

"I don't know of any cases where someone actually died from eating the fruit," Victor amended. "A few years ago, a tourist bit into an apple and got violently ill. It was touch-and-go for a day or so. He and his friend had been downing piña coladas all afternoon, so I don't know if that made it worse or saved him. Maybe the coconut milk coated his stomach lining enough to interfere with the absorption of the poison."

Giovanna's eyes widened. "Susie was admiring those pretty green apples this afternoon. We don't want our guests picking them. Maybe we should put up a warning sign as well as a fence around the tree."

Jim nodded. "An educational plaque. I like it. And having something dangerous on the property adds a bit of mystique, like those English castles with poison gardens."

"What if Claire . . . ?" Giovanna looked at Victor. "Is that plausible from the scene?"

"We won't know until we get the results of the autopsy and the toxicology reports," Victor replied. "But it appears she died of poisoning. The vomiting, the foaming around the mouth—both are telltale signs. Overdose crossed my mind, but the prescription drugs we found in the bathroom were used to control ulcers. No opioids or sleeping pills—the kinds of drugs you normally see with an overdose or a suicide."

"I hope you didn't find any apples in her room." Jim gulped more scotch.

Victor shook his head. "No, the fruit basket didn't contain apples. Looks like she ate a banana and part of an orange."

"We sent the fruit and champagne to her room as a welcome gift." Jim closed his eyes tightly. "I wish this whole thing would go away."

A possible murder will be hard to make go away. Giovanna looked at Victor, loving the way the muted dining room light reflected on his shiny black hair, wishing he were all she had to think about tonight. "Detective Zuniga will wrap up this case as soon as possible."

"That's my cue." Victor stood. "The night shift should be in place. I need to start my interviews with your staff."

Giovanna got up as well. "I'll round them up as you request them."

Jim drained his glass, set it on the table, and pushed back his chair. "Guess I better go keep Maria happy. She's doing a feature about our opening event for the Sunday paper. I hope she doesn't focus it on this unexplained death instead."

"Good luck with that," murmured Victor as Jim headed to the reporter's table.

* * *

Belinda had prepared the conference room and provided Victor with a list of the employees who'd worked the previous evening. Staffing was light because the hotel had not officially opened and few guests were staying on the premises.

Giovanna kept busy leading personnel to the conference room to speak with Victor. She wished she could be a fly on the wall. Feeling responsible for not protecting her guest, she yearned for any snippet of information that would help her understand what had happened to Claire. She shivered thinking someone on her staff might have had a hand in the demise of a customer. *No, it can't be a hotel employee. It must be someone from Claire's team, or her death might turn out to be suicide. Or even accidental. Maybe Claire picked a poison apple.* Giovanna grimaced. If a tree on the resort property had caused the death of a guest, the victim's family might sue for negligence. The company, Jim, and even Giovanna herself.

Victor interviewed Gabriela first. Giovanna noticed the server's shoulders trembled. Walking with her from the Isabela restaurant to the conference room, she put a hand on the young woman's arm. "Don't be nervous. The questions are routine. The detective is talking to everyone."

Gabriela's smile quivered. "I've never been questioned by the police before. I didn't do anything wrong."

"No one says you did." Giovanna opened the door to the conference room and ushered her employee inside. "Victor, you remember Gabriela from dinner? Our excellent server." She hoped her warm introduction would convey reassurance.

"Of course." Victor extended his hand. "Have a seat, Gabriela." When she sank, knees knocking, into the chair, he continued, "How long have you worked at Leisure Dreams?"

"I've been here since the soft opening three months ago." Her shoulders loosened a bit.

"How do you find it?" He winked at Giovanna who remained in the doorway. "Do you like your boss?"

"You don't have to answer until I'm gone." Smiling, Giovanna slipped out and closed the door behind her.

* * *

"I like her." Gabriela's worried expression relaxed into a smile. "Señora Rogers is not like those brash Americans who think they know everything. She's always asking questions, encouraging us to share our suggestions. She even asks for help with her Spanish."

Victor felt a tinge of pride in his girlfriend, although he wasn't surprised to hear Gabriela's assessment. Giovanna was terribly afraid of projecting the image of an "ugly American," and she tried hard not to be one, making an effort to learn about his culture without being judgmental. It was one of the traits that endeared her to him.

Sensing Gabriela would feel more comfortable in her native language, he switched to Spanish and moved to the purpose of his interview. He explained that he'd be recording their conversation as well as taking notes. "Now, señorita, what time were you on duty yesterday?"

"I worked the dinner shift. Arrived at five in the afternoon to set up, and we finished around ten."

"Did you see this woman or any of her crew?" Victor held out his phone to show Gabriela a picture of Claire.

Gabriela barely glanced at it. "I know Claire Costello. I've never met her, but I've watched some of her documentaries. Everyone was excited about her coming here."

"Did you see her yesterday?"

"No. But two of her colleagues came to the restaurant for dinner around six-thirty."

"Which ones?" Victor scrolled to the pictures of the others from Claire's website.

"The pushy young blonde and the man with glasses. They were there tonight too."

Colin and Susie. "How long did they stay?"

"About two hours," Gabriela replied. "Ordered *llapingachos*, dessert, and a bottle of wine, in addition to the catch of the day. I figured they were on an expense account because they weren't concerned about the prices."

Victor figured price was not a big concern for the kind of clientele Jim Roberts strived to attract. "Did you see anyone else from the film crew?"

She pointed to another photo on Victor's phone. "The man with long, scraggly hair came into the restaurant later and ordered a sandwich to go."

"What time was that?"

"Around eight-thirty. He looked over at their table, and I thought he was going to join his colleagues, but he didn't. He turned around and walked toward the kitchen."

"He went into the kitchen?" Victor creased his brow.

"He headed that way while I was waiting on another customer. Later, I saw him leave with a bag."

"What about Jim Roberts?" Victor continued to write.

"He didn't eat dinner here."

Victor looked up. "But did you see him?"

Gabriela's front tooth touched her lip. "He went to the kitchen. I didn't notice what time he arrived, but he left around eight-thirty, also with a bag. His dinner, I guess."

Victor recorded her responses in his notebook. "Do you handle the room service orders, too?"

"Sometimes." She looked down at the table. "I know señor Roberts sent a bottle of champagne to señora Costello."

"Did you take it to her?"

"Me?" Gabriela paled. "No. I couldn't leave the dining room. Belinda took it up."

"Did you see Belinda pick up the champagne?" When Gabriela's face puckered in confusion, he clarified, "Did she put it in the ice bucket? Prepare the tray?"

Gabriela shook her head. "I only saw her leave the kitchen with it. Already on ice. She told me she was headed to señora Costello's room."

"Was there anything else on the tray? Food?"

"A fruit basket."

"And who prepared the fruit basket?"

"Probably Pedro, the sous chef. Or someone working in the kitchen."

Victor shifted gears. "Did anyone else come to the restaurant last night?"

"Some of our regular locals. Chef Gomez is famous around town, and the restaurant is often busy."

Victor handed the young server a business card. "Thank you for your time, Gabriela. Please give me a call if you remember anything else about last night."

She examined the card, then looked up. "Oh, I forgot. That reporter from the *Ayora Times* was here. Maria Vasquez. She's not one of our usual locals. She and her friend met for drinks and appetizers around six, and then I heard her say they were going somewhere in town for dinner."

"What friend?"

"I believe her name is Laurel. Tall, dark-haired woman who does tortoise research at the Darwin. She's a friend of señora Rogers."

"Laurel Pardo?" Victor raised an eyebrow and consulted his notes. "She was here last night?"

"*Sí, señor.*"

Frowning, he thumbed through several pages of notes. "You're sure it was Laurel? Yesterday?" *Why am I not surprised she didn't mention it this morning?*

"*De ley. Claro que sí.*" Gabriela's brown eyes reminded him of a frightened doe as they searched his face. "Is that everything?"

He rose, signaling she could leave. "For now. We know how to contact you if we have more questions." He walked to the door and opened it for her. "Will you please tell señora Rogers she can send in the next person?"

CHAPTER FIFTEEN

Wednesday evening, Leisure Dreams Hotel

Chef Ricardo Gomez entered the conference room dressed in a toque and a white jacket splattered with red sauce. Rosy cheeks and ample girth suggested he enjoyed sampling his own cuisine. Victor wondered whether the stereotypical tall, white chef's hat was Ricardo's idea, or that of Jim Roberts, to lend an air of sophistication to the kitchen.

After introducing himself and shaking hands with the chef, Victor pointed to the cellphone on the table. "Just to let you know, I'm recording all my interviews." Into the microphone, he stated his name, the date, time, and location. "Thank you for your time, Chef Gomez. Can you tell me—"

"I hope you enjoyed your dinner this evening, Detective." The chef leaned toward the microphone. "That tuna was freshly caught."

"Very much, señor. Now—"

"The marinade I use is a recipe I created myself. It's a perfect blend of garlic, red pepper, and citrus, with just a hint of cilantro." He touched his fingers to his lips. "And the secret is not to overcook the tuna, so it stays juicy but retains that grilled flavor."

Victor wondered if the chef was practicing for a Leisure Dreams commercial. "Our meal was delicious, señor. Now, let's talk about last night. Who else came into the kitchen after you started work?"

Chef Gomez harrumphed. Victor couldn't tell if he disliked being interrupted while expounding on his favorite subject—cooking—or if the memory of others coming into his kitchen annoyed him. "My assistant Pedro was there all evening. I put him in charge of the *encebollado*."

"Did Jim Roberts come by?"

The chef rolled his eyes. "Señor Roberts had to inspect everything in the kitchen."

"What time was he there?"

"I don't know. Eight o'clock? I was in the middle of frying plantains for a large order. All the locals love my fried plantains."

"Did you expect him?" Victor asked. "Did you know señor Roberts was in town?"

"We all knew he was coming for the opening, but everyone thought he'd arrive tomorrow. I was surprised when he walked into my kitchen last night."

"What did you talk about?"

"We reviewed the menu for the banquet. He asked if we had all the necessary supplies, and I assured him everything was under control. Señora Rogers had taken care of all the details days ago." Ricardo waved his hands around when he talked as if conducting an orchestra. "I suggested señor Roberts go sit in the dining room and have a waitress serve him, but he said he was going straight to bed. I boxed up samples of the evening's specials for him to try in his room."

"Did he mention any of the guests?"

"He asked Pedro to send a bottle of champagne to the lady's suite. The one who . . . you know . . ."

"Claire Costello?"

The chef nodded; his face solemn.

"Have you ever met señora Costello?"

"Never. I'd never even heard of her, although I've since learned she was a celebrity."

Victor jotted a note. "Where do you keep the champagne?"

"Miguel Ruiz brought some from the wine cellar across the way. We try to keep a few bottles of the most popular wines in the Isabela restaurant, but we didn't have any champagne there last night."

"Was Jim Roberts still in the kitchen when Miguel brought the champagne?"

"He was just leaving. *¡Gracias a Dios!* I'd had enough of his micromanaging."

Victor wrote some notes. "Who took the champagne to señora Costello?"

"Belinda Chavez wanted to take it." Ricardo shut his eyes tightly, squinting his whole face as he spoke.

"Why Belinda?"

"She likes to think of herself as the face of this hotel." As he spoke, the chef stuck out his chest and swiveled from side to side in what Victor suspected was a poor imitation of Belinda. "And señora Rogers was out for the evening. Besides, señora Rogers had also given instructions to send champagne to señora Costello, and Belinda hadn't done it yet." He clucked his tongue. "Typical Belinda. Trying to make señora Rogers look bad."

Victor stopped writing. "Look bad? How? Why?"

Chef Gomez shook his head. "Maybe it's my imagination. Forget I said that." His eyes strayed to the recorder.

The last thing Giovanna needs is a staff trying to undermine her. I should keep an eye on Belinda. Victor forced his focus back to the interview. "I understand there was a bowl of fruit also. Who prepared that?"

"Pedro handles the fruit baskets."

"What time did Belinda pick up the champagne and fruit?"

"Eight-thirty? Nine? I'd already put the soup away and most of the new orders were for dessert. Did you try my chocolate flan tonight?"

"No, señor." Victor consulted his notes.

"That's a shame. It's our signature dessert." Ricardo fidgeted. "Detective, you don't think señora Costello died from something I cooked, do you? There's a rumor going around that she was poisoned."

Victor looked up from his notes and stopped the recording. "We won't know until we get the results of the autopsy and toxicology tests from the mainland." He handed the chef one of his cards. "Thank you for your time, Chef Gomez. Please call me if you remember anything else about last night."

Ricardo looked at the card, pocketed it, and rose. "*Cierto*, Detective."

"When you leave, please ask señora Rogers to send in Pedro Lopez."

"Pedro?" Chef Gomez looked at his watch. "Pedro left. He wasn't feeling well earlier, and after he oversalted the fish stew and burned a steak, I suggested he go home."

CHAPTER SIXTEEN

Wednesday evening, Leisure Dreams Hotel

When Chef Gomez stopped by her office to say his interview had finished, Giovanna was astonished to learn Pedro had left.

She turned to her assistant manager sitting beside her, reviewing the schedule for the opening. "Belinda, I thought you told all the employees the detective wanted to speak with everyone here. Did you know Pedro went home early?"

"It's okay. We're slow right now. He knows we'll need everyone here on Friday for the banquet."

"He's off tomorrow, isn't he?" Giovanna eyed the spreadsheet.

"Don't worry. Pedro will be here on opening night."

Giovanna rose. "He'll have to stop by the police station tomorrow."

Belinda's eyes narrowed. "It's his day off."

"The detective needs to interview everyone who was here last night. Including Pedro." Shaking her head, Giovanna marched out to find busboy Luis Vera, the next name on the list.

* * *

Luis Vera was a small, wiry twenty-something with slick black hair and shifty eyes. He spoke rapidly, embellishing every answer, which gave Victor the initial impression he had something to hide.

Victor quickly concluded Luis hadn't seen much that might be useful—he'd been clearing tables while the welcome basket was prepared—but the busboy was full of conspiracy theories. He'd never met Claire Costello, but he tried to imply that he "almost" knew her. He followed her on Facebook and Instagram.

When the interview was over, Luis kept talking, as if the detective had asked him to be a partner in solving the crime.

Victor rose and handed Luis his card. "*Muchas gracias, señor.* We'll be in touch."

* * *

Aurora Torres, the stout, fifty-ish night maid, displayed the same fearful demeanor at the beginning of the interview as Gabriela, the young server. Victor wondered if these women were intimidated by his stature as a police officer, overwhelmed at being questioned about a possible homicide, or if they were concealing something.

"What does a hotel maid do on the night shift?" he asked. "I imagine few guests need housekeeping services."

Aurora's paralyzed look told Victor his question had sounded accusatory. *Napping on duty, perhaps?*

"I'm not implying your job isn't busy, señora." He used his most soothing voice to restore her trust. "Please walk me through a typical evening shift. Last night, for example."

Her bosom heaved. "I did the turndown service."

"Did you do the turndown service for the Tio Armando suite?" *Where Claire Costello died.*

"No. The *Do Not Disturb* sign was on the doorknob, so I didn't go in."

"What about the other rooms?"

"*Sí, señor.*" She counted them off on her fingers. "Señora Rogers, señor Ashton, señor Thompson, señorita Southworth."

"Did you see señor Roberts arrive?"

"*Sí, señor.*" Her eyes flitted around as if she were deciding whether he'd asked a trick question.

Spying on the clientele? "Did señor Roberts visit any of the other guests?"

Aurora knotted her thick fingers. "I was in the hallway when señor Roberts stopped in front of the Tio Armando suite. He had a bag from the restaurant with him. I thought he was going in, out of habit. But then he stopped. He started to knock but then looked at the *Do Not Disturb* sign and kept walking. He went inside the Marine Iguana suite, and I never saw him leave."

"What time was that?"

"Eight-thirty, maybe nine. A few minutes later, Pedro Lopez delivered a bottle of scotch."

"To the Marine Iguana suite?" When Aurora nodded, he asked, "Did Pedro go inside?"

"No. Pedro knocked. Señor Roberts opened the door, took the scotch, and then Pedro left."

"Where were you when all this activity was happening?"

Aurora pursed her lips. "In the hallway, señor, doing my job."

Victor jotted a note. "Did anyone request housekeeping services while you were on duty?"

"Señor Ashton asked for more towels." She put a hand across her mouth in a vain attempt to hide a disapproving smirk. "He had company. Female."

"What time did you take the towels to señor Ashton?"

"Around eleven."

"And did you notice what time his company left?"

Aurora shook her head. "I think she spent the night."

Victor eyed Aurora. He sensed Giovanna would regard this conversation as validation of her theory about the affair between Colin and Susie. And she might be right. "Any idea who señor Ashton's female companion was?"

A flush crept up Aurora's neck and colored her cheeks. "It was señorita Southworth."

"How do you know?" Victor suppressed an amused smile.

"Her bed had not been slept in."

"You went into her room?" He cocked his head.

Aurora's catty smile morphed into a guilty wince. "Since señor Ashton asked for more towels, I thought I'd check with the other guests to see if they needed any. I'd forgotten Americans use a lot of towels. Señorita Southworth wasn't in her room. I checked again in the morning, right before I went off duty, and there was no sign of her."

"You didn't leave extra towels the first time you entered her room?"

"The room had plenty of towels."

"Why did you go in a second time? You would have wakened her if she'd been there."

Aurora flinched as she glanced at the cellphone on the desk, recording their conversation. "Please don't tell señora Rogers."

Victor made no move to turn it off. "While you were working, señora, did you see anyone go into the Tio Armando suite?"

"Belinda. She brought an ice bucket with a bottle. And a bowl of fruit."

"She knocked despite the *Do Not Disturb* sign?"

Aurora sucked her lower lip. "*Sí señor.*"

"And señora Costello opened the door?"

"I didn't see who opened the door, but Belinda went inside after announcing she had champagne."

"What time was that?"

"Around nine."

"Do you think señora Costello had company? Besides Belinda."

Aurora shrugged. Victor suspected she was curious and would have discovered a way to find out if she could have.

"Did you see Belinda leave?"

"No."

"Did you see anyone else come or go from the Tio Armando suite?"

Aurora shook her head. "I heard voices, but the guest might have been on the phone."

Victor consulted his notes. Laurel had mentioned Claire's phone call, but that was before the champagne arrived. Belinda, however, had said Claire received a call while she was in the room. "Did you ever meet Claire Costello?"

"No. I'd heard of her but never met her. I didn't meet her this time." The maid looked away. "I have no use for people like her."

"People like her? What do you mean?"

"You know. High society. Better than everyone else."

Victor furrowed his brow. "I thought you'd never met her."

A flicker of emotion—anger, fear; Victor couldn't tell—crossed Aurora's face. "I haven't."

He studied her for a moment, trying to decide what her remarks meant, then continued his questioning. "What time did you go off duty?"

"At six a.m."

"Did you pass anyone else in the hall before you left?"

Aurora gave him a knowing look. "Señora Rogers returned around midnight. With . . ." She lowered her lashes and pointed at the detective, her thumb and finger forming the shape of a gun.

Victor chuckled as the maid struggled over admitting she'd seen him go into her manager's suite—for the entire night. "So, you caught us. *Somos culpables.*" He wondered how discreet Aurora was about the comings and goings of the guests. "Did you see anyone else?"

"I passed Belinda as I was getting ready to leave, just before six. She banged on the door of the Tio Armando Suite." Aurora pursed her lips. "Not very professional, if you ask me."

Knowing what had happened next, Victor handed the meddlesome maid one of his cards. "Thank you for your time, señora. Please get in touch if you remember anything else about last night."

CHAPTER SEVENTEEN

Wednesday evening, Leisure Dreams Hotel

Giovanna went to find Nina Morales, the receptionist on duty the night of Claire Costello's death. The dark-haired, thirty-ish woman, with a braid hanging halfway down her back, looked like she could trace her roots to the Incas.

As Giovanna approached the desk, she glimpsed Tyler Thompson heading downstairs. He wasn't carrying camera equipment, which she'd come to view as almost an appendage.

"Good evening, Mr. Thompson," she greeted him.

He nodded her way and headed out the revolving door to a taxi that had just pulled up.

Giovanna turned to Nina. "The detective is waiting for you in the conference room. Belinda and I will watch the desk for you."

"*Sí, señora.* By the way, the security company will be here tomorrow morning at ten to finish hooking up the cameras at the back door."

"It's about time," said Giovanna. "Everyone will feel a lot safer. Thank you for being so tenacious with them." The problems with the security system had been only one of the many delays she'd had to deal with during the last few months, but at last, things were coming together. She glanced at her watch. "Is the back door locked yet?"

"I was just about to." Nina changed course.

Giovanna signaled her to stop. "I'll do it. Go talk to the detective in the conference room."

* * *

Before locking the deadbolt, Giovanna stuck her head out the back door to check the motion-sensor floodlights. She shivered at the thought of a killer sneaking into the hotel and poisoning a guest. Could he or she have come in this way?

A bleat like an off-key trumpet and the stink of dead fish assaulted her senses. She looked down. She'd almost tripped over a fat sea lion curled up against the stucco wall; it lifted its head and bellowed again in annoyance.

"What are you doing here, Harvey?" She flapped her hands in a "scat" gesture. "Go back to the beach."

Not waiting for the pinniped's retreat, she closed the back door and locked it. But were they truly secure? Was she locking evil out? Or locking it in?

* * *

Victor didn't learn much new information from Nina Morales. She corroborated the maid's story about the service calls: Jim's scotch for the Marine Iguana suite at nine, and Colin's request for towels around eleven p.m.

Apart from Jim Roberts, no other guests had checked in during Nina's shift, but dozens of locals had passed through the lobby en route to the Isabela restaurant. Hector Sanchez, the concierge/bellman, had taken Jim's luggage upstairs.

Victor reviewed his notes from other statements. "Do you know the reporter, Maria Vasquez?"

Nina nodded. "She's been around a lot lately. I heard she's writing a feature story about the resort and our opening."

"Was Maria here last night?"

"For a while."

"Was she alone?" It would be good to corroborate Gabriela's story before confronting Laurel about her omission.

"She was with Laurel Pardo, a friend of señora Rogers." Nina creased her brow in concentration. "They were meeting Miguel Ruiz, our groundskeeper."

Victor raised an eyebrow. "What time was that?"

"The women arrived about six-thirty. They asked for Miguel, but he hadn't returned from picking up señor Roberts at the airport. They went into the Isabela restaurant to wait."

"Did Laurel or Maria talk to Claire Costello?"

"I didn't see either of them go upstairs. Nor did señora Costello come down."

Victor felt somewhat relieved. Hopefully, Giovanna's friend Laurel had nothing to do with Claire's death. "When did Maria and Laurel meet with Miguel Ruiz?"

"I'm not sure." Nina looked at her lap. "The ladies left about seven-thirty."

Victor made more notes and then handed Nina one of his cards. "Thank you for your time, señora. Please contact me if you remember anything else about last night."

* * *

When Nina returned from her interview with Victor, Belinda flung her purse over her shoulder and started for the front door.

"Where are you going?" asked Giovanna on her way to summon the bellman for his turn with the detective. "You're not staying over tonight?" Her assistant had spent all week at the hotel to help with preparations for the grand opening.

Belinda threw her boss an apologetic smile. She'd applied a fresh coat of plum-red lipstick and doused herself with jasmine cologne. "Something came up, and I need to go home tonight."

A date? Giovanna wondered. *Anyone I know?* Belinda had never shared much about her love life. "Will you be back in the morning?"

Her assistant nodded. "You'll hardly know I was gone."

"Have fun," called Giovanna as Belinda walked out the door.

* * *

Hector Sanchez entered the conference room, his muscular biceps giving him the air of a bouncer in a rough bar. Victor figured the burly, bearded man's appearance must have assured Jim Roberts of his fitness for the frontline job.

After Victor explained the purpose of the interview and advised Hector that he'd be recording their conversation, he began. "Tell me about a typical workday. Let's start with your arrival at the hotel last night."

"I'm stationed by the lobby door, so I see almost everyone come and go. I provide information about the area for the guests and help them with their luggage."

Victor made some notes, then looked up. "Did you encounter anything unusual last night?"

"No, señor, it was a quiet night. Some of the Americans from the film crew came downstairs and asked for maps and brochures about local attractions."

"Which Americans?"

"A little blonde. Looks like a teenager. Said she was señora Costello's assistant." He stroked his beard. "Told me she had a big role in the film they're making here, and she asked if I'd like her autograph. She seemed disappointed when I said I don't collect autographs."

Victor displayed Claire Costello's website on his phone and navigated to the page containing staff photos. "Do you see her here?"

"*Sí, señor.*" He identified Susie Southworth's picture. Still peering at the phone, he pointed to Tyler's picture. "And then later, this guy came down. He said he's a photographer. Photography is my hobby, so we had a long conversation about cameras. I recommended some scenic viewpoints on the property they could use in their video."

"Did either of the Americans go out after picking up the maps and brochures?"

"The cameraman took a walk around the grounds. Could have been checking out some of the viewpoints I mentioned."

Victor jotted more notes. "Were you here when señor Roberts arrived?"

Hector nodded. "Miguel Ruiz picked him up at the airport. I took his bags from the limo to the Marine Iguana suite."

"Did you pass anyone in the hallway on your way to the suite?"

"Only Aurora, the night maid."

"When you went by the Tio Armando suite, did you see anyone go in or out?"

Hector stroked his beard again as if it helped him think. "No, señor, the *Do Not Disturb* sign was on the door."

Victor paused, reviewing his notes. "Did Miguel come inside the hotel after dropping off señor Roberts?"

"I saw him talking to two women who were on their way out," replied Hector. "A few minutes later, Miguel came inside with two bottles of champagne and headed toward the restaurant."

"Is that usual?" When Hector looked puzzled, Victor clarified, "For Miguel to bring wine from the cellar to the restaurant?"

"No, it's usually the sommelier, but he was already gone for the day. I figured this was a special request from señor Roberts. Whenever the CEO has a special request, he calls on Miguel." The expression on Hector's face conveyed something between amusement and disdain.

Victor furrowed his brow. "Why is that?"

Hector shrugged.

Victor raised his pencil but did not write anything down. "Do you know what time Miguel got off duty?"

"He normally works an early shift and is gone by five or six, but yesterday he came in later because he had to pick up señor Roberts at the airport."

"Miguel had planned to pick up señor Roberts at the airport yesterday?" Victor twirled his pencil. *How did Miguel get the message?*

"None of us knew the CEO was coming in last night, but someone must have told Miguel." Hector touched his beard again. "Like I said, Miguel gets all the special requests."

"Did you see Miguel again after he delivered the champagne to the kitchen?"

"No, señor."

"Did anything else happen last night?"

Hector shook his head. "As I said, it was a quiet night. At least, I thought so."

CHAPTER EIGHTEEN

Wednesday evening, Leisure Dreams Hotel

When he'd finished his interviews, Victor went to find Giovanna, who was still in her office. She looked up with a smile that lit her face. "Are we any closer to learning what happened?"

"The timeline is coming together. Apart from a few discrepancies." He sat down in the chair across from her. "For one, your friend Laurel Pardo."

"Laurel?"

"She was here last night."

Giovanna frowned. "I thought she went out with friends for dinner in town."

"She conveniently left out meeting one of them for drinks earlier. Here, at Leisure Dreams."

Giovanna fiddled with a strand of her long, brown hair that had come loose from the ponytail. "Do you think Laurel visited Claire after all?"

"No one can confirm that Laurel and Claire met. But why didn't she mention being here last night?" He shook his head. "This isn't the first time your friend has omitted crucial details."

"I hope you won't let your personal feelings cloud your judgment." Giovanna knew Victor still stewed about Laurel's disappearing act last year; precious time and resources had been spent searching for a woman who was not lost at sea after all. "Who was with Laurel? Wait, let me guess: Maria Vasquez."

"Right."

"That woman is obsessed."

"She's a reporter. A good one, who smells a story."

"You're cutting Maria a lot of slack." Giovanna eyed him. "Most cops don't like reporters."

He shrugged. "Maria is harmless. She has helped me with cases before."

Watching Victor's face, Giovanna wondered if there had ever been roman-tic feelings between him and Maria. A small population on the island . . . a small pool of eligible love interests. They'd never discussed his previous relationships. She quickly dismissed the unhealthy thought; if the two shared a past, she couldn't change it. "Just Laurel and Maria were here?"

"They were looking for your groundskeeper, Miguel Ruiz. He may have gone into town with them; I'll have to clarify that when I talk to him. In our first interview, Laurel named two other women who joined her for dinner, and she didn't mention Miguel." Victor eyed Giovanna. "Are he and Laurel friends?"

"They used to work together in the tortoise program at the Darwin. From what Laurel tells me, they didn't always agree about research methods." She strained to remember any relevant "Miguel stories" Laurel had told. "Miguel left the Darwin when Jim offered him a job at Leisure Dreams, while the hotel was still under construction. I haven't seen him and Laurel hanging out together since I've been here."

"Why would Miguel go from being a tortoise researcher at the Darwin to a gardener and chauffeur at Leisure Dreams? Seems like a drastic career change."

"Not as much as it appears. Miguel's official role is head groundskeeper, and Jim hired him for his knowledge of the natural systems here, to keep us in compliance with the many environmental restrictions. The chauffeuring isn't really part of his job."

Victor raised an eyebrow. "I didn't realize."

"Of course, the main reason for the career change was money. An American company like Leisure Dreams pays top dollar. Most of the researchers at the Darwin are volunteers or work for low wages. That's not an issue for Laurel, because she comes from a wealthy family and has a generous trust fund."

Victor shook his head. "Why do I think she's up to something?"

Giovanna wagged her finger at him. "Be fair."

"I will be very relieved if Laurel had nothing to do with this."

"Would you like to come upstairs for a nightcap?" Giovanna lowered her lashes. "We could talk it out. Or not."

He grinned. "Tempting. But I know you have a big day tomorrow, with so many guests arriving."

Her sultry smile faded. "Did you talk with everyone you needed tonight?"

"Except for Miguel Ruiz and the sous chef, Pedro Lopez."

Giovanna glanced at her phone. "I tried to reach them both tonight, but no luck. I left messages for them to call me."

"Thanks. You've been a great help."

They stared into each other's eyes, and despite the distraction of today's tragic event, the passion remained. She hoped he was reconsidering her invitation to stay.

There was a knock at the door. Giovanna suppressed a groan. "Come in."

Luis Vera wiped his hands on his busboy apron as he entered the office. "Detective Zuniga, I'm glad I caught you." He held out a now-clean hand to Victor. "You said to get in touch if I remembered anything else about last night."

"Yes. What is it?" Victor picked up his notebook.

"Not exactly last night, but this morning." Luis retrieved a smartphone from his pocket. "Claire Costello has been posting to her social media."

Victor and Giovanna exchanged glances.

"But she died last night." Luis thrust the phone toward Victor. "Look at the time stamp."

Victor peered at the Instagram photo.

"Maybe it was scheduled activity," suggested Giovanna as she displayed Claire Costello's profile on her office computer. "Or maybe someone posts for her."

Luis's dark face deflated. "I thought it was important."

"Thank you," said Victor. "We'll check it out."

Luis hovered at the door. "Her fans need to know what happened. If Claire wanted to fake her death, I could help—"

"Claire didn't fake her death," said Victor firmly. "We'll find out what happened, and I'm sure her staff will put out a statement for her fans once they have more information."

"Don't *you* post anything, Luis," warned Giovanna. "Remember our policy about social media. Wait until there's an official announcement."

"*Claro*," replied Luis.

When the busboy had gone, Giovanna studied the post in more depth. "My hunch is that Claire didn't write this, whether it was scheduled before her death or created afterward." She read aloud, "Check out my awesome new assistant, Susie Southworth, who will appear in my upcoming film about the Galapagos. Stay tuned as we document our amazing journey." The text was accompanied by a radiant photo of Susie in safari attire and high wedge heels, looking more like a petite sportswear model than a filmmaker ready for a nature hike. "Someone made a comment. 'Sounds terrific. But Claire, won't you be on camera, too?'"

"Did she answer?" Victor rose, rounded the desk, and stood behind Giovanna's chair.

"Sort of. The response from 'Claire,' posted at ten-thirty this morning, was, 'Just wait! It will be awesome!!' Claire doesn't seem like the double-exclamation-point type."

Victor stared at Giovanna's screen. "Guess I'll be talking to Susie again tomorrow." He glanced at his watch. "Which will be here sooner than we'd like."

"Sure you don't want to stay?" Giovanna touched his hand, which had crept from the back of the chair to her shoulder.

He sighed. "*Mi reinita*, I better leave while I still can."

She rose and turned to face him. His arms slipped around her, and she returned his embrace. The weight of him pushed her back against the desk as their lips met in a hungry kiss. With one hand, she folded the computer's screen and pushed it aside as they reclined.

* * *

Thursday morning, Leisure Dreams Hotel

Poring over a Spanish-language newspaper, Giovanna struggled to understand the headlines as she sipped her morning coffee. Slowly—too slowly for her liking—her vocabulary was increasing. She picked up a partially nibbled croissant and took another bite.

Michelle and Roberto hadn't told her what flight they'd arrive on, although she expected them today. She'd asked her grandmother to text her the details so she could arrange an airport pick-up, but Michelle had said not to worry. Giovanna hoped they'd bought confirmed tickets instead of flying space-available, one of the perks of Roberto's employment as an airline pilot. Reduced-price airfare was great. The not-so-great part was that standby sometimes meant "standing at the gate and waving goodbye" as Michelle liked to quip.

"Good morning." The voice of Jim Roberts disrupted her reverie. Looking rested and chipper, he eyed her table, set for one. "Where's the good detective this morning?"

Giovanna folded her newspaper and glanced at her watch. "He has a busy schedule today, as you can imagine. And so do we."

"Of course." Jim nodded. "When you're done with breakfast, can we do a walk-through? Make sure everything is in place for tomorrow?"

She smiled. "You're not nervous, are you? We've been working on this event for months."

"I just want it to be perfect."

Giovanna finished her coffee and set the empty cup beside her newspaper. "Before I forget, let me show you that tree we talked about last night."

"You really think it could poison someone?" Jim's face was skeptical.

"Better safe than sorry." She rose.

They left the dining room through the back entrance to the pool area where a sweet, floral scent freshened the air, already growing warm. Giovanna scanned the pool for leaves needing removal. Familiar birdsongs rang from the surrounding bush, calming her nerves.

She led Jim to the head of the beach trail, where sunlight filtered through the shiny leaves of the deadly plant. "This is the infamous tree I told you about. It's called a manzanillo, or manchineel in English."

"But it's such a beautiful tree. Great shade," Jim lamented. "It's part of that postcard view of our property."

"We don't have to take it out. Just put a fence around it, and make a plaque explaining what it is."

Approaching footsteps told them they were not alone.

Giovanna turned to see Tyler, camera around his neck, roaming the grounds. "Good morning, Mr. Thompson."

"I'm glad you're alerting people to the dangers of that tree. Kids might be tempted to climb it or pick the apples." Tyler eyed the manzanillo.

"Thank you for bringing it to our attention," said Giovanna. "It's good that you and your team know so much about the islands. I haven't lived here long, and I appreciate all the help I can get."

The hint of a smile crossed Tyler's normally sour face, and he gave a slight nod.

Before the cameraman moved too far away, she asked, "Who handles Claire's social media accounts?"

Tyler stopped.

"Does she do all her posts herself, or does her team help?"

He shrugged. "My guess would be Susie."

My awesome assistant. Good guess. "If you see Susie this morning, will you ask her to come find me? I have a question."

"I suggest you check Colin's room. They're working on the script." He made air quotes around "working on the script."

"What was that about?" asked Jim, once Tyler had gone.

Giovanna started to answer, then stopped herself, wondering how much Victor would want her to share with her boss about the case. "Oh, just a question Victor had regarding the investigation. I thought I could clear it up for him."

"Great idea," said Jim. "I don't want your detective *friend* harassing our guests."

"He doesn't mean to harass anyone, but he must be objective and investigate all the evidence. The sooner we find out what happened, the less of a media circus we'll have."

Jim jutted his jaw as they headed back inside to continue their walk-through. "This mess needs to go away before the opening. Do whatever you can to speed things along."

CHAPTER NINETEEN

Thursday, Leisure Dreams Hotel

After her walk-through with Jim, Giovanna checked the restaurant and common areas for Susie, but there was no sign of her. She returned to her office and dialed the film assistant's room.

There was no answer. Should she try Colin, as Tyler suggested? Surely, she could come up with an excuse to call him. Yes, there were more details she needed to go over about the role of the film crew at Friday's events. She dialed his room.

The phone rang three times before Colin answered, sounding out of breath.

"Mr. Ashton," she began. "This is Giovanna Rogers, the hotel manager. I hope I'm not interrupting."

He steadied his breathing. "You're fine. What can I do for you?"

"Do you have plans for lunch? If not, I'd like to invite you and your team to the Isabela restaurant at noon. Kind of a working lunch, so we can finalize the details for the opening ceremonies. On the house, of course." When she didn't get an immediate response, she continued, "I know I should coordinate this meeting through Ms. Southworth, but she didn't answer her phone."

During a prolonged silence, Giovanna could hear whispering in the background. Then Colin came back on the line. "Susie's here. We've been reviewing our shot list for the documentary. And yes, we'd love to have lunch with you. Noon sounds perfect."

Giovanna smiled to herself. *He bought it. And Tyler was right about them being together.* "Will you please pass the invitation along to Mr. Thompson?"

"Sure, we'll let him know."

"Wonderful. See you at noon in the Isabela restaurant."

Belinda walked into the office as Giovanna hung up the phone. "*Buenos días, señora.*"

"*Buenos días,*" Giovanna replied. "Everything okay at home?"

"*Sí señora*. Is it a problem that I left last night?"

"Not at all. Glad you had a chance to get away. We've been so busy lately, and I appreciate all your help. You've been going above and beyond." Giovanna shuffled through some papers. "I've put together information for a plaque to label that manzanillo tree by the beach trail. Will you please translate it into Spanish?" Giovanna handed her assistant the English printout.

Belinda skimmed the copy. "Why do we need all this?"

"Because the tree is dangerous. We don't want anyone to get hurt."

Belinda heaved an exaggerated sigh. "Why not just a sign that says, 'PELIGROSO / DANGER'?"

"That should be the heading," agreed Giovanna. "Señor Roberts thought the marker should also contain an educational element. After all, most visitors to the Galapagos want to learn more about the islands. I'll ask Corporate to order us a more permanent, aesthetically pleasing plaque and enclosure, but we need to put up a temporary barricade before tomorrow."

"*Si, señora*." Belinda took the paper from Giovanna and headed for the door.

Again, Giovanna attempted to contact Pedro Lopez and Miguel Ruiz, but neither responded to texts, and her calls went straight to voicemail. *Has Victor had any luck reaching them?*

She wondered what Victor was doing now. *When will we have a chance to be together again? And how will Michelle react to our relationship?* Her grandmother knew she was dating the local police detective, but Giovanna hadn't shared how serious their romance had become.

Snapping back to the work before her, she phoned Laurel at the Darwin Research Station. "Can you talk?"

"Sure. Let me close this cage." Her words dissolved into the muffled sound of cooing to baby tortoises. After the creak of a metal gate, Laurel's voice returned, clearer than before. "What's going on?"

"You didn't mention being here the night Claire died. You said you went out for dinner with three friends in Puerto Ayora."

"I didn't see Claire," Laurel said. "In fact, I didn't even know she'd already arrived."

"So, you didn't know Claire was here until she called later that night, while you were at the restaurant in town?"

"Well, a little before that. Miguel filled me in."

"Miguel Ruiz? My groundskeeper?" Giovanna switched the phone to her other ear. "Did you and Maria talk to Miguel when you were here?"

There was a pause as if Laurel weighed how much she should reveal. "Yes, we met at Leisure Dreams. And then he joined us later at the restaurant."

"Did you tell Victor?"

Laurel sighed. "Miguel joining us was last-minute. I didn't think it mattered."

"Miguel hasn't been back to work since," said Giovanna.

"I wouldn't know about that."

"How did Miguel seem at dinner?" When Laurel didn't respond, Giovanna added, "Was he coming down with a cold? Did he drink too much?"

"I didn't think so."

"What did he say about Claire? Wasn't Miguel the one who told you she was at the hotel already?"

"All he said was that Claire and her crew had arrived earlier in the afternoon."

Laurel was a master at dodging questions; Victor had every reason to be frustrated with her. Giovanna suspected her friend was hiding something. But she couldn't figure out what, and she couldn't read Laurel's body language over the phone. "Had Miguel seen Claire?"

"I'm not sure. You'll have to ask him."

"We plan to. But Miguel's not answering his phone."

"*We?* Are you helping Victor with the investigation now? Is that why this conversation feels like an interrogation?"

Giovanna cleared her throat. "As the manager of this hotel, I have a stake in finding out what happened to our guest. Who will want to stay here if we can't keep people safe? We're all cooperating fully with the police."

"Even Jim?"

Giovanna suppressed the chuckle she knew was inappropriate. "Jim wants this matter to go away as quickly as possible."

"I bet he does. Grand opening tomorrow and all."

"You're coming, aren't you?"

"I wouldn't miss it."

"Don't give Victor a hard time. He'll have more questions for you."

"Can't wait." Laurel changed the subject. "Is your grandmother still planning to come?"

"She's supposed to. And she's bringing her husband, Roberto."

"It will be nice to see Michelle again. What will she say about you and Victor?"

Giovanna sighed. "If she had her way, I'd make up with Timothy."

"She still wants you to marry that guy after what he did?"

"Timothy is the son of her oldest friend. He and I have known each other since we were kids. Michelle assumes our break-up was just a big misunderstanding, and if we'd sit down and talk, we could 'patch things up.'"

"And that's not going to happen?"

"Nope. He took back the ring, and we're over." Giovanna flexed her fingers, glancing at the bare spot where the sparkling diamond engagement ring had once been—a family heirloom she'd never have considered keeping, despite the circumstances of their break-up.

"Do you think your grandmother will accept that?"

"She'll have to," Giovanna declared with more confidence than she felt.

As Giovanna hung up her call with Laurel, Belinda stuck her head in the office door. "I found some contractors to install the barrier, but can you come show them where to put it? I want to make sure I get your vision right." Belinda drew out the word "vision" in the same tone she spoke about the corporate brand.

Giovanna rose and followed her assistant outside. Three workers waited by the trailhead, wire fencing in hand. Pointing to the manzanillo tree, Giovanna pantomimed how she envisioned the fence to surround it. "*Aquí.*"

Belinda let fly a barrage of Spanish, waving her hands in the air. Giovanna could only hope the translation was correct; she was at Belinda's mercy. The workers smiled, nodded, and went to work.

"*Muchas gracias,*" Giovanna told them, and then started inside. "Don't forget the sign," she called to Belinda. "*Peligroso.*"

Chapter Twenty

Thursday, Leisure Dreams Hotel

Giovanna met Claire's team in the Isabela restaurant promptly at noon. She ushered the trio to a table by the window where they had a prime view of the bay's glistening waters. Black fins rose over the waves revealing a school of dolphins swimming by.

Colin pulled out Susie's chair and she flashed him an adoring grin as she sat down.

"Thank you for joining me," Giovanna said as everyone settled at the table. After they'd given the waitress their beverage orders and turned their attention to the menu, she asked, "I trust your accommodations are exceeding your expectations?" She used desired comment-card vocabulary when asking guests about their stay. Nothing like the power of suggestion.

"No complaints," replied Colin, casting a confirming glance at the others.

"Love the scented soaps," Susie added. "And the towels are extra plush."

"First class," Tyler agreed.

"Have you had a chance to explore the area yet?" Giovanna wondered how to ease into the topic of Claire's social media postings. "It's fun to go down by the harbor and watch the people at the fish market. The vendors struggle to keep pelicans and sea lions from sneaking samples. And the Darwin Research Station is a must."

"We checked out some bars last night," said Colin. "And the Darwin is on our shot list, so we'll head there this afternoon."

Giovanna assumed "we" meant Colin and Susie since she'd seen Tyler go out alone. "I imagine there's a lot of administrative work to be done that you hadn't planned on." She peered over the top of her menu. "Has anyone talked to Claire's family?"

"I've been on the phone all morning," said Susie. "Still trying to reach her husband and daughter."

"Ex-husband," Colin reminded her.

"Ex-husband," Susie corrected herself.

"They'll want to make funeral arrangements, but we don't know what to tell them," said Colin. "Any idea when the authorities will release Claire's body?"

"I'll check with Detective Zuniga, but I assume they're still working on the autopsy. The tissue testing is done on the mainland, so it takes more time to get results."

Tyler and Susie locked narrowed eyes.

Before Giovanna could react to the evident animosity between the colleagues, the server came over to take their food orders.

"What's the special today?" Giovanna asked.

"Chef made a scrumptious lobster salad. I tasted some earlier, and it's to die for."

The "to die for" description made Giovanna wince.

Susie's eyes lit up. Colin smiled, and Tyler licked his lips.

"I love Galapagos lobsters," said Giovanna. "They're a little smaller and not as sweet and tender as Maine lobsters, but I find them tasty." She closed her menu. "I'll have the lobster salad."

"Same," said Colin.

"Me too," Susie agreed.

"Make that lobster salad all around," said Tyler. "And I'd like mayonnaise on the side."

Giovanna told the waitress, "Please put everything on my account."

"Very generous of you," said Tyler.

"My pleasure." She turned to Susie. "I guess you handled the bulk of Claire's affairs." Giovanna recognized the irony of the word "affair" after it left her lips. "So much to think about."

Susie puffed her chest, a gesture that reminded Giovanna of a frigatebird trying to attract a mate. "It's a lot of responsibility, but we'll get it done."

Giovanna took a sip of water. "Claire must have a will with instructions on how to distribute her assets and provisions to appoint an executor. But what about things like her email accounts? Social media? How do you shut down those sites? Notify her followers?"

Susie paled.

Giovanna pretended she hadn't noticed the film assistant's uneasiness. "A friend of mine died a couple of years ago, and her family occasionally posts to her Facebook page. I got a reminder about her birthday this year, and friends who didn't know she'd died sent her 'happy birthday' greetings." She made a cringing face. "I know of another guy who died, and someone hacked his account. Two weeks ago, I got a new 'friend request' from a dead guy."

Colin covered Susie's trembling hand with his. "Susie has all the passwords, so we can notify everyone and then close those accounts."

Giovanna pressed on, "One of our employees is a fan of Claire's, and he follows her on several social media channels. He showed me posts about the documentary you guys are making that appeared on Claire's page the morning after she died."

Susie gulped.

Colin turned to look at her.

Tyler smirked.

Giovanna's sweet smile stayed plastered on her face as she waited for an answer.

The waitress brought their lobster salads, artistically displayed in flat china bowls and garnished with slices of avocado. "Can I refresh any beverages here?"

Susie held out her crystal wine glass. "One more Chardonnay, please." Everyone else shook their heads.

Colin tried his salad first. "Good choice." The others dug in.

Giovanna allowed some time for her guests to enjoy the food, then set down her fork. "I can imagine you'd be concerned if someone hacked Claire's account."

Susie finished chewing, then dabbed at her mouth with a napkin. "I do most of her posts. Claire was a busy woman." She took a large gulp of wine. "It was probably one I'd scheduled. Sometimes I write several posts at once and then space them out, to maximize engagement."

Giovanna nodded. "Now that Claire has died, how are you handling the announcement on her page?" She hoped the fact that Claire had met her demise in a Leisure Dreams hotel would be downplayed.

Everyone turned to Susie.

She swallowed, although she hadn't taken another bite. "Once we have more information about what happened, I'll post something. As Colin said, people will ask about funeral arrangements and how they can honor Claire, so I'll need answers."

"Are you the only one with access to those social media accounts?" With the curiosity of a cat toying with a cornered rodent, Giovanna observed Susie's disquiet.

When Susie picked up her fork, her hand trembled. "I think so."

Her colleagues shrugged and held up their hands to indicate they didn't have access.

"Then were you the one who responded to a comment on that post? As Claire? Yesterday morning?"

Susie set down her fork and yanked the napkin off her lap. "Excuse me, I have to make a phone call," she muttered before bolting from the restaurant.

Colin stared after her.

Tyler looked at Giovanna. "That would be a 'yes.'"

* * *

After lunch, Giovanna chatted with Colin and Tyler in the lobby before they headed upstairs. "I hope I didn't upset Susie. The social media postings were brought to my attention, and I thought, as Claire's colleagues, you'd be concerned."

"I'm sure Susie has a logical explanation," said Colin. "We'd like to control the rumor mill and not make any announcements until we have more information."

"Thank you for lunch, Giovanna," said Tyler. "The lobster salad was a winner."

Moments after Tyler and Colin left, Jenny Roberts, one of the CEO's seventeen-year-old twins, bounded out of the revolving glass door. With her khaki shorts and rucksack, long, blond hair in a ponytail, she looked like Safari Barbie.

"Daddy!" She ran to Jim, who had just entered the lobby.

While the two embraced, the next rotation of the revolving door revealed Michelle, Giovanna's grandmother, clad in a stylish beige linen blazer, a poster for the saying, "The sixties are the new forties." Following Michelle was Roberto, her handsome airline pilot husband.

"Michelle!" Giovanna rushed to hug her grandmother and then Roberto. They must have met Jenny at the airport and traveled together to the resort.

The door continued to spin, admitting Elaine Nelson, a short, plump redhead, Michelle's friend from childhood. Elaine's blousy sundress was a kaleidoscope of bright colors that did not occur in nature. Her faux gold bracelets jangled as she crossed the lobby, surrounded by a cloud of strong floral perfume.

What's she doing here? Giovanna wrinkled her nose. *Yikes! That fragrance will be a magnet for flies and mosquitoes.*

She untangled herself from the embrace with Michelle and Roberto to give Elaine a peck on the cheek. "Elaine, what a surprise to see you. Welcome."

"Thought it was time I got a passport and traveled out of the U.S.A.," said Elaine. "Your grandmother talked me into coming. And I wanted to see where you're working now." She gestured at her surroundings. "Manager of all this? At only twenty-six? Such a big shot." Giovanna might have taken exception with the term "big shot," but Elaine's tone conveyed admiration rather than sarcasm.

Giovanna shifted her questioning gaze to Michelle. Then her jaw dropped as the revolving door moved again, spitting out a tall, strawberry-blond man wielding luggage for two. Timothy Nelson—Elaine's son and Giovanna's ex-fiancé.

CHAPTER TWENTY-ONE

Thursday afternoon, Leisure Dreams Hotel

Giovanna felt her face harden. *Seeing him is the last thing I need.* "Timothy, what are you doing here?"

"Giovanna, we need to talk." Timothy's eyes were bright and hopeful as he set down the bags. "I've missed you so—"

Before Timothy could finish, Jim rushed between them to greet Giovanna's grandmother. As Michelle introduced him to Roberto, Elaine, and Timothy, Jim pumped hands like a politician. "So nice to meet you all. I'm thrilled you could come to our big event."

Stepping into the hostess role, Belinda announced, "Come to the desk when you get a chance so we can check you in. And the Isabela restaurant is still open if you want lunch."

"Leave your bags with the bellman," said Giovanna. "He'll take them to your rooms."

"One of us will be happy to give you a tour of the grounds whenever you're ready," Jim said. "Please make yourselves at home." He hugged Jenny closer. "How was your trip, honey?"

"Fine, Daddy. But I'm tired."

"Jim, I'm so sorry your wife won't be able to join us," said Michelle. "We hope she feels better soon."

"Thank you. Janice has had a tough time, but she's on the mend."

"And it was good of Jessy to stay with her," Michelle added. "I know your daughter hates to miss the opening, too."

Jenny shot several photos of the group with her cellphone. "I'm messaging my sister to let her know we're thinking about her and Mom."

Other employees relieved the new arrivals of their luggage. Giovanna recognized Roberto's black roll-aboard suitcase, decorated with Italian flags, and Michelle's well-worn, soft-sided gray one. The flowered trunk-like monstrosity must have contained Elaine's entire wardrobe.

While the others chatted over cups of fruit-garnished ice water, Giovanna sidled up to Michelle. "Why did you invite Timothy? And why didn't you tell me he was coming?"

Michelle patted her arm. "You two will have a chance to talk."

"We've already said everything we have to say." Giovanna gritted her teeth.

"He wanted to come." Her grandmother's smile was unwavering.

"He wouldn't have if you hadn't suggested it."

Michelle's deadpan "Who, me?" expression resembled one of her cats caught on the kitchen counter.

"I've moved on. I'm dating someone here," Giovanna continued. Just seeing Timothy standing in her hotel made her feel disloyal to Victor.

"But you won't be here forever," said Michelle.

"I'm not thinking about forever."

Michelle accepted a cup of ice water from Roberto, who had strolled over. She turned to Giovanna. "Just hear Timothy out. Give him a chance to apologize for the way he handled your business failure. It was a terrible time for both of you, and he's sorry he took it out on you."

"All the apologies in the world won't change who he is." Giovanna could not expel the bitterness from her heart. Her mind replayed their parting scene as if it had happened yesterday. *You're either a crook or an idiot,* he'd shouted. *Which is it?* Timothy had dismissed the fact that he'd signed off on bringing Jerome Haddad in as a partner. But after the con man drained their bank account and forced the clinic into bankruptcy, it became all Giovanna's fault. Was Timothy ready to take all that back?

Michelle sighed and Roberto shrugged.

Giovanna eyed Roberto. "You warned her this wouldn't work, didn't you?"

Timothy and Elaine had already started up the grand staircase toward the guest rooms. Watching their retreating backs, Giovanna wasn't sure whether to be relieved or insulted that her former fiancé wasn't still hovering.

Before she'd had a chance to mull it over, Victor walked into the lobby. Protocol be damned, Giovanna hurried to his side and startled him with a deep kiss.

"I thought you wanted to keep this discreet," he murmured, hands fumbling against her back, his eyes scanning the lobby.

Over her shoulder, Giovanna glimpsed Timothy twist on the staircase and stare. *See, Tim? I'm over you.*

Michelle had turned her attention to Roberto, and they, too, started up the stairs.

Giovanna pulled back from her kiss with Victor. "What brings you here this afternoon?"

"I have to check out a few more things from the scene." He held up an evidence bag.

Giovanna flinched at the thought of the Tio Armando suite designated as a crime scene. And now, more guests had arrived to see it. "Jim asked me how long the tape has to stay up."

"We'll try to take it down by tomorrow," said Victor. "The forensics team has most everything they need, but some of the officers are new, and I want to ensure they were thorough."

"When will we be able to clean the room? Put it back in service?"

"We're working as quickly as possible to make that happen."

Giovanna wondered if guests would be apprehensive about sleeping in a room where a celebrity had died. *I would*, she thought. But then, some morbid curiosity-seekers might go out of their way to book the infamous suite. Like people drawn to poison gardens . . . "Would you like me to go with you, or is this something you need to do alone?"

"You can come. Maybe you'll find something we missed." His puckish grin made her spine tingle. *Would it be too macabre to make love at a crime scene?* "Besides, the door locked automatically when we left yesterday. I need you to open it for me."

They mounted the wide, curving staircase and Giovanna gazed across the majestic lobby: the polished marble floors, plush furnishings, antique vases of fresh flowers. Tall windows revealed ocean and forest views. It was hard to imagine that violence could come to such an idyllic place. But it had before, and now it had again.

Seeing Jenny without her mother and sister reminded Giovanna of the hotel's brutal past and her own near-death experience here at the hands of that madman. With a shiver, she shook off the harrowing memory of Jerome Haddad.

When they reached the Tio Armando suite, Victor pulled back the tape, and Giovanna used her master keycard. The stink of spilled wine hit her. As she closed the door behind them, Victor put on gloves.

"I know Claire's colleagues are going to ask me again about her notebooks," Giovanna said. "What can I tell them?"

"Still working on it. After we've gone through everything, I'll need to assemble the film crew for more questions. I've highlighted entries that need explanation. After that, we'll most likely release the papers."

"They say they need Claire's notes to move forward with the documentary," Giovanna reminded him. "I'd assumed they had their own notes and instructions for what they were planning, but I guess Claire controlled it all. Can they get a copy while you're analyzing the original?"

"I doubt they'll start on the nature documentary until after tomorrow's events." Victor walked about the room, opened drawers, and stooped to look under furniture. "Didn't Jim ask them to film the opening festivities for his commercial?"

"Tyler has already been shooting on the grounds," said Giovanna. "By the way, I had lunch with the whole team today. We talked about those post-mortem social media posts."

"What did you find out?"

"She didn't exactly admit it, but I think Susie made them. The original post I can understand; it was scheduled. But the responses to the comments came after Susie knew Claire was dead."

Victor shook his head, then reached into his pocket and retrieved a pair of nitrile gloves. "Here, put these on."

As the detective worked, Giovanna stood in the middle of the room, unsure whether to touch anything, even with gloves. "What exactly are you looking for?"

"I don't know yet. Something out of place. Something hidden. Something in plain sight we may have overlooked."

"And you'll know when you find it?"

"Maybe. Maybe not."

She crossed the room and unlocked the French doors to the balcony. When she opened them, a blast of fresh, warm air streamed in to help dissipate the odor.

Stepping outside, Giovanna wondered if someone could have come in this way; if so, no one was likely to see them. But how would the intruder have reached the second floor? There was a large scalesia tree nearby, but not close enough for someone to climb it, then leap to the balcony. Unless the person was an acrobat. The tree was much closer to the balcony of her own suite, which gave her pause. She'd been out until almost midnight; could someone have come through her room? She hadn't noticed anything awry, but she and Victor had been preoccupied.

She peered at the ground. No nearby ladder or evidence that one had been used. Maybe a rope? Surely, the police checked for footprints or signs of entry. She called to Victor, "I guess your team considered the possibility of someone entering through the French doors?"

"I'm sure they did."

Before leaving the balcony, Giovanna looked down again. Wedged under the rail was a cigarette butt. She waved Victor over. "I think Claire smoked. I can't say for sure, but that bright coral looks like the same shade of lipstick we saw on the champagne glass."

He joined her outside. "Wonder how the team missed that. Because of the lipstick, I doubt it's one of theirs, and besides, they know not to smoke in here."

"Claire is the first guest to stay in this suite, although Jim Roberts uses it when he visits. He doesn't smoke, though, and he certainly doesn't wear lipstick." She grinned. "At least, not that I know of."

Victor chuckled. "Not that shade anyway." He carefully removed the cigarette butt and placed it in an evidence bag.

Giovanna closed and locked the French doors. She moved to the bed, stripped of its sheets and comforter. The lingering sour smell of day-old vomit made her gag. Salvaging the mattress was unlikely, and she pitied the maid who'd clean the room once the police released it.

Claire's suitcase lay open on the credenza. It was mostly empty. Type A personality that she was, Claire had unpacked before her demise, settling in for several weeks in the Galapagos. In the closet, sundresses, blouses, slacks, and a sparkling, semi-formal gown hung on the padded hangers provided by the hotel. Shoes formed a line on the floor: sandals, heels that matched the gown, sneakers, rubber wading shoes, and leather hiking boots.

The dresser drawers brimmed with Claire's lacy underwear, visors, T-shirts, Bermuda shorts, cargo pants, and swimwear—items that were probably folded neatly before the Puerto Ayora police rummaged through them.

"Did the police find any film equipment?"

"Tyler keeps it all in his room," Victor replied.

Giovanna moved to the bathroom. The medicine cabinet was bare, and there were no personal care items around. Victor had mentioned finding some prescription drugs, but those had been removed. Even the Leisure Dreams-branded toiletries had been taken.

She'd never thought about how to administer a poison. Perhaps putting the toxic agent into a lotion or other personal care product might be an effective way to kill or sicken someone. She turned to Victor. "If Claire was poisoned, do you think the killer might have put something into her skincare products?"

"I'll check with the forensics team, but I think they've already considered that possibility and are running tests. But the vomiting leads me to believe she ingested something toxic."

Like tainted champagne. Giovanna winced.

As they returned to the living room, someone knocked on the door. Before either could respond, a keycard chirped in the lock.

CHAPTER TWENTY-TWO

Thursday afternoon, Leisure Dreams Hotel, Tio Armando Suite

Hand near his holster, Victor strode toward the entrance to intercept the intruder. The door opened and Jim's head appeared.

"Señor Roberts?" Victor's hand relaxed.

Jim craned his neck to see around Victor. "I was looking for Giovanna. The maid said she came in here with you."

"Here I am, Jim." Giovanna stepped closer to the entryway. "How can I help you?"

"Jenny wants to talk to you."

Giovanna turned from Jim to Victor.

He motioned for her to go with her boss.

"You're sure?" She hesitated.

"I'm almost done here."

"What about the tape?" Jim gestured at the yellow plastic ribbon dangling from the door frame. "It makes the guests nervous. The new arrivals are already asking questions."

"I'll remove it soon." Victor picked up the end, ready to re-attach it.

The CEO gazed around the suite before leaving. "We'll need to send in the cleaning crew. I was hoping to use this room during the opening. We're booked to capacity."

Giovanna followed her boss down the hallway. "Jim, we'll manage. Claire had the suite booked all week anyway. Let the police do their jobs. Where's Jenny?"

"In our room."

They reached the Marine Iguana suite. The walls were painted a pale, soothing aquamarine, and the wood furnishings were well-appointed. Picture windows overlooked the pool area, where several guests sunbathed. Giovanna was pleased to see workers near the trailhead, busily installing the protective fence around the manzanillo tree. Now that she knew about its toxic properties, the gnarled manzanillo made her imagine a witches' tree, a harbinger of evil about to befall the resort.

Jenny sat curled on the couch, AirPods in her ears, phone in her lap, eyes closed. On the glass coffee table, an open can of diet cola perspired onto a coaster. Every few seconds, she belted out a few atonal notes.

Giovanna had never felt a strong bond with Jim's daughter, nor did she believe the teenager felt one with her. But now, with Jenny's mother and sister thousands of miles away, Giovanna was the closest thing to a familiar female face. She sat on the couch next to Jenny, touched the teen's knee, and shook it gently to get her attention. "Hey."

Eyes flying open, Jenny turned toward Giovanna and pulled out one of her earbuds. "Hey."

"How was your trip?"

The teenager gave Giovanna a sad smile.

"Your dad is so happy you're here. I'm sorry your mom and sister couldn't make it, but he would have been crushed if you'd stayed home, too."

"It's not fair." Her lower lip protruded.

"The older you get, the more you'll discover that life isn't fair." Giovanna smiled to herself. *Don't I sound like a trite, old philosopher?*

"Can we go see Tio Armando?" Jenny straightened herself on the couch.

"Now?" Giovanna checked her watch, wondering what Jim would think about her taking off so close to the opening festivities. So many details remained to be finalized. "I thought you were tired."

"Please."

The teen's mood shift, from morose to eager, perplexed Giovanna. Had it been that long since she was seventeen? "Let's ask your father. We still have a lot of work to do for the banquet tomorrow night."

"He's the one who suggested it." Jenny blinked, wide-eyed, her face a mask of sincerity.

Giovanna wasn't sure she could trust Jenny. The twins were used to getting their way. "Jim?" she called into the next room.

Her boss had settled at the desk in the bedroom with his laptop, and now he poked his head into the living room. "You rang?"

Giovanna motioned toward Jenny. "Your daughter wants to visit the Darwin Research Station this afternoon. I know we—"

"Excellent idea." Jim clapped his hands together. "Don't worry about things here. You've done most of the work already. Belinda and I will take care of any last-minute details."

"But—"

"And see if the film crew wants to go along." He narrowed his eyes in thought. "The Darwin is on their list of places to shoot for their documentary."

"I think Victor needs to talk to them."

"And ask your grandmother. I'm sure she'd like to show her friend the giant tortoises."

The thought of having Michelle on the excursion appealed to Giovanna; her grandmother had a better rapport with Jenny and could help entertain the teenager. But Michelle would insist on bringing Elaine and Timothy, and she was not in the mood to talk to her ex. "They might be resting."

"Fair enough." Jim nodded, reaching for the desk phone. "But go ahead and ask them. I'll contact the shuttle driver."

* * *

Giovanna stopped by the Penguin Suite where Michelle and Roberto were unpacking.

"Are you up for a visit to the Darwin Research Station?" she asked, leaning on the doorjamb. "Jenny wants to see the giant tortoises, and Jim suggested we organize a group."

"Now?" Roberto cut his eyes to Michelle, who shrugged.

"Sure," said Michelle. "I'll call Elaine."

Roberto turned to Giovanna. "Are you coming with us?"

She nodded. "I'll see you downstairs in half an hour."

"Wait." Michelle placed a hand on her hip. "Tell us about the crime scene tape on the room down the hall."

Instead of leaving, Giovanna plopped down on the couch. No way could this be quick. "One of our guests was found dead in the Tio Armando suite yesterday morning."

Hand pressed against her chest, Michelle sank onto the couch beside her granddaughter. "Oh, no! Giovanna! What happened?"

"Victor is investigating. We don't know the cause of death yet, but poisoning—"

"Poisoning?" Michelle's eyes grew wide. "Murder?"

"It looks like poisoning. But it could be suicide, homicide, or even an accident."

"Good lord." Michelle shook her head. "Don't tell me this is going to be like last time."

"No, Michelle, I'm not a suspect. This is nothing like the *Archipelago Explorer* last year." Giovanna flashed back to the cruise she and Michelle had taken, when she'd first met Victor. She'd been a person of interest in the death of a guide on board their ship. She'd assumed the death she was being questioned about was Laurel's; that her drowned body had been found. Instead, the guide she'd accused of covering up Laurel's disappearance had been found dead at the bottom of the swimming pool.

"Who's dead?" Roberto leaned over the couch.

Giovanna twisted so she could look up at him. "Claire Costello, a nature documentary producer."

"Claire Costello!" gasped Michelle. "I heard she'd be here and was hoping to meet her. We've watched a lot of her nature films." She eyed her granddaughter. "You won't be able to keep a high-profile death like that out of the news."

Giovanna agreed. "Much as Jim would like to." She glanced at her watch. "And much as I'd like to stay and chat, we need to get ready for our visit to the tortoise reserve."

* * *

Within the hour, nine people piled into the hotel shuttle for the thirty-minute ride through a dense scalesia forest leading onto a rural road to the Charles Darwin Research Station. Giovanna hoped she hadn't derailed Victor's plans to question Claire's colleagues again; they were seated inside the van before he could locate and stop them.

Giovanna clung close to Jenny, using the teenager as a shield to keep Timothy from taking the seat beside her. Luckily, his mother sat with him.

As soon as the van pulled out of the driveway, Giovanna sent Laurel a text letting her know to expect visitors and asking if the Leisure Dreams guests could meet Tio Armando. Laurel replied with smiling emojis.

The headquarters of the Charles Darwin Foundation was a sprawling, sixties-era complex of one-story administrative buildings, laboratories, and exhibits situated in a lightly wooded area just outside the town of Puerto Ayora. In addition to the tortoise habitat and displays, the Darwin housed a population of land iguanas. The large, brownish-yellow reptiles resembled their mainland cousins more closely than the iconic Galapagos marine iguanas.

Laurel met the visitors at the entrance. After introductions all around, she led them into the exhibit hall.

"Miss Laurel, are you taking care of Tio Armando now?" Jenny's voice brimmed with awe.

"I'm one of his caretakers," Laurel replied, walking backward to address the group as they passed through the building. "I'm in charge of the giant tortoise breeding program."

"Which I understand has been very successful," said Colin.

With a swoop of her arms, Laurel beckoned the visitors to follow her outside. The park's trails had been marked with signs in both English and Spanish, educating visitors about the flora and fauna of the region. "It has. We found Tio Armando a mate on Isabela Island and brought her here. Fingers crossed that we'll soon have little ones."

Tyler lifted his camera and took a slow, panoramic shot of their surroundings. "Glad he turned out not to be the sole survivor of his species. What a great discovery."

"The news wasn't always so well received," said Laurel. "Tio Armando had become a celebrity, like Lonesome George before him, and I got pushback when I presented my findings. But now everyone is happy about the success of the breeding program."

Giovanna struggled to keep up with Laurel, whose longer legs enabled her to stride briskly toward the tortoise enclosures. Even though Giovanna was five-foot-six and Laurel was only four inches taller, she moved at an accelerated pace.

Timothy and Elaine hung back, taking pictures of everything in sight. Michelle hovered like a mother hen, urging them to stay with the group.

"This place hasn't changed much since Michelle and I visited four years ago." Roberto kept pace with Laurel. "Except that Tio Armando's here now."

"Did you see him at the Beagle Galapaguerra when you were cruising the islands?" she asked. "Most tourist ships used to stop there."

"I guess that's where it was. We went to a tortoise reserve on San Cristóbal." Roberto looked at Michelle, who had just caught up.

Michelle nodded. "We have lots of photos."

They'd reached the deluxe enclosure for the famous tortoise. The huge reptile covered with a mottled brown carapace was the size of a small pony. Contemplating his visitors through dark, beady eyes, the tortoise chewed on a leaf of lettuce, dribbling bits of greenery from his powerful jaws. When Tio Armando craned his wrinkled neck and lumbered toward them, Giovanna remembered his leathery left front foot was missing a toe.

"That thing looks prehistoric," mused Elaine. "And those squatty back legs remind me of an elephant. A short, squatty one."

Ignoring Elaine's musings, Tyler addressed Laurel. "I'd be interested to learn how Tio Armando got moved from the Beagle Galapaguerra on San Cristóbal to the Darwin, via Leisure Dreams. Claire was researching that story for her documentary."

"Yes, Tio Armando's journey remains one of life's mysteries." Laurel's tone was bright, but her face had paled. "Oh, look over here." She pointed at a neighboring enclosure. "Some new baby Pinzón tortoises. See how small they are compared to the juveniles in the next pen."

Chapter Twenty-Three

Thursday afternoon, Charles Darwin Research Station

While the Leisure Dreams guests gathered around Tio Armando's enclosure listening to Laurel explain the tortoise breeding program, Giovanna escaped to a nearby bench to check her email. Knowing so many last-minute details required her attention knotted her stomach, making it hard to relax into tourist mode.

She'd only read a few messages when she caught a whiff of *Acqua di Gio* by Giorgio Armani. When she'd given Timothy the cologne for Christmas a year ago, they'd joked that it was named after her.

"Hey." Her ex-fiancé sat down beside her. "How have you been?"

"Doing well, but really busy now, as you can see." Even though she kept her eyes trained on her smartphone, he'd broken her concentration.

"You're growing your hair out. Looks nice." He reached to ruffle her ponytail, and she flinched.

"Damn." She'd accidentally deleted the email she'd meant to answer. Groaning, she bent to retrieve the message and typed a lengthy response.

Unfazed by her inattention to him, Timothy continued to sit beside her, close enough for her to feel his warm breath on her cheek.

She whirled around, unable to stand it anymore. "Why did you come?"

"I wanted to see you."

"Why? You broke up with me months ago." The gray specks in her blue-green irises glittered like flint. "You said you never wanted to see me again."

"I made a mistake."

Although his face appeared sincere, she would no longer make the mistake of trusting him. She bit her lip. "I tried to tell you that."

"I should have listened," he pleaded. "But I'm here now."

"It's too late." Her muscles tightened and she gripped her phone. "If you'd called or emailed, I'd have saved you a trip."

"It isn't too late." Again, he extended a tentative hand toward her. "We belong together."

Edging away, she eyed him. "You better put on some sunscreen. That fair skin of yours is going to burn here on the equator."

He glanced at a freckled arm, then returned his gaze to her. "Giovanna, I still love you."

What a hypocrite. She set down her phone. "I can't forget all those horrible things you said. How you blamed me for losing our clinic. You made me feel complicit in ripping off our donors. Implied I was as big a crook as Jerome Haddad because I was stupid enough to trust him as a partner."

Timothy wiped his eye, and Giovanna wasn't sure if it was a tear or just sweat. "I know, and I'm sorry. If I could take it all back, I would. When I heard what happened with Jerome—"

"If you really loved me, you'd have stood by me. We could have solved our problems together. Figured out a way to pay back the donors and work with the IRS. Instead, you dumped me."

"And I'm sorry. I was wrong. How many times do I have to say it?" A lock of strawberry-blond hair fell across his forehead, and he flipped it back with a toss of his head. She no longer found it endearing the way a cowlick kept his hair from staying in place.

"You accused me of ignoring due diligence when we accepted Jerome's help with financing. You were so self-righteous," she seethed, refusing to look into the sparkling green eyes she'd once found irresistible. "You even accused me of sleeping with the scumbag."

"Please forgive me." Timothy leaned toward her again.

Writhing out of his reach, she stood. "I can't."

He rose too. "I want to start over. And if you're honest with yourself, you know we can put the financial setback behind us."

"No." She stormed away.

Timothy followed. "Michelle said you're seeing someone here. But you're not going to stay on this island forever."

"That's none of your concern." As she walked toward the tortoise pen to join the group, she jammed her phone into her back pocket. Her hand shook.

* * *

Thursday afternoon, Leisure Dreams

While Giovanna escorted the Leisure Dreams guests to the Darwin Research Station, Victor finished his search of the Tio Armando suite. He found nothing else of interest besides the cigarette butt Giovanna had discovered on the balcony. *Smoking might have affected the way Claire's system interacted with the poison,* he thought.

The detective closed the door and headed to the lobby to meet the health inspector, who had arrived from town to check out the hotel's wine cellar.

Jim marched up to Victor as he greeted the inspector. "Why do you need to go through my wine collection? The cellar isn't part of the crime scene."

Victor suppressed a groan and patiently faced the CEO. "Claire drank champagne the night she died. Where did it come from?"

"Surely, you're not saying our champagne is tainted?" Jim's face reddened. "The Leisure Dreams label exceeds all health and safety standards."

Victor squared his jaw. "If someone tampered with your champagne, wouldn't you like to find out before you serve it to your guests at the grand opening?"

Jim flinched.

"Did anyone else drink champagne around the same time as the victim?" asked the health inspector, heading toward the exit. "Something from the same batch?"

"I'll have to check with the restaurant," Jim replied, keeping pace with the two men. "Locals dine here almost every day, and some drink champagne."

"Belinda said the victim invited her to share a glass but she only took a couple of sips," Victor remarked as they left the lobby. "She said it tasted bad and made her nauseated."

"Belinda doesn't know a thing about fine champagne," Jim grumbled.

"You're welcome to accompany us during our inspection, señor Roberts. But please don't touch anything." Victor kept walking.

Jim scowled. "Okay. Let's get it over with."

Built into volcanic rock on the side of a low hill, the wine cellar resembled a cave. Its underground location kept the temperature stable and substantially cooler than the surface. Tall wooden racks filled with bottles lined the stone walls. A balding, middle-aged sommelier was taking inventory when they arrived.

"Salvador," Jim addressed him. "How's the stock for the banquet tomorrow?"

Salvador's pearly smile would have been perfect except for one missing incisor. "*Todo listo, señor*. As you asked, I ordered extra cases of the special Leisure Dreams label, and it's all here." He gestured toward a towering rack filled with shiny new bottles.

"Do you track which wines are removed and taken to the restaurant?" The health inspector made a slow turn around the cramped cellar, taking in the layout.

"*Sí, señor*." Salvador presented an inventory sheet. "And the person who takes it signs here."

Victor leaned over the inspector's shoulder as he examined the paperwork. Miguel Ruiz, the groundskeeper, had signed for two bottles of champagne on Tuesday, the night Claire Costello died. Pedro Lopez, the assistant chef, had taken two of the same on Monday, and Luis Vera, the busboy, had signed for one on Sunday. "Were all these bottles from the same case?" the inspector asked.

"*Sí, señor.*"

Victor turned to the health inspector. The cellar felt crowded with the four of them huddled together. "They've been serving the same stuff in the restaurant all this week. Have there been any reports of illness?"

The inspector shook his head. "Not to our department."

"That's a relief," said Jim. "I hope you're not planning to ruin my stock by opening up and testing every bottle."

"Does your inventory match what's on the sign-out sheet?"

Salvador tilted his head.

"Are any bottles missing?" clarified the inspector. "Is everything accounted for?"

The sommelier studied the paper and nodded. "Nothing is missing, señor."

"Who has access to the wine collection?" asked Victor. "Can anyone come in?"

"The cellar is locked when I'm not here," replied Salvador. "We keep the key in the manager's office."

"But can anyone pick up wine?" asked Victor.

Salvador rubbed his chin, which showed the beginning of a five o'clock shadow. "Usually, it's Belinda or people who work in the restaurant."

"Miguel Ruiz doesn't work in the restaurant," said Victor.

Jim cleared his throat. "I told Miguel I wanted to send champagne to Claire and asked him to make sure we had some ready."

Victor glanced at the sign-out sheet again. "He took two bottles. Only one went to Claire. Do you know what happened to the other one?"

Jim shrugged. "I can check with the restaurant. It might still be there."

Victor turned to the sommelier. "What time did you leave here Tuesday?" Salvador was not on Belinda's list of employees on duty the night of Claire's death; therefore, he hadn't been questioned.

"I stayed late organizing a new shipment, but I was on my way out when Miguel showed up around seven-thirty."

"What did you do then?"

Salvador responded with a blank expression.

Victor elaborated, "Did you go back into the cellar with Miguel to help him find the champagne?"

"No, señor, he knows where to find it."

"Did you ask him to lock up?"

"Of course, señor."

"Did you give him your key?"

"No, señor. I left the door open for him. It locks when you pull it closed."

Victor nodded and jotted a few notes. "Did you ever meet Claire Costello?"

Salvador squinted. "Who?"

"Claire Costello. The guest who was found dead in her suite yesterday morning."

The sommelier put a hand on his cheek. "Oh yes. I mean, no, I never met her. Never heard of her until today, when everyone was talking about her terrible death. I understand it was suicide?"

"We're still investigating." Victor eyed the racks of champagne bottles. "There were a few drops left in the bottle delivered to her room. We've sent it to the lab to see if they find a trace of toxin. But in the meantime, let's make sure none of the other bottles have been compromised."

"Toxin? Compromised?" Salvador paled as he groped for a nearby folding chair.

Jim pressed his fingers against his temples. "Crap!" He eyed the inspector. "My grand opening is tomorrow. This has to be resolved before then."

* * *

Thursday afternoon, Charles Darwin Research Station

While the others toured the grounds, the film crew set up to take video of the tortoises, and they recorded Laurel's spiel about Tio Armando. The daughter of a film producer herself, Laurel was no stranger to miking up and performing for the camera.

Jenny's mood improved at the park. Her face lit up when Laurel showed her a group of baby tortoises, and it glowed even brighter when Laurel let her feed them.

But on the van ride home, the teen brooded.

Giovanna patted Jenny's shoulder. "Did this outing help? You got to see Tio Armando."

Her eyes brimmed with tears. "I keep thinking about Mom and Jessy."

Giovanna had been thinking about Janice and Jessy too. "You'll all come down here another time."

Jenny stared at her phone.

"I saw you taking pictures. Did you send some to your mom and sister?"

Jenny nodded, then nudged her. "Is that guy your boyfriend?"

Giovanna turned around in her seat. "Who?"

"The tall blond dude who came down here with Michelle and her husband. And his mother. He told us he was your fiancé."

"Ex-fiancé."

"He's cute. And how romantic that he came all the way here to be with you."

Giovanna grimaced. *Timothy's timing couldn't have been worse.*

"Daddy said you're dating that cop now. Victor."

Giovanna straightened in her seat. "Victor Zuniga." She and the Roberts women had met Victor last year when he'd come aboard their cruise ship to investigate the guide's death. Giovanna, Jessy, and Janice had all interacted with the dead man shortly before his fatal fall into the swimming pool. Because Jenny hadn't been near the scene, she hadn't experienced the same scrutiny as the others. Still, the dogged detective wasn't easy to forget.

"Daddy said Victor saved your life." Jenny pantomimed firing a gun. "He shot the bad guy who stabbed my mom and tried to kill you."

"He did."

"Is that why you're dating?"

Is it? Giovanna stared out the window as various species of ferns and cacti lining the two-lane road passed by in a blur. She remembered lying on the hard ground, grasping for a rock just out of her reach. Jerome Haddad straddled her body, brandishing the bloody knife, evil in his ice-blue eyes. Then a shot rang out, and Victor appeared at her side. Their kiss, like Prince Philip awakening Sleeping Beauty from her coma . . . "It's much more than that." *Victor appreciates me for who I am. He's not trying to mold me into his perfect woman. Like Timothy.*

"What about your fiancé?" Jenny's voice burst her reverie.

"Ex-fiancé."

"So that's it? The cutie came all the way here, and you're not getting back together?"

"I didn't invite him." Much as she hated to admit it, Giovanna was flattered that Timothy had come to the Galapagos. The journey was expensive, and he wasn't particularly adventurous; his idea of a vacation was a golf or ski resort close to home.

Jenny stole a glance at Timothy. "I bet he won't give up. He hasn't taken his eyes off you."

With a Mona Lisa smile, Giovanna gave Jenny's ponytail a playful tug.

* * *

Thursday afternoon, Leisure Dreams

By the time the group of nine returned from their excursion, more guests had checked into the hotel. Giovanna felt guilty for being gone so long, even with the CEO's blessing. But he liked being in the middle of things, and Belinda enjoyed playing hostess.

Waitresses circulated through the lobby with trays of colorful cocktails and fruit punch for the arriving guests. When the group stepped off the shuttle, one of the workers scurried back to the kitchen to replenish the refreshments.

Drinking chilled guava juice, Michelle and Roberto chatted with the others for a few minutes, rehashing their visit to the Darwin, and then excused themselves to their room to rest.

Jenny set her empty glass on a tray. "Think I'll put on my bikini and go to the pool. There's still time before the sun goes down."

As Jenny headed to her father's suite, Elaine sauntered over to Giovanna, cocktail in hand. "Honey, this was so much fun. It's like you live in an amusement park."

Giovanna laughed. "An amusement park?"

"Well, a zoo."

"I do love all the wildlife. One of the benefits of working in the Galapagos."

Timothy sidled up next to his mother. Elaine put a hand on his shoulder. "Have you two had a chance to talk?"

"No." Timothy gazed at Giovanna.

"Yes, we did." Avoiding Timothy's eyes, Giovanna gave Elaine a tight smile. "You two must be exhausted from your trip. Everyone's going for a nap."

Elaine yawned and surrendered her glass to a passing server. "Excellent idea."

"I'm not tired." Timothy's eyes swept Giovanna from head to toe.

"Take a stroll around the grounds then. If you'll excuse me, I have to work." Not waiting for Timothy to protest, Giovanna headed toward her office.

* * *

Belinda was laying some invoices on the desk when Giovanna entered her office. She sank into her armchair. "Thanks for holding down the fort."

"The fort?" Belinda's face puckered like a dried fruit as she mouthed her manager's words.

"Sorry. It's an expression. Thanks for filling in and greeting the new arrivals while I was gone."

"Only doing my job."

"And you're doing it very well." Giovanna's assistant thrived on compliments, so it was important to give them. "By the way, have we heard anything from either Miguel Ruiz or Pedro Lopez?"

Belinda shook her head. "Neither of them answered their phones."

"I hope they're okay. Do they both live alone?"

"Pedro lives with his parents, but they're visiting relatives on the mainland." Belinda's face softened. "Miguel . . . he lives alone."

Belinda's starry-eyed gaze made Giovanna suspect her assistant had a romantic interest in Miguel. "I think we should send someone to check on them."

Belinda shook her head vigorously, lips pressed together. "They'll be back for the opening."

"Victor still needs to speak with them." Giovanna wondered how she'd have felt if an employer checked up on her when she called in sick. She'd had no chance to find out because she'd rarely been absent during her short corporate career. But then, there had never been a murder investigation at her place of business.

Belinda's cellphone rang. "*Hola*." As she listened, her face tightened. "*Dios mío*." Her eyes grew wide as melons.

"What's wrong?" Giovanna asked.

"The health inspector just left our wine cellar."

Chapter Twenty-Four

Thursday afternoon, Leisure Dreams

By the time Victor and the health inspector finished with the wine cellar, Giovanna and the hotel guests had returned from their visit to the Darwin. Resisting the urge to stop in Giovanna's office and be reenergized by her smiling face, he headed outside to search for Claire's colleagues before they left again.

He found them sitting by the pool chatting with Jenny Roberts.

Tyler peeked up from his book on photography as Victor approached. "*Hola, señor.* I wondered when we'd see you again."

Victor gestured to Susie. "Ms. Southworth, may I have a word with you alone?" He used his most genuine tone and a smile to match.

Susie's eyes flashed panic at Colin, but he just shrugged. She rose from her lounge chair and, feet shuffling, followed Victor.

He led her to a secluded part of the patio and motioned for her to sit in one of the Adirondack chairs. "Can you please walk me through your movements on Tuesday evening again? After you and your colleagues arrived at the hotel."

She let out an exaggerated sigh. "Detective, I already told you everything yesterday. I was tired from traveling and went to bed early."

"You never left your room?"

"No." She studied her manicured nails.

"You didn't go downstairs to talk to the concierge about local attractions?"

Her cocky tone wavered, but she continued to scrutinize her fingernails. "Well, that was early, shortly after I checked in. I wanted to get some maps and brochures about places we should include in our documentary."

"Didn't you already have an agenda mapped out?"

"Well . . . I wanted to see what else there was to do here."

Victor consulted his notes and revisited the statement from Hector, the doorman. "And what time was that?"

"Maybe around six."

"And after you talked to the concierge, where did you go?" He consulted his notes.

"I . . ." She bit her lip.

"Did you have dinner?"

She took a breath, the cockiness gone. "I was on my way upstairs, and I ran into Colin. He was going to the restaurant and asked me to join him. To talk about work stuff."

"What time was that?"

"I don't remember exactly. Six-thirty?"

Victor nodded. "So, you and Colin had dinner together in the restaurant." His mouth twisted into a smile. "After meeting by chance in the lobby around six-thirty?"

Susie straightened in her deck chair. "Yes. I already told you we had to plan for the upcoming days."

"But you didn't call Claire and ask her to join you for this impromptu meeting?" Victor raised an eyebrow. "Didn't you do the project planning before you got here?"

"She's . . . she was . . . a 'big picture' type. She liked to articulate her vision and then leave the details to us." A hint of resentment rang in Susie's voice.

"So, that's a 'no'?"

"Right. We didn't call Claire. We never saw her again after we checked into the hotel. She likes to do her own thing. Meditate, or whatever." Again, a disrespectful tone tinged her voice.

"Did any of your other colleagues come to the restaurant while you were there?"

"Tyler? I didn't notice him if he did. And I told you we didn't see Claire."

Victor nodded. "How long did you and Colin stay in the restaurant?"

"I guess we were there for a couple of hours." Susie glanced at Victor's face for the first time during their interview. "The service was slow."

"Slow? I thought it wasn't busy."

"Well . . . it seemed slow."

Susie's lip trembled whenever he poised his pencil to write, so he took his time to gather more details than usual. "You were in the restaurant for a couple of hours. So, you left about eight-thirty? Nine o'clock?"

"About then, I think."

Instead of writing, he kept watching her.

She cleared her throat. "Nine o'clock."

"Did you and Colin leave the restaurant at the same time?"

Susie blinked, then nodded.

"That's a 'yes'?"

"Yes."

Her lip trembled again as he lowered his pencil. "After dinner, where did you go?"

"To my room."

Victor raised an eyebrow. "And did you stay in your room the rest of the night?"

She squirmed as if the deck chair were no longer comfortable. "Yes."

He studied her face.

Susie shifted her gaze back to her fingernails.

Victor kept staring at her. According to the maid, Susie had not been in her room all night.

She raised her head but did not meet his eyes. "Are those all the questions you have for me?"

"So, you didn't go to Colin's room after dinner?"

Susie's ivory complexion turned bright pink.

"It's okay. I'm not judging you." He suppressed a chuckle. "In fact, if Colin corroborates your story, you have a better alibi."

"Alibi!" Her baby-blue eyes watered. "I didn't mean for it to happen. Colin came on to me. Claire was too demanding." A tear trickled down her cheek. "At first, I tried to resist him but Claire's just so . . . ugh . . . she was a hard person to work for. Colin and I bonded over that."

Victor nodded. "I can imagine." Giovanna's instincts had been spot-on. "I take it, Tuesday night wasn't the first time you and Colin were together?"

Susie dabbed her eyes with the back of her hand, careful not to smear her mascara. "We didn't want anyone to know. We never meant to hurt Claire, but Colin wasn't in love with her anymore. She treated him like a lap dog, not a real partner."

The detective locked eyes with Susie. "Did you want to get rid of Claire? It would have made things easier for you and Colin."

"No, I swear. We didn't do anything to Claire." She sniffled. "I mean . . . except . . . you know."

"The affair?"

Susie paled. "Yes."

Victor turned a page in his notebook. "Let's talk about Claire's social media accounts. I understand you had access to them?"

Susie took a snot-filled breath. "I handled most of her posts, yes. A lot of busy celebrities hire assistants to—"

"Right." Victor waved his pencil to cut her off. "It's been reported that a post went out the morning Claire died."

"The post had already been scheduled, and I didn't think to stop it. I was so shaken by the news of her death."

"That's understandable. But there was a reply to a comment on that post, purportedly from Claire, made around ten-thirty the morning after she died. Obviously, Claire didn't write it, and you already knew Claire was dead."

Susie steepled her hands. "I don't know how it got there."

"Are you saying you didn't post the comment?"

"No." Biting her lip, she feigned interest in an insect crawling across the pavement.

Victor marveled at the gamut of emotions Susie had displayed during their talk. *What is she hiding? The affair is no longer a secret.* "So, you *did* post the comment." He waited to see if she'd contradict him.

"I was in shock." Her voice had become shrill, almost pleading. "I'd just found out my boss was dead. I checked her social media. I thought about posting a message to her fans, but I didn't know what to say."

"How about nothing?"

"I must have replied on autopilot. To boost engagement, I try to respond to every comment." She shook her head. "I know it sounds bad. But it's the truth."

Not changing his expression, Victor studied her face.

"Colin and I had nothing to do with Claire's death."

Unless we determine she killed herself over a broken heart. Victor was tempted to say those words, but he controlled himself. If Claire's death turned out to be suicide, he couldn't arrest Susie and Colin for cheating on her.

As he walked Susie back to the poolside group, a flicker of familiarity passed between her and Colin. An almost imperceptible nod, with not quite a smile, not quite a wink. Like a coded message.

Victor tapped Colin next. Rising, the young man pushed up his glasses and looked down his patrician nose at the detective, as if another interview was a complete waste of his time.

"Thank you for speaking with me again," Victor said, as they settled into deck chairs in the cozy corner of the patio where he'd questioned Susie. "I'd like to clear up some details from your story about the night your colleague died."

"Of course." Shoulders back, Colin sat erect, not quite comfortable in the Adirondack. "We all want to find out what happened to Claire, and we'll cooperate fully with your investigation."

Victor gave Colin a sidelong glance. "Actually, you and Claire were more than just colleagues, weren't you?"

Colin swallowed. "I think it's common knowledge that we were lovers."

The way Colin pronounced the word "lovers" made it sound dirty. Victor eyed his arrogant face. "So, as her *lover*, were the two of you together Tuesday night?"

"No. She needed some time to herself, and I told you I stayed in my room all night." Colin shifted his six-foot frame in the chair, still fighting for a comfortable position.

"Alone?"

Colin tightened his jaw. "I didn't see Claire."

"That wasn't my question."

Colin stared straight ahead.

"Did you have dinner?"

Colin took off his glasses and wiped them on the tail of his button-down shirt. "Yes, I had dinner in the restaurant Tuesday night." His steel-gray eyes glinted. "I thought you were questioning me about later, when Claire died."

"We don't really know what time she died."

"I heard it was after she drank the champagne."

"You know about the champagne?"

"I think everyone knows about the infamous bottle of bubbly. And we saw the lady take it up to her."

"Who?"

"Who took the champagne to Claire?" Colin ran a finger over his smooth chin. "I think it was that sassy little assistant manager chick . . . Belinda, I believe is her name."

Victor nodded and wrote. "So, you saw Belinda take the welcome gift to Claire?"

"Sort of. We saw her leave the restaurant with it, and someone mentioned it was for Claire."

"You said 'we.' Were you with someone?"

Colin swallowed. "I ran into Susie downstairs. We had to discuss the film project, so I asked her to join me for dinner."

Victor stifled a chuckle at Colin's attempt to paint the relationship as strictly business. "How fortunate that you ran into each other then."

"We were able to get a lot accomplished. Of course, little did we realize what roadblocks lay ahead." Catching the coldness of his choice of words, Colin amended, "Claire's death is a tragedy—both personal and professional for us all. My first instinct was to head back home and grieve, but I knew she'd want us to continue with our project. She worked so hard on it, and she wouldn't want our trip to be in vain."

Victor twisted his pencil while listening to Colin's speech. The man was as talented as any telenovela actor, and the detective was enjoying the performance.

"Is that all you have for me? You've stopped writing."

Victor tapped his notepad with his pencil. "What time did you leave the restaurant?"

Colin shrugged. "Around nine, I think."

"Belinda had already left with the champagne?"

Colin nodded.

"Did you pass Belinda on your way upstairs?"

With an exaggerated sigh that signaled Belinda's whereabouts were of no interest to him, Colin responded, "No. Guess she made a quick delivery."

"And after dinner, did you and Susie go to your separate rooms?"

Colin shifted in his chair again.

"Or did you continue planning the project?"

Colin narrowed his eyes at the detective. "Susie told you, didn't she? You forced her to tell you."

Victor shrugged. "We're not talking about her version of events right now. I'm asking for yours."

Resigned, Colin leaned back in the chair. "Yes, Susie came to my room to continue our discussion." Then he winked at Victor like a frat boy bragging about his conquest, as if Victor would be impressed or even envious that he was juggling two women.

Refusing to engage in the overture of macho camaraderie, Victor began writing again. "What time did the young lady leave?"

Colin lost the frat-boy leer. "I don't remember."

"The next morning, perhaps?"

Colin scowled.

"I take it, this wasn't the first time you two had met behind Claire's back?"

Colin kneaded his forehead. "We never meant to hurt Claire." He dropped his hand in alarm as if he'd just realized the implication of his words. "That way, I mean. Betrayal. And we had absolutely nothing to do with her death."

"Well, it's good to know you have your principles." His smile dripping with sarcasm, Victor stood. "Please let me know if you think of anything else that might help our investigation. And if you know of anyone, besides you and Susie, who might have a motive to be rid of Claire."

Colin rose as well, regaining his haughty demeanor, towering over Victor by several inches. "There is someone, Detective. Tyler. Claire was planning to fire him after this project wrapped."

Chapter Twenty-Five

Thursday afternoon, Leisure Dreams

As soon as Colin and Victor returned to the group by the pool, Tyler closed his book and got up from his lounge chair. "I guess you're ready for me now." He extended his long arms in an exaggerated manner, as if they were bound, and plodded after Victor like a pirate's prisoner walking the plank.

As they passed Colin, Victor could almost feel the flames from the glare the colleagues exchanged. He tried to recall when he'd observed other instances of animosity between the two men and wondered how they'd functioned as a cohesive team when Claire was alive.

Some other guests had claimed the deck chairs where he'd interviewed Colin and Susie, so he led Tyler to an out-of-earshot clearing. They sat facing each other on large, volcanic boulders.

"Fire away," said Tyler. "I'm sure you'll find me more forthcoming than those two."

"*Fire away*. Interesting choice of words," Victor mused.

Tyler furrowed his brow, not picking up the reference to Colin's assertion.

Victor studied the cameraman. "How was your employment relationship with Claire Costello?"

"Great. We worked together for over a decade." He sounded sincere enough.

"And lately? Everything was fine?" There had to be a reason Colin thought Claire was going to fire Tyler. Unless he'd made up the story to deflect attention from himself.

"Sure. Why would you ask?" Tyler's eyes flitted to a striped lava lizard scurrying across the rock. "We disagreed from time to time, perfectly normal among strong-willed creatives in a business like ours."

Victor followed Tyler's gaze to the reptile, which resembled a miniature land iguana. "Any recent disagreements?"

Tyler snapped his head up and turned back to Victor. "Colin! Did that snake tell you Claire was going to fire me?"

"Is it true?"

"Wishful thinking," Tyler scoffed. "I'm part-owner in her company, so it wouldn't have been that simple, even if she'd wanted to fire me. Colin may not know that. He's been pestering Claire for months to get rid of me."

"Why do you think that is?" Perhaps Tyler was not an easy person to get along with.

"He wants to bring in his own people." Tyler twisted on the boulder. "A 'yes' man. Another photographer who'll give him more control. Someone not so critical of him. The man doesn't have as much talent as Claire attributed to him. That fancy degree from Auburn and a handful of film credits might have impressed her, but not me." He shook his head. "And Colin had a guilty conscience for cheating on Claire with Susie. He was afraid I'd tell our boss, and she'd dump him. Claire was his meal ticket, and he still needed her. Susie was just the candy bar in the closet."

Victor widened his eyes with interest, encouraging the cameraman to continue.

Tyler twisted to face Victor. "Susie was useless as an assistant; she has no idea what it takes to make a nature documentary. Claire only hired her because she's the daughter of one of our sponsors, and it helped us get more funding for this project."

Victor raised an eyebrow as he absorbed the new information. "The other day, you told Colin that Claire knew about his affair with Susie."

Tyler ran his hand through his mop of hair. "She did. I didn't tell her, but she figured it out. She wasn't stupid."

"How did she figure it out?"

Tyler stroked a lone tendril of hair hanging from his chin, a feeble attempt to grow a goatee. "Women sense these things. A lie here, an unexplained absence there, another woman's scent on a lover's clothing. It was all coming together right before we left for this trip. She stewed about it the whole flight down, but those two flirted like she couldn't see them."

Balancing his pad on his knee, Victor made some notes. "Once Claire knew about the affair, what did she plan to do?"

Tyler traced a crack on the side of the rock beside his leg. "She didn't share her plans with me, but Claire wouldn't stand by for long and let them make a fool out of her."

Victor nodded. "I never met the woman, but it sounds like she'd have been tough on them. I suppose you'd be happy to see them both go?"

Tyler shifted his weight. "I have nothing against Colin and Susie, apart from Colin's gigantic ego. But I hated to see them take advantage of Claire."

Victor had to agree about Colin's ego. "You were quite protective of Claire, weren't you?"

"She got sick a lot, and I always took care of her." Tyler's voice had grown husky.

Victor raised an eyebrow. "Sick? How so?"

Tyler cleared his throat. "Claire had stomach issues. Ulcers, mainly. Nothing that kept her down too long. My mother had ulcers too, so I was familiar with the common remedies and could usually find something to make her feel better."

"Were you and Claire ever involved romantically?"

The cameraman crossed his arms. "Our relationship was strictly professional."

Victor studied Tyler's face for a moment, trying to decide if he believed him; the denial was a bit too forceful. "I know we went over this before, but I'll ask again. Did you see Claire after you checked into the hotel? Maybe for dinner? A nightcap?"

"No. I called her room and asked her to dinner, but she wanted to stay in and relax. When I offered to bring her something from the restaurant, she said she wasn't hungry." He stared off at the water. The wind was calm, and the sailboats were barely moving. "I took the hint that she didn't want to be disturbed."

"So, you had dinner by yourself that evening?"

Tyler nodded. "I got restless sitting in my room. Went downstairs and talked to Hector, the concierge, about the local attractions. He's a photography buff and was impressed that I earned my living as a cameraman. He gave me ideas about scenic viewpoints we could use in our film."

"Did you check out those viewpoints?"

"Right before sunset, I walked down to the beach, by those rocks where the sea lions hang out. Shot some nice footage of pelicans diving for fish."

"And after that?"

"I went to the restaurant and started to go inside, but then I saw Colin and Susie huddled at a corner table, all lovey-dovey. I didn't want to be around all that PDA, so I ordered a blackened grouper sandwich and took it to my room."

Victor nodded and wrote. "And on the way back to your room, did you stop to check on Claire? Find out if she'd changed her mind about having company?"

"Wish I had, but no. She'd put out the *Do Not Disturb* sign, and I respected her wishes."

Victor reviewed his notes. The timeline of Tyler's story fit with what he'd learned from others. "One more thing." He locked on Tyler's face. "Ms. Rogers mentioned you knew about the dangers of the manzanillo tree on the property."

Tyler gestured toward the imposing tree near the trailhead. "I'm glad she put a fence around it. That was fast."

"She's very efficient." Thinking about Giovanna gave Victor a warm feeling. "How did you know about the toxic properties of that tree?"

"Claire and I have traveled all over the world, making nature documentaries. We featured the manchineel in one of our films about the Caribbean. I recognized it immediately."

"Claire was also aware of the tree's dangers?"

"Yes." Tyler blinked. "Why? Is that important?"

"Then she wouldn't have inadvertently eaten one of the apples?"

Tyler shook his head. "Claire would never do that. She knew better."

"Unless she meant to kill herself."

The cameraman gasped. "You think she poisoned herself?"

"Unlikely," said Victor. "But we haven't ruled anything out yet."

Tyler stared at the tree. "I don't think Claire even left her room, but I guess it's possible."

"You said you didn't believe Claire would commit suicide."

Tyler swallowed. "I don't want to believe it. But then, I don't want to believe someone killed her. Certainly not on purpose."

"Not on purpose?" Victor frowned. *What does that mean?* "What do you know about the medications she was taking? Perhaps, combined with alcohol on an empty stomach, something caused an adverse reaction."

"As I said, Detective, she had ulcers. She took several prescription medicines. But I'm not a physician and don't know if any of those substances would make a lethal combination with alcohol." Tyler fiddled with the stray hair on his chin. "After her last physical, Claire mentioned her glucose was high, and the doctor suggested she might be pre-diabetic. He wanted to run more tests. She never went back for a follow-up visit; *diabetes* wasn't a word she wanted to hear."

"You seem to know a lot about her medical history."

"As I said, Claire and I traveled all over together. We shared a lot."

A greenish-gray Darwin's finch hovered in the spray from the rock waterfall beside the pool and then fluttered away.

Victor's eyes abandoned the fleeing bird. "What's going to happen to the film company now that Claire is gone? She's been the face of these documentaries for a long time. You said you're a part-owner, so you must have thought about it."

"I don't know. I'll have to talk to the other investors. Claire's ex-husband, for one. Of course, Claire owned the majority stake, so her beneficiary will have final say. Whoever that is." Tyler sighed. "It's too soon to think about it."

"I imagine you have many decisions ahead," said Victor.

Tyler made a fist. "My first priority is to find out why Claire died."

CHAPTER TWENTY-SIX

Thursday afternoon, Leisure Dreams

Before leaving the hotel, Victor stopped by Giovanna's office. She looked up from her computer and smiled. "I didn't realize you were still here."

"I had to speak with Claire's colleagues again."

"I'm sorry I whisked them away earlier," she said. "Jenny wanted to see Tio Armando, and before I knew it, Jim had organized a big production. Most of the hotel guests, including the film crew, went to the Darwin with us."

"Was Laurel Pardo on duty there?"

"Yes. Why?"

"She's next on my list." Victor glanced at his pocket notebook.

Giovanna wasn't surprised. The inconsistencies in Laurel's story needed clarification. "Since she didn't see or speak to Claire while she was here earlier in the evening, she didn't think it was important to mention."

"You talked to Laurel about the case?"

"You said there was a discrepancy in her story." Giovanna gave him a tight-lipped smile, and some of the magic in their eye contact dissipated. "I thought I was helping."

"I'll let you know when I need help."

She frowned, and the look she gave him was strictly business. "Is our wine safe to serve?" Seeing his puzzled expression, she continued, "You went through the cellar with a health inspector. Jim will have a fit if the government shuts down his champagne supply right before our opening festivities."

"He'll have an even bigger fit if his wine's contaminated, and his guests get sick—or worse."

"I don't even want to think about that." Giovanna ran her hand across her forehead. "So, what did you find? Is our champagne safe to serve?"

"We didn't find evidence of tampering with any of the bottles, and champagne from the same batch has been consumed all week without incident. So yes, I believe your wine supply is safe. The bottle was already open when Claire received it; someone could have poisoned it in the kitchen, inside her room, or en route. And we still don't know for sure the champagne was the culprit."

"I guess that's a relief." Giovanna touched her hand to her heart. "When I heard you'd gone to the cellar with an inspector, I was afraid the perpetrator was trying to sabotage our grand opening."

"It appears Claire Costello was the target."

"Now we need to find the motive."

"We?" He raised an eyebrow.

Giovanna winked. "You need me on the case. Admit it."

He flashed the quirky, lopsided grin she found so endearing. "I'm going to try to catch Laurel before she leaves the Darwin today."

Giovanna rose to walk him out. "I'd love it if you'd come for dinner later. You could meet Roberto and get better acquainted with Michelle."

Victor pecked her cheek. "I think your guests would appreciate time alone with you tonight. I'll meet them tomorrow."

* * *

Thursday evening, Charles Darwin Research Station

When Victor parked in front of the research station, Laurel was leaving. "Ms. Pardo?" he called as he got out of his car.

She stopped. "Detective, what are you doing here?"

"We need to talk," he said, walking toward the building.

"It couldn't wait until tomorrow?" She jingled her car keys. "You didn't ask if I had plans for the evening."

"This won't take long if you cooperate."

Laurel unlocked her office and, sweeping her arms with a dramatic flourish, ushered Victor inside. "I'm cooperating."

He took a seat and motioned for her to join him. "Let's review your statement from our talk yesterday. Tell me again where you were on Tuesday evening. Start with when you left work."

"I met friends for dinner."

"And before that?"

"Maria and I had drinks." She didn't meet his penetrating gaze.

"Where?"

Laurel lowered her voice to almost a whisper. "Leisure Dreams."

Victor nodded. "Why didn't you tell me that before?"

"Like I told Giovanna, I didn't think it was important."

He closed his eyes and shook his head. "You knew Claire Costello died that night at the hotel. Why didn't you think telling me you'd been there was important?"

"You asked if I'd had any contact with Claire," she replied. "I told you about our phone call while I was at dinner. Bahia Mar was the restaurant; I believe you know that already. When Maria and I were having a cocktail at Leisure Dreams, I had no idea Claire had checked in."

"When did you find out she'd arrived?"

"Miguel told me. Not long before Claire called."

"Miguel." Victor flipped through his notebook. "Was he one of your dinner companions? You didn't mention him before." He read the names, all women, that Laurel had provided at their first interview.

"I guess I forgot. He joined us later." She looked down at her wooden desk.

"You forgot." Victor let the words hang in the air.

Laurel fingered the cellphone lying on her desk. "Sorry."

"Have you seen Miguel Ruiz since Tuesday night?"

Laurel swallowed but did not respond.

"Giovanna said Miguel didn't show up for work today, and she hasn't been able to reach him. Have you checked to see if he's okay?"

"I haven't seen him."

"But you've spoken to him?" Victor glanced at his notes. "You're friends, aren't you? You used to work together. You had dinner together the other night."

Laurel's cellphone vibrated. She glanced at the screen but didn't pick up.

"Go ahead and get that. I'll wait." Victor had glimpsed the caller ID.

She eyed the device. "They hung up already." She nonchalantly doodled on a pad of Darwin-branded paper as if she hadn't noticed the caller.

Victor smiled. "Is Miguel at home?"

CHAPTER TWENTY-SEVEN

Thursday evening, Leisure Dreams

Jim had invited Giovanna and her guests to dinner in the Isabela restaurant. The staff prepared a round table in the middle of the room with a centerpiece of white and purple passion flowers.

To avoid sitting beside Timothy, Giovanna positioned herself between Michelle and Roberto. Nevertheless, she and her former fiancé had a clear view of each other from across the table despite the obstruction of the flower arrangement.

Seated next to Timothy, Jenny rested her elbow on the table, hanging on his every word. "I want to be a veterinarian someday. I love animals. Is veterinary school hard?"

Timothy had been gazing at Giovanna, who refused to look his way. "It's not too hard if you study and apply yourself." Although he replied to Jenny, his eyes never left Giovanna.

As they dined, Giovanna chatted with Michelle and Roberto about their latest travels in South America, and she tried to shut out Timothy's conversation with Jenny. She was grateful to the teenager for diverting his attention. But he should not have inserted himself into her social circle again like he was part of the family. Victor should be there instead.

Chef Gomez stopped by the table, sporting his white jacket and toque like a celebrity posing for photos. "How is everything?"

"Excellent." Michelle held up her fork. "I especially love the cream sauce you served with the whitefish. Do I detect a bit of nutmeg?"

"*Sí, señora!*" The chef touched his chest. "You're the only one who's been able to guess my secret ingredient."

"My wife loves to cook, and she's always experimenting with new recipes." Roberto placed a hand on Michelle's shoulder. "Nutmeg is a staple for her."

The chef grinned. "Señora, we must talk later. You're welcome to stop by my kitchen any time."

Giovanna smiled at her grandmother. Chef Gomez rarely tolerated outsiders in the kitchen.

After leaving their table, Chef Gomez made rounds through the restaurant, introducing himself to diners and asking them if they had questions, but mainly soliciting praise for his cuisine.

Jim watched for a few moments, then turned back to his guests. "That Chef Gomez is a keeper, don't you agree?"

Glasses were raised all around in a toast.

"To the chef," said Roberto.

"And to the success of your grand opening," said Michelle.

"To the Galapagos," said Elaine. "My first trip out of America."

"Well, you're in *South* America. The Galapagos Islands are a part of Ecuador." Giovanna couldn't help correcting her, even though she knew her remark sounded bitchy. Elaine shouldn't have come. Or at least, she shouldn't have brought her son. "But you're a long way from the *United States* of America."

Gabriela came by to refill water glasses. As she bent to fill Timothy's, he turned to ask her a question, and her long black hair grazed his cheek. She blushed. "Excuse me, señor."

"No, it's okay." He smiled. "I never know which fork to use first. Maybe you can help me?"

"Start at the outside and work inward. Looks like you managed." She leaned over his place setting and pointed. "The dessert fork is here on top."

"Thank you so much, uh . . . señorita." Timothy grinned, and their eyes met.

Is he flirting with her? Giovanna wondered. *Does he think he can make me jealous? Ha!*

Luis Vera, the busboy, whisked away dirty plates and silverware as soon as guests finished with a course. After he'd cleared the main course plates, he sidled up to Giovanna. "Señora, was your detective friend able to use my information about Claire Costello's social media postings?"

"*Sí, señor. Muchas gracias.*" Giovanna smiled. "The detective appreciates your help."

Michelle shot her granddaughter a curious look, but Giovanna waved her away, mouthing, "We'll talk later."

Chef Gomez appeared again, followed by Gabriela and Luis. "My special apple pie for dessert. Made fresh today."

Giovanna felt the blood rush from her face. Everyone admired the golden-crusted apple pie as juicy slices appeared on china plates before them. "Ricardo," she began. "Where did you get the apples? Are they locally grown?"

Chef Gomez set a slice of pie in front of her. "Of course not, señora. No edible apples grow here in the Galapagos. These were imported from Washington State, in your country. They arrived fresh this morning."

Giovanna felt her circulation return. *No poison apples, thank you.*

* * *

Timothy caught up with Giovanna as the group disbanded and the guests made their way upstairs or went outside for after-dinner strolls. "Walk with me," he begged. "For a few minutes. Hear me out."

Rather than make a fuss, Giovanna agreed. "The lights are pretty by the pool, but otherwise, you won't see much of the property in the dark."

"That's okay. I like listening to animal sounds at night, and if it's that dark, maybe we'll see some stars and planets."

Giovanna also enjoyed listening to nocturnal animal sounds and identifying constellations, but she didn't admit it to Timothy. Remembering their many common bonds opened old wounds.

They strolled outside into the warm night air. "Are you building your practice back up?" she asked. Timothy had all but left his veterinary practice to his partners in order to found a low-cost spay/neuter clinic with Giovanna. After the clinic went bankrupt and the scandal broke, his partners were afraid to take him back. The IRS was still investigating how the clinic owners had squandered hundreds of thousands of dollars in donations and then shut their doors. Their building and equipment had been seized, and all the remaining money Timothy and Giovanna had invested had gone to settle claims. Their partner, Jerome Haddad, who had drained their accounts and left the country, had never been prosecuted. At least he was dead now, but Jerome's death hadn't solved their financial problems.

"It's been slow," Timothy said. "But coming along. The partners understand none of it was my fault."

No, you told them it was all my fault. "They must have felt better after you cut me loose."

He stopped to face her. The shadows distorted his features so that he looked like a stranger. "I told you I was sorry."

"Sort of." She kicked a pebble down the path. *Too little, too late.*

Timothy gripped her shoulders. "I should have known you had nothing to do with the fraud."

"You did know." She shrugged him away. "But you blamed me for what Jerome Haddad did to our business."

"You brought him in as a partner."

"Aha!" Giovanna waved her finger at Timothy. "You're still angry about that."

"I'll never forgive Jerome. But I forgave you." Timothy clenched his jaw.

"I did nothing wrong, so there's no need for you to forgive me." The old anger welled up inside, flushing her face. "I made a bad business decision—a fatal one. But you approved it."

Timothy touched her shoulder, more gently this time. "Can't we get past this?"

"I told you, I can't. Not now." They reached the pool, and she sat down on a nearby boulder. "I'm sorry you came all this way hoping for a reconciliation."

"But I love you. I've never loved anyone else."

She shook her head. "Your love is conditional. Real love is unconditional." She waited for him to say, "Get a dog," like he used to when they'd joke around, but he didn't.

He sat down beside her, uncomfortably close. "I won't give up." He nudged her like they did to each other when they were children. "You know I don't give up."

She smiled despite herself. "That's your prerogative."

Gently, he lifted her chin until their lips brushed against each other; before she realized what was happening, he pulled her into a kiss.

Giovanna shoved him away. His gesture had failed to ignite any of the old passion she'd once felt; on the contrary, it fueled her anger. "What are you doing?" She stood up.

"Kissing you." He stood too.

"Don't."

"Admit it, you liked it. You've missed me as much as I've missed you."

She started toward the main building. "Honestly, I haven't thought about you in months." She knew Timothy was following her, but she kept walking.

When they were back inside, she busied herself conferring with the concierge and the receptionist about the evening's arrivals. Several of the Leisure Dreams corporate staff had checked in, and the Chief Marketing Officer was supposed to get a welcome basket. *Dare we send him champagne?*

Timothy loitered in the lobby for a few minutes, then retreated upstairs.

* * *

Hearing voices as she passed Michelle's suite, Giovanna knocked. She could really use a conversation with her grandmother right now.

Michelle opened the door wearing a pale blue robe. Her face lit up. "Giovanna, come in. Roberto just made herbal tea. Would you like some?"

"Sounds great." Giovanna entered the suite, and Roberto set out another cup. "I know you two have had a long day, and I don't want to keep you up."

"Sit," said Michelle. "Tell me more about our hotel murder mystery."

Roberto set down the teapot. "If you'll excuse me, I'm going to go read about a murder that's already been solved." With a wave, he withdrew to the bedroom with one of his Ann Rule true-crime books.

Giovanna wanted to complain about Timothy rather than discuss the death in her hotel, but she knew she'd have to indulge her grandmother's curiosity. "I'm not a suspect."

"That's a relief. You're sure?" Michelle took a sip of the steaming tea.

"I never met the victim and have no motive. And besides, Victor is my alibi." Giovanna stirred a lump of brown sugar in her cup, watching its crystals dissolve in the hot liquid. "Tuesday, we spent the whole day hiking on the other side of the island, and we had a picnic on the beach at sunset."

Michelle's smile looked forced. "Sounds romantic."

"Very."

"But do they know the time of death?" asked Michelle. "Didn't you say Claire Costello was found dead the next morning? The police could still say you had opportunity. Remember last time."

Giovanna shook her head. "Victor came back to the hotel with me. We spent the whole night together." She looked her grandmother in the eye, gauging her reaction.

Tea sloshed from Michelle's cup as she set it down. "I see. So, that's why you're not thrilled about Tim being here."

"Regardless, I wouldn't have been thrilled to see Timothy. Why did you let him come?"

"It was his idea."

"But I'll bet you suggested it." Giovanna's eyes blazed like sunlight on metallic paint. "How could you do this? You didn't even ask me."

Michelle touched her granddaughter's knee. "I'm sure the detective is a nice man, but think about the future."

Giovanna blew on her tea and took a drink.

Michelle withdrew her hand from Giovanna's knee and picked up her teacup. "Fine. You're young; you're having fun. I get it. I'm not one to talk. But don't burn your bridges; that's all I'm saying." She took a sip. "Is Victor sharing any details about the investigation with you?"

"He gets into 'cop mode' sometimes, but yes, he shares a lot with me," Giovanna replied. "Because of my role as hotel manager, he has to rely on me for information about staff, entry to secure areas—he needs my cooperation."

"What have you learned? Was it poisoning?"

"Most likely, but they're still waiting for the toxicology report."

"Do you have suspects?"

Giovanna stirred her tea; some sugar had settled to the bottom of her cup. "He still hasn't talked to everyone who was on duty that night. But yes, I think there are suspects."

CHAPTER TWENTY-EIGHT

Thursday evening, Puerto Ayora

Miguel Ruiz lived in a tiny, mid-twentieth-century wood-frame house on the edge of town with a lawn of mostly weeds. A dented, decades-old Volkswagen Bug was parked in the gravel driveway.

Victor strode up the pebbly walkway, wondering if Miguel would answer the door, or if he was even home. Laurel most likely alerted him as soon as the detective left her office.

The porch light contained no bulb, and only a dim glow filtered through the translucent curtains. Victor knocked on the unvarnished door. Rock music played inside. "Miguel Ruiz?"

No answer, but someone lowered the volume.

Victor rapped louder. "Miguel? Police! Open up."

Boards creaked under footsteps crossing the wood floor.

The door cracked open, and incense-masked marijuana smoke seeped out. A head with close-cropped, dark hair peered through. The shirtless Ecuadorian man, who appeared to be in his late thirties, wore faded jeans and held a Pilsener in one hand. "What do you want?"

"Detective Zuniga." Victor displayed his badge. "May I come in? We need to talk."

Miguel opened the door and stepped aside to admit Victor into the entryway. "What's this about?"

Victor wished automatic mistrust of the police wasn't so common among the islanders, but he could hardly pretend he'd come on a social call. He scanned the room and concluded they were alone. "When was the last time you were at the Leisure Dreams resort?"

Miguel paused as if consulting an internal calendar. "This past Tuesday. I was supposed to work this morning, but I called in sick."

The man looked perfectly healthy to Victor. "I'm sorry. I hope you're feeling better."

Miguel smirked. "Yes, thanks. Just one of those twenty-four-hour bugs."

"That's good. You'll be there tomorrow for the opening?"

"*Sí*, but I didn't know management had started sending the police to check up on absent employees."

"That's not why I'm here. Tuesday night, one of the hotel guests died."

Miguel's face revealed nothing. Not guilt, not sadness, not surprise.

"We're questioning everyone who was on the property that day and evening. Routine."

"Of course."

"Did you hear about the death already?"

Miguel scrunched his face. "Suicide, wasn't it?"

"We're still investigating." The detective gestured toward a worn leather couch against the wall. "May we sit?"

Miguel walked to the couch and sat down. He took another sip of his beer.

Victor followed. "Did you know Claire Costello?"

"I've heard of her." Miguel shifted his position, increasing the space between him and the detective.

"Only heard of her? Your paths never crossed?" When Miguel didn't respond, Victor added, "She's been to the Galapagos several times to produce nature documentaries, and you used to work at the Darwin Research Station, where her company filmed."

"Oh. We may have met then." Squirming, Miguel picked at the label on his beer bottle.

"Did you know she was coming here?"

The groundskeeper set his beer on the coffee table and ran his finger across a tiny hole in the leather couch. "I was driving the CEO around when señora Costello arrived."

Victor's gaze stayed focused on Miguel's face, but Miguel wouldn't look him in the eye. "She was a VIP guest, wasn't she?"

"I suppose so."

"Since Claire was such an important guest, did señor Roberts want to do anything special to welcome her?"

"She got the VIP treatment, yes. Señora Rogers had already arranged it."

"And what exactly did that entail?"

Miguel shrugged. "Best suite. Fresh flowers in her room. More personal attention from the staff."

"That's it? Any welcome gifts? Like a fruit basket, wine?"

"Señor Roberts wanted to send her a bottle of his best champagne."

Victor nodded as if this were news to him. "And did he?"

"He asked me to get some out of the cellar because there wasn't any in the kitchen."

"Why not? If señora Rogers had already requested it?" Victor remembered Giovanna's phone conversation with Belinda the morning they found Claire's body.

Again, Miguel shrugged.

Victor sensed he'd have to dig to get more than minimalistic responses. "So, did you get champagne from the cellar?"

"Yes, I brought up two bottles."

Victor tapped his tooth. "Did you notice anything unusual about either of those bottles?"

Miguel's expression flickered, like the bulb in a short-circuiting socket. "No, they were the standard Leisure Dreams premium reserve."

"And did you take the champagne to señora Costello?"

His face paled. "No, I was off duty by then."

"Did you see who took it to her?"

"No. I gave both bottles to the sous chef. After that, I clocked out and left." Miguel crossed his legs and then uncrossed them.

"Home?"

"I met some friends for dinner."

"Who?"

"Is that relevant?" Miguel scowled.

"I'll decide whether it is."

"Laurel Pardo and Maria Vasquez. And a couple of other young ladies from town. I don't remember their names."

Victor wrote, then flipped back through his notes. "You never answered my earlier question: Did you see or speak to Claire Costello at any time on Tuesday?"

"I didn't see her."

Victor's mouth twitched. Getting answers out of Miguel was no easier than questioning Laurel. "Did you talk to her? Perhaps over the phone?"

"Not me." Miguel looked away.

Victor was not convinced. But why would Miguel lie?

CHAPTER TWENTY-NINE

Friday morning, Leisure Dreams Hotel

Giovanna rose before dawn, and not long afterward, the hotel buzzed with activity. Extra staff—temps from a local restaurant and employees from the Quito property—had come to help with the grand opening.

"What can I do?" asked Michelle when she came down to the lobby. "Feel free to put us all to work."

"Thank you," said Giovanna. "Normally, I'd say relax and enjoy the resort, stay out of our way, but this is so . . . important." She could feel her blood pressure spiking.

Michelle pushed a strand of light brown hair out of her granddaughter's face. "I know, honey. This is a huge day for you and your hotel."

Giovanna bit her lip. "Especially after a guest died on my watch. If something else goes wrong—"

"So, let us help," offered Michelle. "We can knock out some last-minute tasks to keep you from feeling stressed."

"Okay, I'll take the free labor. You and Elaine can help Belinda set up for the banquet in the restaurant. She can use someone to keep her focused. Sometimes, she's a scatterbrain."

"Your assistant, Belinda, right?" Michelle gestured across the room to where Belinda was giving instructions to several new barmaids. "She's a perky little thing, isn't she?"

Giovanna smiled. "She and Elaine should get along great. They're a lot alike."

Michelle and Giovanna exchanged amused glances.

Giovanna twisted her hands together. "Roberto's still into gardening, isn't he?"

Michelle nodded. "Ever since he earned his Master Gardener certification, he's been analyzing the pruning techniques of horticulturists around the world. He'd love an opportunity to make his mark."

"Great." Giovanna grinned. "Roberto can help Miguel prune the bushes around the front. He was supposed to do them yesterday, but he called in sick. I'm glad he made it in this morning. Early, even." As soon as Miguel had arrived, she'd texted Victor to let him know.

Just as Michelle took off to tackle her assignment, Jim appeared at Giovanna's elbow. Trailing behind him were three members of the Leisure Dreams marketing department and Kevin Franklin, Director of Corporate Communications. "Ms. Rogers," said Jim. "Will you be joining us for the meeting with the sales team?"

Giovanna offered her hand to Kevin—a lanky, fair-haired man in his late forties, tall enough to appreciate the hotel's high doorways. "The conference room is ready." Pointing, she stepped toward the business center and beckoned the group to follow. "How are your accommodations?"

"Very nice," said Kevin, adjusting his gold wire-rimmed glasses as the executives crossed the lobby's beige marble floor. "Even though this property is more like a boutique hotel, it maintains the same luxurious feel and attention to detail that the Leisure Dreams brand is known for."

When everyone was seated around the granite conference table, Jim began, "Most of the representatives from the local tourist board will be here this afternoon, as well as several travel agents and government officials from the mainland, who will be staying overnight." He looked at Giovanna. "I trust their rooms are ready?"

"Yes, sir."

"We've invited spokespeople from the Charles Darwin Research Station." Jim gestured at a stack of flyers advertising the wildlife center. "Leisure Dreams has a special partnership with the organization as part of our focus on education and conservation. Not to mention, the Darwin is the main tourist attraction on this island."

Giovanna nodded, marveling at how Jim could utter brochure statements with a straight face as if he'd written them.

"Excellent," said Steve Blackstone, the silver-haired Leisure Dreams Chief Marketing Officer. He was a large man in his fifties with broad, powerful shoulders and a cleft chin. His piercing gray eyes swept the room as if taking measurements, evaluating every feature against corporate standards.

"We plan to visit the Darwin Research Station while we're here," said Andrea Horton, his spindly, middle-aged assistant with a beak-like nose and short, mousy brown hair. "I can't wait. I love giant tortoises."

"It's not to be missed," agreed Olivia Martinez, the forty-something sales director for the South American region. Her thick dark curls were tied at her nape with a bright red ribbon that matched her full skirt, reminding Giovanna of a flamenco dancer. "If you don't get to any other islands, at least you'll see a good sampling of the unique Galapagos wildlife."

"Speaking of wildlife, we need to talk about the elephant in the room." Kevin poured himself a cup of coffee from the carafe in the center of the table.

Andrea looked at Jim. "Is it true about Claire Costello? There hasn't been much news back in the States."

Jim's eyes shifted to his hotel manager. "Giovanna, why don't you brief them about our unfortunate . . . uh . . . situation?"

She cleared her throat. "There's not much to tell yet. Claire Costello and her team arrived Tuesday afternoon. The next morning, when Claire failed to respond to her requested wake-up call, my assistant found her dead in her suite."

A collective gasp halted the conversation. Kevin kept pouring after his cup was full, sloshing coffee onto the table.

Giovanna passed him a handful of paper napkins bearing the resort's logo. "We're cooperating with the police investigation, but the case has yet to be resolved." She reached for the pitcher of ice water and poured herself a glass.

Steve's hand shook when he took the pitcher from her and served himself. The way he glared made Giovanna wonder if he blamed her for the tragedy.

"How . . . how did Ms. Costello die?" Andrea asked.

"The police haven't confirmed it, but signs point to poisoning," Giovanna said.

"Poisoning!" Steve slammed his glass onto the table. "Are we liable?"

"Poisoning in . . ." Kevin sat up straighter. "Something she ate? Here?"

"Could it have been an accidental overdose?" suggested Olivia. "Natural causes?"

Giovanna cast her eyes toward Jim, who was no help. He had delegated full responsibility for the difficult conversation to her. "We don't know yet. The police detective in charge of the investigation should be here later, and he can answer more of your questions. We're trying to do damage control with the media."

"Who's your local media contact?" asked Kevin.

"Maria Vasquez, with the *Ayora Times*." Giovanna watched him jot down the name. "She's coming to the banquet tonight and has already been here asking questions."

"I'll get in front of it." Kevin's jaw stiffened.

"How was Claire poisoned?" asked Andrea.

"We don't know. But we delivered a fruit basket and a welcome bottle of champagne to her room." Giovanna took a sip of water. She wished Victor were here to help her field the questions. "The champagne and some fruit appear to be the last items she consumed."

"Our champagne is tainted?" thundered Steve. His face reddened, and the veins in his neck bulged above his collar. "What will we serve tonight?"

"The health inspector and the lead detective searched our wine cellar yesterday and found no evidence of tampering," Giovanna assured him. "They believe our wine supply is safe."

"So, do we have a killer on the property?" Steve ran his hands through his thick, silver hair. "One of our employees is a murderer?"

Giovanna bristled. She had been instrumental in hiring many of the employees, or at least supervising them, getting to know the individuals and their families. Calling one of them a murderer felt personal. "Claire's colleagues had issues with her, and they're on the suspect list too. If, in fact, her death turns out to be murder."

"Claire and her team were on my flight from the States the other day," said Olivia. "I stayed over in Guayaquil, but they flew straight here. On the plane, Claire acted like a royal bitch. Snapping at them, degrading them, embarrassing them in front of the whole first-class cabin. Any one of her employees might have wanted to kill her."

Kevin held up his hand. "Please, keep all the speculation inside this room. The less we theorize, the better. If you express an opinion about this case in front of a reporter, the next thing you know, you'll be quoted as a company spokesperson, and your statement will be viewed as fact. The last thing we need right now is a media circus."

"All I've told Maria is that we're cooperating with the police, and she needs to check with them for more details," said Giovanna.

"Good," said Kevin. "We need to keep this situation contained."

Jim nodded his approval, which Giovanna took as encouragement. But was it enough? Could she pull off this event without another disaster?

* * *

Giovanna's next order of business was to arrange a meeting between the Leisure Dreams corporate team and Claire's documentary film crew to discuss promotional shots during the opening ceremonies. She explained to Kevin and Steve that she had to oversee last-minute banquet details and assured them they could handle the meeting on their own. "Text me if you have questions or need access to any nonpublic areas," she said, after making the introductions.

She headed into the kitchen to check on the food preparations. Chef Gomez stirred a kettle of fish stew and barked orders at staff as they scurried around the work area, trying to avoid his sharp tongue by looking busy and performing their duties correctly.

Giovanna surveyed the flurry of activity. "*Buenos días, señor.* Do you have enough help? Is there anything you need?"

"We have everything we need, señora."

She watched the staff come and go for a moment. "Any word yet from Pedro Lopez?"

The chef shook his head. "No, señora. I called his house this morning, but there was no answer. I could really use his help today."

The sous chef's absence troubled her. Could something be wrong? "I can send my grandmother in to assist you."

"*Su abuela?*" Gomez quirked an eyebrow. "Will she follow instructions?"

"She's a good cook and likes to experiment in the kitchen. If you speak to her nicely, she'll probably do what you ask."

"Señora, I always speak nicely." He flashed a cheeky grin.

One of the young men chopping vegetables looked up and scowled.

Giovanna gestured at the hustling kitchen staff. "Shall I ask for a second opinion?" With a smile, she headed into the dining area.

Michelle, Belinda, Elaine, and several waitresses spread tablecloths and arranged centerpieces.

Giovanna approached Michelle. "I have a task you might find more appealing if you're up for a challenge."

Michelle turned to her granddaughter. "Since you know I'm not the artsy, interior decorator type?" As she spoke, Belinda walked by and straightened the centerpiece Michelle had just placed.

"I didn't say that." Giovanna put her hand on her grandmother's shoulder. "How would you like to help Chef Gomez? I know you like to learn new recipes, and his sous chef didn't show up again today."

"Are you sure you want me in the kitchen?" asked Michelle. "Aren't there some labor laws or liability issues we'd be violating?"

"Probably." Giovanna chuckled. "But I'm the manager of this hotel, and the CEO is here to back me up. Besides, the chef likes you. You're the only one who could detect the nutmeg in his fish sauce last night."

Michelle set down the tablecloth she had just picked up. "See you later, ladies." She put a hand on Giovanna's shoulder. "I hope the sous chef will be okay."

Giovanna led her grandmother to the kitchen. "I'm starting to worry. No one has seen or heard from Pedro since Wednesday, the night after Claire Costello died."

* * *

Friday afternoon, Puerto Ayora

After verifying with Giovanna that Pedro Lopez had again failed to show up for work, and no one had been able to reach him, Victor decided to pay him a visit. Something was off. Was the man in hiding?

Pedro lived with his parents in a small stucco house near Miguel Ruiz. The run-down, unfinished condition of the neighborhood was similar.

Victor strolled up the walkway and knocked on a weathered front door badly in need of paint. There was no response. Inhaling the fragrance from an overgrown yellow Cordia bush next to the stoop, he pressed an ear to the door but didn't detect any sign of movement.

Next door, an elderly woman appeared on her porch. She eyed Victor suspiciously as she began to water the potted plants.

"Señora," he called to her. "Do you know your neighbors who live in this house?"

"*Sí, señor. La familia López.*"

"Are they home?"

"No, señor. They left for the mainland last week. A funeral, I believe."

"Pedro too?" According to Giovanna and Belinda, Pedro had been at work on Tuesday night, and part of Wednesday, which meant he had not accompanied his parents to the mainland.

The woman shrugged and went back inside.

Victor circled the house and peered through the windows. The rooms were too dark to make out much.

He called the police station. "Have someone contact the airlines and check the passenger rosters for the past two days." Maybe Pedro Lopez had joined his family on the mainland.

"*De acuerdo, señor,*" agreed the officer.

Victor had an uneasy feeling about the sous chef. If he was attending a funeral on the mainland, why wouldn't he have told his employer? Giovanna said Pedro was reliable; this was the first time he'd failed to show up for work. Once car trouble had caused him to be late, but he'd called to let her know and even offered to make up the time.

Before leaving, Victor tested the front door. It was locked.

As he started down the walkway, a twenty-something man passed on foot. His head turned toward the Lopez house.

"Señor," Victor called to him. "Do you live around here?"

The man pointed to a house two doors down.

"Do you know Pedro Lopez?" Victor walked over and displayed his badge.

"*Sí, señor.* Is there a problem?"

"Is he home?"

The neighbor shrugged. "I haven't seen him since Wednesday night. He got home from work a few hours early."

"Did you talk to him?"

"No, señor. Except to wave hello."

"Was he alone?"

"Some guy came over shortly after Pedro got home." The neighbor's eyes flitted around, as if on the lookout for something or someone.

"What did Pedro's visitor look like?"

"Medium build. He had on a baseball cap and a black shirt. I couldn't see him very well in the dark."

"Does Pedro have family or friends living around here?" asked Victor.

"He has many friends who come around a lot. I don't know all their names." The neighbor pointed at the house. "They keep a key under one of those flower pots."

"*Gracias, señor.* You've been very helpful." Victor turned back toward the porch. After lifting several flower pots, he found a rusty key. He picked it up and tried it in the lock. The door opened.

An overpowering stench hit him like a blast from a furnace, causing him to gag. The heat was stifling; there was no air conditioning, no ventilation.

Hand on his gun, Victor stepped into the house. "Pedro Lopez?" he called. "Police."

Victor stepped through the living room, holding his breath, his burning eyes peeled for clues. *Like walking into hell.*

The bedroom door stood ajar. Victor peered inside.

A partially clothed man's body lay sprawled across the bed. His unseeing eyes were open, and his mouth crusted with dried vomit. Just like Claire Costello.

In his line of work, Victor had seen his share of dead bodies. It never got easier. Raising his cellphone, he called for the crime scene unit.

CHAPTER THIRTY

Friday evening, Leisure Dreams

Giovanna glanced at her watch again. She'd expected to hear from Victor by now. Of course, his priority had to be the investigation, one of the drawbacks of being involved with a police detective.

Michelle strolled up, untying the strings of her apron as she walked. "I'm heading upstairs to shower and change. What time do you want us back down here?"

"The cocktail party begins at five, but you don't have to be here right when it starts unless you want to." Giovanna consulted her clipboard. "Jim will make his speech at six-thirty, and we'll serve dinner at seven."

"Got it. Have you seen my husband?" Michelle wriggled free of the apron. As she spoke, Roberto walked into the lobby.

"Are all my plants properly pruned now?" Giovanna grinned.

Roberto removed his garden gloves. "Miguel does a good job. I didn't see any vegetation massacre."

"Thank God for that," laughed Giovanna. "You won't see any 'crape murder' around here." Roberto relished taking photos of improper pruning in his travels, but his biggest complaint was how his fellow Georgia residents topped their crape myrtle trees—"crape murder," as he called it.

Giovanna's phone buzzed with an incoming call from Victor. She waved at Michelle and Roberto as they headed upstairs and turned her attention to her caller. "*Mi hombre!* Please tell me you're on your way."

"I'm at the station," he replied.

She switched the phone to her other ear. "Did you ever get in touch with Pedro Lopez?"

"I saw him."

"Good. What did he have to say?" She needed everyone on duty for the opening events, and Pedro better have a good excuse for not showing up.

"I didn't speak to him."

"I don't understand." Giovanna's hand shook. There was an ominous tone in Victor's voice. "What's wrong?"

"He's dead."

She felt the blood drain from her face. "What did you say?"

"Pedro Lopez is dead."

"Oh, my God!" She touched her pounding chest. "What happened?"

"That's what we're trying to find out. He'd been dead for a while when I found him this afternoon. Decomposition had begun. And Giovanna . . . his death reminds me a lot of Claire's."

Giovanna gasped.

"Listen, I understand if you want to hold off telling your staff until tomorrow. This news will undoubtedly dampen their spirits tonight."

Giovanna shuddered thinking about Ricardo Gomez, Michelle's new best friend. The mercurial chef would be devastated to learn about the loss of his protégé. And she hadn't begun to think about a communication plan for the staff. But of course, they'd have to be told. And perhaps questioned. Again. "Thanks. Jim will blow a gasket when he finds out."

"Yes, better wait until tomorrow to tell him. Unless he asks about Pedro, of course."

"I doubt he will. He isn't keeping up with who's at work, who's been questioned already, and who hasn't. He just wants this whole mess to go away."

"But now it's worse. You know I'll have to speak to Pedro's co-workers tomorrow."

Giovanna groaned. "Could this be connected to Claire Costello's death? You said it looked like the cause was similar."

"We can't rule it out. Two untimely deaths so close together, on an island where there's hardly any—" Victor's words trailed off amidst voices in the background. "Never mind. I don't want to spoil your party."

"Are you still coming?"

"I'll try. I don't think Jim will miss me if I don't make it."

"But I will."

"I'll do my best. Worst case, I'll be out there tomorrow to interview staff."

"That doesn't sound like as much fun." She made one last attempt, "I'd really love to see you here tonight. Whenever you can get here."

"*Mi reinita,* I'll try."

As she ended the call, Jim walked up. "Have you seen Jenny?"

Giovanna shut her eyes, trying to recall her last Jenny sighting. "It's been at least an hour. Maybe she went upstairs to get ready?"

"I'm headed to the room now, so I'll check." He stopped and patted Giovanna on the shoulder. "The place looks stunning. Great job."

Gazing around the lobby at the vases of fresh flowers, custom balloons, carefully hung photographs of iconic Galapagos wildlife, she agreed. The hotel looked beautiful. Even though the staff had done most of the work, the CEO was giving her credit. "Thanks. It was a team effort." As he walked away, she called, "Good luck tonight."

He turned. "People make their own luck."

* * *

Giovanna thought about Jim's statement as she stood in the shower, letting the warm water wash over her slender body, droplets beading on her tanned skin. Had she made her own luck by persuading Jim Roberts to give her this job? After her bankruptcy and the accusations of fraud, few companies would have hired her, and certainly not in the financial field for which she'd trained.

But Jim's situation was unique. His own wife had also been victimized by Jerome Haddad; in fact, if Jim and Janice Roberts had focused on bringing Jerome to justice back when he'd scammed Janice's nonprofit, he might never have gone on to swindle others. Giovanna had used Jim's guilt to her advantage.

Someone knocked on the door, but Giovanna ignored it. She massaged her scalp with almond-scented shampoo and closed her eyes as suds dripped down her cheeks.

A keycard unlocked the door. Footsteps crossed the room.

"Who's there?" Giovanna's pulse quickened. In her haste to prepare for the evening, she had forgotten to lock the deadbolt and put out the *Do Not Disturb* sign. An image of the shower scene in the old Hitchcock movie, *Psycho*, flashed before her eyes.

In a moment, the door closed, and the footsteps faded.

She rinsed off and stepped cautiously out of the tile shower onto the fluffy bathmat. As she dried herself, she listened for movement, some sign that some-one was still in her room. "Anyone here?"

Satisfied that she was alone, wrapped in a thick bath towel, she proceeded out of the bathroom. Perhaps one of the maids had come in to tidy up, thinking she wasn't in the room.

Her eyes surveyed her surroundings. In the center of her glass coffee table sat a huge bouquet of fresh flowers artfully arranged in a white ceramic vase. She sank to the couch. The towel slid away as she read the card, "Good luck tonight. Thinking of you always."

The card wasn't signed. She studied it, then searched around the table for evidence of who had sent the flowers. Victor? She could only hope, but it seemed like a frivolous expense on his police salary. And if he sent flowers, did that mean he wasn't coming? She still held out hope of seeing him tonight.

Could the sender have been Jim? Possibly, except he wouldn't add, "Thinking of you always." Jim was a father figure, not a potential love interest, and he was deeply devoted to his family. Also, he would have signed the card, or at least had his name printed by the employee who'd ordered the flowers on his behalf. Jim would want credit.

What if the flowers were from Timothy? If so, he'd refused to take her not-so-subtle hints that she wanted nothing more to do with him. But since he hadn't signed the card, there was no need to seek him out tonight and thank him.

She sniffed the fragrant flowers—a mix of gardenias and lavender. Timothy knew she loved gardenias. Regardless of who had sent them, the white and purple blooms brightened her room. She'd get the staff to divulge the sender; she wouldn't need a police detective to help her solve that mystery.

* * *

Laurel and Maria were among the first guests from town to arrive. Giovanna wondered if Maria had heard about the death of Pedro Lopez. If not, she certainly wouldn't be the one to break that news to the reporter.

Giovanna exchanged cheek kisses with Laurel. "Thanks so much for your impromptu tour of the Darwin yesterday. Our guests really enjoyed it."

"No problem," said Laurel. "You know how I love talking about tortoises." She touched Giovanna's sleeve. "That little black dress looks great on you."

"Thanks." With a smile, Giovanna smoothed the fitted skirt against her thigh.

Laurel's eyes swept the room. "Where's Romeo?"

Giovanna felt her face flush. "He's busy with work, but he'll come by later."

"I was beginning to think Leisure Dreams was his place of business." Laurel winked at Maria, who returned a cryptic grin.

At that moment, Olivia Martinez passed by, and Giovanna tapped her shoulder. "Olivia, I'd like you to meet Laurel Pardo, one of the tortoise researchers from the Darwin, and head of the giant tortoise breeding program." She turned to Laurel. "Laurel, this is Olivia Martinez, our sales director for the South America division."

"Laurel." Olivia extended her hand. "So glad to finally meet you. We're excited about the partnership between Leisure Dreams and the Darwin, and all the educational opportunities we can provide for our guests."

As the two shook hands, Giovanna extricated herself from the conversation and slipped into her hostess role. She greeted some local government officials she vaguely recognized and waved over a waitress carrying a tray of drinks.

Out of the corner of her eye, she glimpsed Timothy descend the stairs. He looked handsome in his dark suit and bright cardinal tie, dressed more formally than the other guests, who were wearing a mix of "cocktail casual" and "island chic." She thought again about the flowers delivered to her room and wondered if she should say something.

Instead, Giovanna averted her gaze and went to greet a woman from the Galapagos Tourist Bureau. The woman lavished praise for the layout of the resort and asked for extra brochures to pass out to visitors.

Giovanna was relieved the woman hadn't mentioned the celebrity death. Perhaps the news hadn't reached her yet. Or maybe she was too polite to bring it up tonight.

"Señora Rogers." Maria appeared at Giovanna's elbow. Without Laurel at her side, Maria was all business.

"Señora Vasquez, how can I help you?" Giovanna kept her tone businesslike as well.

"What's the status of the investigation into Claire Costello's death?"

Giovanna smiled through gritted teeth. "No updates since we last spoke. Have you checked with the police?"

"I understand a health inspector went through your wine cellar yesterday. Why was that?"

"As you've heard, Claire drank champagne from our reserve shortly before she died. They wanted to ensure nothing was wrong with our stock." Giovanna lowered her voice, encouraging Maria to reduce her volume as well. "Out of an abundance of caution."

"And what did they find?"

"Señora, they found nothing to suggest that any of our wines were tainted or had been tampered with. The inspector assured us we could serve it tonight as planned." As Gabriela walked by, balancing a tray of full champagne glasses on her arm, Giovanna picked up two and handed one to Maria. "Will you join me in a toast?"

Maria took the glass but waited for Giovanna to take the first sip.

Giovanna touched her glass to Maria's. "To the grand opening of Leisure Dreams - Galapagos, and may the police quickly solve the mystery of Claire Costello's death." She tilted the glass to her lips.

Maria followed suit, still watching Giovanna and the other guests who were partaking of the champagne. Her eyes narrowed as Tyler entered the lobby through the front door, camera in hand.

"If you'll excuse me, I need to speak with the cameraman." Giovanna set down her glass. "Enjoy your evening, Maria."

Giovanna caught up with Tyler and pointed out key guests. "Be sure to get some photos of Jim with the American ambassador," she reminded him.

"I've been shooting people as they arrive," Tyler said. "I have a list for you."

Giovanna cringed at the expression "shooting people," but she understood what Tyler meant. "Thanks."

"What time do the speeches start?" he asked.

"Jim plans to kick it off about six-thirty."

"Will you be speaking, too?" Tyler smiled.

"He wants me to say a few words." Giovanna glanced around the room. Although she'd been comfortable speaking in front of groups during her three-year corporate career, she hadn't done it in a while. The last public speeches she'd given were to tout her nonprofit spay/neuter clinic, trying to persuade potential donors to support her fledgling charity. And after Jerome Haddad drained their accounts and forced her into bankruptcy, she felt like a charlatan. A wave of jitters hit her.

"Picture them naked, and you'll do great. That's what Claire always said." Tyler patted Giovanna's shoulder and moved away to take more video of the cocktail party.

CHAPTER THIRTY-ONE

Friday evening, Leisure Dreams Grand Opening

Giovanna surveyed the lobby to ensure all the guests engaged in conversation, and that champagne and *hors d'oeuvres* were readily offered. Belinda had begun ushering people inside the lavishly adorned Floreana ballroom to take their seats for the ribbon cutting and speeches.

Stealing a moment for herself, Giovanna slipped outside into the warm evening air. So far, the event was progressing smoothly. Nevertheless, she couldn't blot out thoughts about the two deaths connected with the hotel on her watch this week.

She headed for the lookout point over the harbor. Few boats remained on the bay, and the streetlights of Puerto Ayora were gradually blinking on. As she passed the pool, a flutter of dark wings swooped down, and a Galapagos Hawk plucked a lava lizard from the rocks. Though frequently spotted on some uninhabited islands, Galapagos Hawks had once been thought extinct on Santa Cruz. Giovanna gasped as the majestic bird flew off into the sunset with its prey in its talons.

Raised voices arguing in Spanish pierced her reverie. She listened as they approached from the trail leading to the water. Did one of those voices belong to Laurel?

Straining to tune in to the rapid-fire conversation, Giovanna deciphered a few words, but not enough to understand what the man and woman were quarreling about. She moved toward the trailhead, closer to the sound of the voices.

Laurel Pardo and Miguel Ruiz, almost nose to nose, shouted at each other.

From the crest of the hill, Giovanna called, "Is everything okay?"

Laurel's face transformed from angry to affable as she relaxed her jaw and pasted on a smile. "Everything's fine, Giovanna. Miguel and I were discussing what the film crew needs to cover with *my* tortoise breeding program."

They joined her at the top of the hill and headed toward the hotel.

Giovanna wondered why Miguel would care about the film crew's coverage of the breeding program. He hadn't worked with tortoises since before being hired at the resort as a groundskeeper. "You mean, how much to tell them about Tio Armando's history?"

Miguel's eyes popped and Laurel's face pinched.

"I thought I heard you mention Tio Armando." Giovanna studied their faces as they walked. *From their reaction, I must have guessed right.*

"Tio Armando is a big part of the program," Laurel said. "Don't you agree, Miguel?"

Miguel scowled at her and turned to Giovanna. "Señora Rogers, is there anything you need me to do?"

"Not at the moment." She gestured at the shrubs lining the beds around the hotel. "Nice job today with the pruning. Roberto was impressed with your horticulture skills."

He grinned. "Your father knows quite a bit about gardening himself."

Giovanna did not correct him. Most people assumed Michelle and Roberto were her parents. They had raised her. It was too much trouble to explain that Michelle was her paternal grandmother, married to Roberto; he was the closest relationship Giovanna had to a father.

As they neared the pool area, she remembered what she'd wanted to discuss with Miguel the day before. "Miguel, the cameraman on Claire Costello's film crew noticed we have a manzanillo tree on the property, near the beach trail."

Miguel stopped.

"Did you know the fruit is poisonous? And the bark can cause skin irritation, so we don't want our guests to go near it."

"How—?"

"I asked the workers to build a fence around it, and Belinda made a sign to explain its dangers. But it's a makeshift job, so we could have something done in time for the opening."

"Señora—"

"You know about the manzanillo tree, don't you, Miguel?" Laurel taunted.

Miguel mumbled something unintelligible in Spanish.

As they detoured to the problem tree, Giovanna pointed to the crude picket fence and hand-lettered sign in English and Spanish. Belinda had misspelled "poison" by adding an extra "s," and Giovanna cursed herself for not checking it closely before the sign was posted.

"I've asked Corporate to send us a more professional-looking plaque," she told Miguel. "I can't imagine why the construction crew left that tree here."

"It's a beautiful tree," said Laurel. "I see why they left it. The manzanillo is common enough here that the workers would have known to avoid it."

They entered the hotel through the back door. Giovanna stopped in the restaurant to check on the dinner's progress before heading for the ballroom, where close to a hundred guests had assembled to celebrate the resort's grand opening.

"Ladies and gentlemen, may I have your attention, please?" Jim stepped onto the flag-draped podium and tapped a spoon against a champagne glass.

The chandeliers dimmed, and a hush fell over the ballroom.

"I want to welcome everyone and thank you for coming to the grand opening of Leisure Dreams - Galapagos, our little oasis in the Pacific. Every room is a luxury suite with a stunning ocean view, and you'll find all the amenities Leisure Dreams customers around the world have come to expect." Jim beamed in full public relations mode. "For those of you visiting for the first time, prepare to be amazed. The Galapagos archipelago is an ecosystem filled with unique flora and fauna found nowhere else on earth."

He paused for effect and applause. A showman at heart.

"Those of you who live here and love the Galapagos will be pleased with how we've tried to be a good neighbor by protecting the environment every step of the way. From our low carbon footprint, use of natural materials, preservation of the surrounding vegetation, to our focus on education paired with tourism. We've created good-paying jobs for over forty local workers. I think you'll agree Leisure Dreams is an asset to the community."

His eyes scanned the audience, locking briefly on key individuals with a gracious smile, encouraging more applause.

"Leisure Dreams is pleased to partner with the Charles Darwin Research Station, by providing free shuttle service from the hotel to the park several times daily. We've also forged a partnership with the Galapagos tourist bureau to offer organized boat trips to neighboring islands." He looked straight at the woman from the tourist bureau and nodded. "Our goal is to give our guests a well-rounded, first-class vacation, where they can not only relax in splendor and have fun but also learn about nature and the environment."

Another pause, more clapping.

"And now, let me introduce Puerto Ayora's mayor, Carlos Hernandez, who will cut the ribbon and pronounce this resort open." Jim stepped aside to make room on the stage for a stocky, middle-aged Ecuadorian, grinning from ear to ear.

Amid a flood of flashbulbs, the mayor sliced the teal satin ribbon draped across the stage with an oversized pair of scissors. "I hereby declare this resort open."

"Ladies and gentlemen, please join us in a toast to the grand opening of Puerto Ayora's first resort hotel, Leisure Dreams - Galapagos." Jim raised his glass.

"Here, here." The Chief Marketing Officer raised his as well, encouraging others to join in.

Glasses clinked. Giovanna held her breath as she looked around the room, envisioning guests becoming violently ill after the champagne touched their lips. But nothing untoward happened.

"Now, go out and tell your friends!" Jim again raised his glass as he stepped off the stage.

CMO Steve Blackstone gave the next speech, explaining in more depth about the Leisure Dreams product and plans for expansion in South America, complete with statistical data. Giovanna found his talk a bit dry, and she noticed several private conversations start up among the guests as Steve droned in more detail than anyone cared to hear.

When it was her turn to speak, Giovanna kept her message concise to get the program's timeline back on track. "Ladies and gentlemen, it's a privilege to manage such a first-class resort in one of the most fascinating places on earth. For those of you who are staying here, if there's anything you need, please don't hesitate to ask me or members of our excellent staff. It's our goal to make your stay comfortable and memorable. For those of you who live in town, and haven't tried our restaurant yet, you're in for a treat tonight, which I hope will keep you coming back regularly and—"

"Excuse me." The voice of Maria Vasquez carried from across the room, and a few nearby heads turned to look at the reporter in the audience instead of the hotel manager on stage.

Giovanna had been seconds away from finishing her remarks, stepping off the podium, and herding the crowd into the Isabela restaurant for dinner.

"Señora Rogers, can you assure the guests will be safe here?"

Jim, Steve, and Kevin rose and moved toward Maria.

"Señora Vasquez," replied Giovanna. "Of course, the security of our guests is of the utmost importance."

"Are you sure?" Maria eyed the executives weaving among the chairs to reach her. "After the death of one of your guests earlier this week, the police still don't know what happened."

The attentive crowd dissolved into whispers as dumbstruck guests repeated Maria's words and turned to each other for clarification. Some scrolled through their smartphones. Steve wiped his forehead, and Jim's face looked petrified. Kevin rolled his eyes.

Giovanna tapped on the microphone to quiet the crowd. "Ladies and gentlemen, please allow me to explain." She waited for the murmurs to die down before continuing. "Unfortunately, we indeed had a guest pass away on the premises earlier this week. The police have yet to confirm the cause and manner of death, but the entire staff has been cooperating with law enforcement, and we'll continue to do so until the investigation is completed."

A deep voice bellowed, "Who was the guest?"

"Claire Costello, an American film producer." As she replied, more people pulled out phones. "Our hearts go out to her family and friends."

Someone shouted, "Do the police suspect foul play?"

"Is there a murderer here at Leisure Dreams?" came a shrill voice.

More panicked whispers ensued.

"Ladies and gentlemen," said Giovanna. "Local law enforcement is working diligently on this case, and you can rest assured that our resort is safe." She gazed longingly at the entrance. Now would be a good time for Victor to walk in and save the day, but he didn't. "And now we'd like to welcome you to our dining room, where you'll sample some of the specialties prepared by our renowned chef, Ricardo Gomez." She stepped off the stage and gestured toward the ballroom exit à la Vanna White on *Wheel of Fortune.*

Michelle pushed her way through the crowd and addressed her granddaughter. "I can't believe the gall of that reporter." She touched Giovanna's shoulder, which was shaking. "Are you okay? You handled yourself very well, considering."

Giovanna shook her head. "Maria is like a dog with a bone. I should have known she'd grandstand like that." She nodded toward Maria, surrounded by inquisitive guests. "Looks like she's fishing for statements."

Jim appeared next to Giovanna. "What are we going to do about that reporter? Someone needs to silence her."

Giovanna sighed. "The police must not have given her enough leads, so she thinks she can get a better story by pestering us."

Out of the corner of her eye, she glimpsed Miguel Ruiz chatting with Roberto; after their day of gardening together, they'd become quite chummy. As Maria walked by, Miguel shot her a venomous look, like spit from a coiled cobra. Giovanna wondered if Roberto had noticed.

CHAPTER THIRTY-TWO

Friday evening, Leisure Dreams restaurant

Giovanna stood near the entrance of the Isabela dining room as guests funneled in and found their places. Belinda and her team had decorated each table with centerpieces of native Ecuadorian orchids, choosing shades of cream and lilac that complemented the Leisure Dreams peach tablecloths. The matching peach linen napkins, each folded to look like a blooming tulip, were flecked with teal, the resort chain's other trademark color. Smooth jazz played softly through the speakers.

Michelle and Roberto strolled in, and Giovanna touched her grandmother's sleeve. "Do you know where you're sitting?"

"Over there with Elaine." Michelle pointed to her friend, waving like a flagman at a large table across the room. "Victor's not coming?"

"He'll be here," Giovanna replied.

Michelle cocked her head as if she didn't quite believe her as she and Roberto left for Elaine's table.

When most of the guests had entered the restaurant and were getting settled, Giovanna moved to the small table she and Belinda had reserved as a command center. Near the entrance to the kitchen, it gave them a view of the entire room.

She set her clutch purse on the chair beside her to save a place for Victor and then checked her phone for new texts.

In a moment, Timothy appeared. He placed a hand on Victor's chair. "Is this seat taken?"

"Yes."

He raised his blond eyebrows. "Who's sitting here?"

"Your seat is over there, with your mother and Michelle." Phone in hand, she gestured toward Elaine's table.

Timothy followed her gaze. "No more room. My mom invited that couple from the film crew to sit with them."

Waiters began filling wine glasses and passing out plates of ceviche marinated in a citrus and cilantro dressing.

"This seat's empty." Belinda patted the fourth chair at their table. "Giovanna, you haven't introduced me to your friend yet."

Timothy pulled out the chair Belinda had indicated and planted himself in the empty seat before Giovanna could protest. "Thank you, Miss—"

Giovanna narrowed her eyes at Timothy and then addressed her assistant. "Belinda, this is Timothy Nelson, a childhood friend. He and his mother flew here with Michelle and Roberto. Tim, this is Belinda Chavez, my assistant manager."

Timothy extended his hand to shake Belinda's. "A pleasure to meet you, Belinda. Tell me, what's it like to work for Giovanna? She was terribly bossy when we were kids."

Giovanna shot him a glare and rose. "Please excuse me."

Belinda's eyes widened. "Is something wrong, señora? Do you need my help?"

"Sit," said Giovanna. "Entertain Timothy. You invited him."

She escaped behind the swinging door into the kitchen, a beehive of activity. Bright lights glinted off state-of-the-art, stainless-steel appliances. Workers zigzagged through the galley, rattling pots and balancing plates as if in a choreographed dance routine. An aroma of garlic sautéing in butter dominated the room. Steam rose from a simmering pot of *encebollado*.

Chef Gomez barked orders in rapid Spanish while juggling two pans. When he looked up, he sloshed some sauce onto the burner which sizzled and quickly hardened into a charred crust. "Señora Rogers, what can I do for you?"

"How can I help?"

The chef wiped his broad forehead with a peach-and-teal checkered bandana. "I could sure use Pedro right now. He's worth three of these other *vagos. Bueno para nada.*"

"I'm sorry." Giovanna hoped none of the kitchen workers had overheard the chef's negative assessment of them; she needed morale to remain high.

"Turn the fire off under that fish," he yelled at one of his helpers. "You're going to overcook it! And don't forget that last shot of Sambuca." He turned back to Giovanna. "Any word from Pedro today? I thought he'd be back by now. It's not like him to disappear. He knows how important tonight is."

Giovanna bit her lip. She had intended to wait until dinner was over to break the news about the sous chef.

"Señora Rogers, what is wrong?"

She shook her head. "It's not good. The police went to his house and found him. He was—"

Ricardo paled and put his hand across his heart. "*Dios mío!*"

"I'm so sorry. I didn't want to tell you until—"

"Of course, you should have told me. What in God's name happened? *Pobrecito! Su familia!*" The chef's head jerked around so he could glare at one of his helpers. "Don't let that garlic burn!" He wiped his brow again. "*Dios mío!*"

"I don't know anything more than what I just told you." Giovanna dodged a worker rushing toward the stove. "The police are investigating, and I'm sure they'll contact Pedro's parents."

Ricardo hyperventilated, and Giovanna led him to a stool next to one of the Sub-Zero refrigerators, where he almost collapsed. Several staff members looked in their direction. She motioned them to continue cooking. Busboy Luis Vera brought over a glass of water.

"I'm so sorry, Chef," Giovanna said again. "I know you were fond of Pedro. It's a loss for us all."

Ricardo hung his head. "I had a dream that something was wrong."

"Señor," began one of the kitchen helpers. "I believe the fish is done."

Ricardo waved her away. "Then take it off the fire, *idiota!*"

Giovanna looked at the helper. "Please go ahead and take it off the stove and get it ready to serve."

Ricardo's nose wrinkled like a rabbit in a garden. "I smell garlic burning." He set down the glass of water and rose from the stool. "*Idiotas!*"

"Are you feeling better?" asked Giovanna, still concerned the chef might keel over any moment.

He rushed to the stove, pushed one of his helpers out of the way, and grabbed the pan of charring garlic. "The show must go on!"

* * *

Giovanna rechecked her phone for a message from Victor. Nothing.

Instead of returning to her table, where Timothy still chatted with Belinda, she cruised the dining room, asking guests how they were enjoying their dinner.

"Was that octopus in the first course?" inquired the American ambassador's wife.

Giovanna nodded. "One of our specialties."

"The octopus I've had in the past was not this tender," said her husband. "Your chef did an excellent job."

"He'll be happy to hear that." Giovanna smiled and moved to another table, sidestepping busboys clearing soup bowls as waiters followed to serve the main course.

After visiting several other tables, she swung by Michelle's corner of the restaurant. "How's everything here?"

"The sea bass is divine." Taking a bite, Michelle winked at her granddaughter. "And now I know how Ricardo makes his sauce."

Elaine looked up from her conversation with Susie and Colin. "Do you know my goddaughter, Giovanna? My almost daughter-in-law." She waved her half-empty wine glass, and Giovanna suspected it was not her first. Or second. "Giovanna, did you know Susie and Colin worked with Claire Costello? They've been telling me some great stories."

Giovanna gave a polite smile. "We've met."

"Every course has been wonderful," said Colin. "Especially that fish stew."

"I'm glad you're enjoying it." From the corner of her eye, Giovanna noticed Roberto had gone to talk to Laurel and Miguel at their table. Everyone was laughing, so whatever the two had argued about earlier must have been set aside.

Out of excuses to stay away, she returned to her own table.

"Everything okay?" Timothy asked as she sat down.

She nodded without looking at him. "Everything's fine."

"You haven't eaten anything."

"I've been busy." She gazed at his cleaned plate.

"I asked the waitress to hold yours until you're ready. Want me to call her over?"

Eating her missed courses in front of her ex-fiancé was the last thing she wanted to do right now. Before Giovanna could think of a reason to get up again, Gabriela touched her shoulder. "Señora Rogers, Chef Gomez would like to see you back in the kitchen."

"*Gracias,*" she thanked Gabriela. To Timothy and Belinda, she announced, "Don't wait for me."

Giovanna pushed her way through the swinging doors once more, wondering what to expect. Had Ricardo's burst of energy faded back into grief over the loss of his colleague?

To her relief, Ricardo was putting on a virtuoso performance, back in the role of maestro. The kitchen help scurried about, weaving around each other with great efficiency as they drizzled caramel sauce over custard mounds and prepared to serve the *flan de piña* for dessert.

"Señora Rogers." Ricardo stopped when he saw her. Slipping an arm around her shoulder, he led her to a corner of the kitchen. "I can't stop thinking about Pedro Lopez."

"I know, señor, and I'm deeply sorry."

"His death is such a shock. It took me a while to process."

"What is it you wanted to tell me, señor?"

"I think I know why Pedro was murdered."

CHAPTER THIRTY-THREE

Friday evening, Leisure Dreams kitchen

Giovanna stared at Chef Ricardo Gomez. The lingering odors of garlic and fish no longer enticed her. "Why did you say Pedro Lopez was *murdered?*"

Ricardo removed his arm from her shoulder. "Didn't you say?"

"The police found him dead in his home. They don't know—" She watched one of the kitchen workers load a waiter's tray with plates of caramel-coated flan.

"You said the police are investigating."

"As they would with any sudden, suspicious death. But they're not certain Pedro's death was a homicide."

Ricardo put his hand to his mouth. "He had such a bright future as a chef. He was young, healthy . . ."

"So was Claire Costello."

"And she was murdered." He moved his hand from his mouth to his hip.

"They don't even know *that* for sure." Giovanna still held out hope for a less sinister conclusion.

Ricardo waved his finger at her. "Señora, they've spent too much time investigating for it to be anything else. The maids tell me the Tio Armando suite is still covered in crime-scene tape."

Much to Jim's chagrin. "Detective Zuniga will be here later tonight or early tomorrow to talk to the staff who worked with Pedro." She eyed the chef. "Why do you think your sous chef was killed?"

Ricardo seemed less enthusiastic now. He shuffled across the floor.

"If you know something, you should tell Vic . . . Detective Zuniga. Or tell me now, and let me pass it on to the police."

"I believe it had something to do with the champagne."

"The champagne?" Giovanna wasn't surprised word about the fateful welcome gift had circulated.

"The night that woman died, she'd been drinking our champagne."

"What does it have to do with Pedro? Did he drink the champagne too?"

Ricardo snorted. "Señora, no, of course not. He was on duty."

"I didn't mean to suggest—"

"But he saw something." Ricardo pointed at one of the workers who was garnishing plates of flan with artful drizzles of caramel sauce. "Be careful with that caramel!"

"What did Pedro see?" asked Giovanna. "I understand he opened the champagne and set up the tray with the fruit before Belinda took it to señora Costello's room."

"He didn't tell me," Ricardo admitted. "But he was upset the next night when he heard what happened. I told him to talk to the detective, but Pedro said he had to check out something first."

Giovanna pushed a lock of hair off her forehead. Despite several fans circulating the air, the kitchen remained stiflingly warm. "Did Pedro make a phone call before he left? Or get a phone call?"

Ricardo blotted the sweat from his brow with his bandana. "Now that you mention it, he might have been on his phone. I usually don't allow it in the kitchen, but we were slow."

"Did he leave after the phone call?"

"I think so. Maybe he was talking to his parents. They're over on the mainland." Ricardo winced. "Such fine people; they were so proud of him. *Dios esté con ellos.*"

Giovanna didn't envy Victor's job of delivering the news to Pedro's parents. And what if their son was murdered, as Ricardo had implied?

"You said Pedro went home early because he felt like he was coming down with the flu," said Giovanna. "Was that not true?"

Ricardo snapped his fingers at a passing busboy. "Make sure to put the rest of that *encebollado* in the refrigerator." He turned back to Giovanna. "Pedro told me he had to check something at the house for his parents. But he also said he might be coming down with the flu. The last thing we need here is a kitchen employee working while he's sick, so I had no choice but to let him leave."

"I agree, señor. But I wish he'd talked to the detective before he left."

Ricardo wrung his hands. "I'm sorry, señora. Pedro ran out in such a rush."

"And now he's dead."

"*¡Chuta!* If only I'd insisted he tell the police what he knew." Ricardo looked at the ceiling. "Maybe the murderer would be caught, and Pedro would still be alive."

* * *

By the time Giovanna returned to her table, most everyone had finished dessert. Some guests were sipping coffee and chatting; some were visiting neighboring tables. Others strolled the grounds or had wandered back to the Floreana ballroom, where a local band played Latin dance tunes.

Victor's unused place setting had been removed, and Timothy sat alone at the table. He smiled when she sat down in front of a magazine-worthy caramel-topped flan. "It's about time. I was getting ready to eat your dessert."

Giovanna's appetite had long since vanished. She pushed the plate toward Timothy. "Go ahead. *Buen provecho.*"

He rubbed his eyes. "Seriously?" Leaning over, he put a hand on her forehead. "Do you feel okay? You're offering me your flan? Giovanna Rogers, the woman who ordered two last time we went to Pascal's? And didn't share a bite?"

She jerked her head away. "Don't eat it if you don't want it."

He picked up his fork. "Wait a minute . . . it's not poisoned, is it?"

Her face hardened. "That's not funny." She rose to leave.

He tugged her sleeve, propelling her to sit back down. "Hey, what's wrong? You're no fun anymore. Remember when my mom tried her new quiche recipe, and we—"

"May I remind you that we're in the middle of a death investigation? Possible poisoning?" She snatched the dessert plate from Timothy. "Give me back that flan."

"I'm sorry. Too late." He lifted his fork and sank it into the custard.

"Hey, the caramel is the best part." She picked up her fork and held it like a shield.

Their forks clashed as if in a swordfight. Timothy picked up a spoon with his other hand, slipped it behind the tangled cutlery, and brought it back with a mound of custard.

"Mmm . . ." he purred. "This is heavenly."

Taking advantage of his distraction, she scooped up a bite, savoring the creamy sweetness tinged with the tartness of pineapple.

Timothy let his utensils fall and clutched his chest. His head lolled to the side. "Ooh . . ." he groaned.

Giovanna touched his shoulder. "Tim? What's the matter?" She loosened his tie and collar. "Timothy!"

He lifted his head and grinned. "Gotcha."

She pounded her fists against his shoulder until he clasped her hands and pushed her away, immobilizing her blows.

"I told you, that's not funny." But despite her fury and determination not to let him back into her life, she laughed. "Really, it wasn't funny."

He grinned. "At least you still care enough about me to save my life if it needed saving."

She shook her finger at him. "Don't be so sure."

"No use letting a scrumptious dessert go to waste." He cut off another large bite.

She seized her fork again and staked off the rest of her flan.

* * *

Timothy and Giovanna were the last ones to leave the dining room. Guests networked in the lobby, and many gathered around Hector Sanchez at the concierge desk. The woman from the tourist bureau had dropped off several boxes of brochures featuring island attractions to fill the display racks.

"Why don't you see what your mom is up to?" Giovanna suggested to Timothy. "She might want to dance."

"Think I'll take a walk," he said. "Want to come? You could show me around the grounds."

"No thanks. I need to mingle." She looked away as Timothy took the hint and headed toward the door.

Jim and the other Leisure Dreams executives had made themselves comfortable on the couches near the lobby bar, sharing after-dinner drinks with local officials. Soft music played in the background, barely audible above the low din. Most of the Ecuadorians were dancing the *pasillo* in the ballroom.

As Giovanna neared her boss, Steve leaned toward Jim. "You must admit, she doesn't fit the Leisure Dreams brand. And after the fiasco with Claire Costello, the prudent move would be a management change."

Giovanna froze, watching Jim's face as he listened to his Chief Marketing Officer. Did he agree?

She sprang into action, not allowing them to finish the conversation, not allowing the seed of doubt to take hold. "Gentlemen, why aren't you dancing?"

Chameleon-like, the two executives lost their serious mien. Rising, Jim grinned. "I suppose I should find my daughter before she gets cozy with one of the local boys."

When he'd gone, Giovanna turned to Steve. "Mr. Blackstone, if you notice anything about the resort that doesn't fit the Leisure Dreams brand, I hope you'll let me know. My whole team is committed to excellence."

Andrea scooted across the couch toward her boss. "Dancing sounds like a great idea." She winked at Giovanna.

With a nod, Giovanna watched them head toward the ballroom. Her heart pounded, out of sync with the drumbeats from the band. Was she going to be fired?

Needing to clear her mind, she headed for the revolving door and slipped through, emerging from the air-conditioned hotel into the steamy night air. Not paying attention to where she was walking, she bumped smack into Timothy.

"Whoa." He held out his hand to help restore her balance.

"Sorry." She caught the black shawl that had slid from her shoulders.

"Full moon," he observed. "Look how the water on the bay glistens. Isn't there a path down to the beach?"

"There." Giovanna pointed toward her favorite trail, which she'd hoped to descend alone, to lick her wounds and regroup. "But it's not designed to be walked at night. There are no lights like there are on the steps to the dock."

"Show me."

Moonlight shone on the path. It was steep and narrow, forcing them to walk single file, which was fine with her.

"I'd like to come back here in daylight," Timothy said.

"Then go back inside and come out here tomorrow."

"I want to be with you. And I can tell by the way you're tucking your shoulders that something's wrong."

As she turned to reply to her ubiquitous ex-fiancé, Giovanna stumbled over something in the middle of the path, shadowed from the moonlight by a scalesia tree. She shrieked.

"Giovanna!" Timothy grabbed her arm to keep her from falling flat on her face. "What was that?"

Balance restored, she activated her phone's flashlight and shone it on the obstruction; a shoeless leg protruded from the brush. As she moved the light closer, a black stiletto appeared, heel bent. The woman lay sprawled, face down, arms spread to her sides. Silver sequins from her tight-fitting evening dress sparkled in the artificial light.

Giovanna let out a scream. Maria Vasquez wasn't moving.

Timothy knelt and flipped the woman over, checking for a pulse. "She's still alive, but barely. Call an ambulance!"

While Giovanna fumbled with her phone, Timothy rolled up his sleeves, cleared Maria's airway, and began a series of chest compressions.

In a mixture of English and broken Spanish, Giovanna attempted to explain to the emergency operator where she was and what had happened.

Timothy continued his rhythmic compressions, mouthing the disco song, "Staying Alive," his strong arms pumping life back into Maria. Watching,

Giovanna remembered his expert, caring bedside manner with the animals in his veterinary practice.

He stopped, pressed his ear to Maria's chest, then looked up at Giovanna. "She's breathing on her own again. But she's still unconscious. Do we have anything to cover her?"

"Here, put this over her." Giovanna handed him her shawl. "Hopefully, help is on the way." She knelt and gazed at Maria's bruised forehead. "Maria, can you hear me?"

No response.

Timothy tucked Maria's dark curls behind her ears. "Maybe she fell? Or was pushed? Whatever happened, it knocked her out." He picked up the broken shoe beside her. "I don't know how she could even walk out here with these."

Giovanna eyed the stiletto heels. She was having a hard enough time walking the trail in her one-inch pumps. "Maria wears those most of the time. I think she wishes she were taller."

Timothy shook his head and turned his attention back to Maria, watching for signs of a return to consciousness.

Despite the warm evening, Giovanna felt a chill without her wrap. "What is happening? First Claire, then my assistant chef, now this. And I'm probably getting fired."

Timothy leaned across Maria and took Giovanna into his arms; she did not resist. "You didn't tell me about losing an assistant chef. And what's this about getting fired?"

She felt tears welling in her eyes. "This is a nightmare."

He stroked her hair, kissed the top of her head.

"Giovanna?" Victor's voice pierced the night air, drowning out the sounds of crickets and buzzing insects.

"Victor!" She straightened, pulling away from Timothy. She glanced down at her phone, which she hadn't checked since her emergency call. She'd missed a text from the detective. "Oh, Victor, it's Maria. I called for an ambulance."

He rushed down the path to join them.

"She's breathing, but she's unconscious," Timothy said.

"Timothy did CPR," explained Giovanna.

"That's good." Victor eyed them. "How did you find her?"

"We were walking." Giovanna winced at how that must sound. "I almost tripped over her. She wasn't breathing at first, and I thought she was dead." She reached for Victor.

He stiffened. He'd pulled out his phone and was already speaking into it in rapid Spanish.

"Was Maria at your event this evening?" Victor asked when he'd finished his call.

"Yes, she came with Laurel Pardo. They were in the dining room, but I don't remember seeing her after dessert." Giovanna searched his face, wondering how he was processing the sight of her with Timothy. In his arms. "I spent much of the evening in the kitchen, and I told Chef Gomez about Pedro. I know we agreed not to say anything until later."

"It's okay," said Victor. "He would have found out soon enough." The detective knelt beside Maria and spoke softly to her.

Her eyes remained shut, her lips unresponsive.

Victor touched Giovanna's shoulder. "You two go back inside and corral the guests. Don't let anyone leave. Especially not Laurel. I have some questions for her."

"Got it," said Giovanna. She racked her brain for an excuse to keep the guests there. "I'll tell them it's time to draw the raffle prize." *Jim will be livid,* she thought. The last thing Leisure Dreams needed was another incident. On opening night. One more reason for Steve to recommend her termination. And the executives still didn't know about the death of Pedro Lopez.

She started back inside with Timothy at her heels.

CHAPTER THIRTY-FOUR

Friday evening, Leisure Dreams grounds

After watching Giovanna and her ex walk away, Victor turned back to Maria. "Hang on, *nana*." He addressed her with the Quechan term of affection similar to "sister." In many ways, she was like a sister to him.

Although still breathing on her own, the reporter remained immobile.

Soon, two paramedics wearing headlamps descended the hill, balancing a backboard. They knelt at Maria's side to check her vitals. Then they carefully lifted her onto the stretcher and strapped her in.

Be strong, Maria, Victor thought. *She's so still.*

The sound of girlish giggles grew closer, followed by a low masculine voice. And then more giggles. Victor turned.

In a glow of cellphone flashlights, Susie and Colin appeared on the path, trudging uphill from the beach. They stopped abruptly, and so did their laughter.

"Good evening, Ms. Southworth, Mr. Ashton." Victor took a step toward them.

Susie eyed the commotion. "What happened? Is someone hurt?"

"Who is that?" Colin squinted at the figure being tended to by paramedics.

"How long have you two been out walking?" asked Victor.

"What is this? Another inquisition?" grumbled Colin.

Susie touched her colleague's arm. "We came outside about an hour ago. We walked down to the beach and were on our way back."

"Did you see Maria Vasquez when you came outside?" Victor gestured toward the woman on the stretcher.

Susie gasped again. "Maria, the nosy reporter. Is that her?"

"We didn't see her."

Colin's answer was a little too quick, Victor thought. "Did you speak to Maria this evening?"

"At the cocktail party," said Colin. "During dinner, she was on the other side of the room."

"Do you remember who she was sitting with?" Victor found it hard to read Colin's expression in the dark with moonlight casting unnatural shadows.

The pair looked at each other, then Colin replied. "That woman from the Darwin place, and some other people I didn't recognize."

"I think the lady from the tourist bureau was at their table," added Susie. "I met her, but I don't recall her name."

"Did you notice when Maria left the party? And if she was with anyone?"

Shifting his feet back and forth as if anxious to get going, Colin shook his head.

Susie said, "She was gone when we left the dining room. And we didn't pass anyone on our way outside."

"I'm afraid we're not much help," said Colin. He touched Susie's waist and took a step up the hill.

Victor glanced at their shoes, which were covered in sand and scalesia leaves. "What's that on your feet?"

"We told you we've been walking on the beach." Colin lifted a foot and wiped off some sand with his hand.

Victor studied Colin's body language. He didn't trust either of them but wasn't sure what they might be hiding.

"Okay if we head inside now? Got a big day tomorrow." Colin clicked his tongue.

"Just one more thing," said Victor. "Since you arrived, have either of you left the hotel grounds?"

Susie answered for them. "We visited the Darwin Research Station on Thursday afternoon. It was a big group: the CEO's daughter, Ms. Rogers, and her family."

"That's it? No other outings?"

"Why? Are we suspects in *another* murder investigation?" Colin put a hand on his hip.

Victor eyed him. "Why would you say there's another murder investigation?"

Colin swallowed. "No reason."

* * *

As they entered the hotel, Giovanna turned to the doorman. "Don't let anyone leave. We need to talk to everybody in the ballroom, so please direct them there."

"*Sí señora*," replied Hector.

Jim caught Giovanna's eye as she and Timothy came into the lobby. "What's wrong?"

"It's Maria Vasquez," she began.

"What is that woman up to now? I thought she'd agreed to downplay the murder speculation." Jim grimaced. "There are plenty of positive things she can write about our event."

"Maria had an accident."

Jim's eyes popped.

Giovanna cupped her hand over her mouth and raised her voice so her boss could hear her over the music. "Maria is unconscious. She fell—or was pushed—on the beach path."

"Unconscious? What—?"

Timothy piped up, "An ambulance is on the way."

Jim glanced at Timothy and Giovanna. "Where is Maria? Is someone with her?"

"Victor," said Giovanna.

"He's back?"

"Just in time. And he wants to talk to our guests. We can't let anyone leave."

Jim cast his eyes skyward. "And I thought the evening was going so smoothly."

"Let's tell them it's time for the raffle."

"Raffle?" His eyebrows shot up.

"A free weekend at the property of their choice. Must be present to win." She turned to Timothy. "Will you help us gather people in the ballroom? Get your mom and Michelle involved." She glimpsed Belinda snaking through the lobby, playing the gracious hostess. "There's Belinda. Let her know what we need, and she'll take over."

When Timothy had gone to speak with Belinda, Giovanna added, "Sir, there's something else I haven't had a chance to tell you yet."

Jim's face froze.

She had no need to preface her words with fluff, so she launched right in, "Pedro Lopez—Ricardo's sous chef—was found dead in his home earlier today."

Jim's eyes widened. "The employee the police were looking for?" When Giovanna nodded, he murmured, "That's awful." And then, "Well, at least it didn't happen on the resort property. I hope you're not going to tell me he was poisoned by something he ate or drank here."

"They don't know what caused his death," Giovanna replied.

"I suppose his connection with Leisure Dreams will generate buzz in the media." Jim rubbed his forehead.

Steve and Andrea came out of the ballroom, still swaying to the music, drinks in hand. "Hey, Steve." Jim beckoned his Chief Marketing Officer. "We have another situation."

Steve turned to Andrea. "Go find Kevin and Olivia."

* * *

The Leisure Dreams management team convened in Giovanna's office. Claiming the armchair behind her desk, Giovanna felt more in control. She was grateful to be able to address the group all at once, instead of recounting the latest incidents multiple times.

"Did the reporter know about the death of the assistant chef?" asked Kevin.

"Not that I know of," replied Giovanna. "She didn't question me about it."

"Who else knows?" asked Steve.

"Vic—Detective Zuniga agreed we could wait until tomorrow to tell the staff," Giovanna said. "But I ended up telling Chef Gomez during dinner. He was devastated, as you can imagine."

"Is there any connection between the death of this employee and what happened to the reporter?" asked Olivia.

"And Claire Costello," added Steve. "They could all be connected. A major scandal."

"We don't know yet," replied Giovanna.

"Maybe it's a single perpetrator," suggested Andrea. "The sooner the police catch him, the better."

"Or her," Steve added, narrowing his eyes at Giovanna.

Kevin tapped his hand on Giovanna's desk. "We need to do some serious damage control. Whether there's a connection or not, people will look for one, the media might even manufacture one, and our brand will suffer."

A knock interrupted their speculation.

"Come in," said Giovanna, wondering if one more person could squeeze inside her crowded office.

The door opened and Victor stood before them. "Detective Zuniga, have you met the executive team yet?" Before he could answer, she briefly introduced each player.

Victor nodded in acknowledgment. "Good, you're all here."

"How's Maria?" Giovanna asked him. Their eyes met with a hint of a spark, a brief reminder of the intimacy they'd shared; maybe it was only her imagination.

"The ambulance is on the way to the hospital. Maria didn't regain consciousness while I was with her, but she was still breathing."

"I hope she'll recover soon," said Olivia. "Then she can tell us what happened."

"It must have been an accidental fall," said Jim. "That path is quite steep. And those heels she was wearing . . ."

Victor eyed the CEO. "How did you know where she was when she fell?"

Jim shot a panicked glance at Giovanna. "Giovanna, didn't you say?"

Giovanna couldn't remember what she'd said about the location of Maria's accident. She bit her lip. "Maybe."

"Did you find Laurel Pardo?" Victor looked straight at Giovanna. This time, it was all business.

Since coming back inside, she hadn't had a chance to talk to anyone but Jim and the executive team.

Before Giovanna could answer, Andrea spoke up. "Laurel left a while ago. She was talking with some guy, and I saw them walk out together."

"Was Maria Vasquez with her?" Victor turned to Andrea.

Andrea looked thoughtful. "Earlier. But I didn't see Maria when Laurel left."

"Okay," said Victor. "I want everyone to think about the last time you saw Maria Vasquez this evening. Did anyone see her leave?"

Heads rotated from side to side as everyone traded glances with their colleagues.

"Wait!" Olivia held up her finger, then touched her forehead as if it were a crystal ball. "I saw her talking to a man near the entrance. They might have left together, but I can't be sure."

"What time was this?" Victor took out his pocket notebook.

She squinted as if the image might re-emerge. "Right before the music started." She nodded. "They might have stayed for a few minutes after the dancing began, and then I didn't see either of them again."

"What time did the dancing start?" Victor looked at the others for confirmation.

Shrugs all around. Then Jim offered, "About nine o'clock. Belinda can verify. She's handling the music."

Victor nodded as he wrote. "Who was the man Maria was talking to?"

"I don't know," said Olivia. "I think he works here, but I didn't meet him."

"Can you describe him?"

Olivia shrugged. "Dark hair. Longish. Not tall, but taller than Maria. Thirties, maybe early forties. Not very dressed up. He sat by Laurel at dinner."

"Not one of the men from the film crew?" said Victor.

"No," replied Olivia. "But wait . . ." She touched her forehead again as if a new vision were forming. "That cameraman . . . What's his name? Tyler?" She turned to the others for confirmation.

"Tyler Thompson," said Giovanna, "is the cameraman. And he wasn't dressed up tonight. I don't think he owns formal attire."

"Yes," Olivia agreed. "Last time I saw Maria, she was talking to him."

"And did you see Tyler again after that?" Victor asked.

Another tap. No visions emerged; it appeared Olivia's crystal ball had gone hazy. "Not that I recall. But I wasn't paying him much attention."

"He was in the ballroom taking pictures of the dancers right before we heard the news about Maria," said Andrea.

Victor gazed around the room, making eye contact with each person. "Did you notice Maria Vasquez in serious conversation with anyone else this evening?"

Surreptitious glances passed between Andrea, Olivia, and Kevin.

Kevin cleared his throat. "I had a long chat with the lady right after dinner."

Victor turned his attention to Kevin. "About?"

He looked at his lap. "The newspaper's coverage of Claire Costello's death. I tried to convince Maria that a positive story about our opening—which represents a great boon to the local economy—deserves higher placement in the newspaper than the death of a foreign visitor, about which we still don't have all the facts. She caused quite a scene during the speeches when she brought up the death investigation."

The corners of Victor's mouth twisted. "How did she respond to your request?"

Kevin frowned. "We didn't exactly reach a meeting of the minds."

"Well, now there'll be no story tomorrow," said Jim. "At least not by Maria."

Everyone stared at the CEO.

He shuffled in his chair. "Well, with Maria in the hospital . . ."

"The paper will be more likely to cover the story of Maria's accident at our grand opening than Claire Costello's death, which by now is old news," said Kevin. "Neither is good for our brand."

Victor clenched his jaw. "Right now, I'm more concerned with what happened to Maria Vasquez than your *brand*."

Giovanna said, "We've asked people to gather in the ballroom for a raffle. You can make your announcement there."

Jim and Steve looked at each other. Steve threw his head back and groaned.

Giovanna eyed him. "Unless you have a better idea?"

"The news should be delivered by a Leisure Dreams spokesperson," said Steve. "Kevin, as Director of Communications, will make the announcement."

Giovanna turned to Victor. "Are you okay with that, Detective?"

"Fine with me."

"Where do you want to conduct the interviews?" asked Giovanna. "In here?"

"Are you finished with us, Detective?" asked Olivia.

"For now," said Victor. "But don't leave the islands yet."

Giovanna exchanged places with him, their shoulders lightly grazing as they passed each other, making her long for this all to be over, for them to get back to the way they were before Claire's death.

The Leisure Dreams corporate team filed out, leaving Victor behind Giovanna's desk. Belinda came into the office as they were leaving. "What's going on?"

"Sit down," said Victor. "You're just the person I want to see."

She frowned. "Some new developments about Claire Costello's suicide?"

"Not yet." He eyed her. "Why do you keep saying her death was a suicide?"

"Well, I understand she was quite troubled. I mean . . . you don't think it was suicide?"

"We haven't ruled it out, but that's not what I want to talk to you about."

She raised her eyebrows.

"What time did the band start playing dance music tonight?"

She relaxed her shoulders. "Nine o'clock. Just as señora Rogers asked."

Listening for a tone of disrespect at the mention of Giovanna, he jotted Belinda's answer in his notebook. "Did you see Maria Vasquez leave?"

Belinda leaned on the desk and tucked her chin in her hand. "No, but it must have been a while ago."

"When was the last time you saw her?"

"At dinner. But Maria was across the room. I sat next to señora Rogers and her boyfriend."

Victor's mouth tightened.

"Oh, I'm sorry." Belinda sucked on her lip. "Her fiancé . . . ex-fiancé. You know . . . Timothy . . . the guy who came down from the States with her family."

Victor cleared his throat. Seeing Giovanna in Timothy's arms under the moonlight was the last thing he wanted to think about right now. "You saw Maria Vasquez at dinner. Did you see her leave the dining room?"

"I don't remember. I had so much on my mind, I wasn't keeping track of everyone's comings and goings. Timothy told me something happened to Maria Vasquez, which was why we had to get everyone into the ballroom."

"She had an accident." Victor watched Belinda's face for a reaction.

Belinda touched her gaping mouth. "Oh, no! Will she be okay?"

"She's been taken to the hospital."

"What happened?" Her surprise and concern appeared genuine.

"That's what I'm trying to find out." He tapped his pencil on his notebook. "You know the drill. Everyone has been asked to stay until I've talked to them, or at least have their contact information. I'll need your help rounding people up and bringing them to me. Will you do that?"

"Of course." She stood. "Are you ready for the next victim?"

He arched his eyebrow. "Victim? Is that a good choice of words?"

"It's how I feel sometimes when you question me."

He gave her a half smile. "Just one more thing."

She had started for the door but stopped.

"When was the last time you left the grounds?"

Belinda blinked. "I've been at the hotel all week getting ready for the opening."

"You haven't been home?"

"Not since Monday." She averted her eyes.

"But did you leave the Leisure Dreams property?"

She shook her head but looked away.

He sensed she was hiding something, but he'd decide later if it was important enough to pursue. "That will be all for now. Please send in the next 'victim.'"

CHAPTER THIRTY-FIVE

Wee hours of Saturday, Leisure Dreams Hotel

Victor reviewed his notes and concluded most of the guests and staff had little to offer regarding Maria's movements on Friday evening. Everyone remembered who she was, but after her outburst about the murder investigation during Giovanna's speech, most people avoided her. Both Steve Blackstone and Kevin Franklin had spoken with the reporter at length. However, no one suggested her interactions with the executives appeared threatening, and neither man had left the building all evening. Laurel Pardo's name had come up, but no one saw her leave with Maria.

After the interviews, Victor strode to the concierge desk to talk to Hector Sanchez, who would have had the best view of anyone using the main entrance. "Thanks for your help with crowd control, señor Sanchez," he said. "I talked to most of the guests and staff before they left, or at least got their contact information."

"*De nada*," replied Hector.

"Do you remember when Maria Vasquez, the reporter from the *Ayora Times*, left the party this evening?"

"Vaguely. I was talking to one of the women from the bureau of tourism when señora Vasquez headed out." Hector scratched his head. "She was in a hurry."

"What time was that?"

Hector twisted the watch on his wrist. "Must have been around nine."

"Was she with anyone?"

He scrunched his face in thought. "I think she left alone."

"Did you see her speaking with anyone before she left?"

Hector touched his chin with his index finger. "Miguel Ruiz."

His name keeps coming up. "Tell me about their conversation. How did they sound?"

Hector shrugged. "Sorry, I didn't pay much attention."

"Did you see Miguel after Maria left?"

"No. I figured he went home."

The elusive Miguel. The one who handles "special requests" for Jim Roberts. Victor jotted some details in his notebook, then looked up. "Thank you, señor." As he turned to walk away, he found Giovanna at his elbow. Their eyes met.

"Can you come up?" She touched his arm, and a bolt of warmth shot through him. "If you're finished with your interviews."

He hesitated. *Where's Timothy?* "What about . . . your boyfriend?"

"You're my boyfriend." She looped her arm through his.

"You don't care what the staff will say about us?" He'd seen the knowing looks and heard the derision in Belinda's tone.

"They're already saying it."

He put his hand on her slim waist. She looked hot in that little black dress. "Let's go then."

* * *

As soon as the door to her suite closed behind them, they fell into each other's arms, covering each other's faces with hungry kisses.

Giovanna ran her fingers through Victor's shiny black hair. "Do you know how hard it is to keep myself from doing this when you're trying to conduct your interviews?" she murmured.

He kissed her lips, her nose, her eyes, and then her lips again. "Do you know how hard it is to focus on those interviews whenever I see you walk into a room?" He eased her to a vantage point at arm's length, studied her flushed face, then pulled her close again. "All I want to do is this."

Lips locked, they moved in tandem toward the couch. Their bodies had just reclined against the cushions when a knock at the door intruded into their moment.

Giovanna groaned. "I put out the *Do Not Disturb* sign."

"Giovanna . . . can we talk?" Timothy's voice sounded tentative.

She placed a hand on Victor's shoulder to implore him to stay, then rose and went to the door. She cracked it open. "I'm not dressed."

Timothy grinned. "That's even better."

Giovanna let out an exasperated breath. "And I'm not alone." As Timothy's face fell, she added, "It's late," and closed the door.

Timothy's footsteps retreated down the marble hallway. Giovanna returned to the couch and snuggled up to Victor. "Where were we?"

Victor winced. "You burn bridges, don't you?"

Her answer was a kiss. "Timothy and I are over. I told you that when we met."

"It doesn't look like it. Not to him."

She leaned against the cushions. "He wants to get back together; let bygones be bygones. It's not happening. He showed his true colors, and I can't reset the clock."

"I suppose he has asked you to forgive him?"

"Yes."

"Don't you forgive people who have hurt you?"

She picked up a throw pillow and held it against her chest. "You make me sound so cold."

"Everyone needs forgiveness sooner or later."

She squeezed the pillow tighter. "I might forgive Timothy someday, but that doesn't mean I should marry him."

"He still loves you. It's obvious, even to me."

"And the next thing you'll say is that I still love him."

"Do you?"

"Not the way he wants me to."

There was another knock at the door.

Giovanna sighed, then called out, "Timothy, I told you—"

"Señora Rogers?" came Belinda's voice.

"What the—?" Giovanna rolled her eyes at Victor.

A pause. Then, softly, "Is Detective Zuniga with you?"

They both straightened and smoothed their hair and clothing. Giovanna got up, walked to the door again, and cracked it open. "What is it?"

Belinda craned her neck as if hoping to see a show. "Hector remembered something else about this evening. He said—"

Victor joined them at the door. "Where is Hector now?" With a resigned shrug, he followed Belinda down the hallway.

Giovanna waved from the open doorway. "I'll be awake for a while."

CHAPTER THIRTY-SIX

Wee hours of Saturday, Leisure Dreams Hotel

Hector Sanchez still stood at the concierge desk where Victor had interviewed him earlier. He smiled when Belinda returned with the detective. "Sorry to summon you, señor, but I just remembered something you might find important."

"No problem. What is it?" Victor took out his notebook. He nodded to dismiss Belinda.

"The cameraman," Hector began. "Señor Thomas? Thompson?"

"Tyler Thompson. What about him?"

"I don't know when he left or how, but I saw him come back inside. About ten minutes before señora Rogers and her friend reported finding Maria Vasquez."

Victor flipped through his notebook to reread the transcript of his conversation with Tyler Thompson. Tyler had not mentioned going outside and said he had not spoken to Maria Vasquez all evening. "Why did you just now remember this?"

Hector shrugged. "I didn't see him with the reporter, so I wasn't sure it was important."

Victor raised his brow. "Señor Sanchez, why did you decide this was important now?"

"The man acted different. The night the film crew arrived, he was friendly, and we talked a lot about photography. Tonight, when I greeted him, he hardly looked at me. I asked him if he'd had a chance to check out any of the scenic viewpoints I told him about, and he acted like he didn't hear me." Hector pursed his lips. "And he was sweating."

"Well, señor, it's quite warm outside."

"There were grass stains on his shirt, and it was untucked like he'd fallen or been in a fight. I asked him if something was wrong, but he didn't answer."

"And you didn't think to tell me this earlier?"

Again, Hector shrugged.

"Did you see where señor Thompson went after he came inside?"

"Up to the guest rooms, I suppose." Hector shook his head. "I wanted to ask him how his trip to town went, but someone else walked up."

"Trip to town?" Victor waved his notebook in the air. "When did Tyler leave the resort?" While questioning guests and staff about their interactions with Maria, Victor had slipped in questions about their whereabouts the previous two nights to eliminate suspects in the death of Pedro Lopez. None of the hotel guests had mentioned leaving the grounds. "I know a group of them visited the Darwin Research Station yesterday afternoon—"

"It was the night before. The cameraman asked me to arrange a car for him to go into town. His colleagues also went out Wednesday night, but they arranged their own transportation."

This is new information. The whole film crew was in Puerto Ayora the last night anyone saw Pedro Lopez alive. "What time did Tyler leave the hotel?"

"Around eight o'clock."

"And when did he return?"

"Right about midnight."

Victor paused in his writing. "Didn't you ask him then how his trip into town went?"

"I did. He said it was 'productive.' Maybe it had something to do with his film."

"How did Tyler seem when he got back?"

"Bloodshot eyes, like he'd been drinking or was exhausted. I didn't want to keep him from his bed."

"But you thought he'd have more to say about it tonight?"

"Maybe."

Victor nodded. "Thank you, señor. Is there anything else?"

Hector smiled. "Have I been helpful?"

"*Sí, señor.* We'll see what señor Thompson has to say." Victor looked at his watch.

As he debated whether to go back to Giovanna, rouse Tyler, or head home, he spotted the cameraman starting up the staircase.

* * *

Giovanna settled onto the couch with a book and wondered if Victor would return. Thoughts of the two deaths on her watch, Maria's accident, and her future at Leisure Dreams broke her concentration. Another knock at the door interrupted her rumination.

Letting the book fall to the floor, she jumped up expectantly and threw open the door with a broad smile and sexy pose.

Michelle stood in the hallway. When Giovanna's face fell, she said, "Don't look so disappointed."

Giovanna sighed, then stepped aside to admit her grandmother. "Have you been watching me?"

"I talked to Timothy, and then I saw your detective friend leave."

"So, the answer is yes."

"Not on purpose. I went down the hall for ice."

"Want some tea?" Without waiting for an answer, Giovanna turned on the electric kettle to boil water, then spooned some loose oolong into her tea infuser.

Michelle sat down on the couch. "Your grand opening was . . . interesting. Do you think it was a success?"

"Considering we've had two mysterious deaths this week and one mysterious accident, which I hope doesn't turn into a third death."

Michelle sighed. "Shall we go for 'memorable'?"

"'Memorable' is a fitting word." Giovanna checked the kettle.

"Have you had a chance to talk to Timothy?"

Giovanna rolled her eyes. "Talk to him? I can't get rid of him. For a supposedly bright guy, he can't take 'no' for an answer."

"Can you honestly say it's completely over? You two have been friends since you were ten."

"And maybe we'll be friends again someday. *Friends*." Eyeing her grandmother's earnest face, she added, "Michelle, I know you and Elaine were hoping for a wedding. A happily ever after for Timothy and me. But that's not the way the movie ended."

The kettle whistled. Giovanna rose to pour boiling water into the teapot. She took a carton of milk from her small refrigerator and carried it to the coffee table.

"So, tell me about you and Detective Zuniga," said Michelle.

Balancing the teapot, cups, and saucers on a tray, Giovanna stepped from the kitchenette to the living area like an acrobat on a tightrope and unloaded the items onto the coffee table. She sat down next to her grandmother.

"Is it serious?" Michelle pressed.

Giovanna checked the teapot. "Maybe." She poured tea into the cups and handed one to her grandmother. "Things have been hectic lately, but I love being with him. We have so much fun together when we're not consumed by a murder investigation."

Michelle poured milk into her teacup and stirred until the dark brown liquid changed to a creamy tan. "How long do you think you'll stay in the Galapagos?" She gestured around her granddaughter's hotel suite. "Your accommodations still seem temporary."

Giovanna shrugged. "I'm in no hurry to move back to Georgia. I'm still a pariah after the bankruptcy. I'll stay here as long as Jim needs me, and I'll get a place in town once everything's up and running smoothly." She hoped Jim would disregard the comments his Chief Marketing Officer had made about her.

Michelle sipped her tea. "I guess I shouldn't give you grief about planning your future. You're a lot more mature than I was at your age."

"Thank you. And weren't you almost forty when you married Roberto?"

"But I didn't have someone like Timothy when I was your age."

"Maybe that's the problem." Giovanna set down her cup. "I've known Timothy most of my life. I've hardly dated anyone else. What's wrong with exploring what's out there?"

* * *

Victor quickened his pace to catch up with Tyler on the staircase. "Señor Thompson?"

Tyler gripped the banister until his knuckles whitened. He turned to face the detective.

"May I have a word?" Victor gestured toward one of the lobby couches. "It won't take long."

"What now?" Tyler's nostrils flared. "It's been a busy day, and you've already questioned me tonight. I don't know what else I can add."

They sat down on the couch, several feet apart, and Victor took out his pocket notebook. "Earlier, I asked if you'd spoken with Maria Vasquez this evening."

"And I told you no. I try to avoid speaking with her. That woman annoys me."

Victor raised his brow. "Why?"

"She's so . . ." Tyler sucked in some air between his teeth. "I'm not sure why. Maybe it's that high-pitched, know-it-all, gotcha voice. The way she tries to make a scandal out of nothing. She rubs me the wrong way."

"Would you like to get rid of her?"

"I wouldn't be sorry if she went away." Tyler's eyes darted to Victor's notebook. "No, I didn't have anything to do with her accident, if that's where you're going with this."

"When we spoke earlier, you told me you hadn't left the hotel this evening. Do you stand by that statement?"

"Does 'the hotel' include the grounds?"

"You went outside?"

"Is that a problem?"

"What time did you go outside?" Victor rapped his pencil against his notebook.

"Honestly, I don't remember. I don't wear a watch." Tyler pointed to his bare wrist. "The loud music gave me a headache, and I wanted some fresh air. I'd already taken plenty of footage for Mr. Roberts's commercial."

Victor jotted a note. "Where did you go?"

"Out back by the pool. I was going to walk down to the beach, but I didn't trust myself on that steep path. They really should put some lights out there."

Victor refrained from commenting on the hotel's shortcomings and continued his questions. "What did you do instead of walking on the beach?"

"I had a smoke and then came back inside."

"Through the back door?"

"No. I went out that way, but I came back in through the front."

"Who did you see while you were outside?"

"I saw two couples strolling. Not all together. Each couple . . . you know."

Victor waved his pencil. "Right. Two separate couples. Go on."

"I couldn't make out their faces or what they were saying, so don't ask me to identify anyone."

Victor tapped his wooden pencil against his tooth. "Did you see Maria Vasquez?"

Tyler shrugged. "She might have been one of the women I saw. Part of one of the couples. But I couldn't say for sure."

"Did you speak with anyone while you were outside?"

"I said no."

"Did you fall?"

"What makes you think I fell?"

"Someone said you looked disheveled when you came back inside." Victor studied Tyler's attire. "Either that person was mistaken, or you've changed clothes."

Tyler gave a thin smile. "People tell me I present a disheveled appearance."

"So, you didn't fall? Or get into a scuffle?"

"Really, Detective. What are you implying?"

"I'm not implying anything; just asking." Victor looked him in the eye. "Trying to figure out where everyone was when Maria Vasquez had her accident."

"I wish I could help you, Detective, but I didn't see what happened. Sorry."

Victor wrote more in his notebook, then flipped a page. "Since you arrived at the hotel, have you been off the premises?" He smiled. "Not including strolling the grounds."

"A group of us toured the Darwin Research Station yesterday afternoon."

"What about the night before? Did you leave the property?"

Tyler looked down.

Victor waited, remembering what Hector had told him.

"I went into town. Thought I'd check out some of the nightlife."

"Where did you go?"

"A few bars. I don't remember what they were called. One had a picture of a pelican on the sign."

"El Pelicano?" It was a favorite watering hole among the police squad, and tourists flocked there too.

"Maybe."

"Were you alone?"

"Define 'alone.'"

Victor continued to stare at the cameraman. *If he'd kept to himself all night, he could have answered that question.*

Tyler cleared his throat. "I talked to a few locals."

"Names?"

"Didn't get them."

"Anyone who works at the resort?"

"We didn't talk about Leisure Dreams."

"Did you see anyone you recognized from the hotel? Employee or guest? Maybe your colleagues?" Hector had mentioned seeing Susie and Colin leave the property that night also.

Tyler scrunched his face in thought. "A man on a nearby bar stool. But I didn't know until tonight that he works here."

"Who was that?"

"I think his name is Miguel. I heard he's the groundskeeper."

Victor nodded and wrote. "What time did you see Miguel?"

Tyler pressed his head against his hand. "Gosh, this feels like I'm back in college, taking an exam." He sighed. "Miguel was with some other guy, and they left before I did. I couldn't hear their conversation, but it seemed intense. It's the only reason I noticed him. I didn't want to hang around if a fight broke out."

A fight? The conversation was that intense? "What about the other man?"

"Never saw him before. Or since."

Victor jotted more notes. "When you recognized Miguel this evening, did you speak? Did you mention seeing him at the bar two nights ago?"

"What if I did?"

Victor gave him the interrogation stare.

"Really, I don't get where you're going with this. You asked me about Maria Vasquez. I'm trying to cooperate. What does my trip to town have to do with the reporter's accident?"

"Nothing, señor."

"Then why—"

"Pedro Lopez, the Leisure Dreams sous chef, was found dead in his home yesterday. I'm trying to establish a timeline."

Tyler's mouth flew open. "And I'm a suspect because I went into town? I don't even know Pedro Lopez."

Victor took out his phone and located a photo Giovanna had texted from Pedro's employment file. Since he'd never seen Pedro alive, he had no idea how good a likeness it was. "Did you see this man when you were in town last night?"

Tyler peered at the photo. "Hard to say. He might have been the man arguing with Miguel."

"Thank you, señor. You've been more helpful than you meant to be."

"I always mean to be helpful." Tyler stifled a yawn. "By the way, how are you coming with your investigation into Claire's death?"

Victor's phone buzzed. "Excuse me." He glanced at Tyler. "*Hola.*" He listened for a minute while continuing to watch the cameraman. "She's awake? I'll be right over."

Tyler's face had grown pale gray.

CHAPTER THIRTY-SEVEN

Early Saturday morning, Puerto Ayora Hospital

Before starting the engine of his police car, Victor sent Giovanna a quick text to let her know he wouldn't be back that night, in case she was waiting up for him. *Or maybe her former fiancé returned. He's still in love with her, and he's not giving up.*

She answered the text immediately with a heart emoji, followed by, "Good news about Maria. Hope you get some answers."

He smiled to himself, his faith in her feelings restored.

* * *

The Puerto Ayora hospital was a small, mid-twentieth-century two-story building with straight-backed Naugahyde chairs in the dingy but tidy lobby. Although the island boasted state-of-the-art decompression apparatus to help save divers who'd gotten into trouble, most other emergency facilities were limited.

A nurse ushered Victor into the recovery room where Maria lay. Abrasions and bruises covered her face, but she brightened when he walked in.

"Detective Zuniga." Her voice scratched like the needle of a turntable against an old vinyl record. The right half of her upper lip had swelled to twice the size of the left.

"You gave us a scare, Maria." He smiled. "How are you feeling?"

She touched her head and grimaced.

"I'd like to ask you a few questions if you're up for it. Is that okay?"

She nodded slowly as if it hurt to move her head. "I have questions for you, too."

He took out his notebook. "We'll help each other like we always do. But let me start. Do you remember what happened?"

"Not much."

"Just tell me what you recall." He waited.

Her eyes flitted around the room and blinked at the bright lights. "I fell. I felt my feet fly from under me, and the next thing I knew, the ground smacked me in the face." She patted the rail of her adjustable bed. "I'm in the hospital."

Victor nodded. "This is it. Have you ever been here?"

"Not as a patient."

"For a story?"

"Felipe Santore last year. After his business partner stabbed him. You remember."

Thoughts of Jerome Haddad's murderous rampage surfaced again. After stabbing his wife, his partner Felipe, and Janice Roberts, that madman had kidnapped Giovanna and almost killed her. Shaking his head, Victor tried to dismiss memories of the manhunt; how terrified he'd been that they wouldn't find her in time. He'd shot a man to death, and at the time, he'd felt nothing but relief.

That nightmare was over; he needed to focus on the situation at hand. "Let's talk about your accident, Maria. What happened before you fell?"

Maria closed her eyes as if reading the answers from the insides of her eyelids. "I was at a party. I didn't see you there, though. Leisure Dreams, the grand opening."

He'd missed it, disappointed Giovanna. He'd wanted to be there to support her. "Good. What else do you remember?" He pointed to a plastic cup and pitcher on the nightstand. "Want some water?"

"Please." With another wince, Maria raised herself to a semi-sitting position.

He filled the cup and handed it to her. "Can you manage?"

She took a sip of water. "Your girlfriend made a speech. You would have been proud."

He ignored the cattiness in Maria's voice. "I'm sorry I missed it."

"She's not right for you, but I can tell you're smitten."

He cocked an eyebrow at Maria. "Let's stick to the subject. What else do you recall about the evening?"

"I'm afraid I behaved badly."

"How so?"

"I interrupted her. Asked about the status of the investigation into the death of Claire Costello." She took another sip of water. "The bigwigs didn't take it well. Those goons meant to silence me."

Victor imagined the discomfort Giovanna must have felt, and he hadn't been there to jump to her defense, to deflect the inquiries to the police investigation. She had not mentioned Maria's outburst when they spoke, but their time together had been cut short. "Let me guess: Giovanna told you to direct your questions to me?"

"Right. And what's your answer?"

"We'll talk about that later. What time did you leave the party?"

She shrugged against the flat, white pillow. Her shiny black hair, now loose from her chignon, flowed around her shoulders. "I don't know. Almost everyone had gone into the ballroom to dance."

"Were you with someone?"

"I went to the party with Laurel."

"Did you leave with her?"

Maria squinted. "I don't know where Laurel was when I went outside. I was talking to Miguel . . ." Her voice trailed off as if the picture in her mind had faded.

"Did you go for a walk?" Victor asked. "You weren't near the parking area when we found you."

She shook her head. "I don't remember."

"Did you talk to Miguel about Claire Costello?"

Her pallor returned. "I'm supposed to be asking *you* about Claire Costello."

"Did Miguel know Claire Costello before she arrived here?"

"Of course. We all did. She's made documentaries in the Galapagos before; Miguel and Laurel have helped her with research."

"Did you know the rest of Claire's crew?"

"That camera guy has been working with Claire for a long time. I always thought he was creepy." Maria took another sip of water. "The way he hovered over Claire. She'd often get sick right after they arrived, and he played the nursemaid. The situation smacked of Munchausen. Or maybe even Munchausen by proxy."

Victor felt his breath catch in his throat. "What? You think he was deliberately making her ill?"

The reporter licked her lip and then flinched as her tongue touched the wound. "I have no proof. Claire had a sensitive stomach and loved trying new food and drink, so most likely, that was why she frequently got sick when she traveled. She pushed herself."

Still mulling over the new information, Victor continued, "Did Claire share the subject of this new documentary with any of you?"

"I assumed it had to do with the resort's opening. Why else would Jim Roberts be sponsoring it? And it appears that's what her staff is working on now."

"Laurel mentioned Claire wanted to talk about Tio Armando."

"Laurel and I both thought that. As you know, the tortoise has a connection with Leisure Dreams that has never been fully explained."

"Tell me more about Miguel. What did he know about this connection? Did he have a reason to silence Claire?"

"You're the detective." Maria weakly waved a finger. "It's your job to find out what happened to Claire Costello."

Victor smiled, revealing his chipped tooth. "Let's get back to your accident. Could you have been pushed?"

"It's possible. It was dark, and I wasn't my most alert."

"But did it feel like someone pushed you?" He picked up the cup she had set down. "More water?"

She nodded. "It might have been that nasty cameraman."

Victor refilled the cup and gave it to Maria. "The cameraman? Tyler Thompson?"

"I didn't see him when I went outside, but I'm sure he was the one who tripped me the other day."

"The other day? What are you talking about? What happened?"

"Your girlfriend was giving the film crew a tour of the grounds on Wednesday, and I tagged along to see what I could learn about Claire. Somehow, I tripped over his foot and fell off the pier, into the water." She made a sour face. "Your girlfriend pulled me out."

"Her name is Giovanna Rogers." Victor suppressed a smile. "That must have been quite a scene."

"Ha, ha, ha. Everyone laughed except me. But that man has a mean streak. You should keep your eye on him, Detective." She set down the cup.

Victor grew serious. "When did you last see Tyler?"

Her eyes flitted to the ceiling, where a large insect buzzed around the light bulb. "I don't know."

"Did you speak to him at the event?"

She shook her head. "I told you, it's all a blur. I had a few glasses of champagne, well over my limit. I was outside talking to Miguel, waiting for Laurel, then the next thing I knew, I woke up here."

"Except you said you remember falling."

"Yes, that."

Victor tapped his pencil on his notebook. "Do you know a man named Pedro Lopez?"

"Is that someone who works at Leisure Dreams?"

"He was the sous chef. He's dead now."

She leaned back against the pillow. "Dead?"

Victor nodded.

She took a breath as if still digesting the news. "How? Do you think his death and Claire's are related?"

Victor shrugged. "I'm trying to find out."

"And my fall?"

"I don't know. But you need to be honest with me."

Maria let out a long sigh. "Wow. This is a bigger story than I thought."

He patted her knee through the sheet. "You'd better get some rest so you can write it."

CHAPTER THIRTY-EIGHT

Saturday morning, North Seymour Island

As scheduled, a minibus from the tourist bureau arrived at the hotel at eight the next morning. Giovanna was excited to join the group on their excursion to North Seymour Island. Guests included the corporate team, the film crew, and friends and family of the hotel management.

Jim had assuaged Giovanna's guilt at leaving her post for the day. "Belinda and the rest of the staff can handle whatever arises. Go enjoy yourself. Besides, you're the face of Leisure Dreams here, so consider yourself on duty."

Giovanna could have argued that *Jim* was the face of Leisure Dreams, not her. And the trip included executives much higher on the corporate ladder who could represent the company. But it felt good to know the CEO had confidence in her and still viewed her as his hotel manager. The CMO's words last night must not have resonated with him. She also suspected Jim had no interest in the outing, and his ulterior motive was for her to entertain his teenage daughter and the corporate visitors while he spent the day working without interruptions.

Giovanna helped the guide usher guests into the minibus. She avoided sitting beside Timothy by seating him next to his mother, and Jenny at her side. She and Jenny sat directly behind the guide and Tyler. Michelle and Roberto, in the seat behind her, served as a buffer between her and Timothy.

Ready for a day of adventure, Jenny had brought her GoPro camera and some high-power binoculars. She turned to Giovanna. "This will be fun." Most of the previous wistfulness was gone from her smile.

The bus headed north across Santa Cruz Island to the Itabaca Channel, the narrow body of water separating Santa Cruz from Baltra Island, where the airport was located. During the hour-long ride, the terrain and vegetation ranged from arid to semi-tropical as they passed through various elevations. When the bus drove into the highlands, both Jenny and Tyler snapped pictures of Los Gemelos, twin craters—looking more like sinkholes—formed by the collapse of an ancient magma chamber. Lush green lichens and scalesia forests stood out against the dark grey volcanic walls.

Tyler chatted with the guide in Spanish. Although his accent was distinctly American, Giovanna was impressed with his command of the language—certainly much better than hers.

Michelle leaned forward and tapped Giovanna's shoulder. "I'm so glad you got to come along."

Giovanna touched her grandmother's hand and turned to look at her. "Me too."

"I've been worried about you working too hard," Michelle said. "I know you live in a beautiful place, but do you get time to enjoy it?"

"Victor and I went hiking on Tuesday. I took the whole day off." *Just before my life ran off the rails.*

Michelle and Roberto exchanged glances, and he diverted his wife's attention to a soaring Galapagos Hawk before she could comment on her granddaughter's love life.

When they reached the Itabaca Channel, a large, motorized Catamaran-style yacht awaited them, ready to take the group to North Seymour Island. Giovanna again avoided eye contact with Timothy as she hung back with the guide to help the passengers negotiate the boarding bridge between the pier and the vessel.

After a brief safety drill with the captain, they were on their way, cutting across the indigo water, on the lookout for whales, dolphins, and sharks. Jenny spotted the first splash, and others rushed to the side of the boat where she'd seen it, many missing a bigger splash on the opposite side.

Tyler photographed a blacktip reef shark in mid-air during a particularly spectacular vertical jump. After he'd shown everyone his incredible shot, Jenny remained glued to his side, asking for photography advice and comparing equipment.

The guide, a sturdy, twenty-something Ecuadorian woman, gave an overview of their destination to the few passengers listening to her. "North Seymour Island, named for an English nobleman, Lord Hugh Seymour, isn't volcanic in nature like many of the islands in the Galapagos archipelago—such as Santa Cruz, the one we just left. North Seymour was formed by seismic uplift." She scanned the crowd as if to determine whether it was worth continuing her spiel.

Giovanna gave her an encouraging smile.

"Is there a South Seymour?" asked Andrea.

"*Sí, señora.* But we know it better as Baltra. It's the island we're passing on your left."

"Baltra is where our plane landed," Olivia explained to her colleague. "It looks different from this angle."

The guide added, "During World War II, the United States established an air base on Baltra."

Roberto said, "Ecuador still uses Baltra as a military base, doesn't it?"

"*Sí, señor.*" The guide brightened as if pleased that at least one of the tourists knew something about her country. "The whole island of North Seymour is less than two kilometers long and has a maximum altitude of twenty-eight meters. You'll see lots of low, bushy vegetation, and right where we make our dry landing, you'll walk through a forest of silver-gray, barren-looking Palo Santo trees."

"What do you mean by a 'dry landing'?" asked Andrea.

The guide smiled. "We can transfer directly from the boat to land without getting wet. On some islands, there's nowhere to dock, so you must wade through several feet of water to get ashore."

"Will we see blue-footed boobies?" asked Timothy, referring to the iconic poster bird of the Galapagos, renowned for its bright blue feet.

The guide's smile revealed a gold-rimmed tooth. "*Sí, señor. Piqueros de patas azules.* Isla Seymour Norte is a great place to see the blue-footed boobies. It's one of their favorite nesting grounds." She pointed at a flock of flying birds. "Those are boobies over there."

Timothy squinted. "They look like ducks. I can't see their blue feet."

"They tuck them in when they're flying." The guide smiled again. "You'll get a good look at their feet when we go ashore."

The yacht anchored a few meters from shore, where they transferred in shifts to a panga, a skiff with an outboard motor. Giovanna had not noticed Susie's shoes when they left the hotel, but as soon as she saw the three-inch wedge heels on open-toed sandals, she envisioned disaster. *For someone who works on nature films, what was she thinking?* "Don't you have—?"

Before Giovanna could finish her sentence, Colin helped Susie into the panga. Susie flashed a regal smile at the rest of the passengers which reminded Giovanna of the photo she'd posted on Claire's social media.

Moments later, with a noisy escort of sea lions, pelicans, and frigatebirds, they docked at a crude pier made of black basalt. "Be careful going ashore," the guide cautioned. "The rock steps are uneven, and they can get slippery." She raised her voice. "Wait for me at the top of the hill. The Galapagos Park Service requires us to keep together as a group, and everyone must stay on the trail."

Giovanna held her breath as Susie carefully negotiated the steps, teetering like a clown on stilts. She was tempted to hold out an arm for support, but Colin already clung to his paramour.

On the final step, Susie's foot slid off its sandal and made contact with the rock, throwing her off-balance. Colin tightened his grip on her arm, but gravity won, forcing him to let go or be pulled down with her. Susie tumbled off the incline and landed with a thud on the packed sand below, narrowly missing a napping sea lion. Barking with annoyance, the pinniped edged away. Three nearby pelicans flapped their massive wings and took off for the sky.

"Susie!" Giovanna and Colin cried in unison, dashing down to the sand.

Winded, Susie propped herself up on her elbows.

Colin grabbed her foot. "Where does it—"

"Ow!" Susie yelled.

Her knee was scraped, and her ankle appeared to be swelling.

"Is she okay?" called the guide. "I have a first aid kit." She started toward them.

Susie glared sullenly.

"I'm sorry that happened," said Giovanna. She picked up the shoe that lay several feet away. "You know—"

Colin took Susie's hand. "Can you get up?"

She attempted to rise but moaned and stayed put.

The guide opened her first aid kit, then took out antiseptic and a bandage.

Colin addressed their guide. "How long is the hike?"

"The trail around the island is about two kilometers." She applied an antiseptic to Susie's scraped knee. "Some of the terrain is irregular." The guide eyed Susie's swelling ankle. "You should have that checked out when we get back. It might be sprained."

Susie groaned, and Colin shook his head. "I don't think she can make the hike. But y'all go on. We'll wait here until you're done."

"You're kidding me," said Tyler, who had started back down the rocky steps. "I need help with some of the shots. Who's going to handle the sound and take notes?"

Susie's lip quivered. "I didn't fall on purpose, Tyler."

"Maybe not, but if you'd listened last night when they told you how to dress for a hike, you might not have fallen." He pointed to the shoe in Giovanna's hand. "And didn't Claire give you a packing list for this trip?"

Susie touched the other shoe, still strapped on her foot. "I'm not used to hiking, and I didn't bring any tennis shoes. They look goofy on me."

Tyler huffed. "Well, you look goofy now, splatted on the beach with the sea lions."

The guide consulted her watch. "We need to get started if we're going to do this walk. And I know you need to set up your filming. Who's coming?"

"Colin, go with Tyler," Susie pleaded. "Otherwise, we'll never hear the end of it."

"I can't leave you by yourself." He observed the rest of the group waiting at the trailhead.

Giovanna clenched her teeth. "I'll stay with her, Colin. Tyler needs your help."

The guide eyed her gratefully. "You're sure, señora?"

Giovanna nodded, silently cursing Susie and her shoes. She glanced at the top of the ridge as the others set out on the hike. Timothy and Michelle cast regretful looks in her direction before joining the chattering group. At least she wouldn't have to spend the day fending off Timothy's advances.

When the others had gone, Susie turned to Giovanna. "Thank you, Ms. Rogers. I'm sure you'd rather be up there showing your friend around."

"Call me Giovanna, please."

"Giovanna," Susie repeated. "I'm sorry to be such trouble."

"It's okay."

"Tyler can be so mean."

She sounds like a third-grader. Where did Claire find her? Giovanna made herself comfortable on the sand. "It must be a trying time for all of you."

"He blames me for Claire."

Giovanna studied Susie's face. *Might as well see what I can learn while we're stuck here together.* "Why would he blame you?"

Susie's eyes watered. "Because of Colin."

"The affair?"

Susie sniffed, showing no surprise that her clandestine romance was out in the open. "Claire didn't treat Colin right; she didn't deserve him. Tyler couldn't see it. He worshipped Claire."

"Really?" Giovanna sensed Tyler had professional respect for Claire, but "worship" didn't seem to fit. She watched a sea lion pup nuzzle against its mother, who rolled away, having had enough of her offspring for the moment. After the brief disruption of humans entering their space, the animals returned to their routines.

"If only Claire had reciprocated Tyler's affection, things might have turned out differently," Susie declared.

Giovanna creased her brow. "Tyler's affection? Why do you say that?"

With a shrug, Susie doodled in the sand.

"Were Tyler and Claire ever a 'thing'?"

Susie scoffed. "In Tyler's dreams."

"You know that for a fact?" Giovanna wondered how much of Tyler's adoration for Claire existed only in Susie's imagination. Maybe it was her way to justify going after Colin.

"Claire was a hypochondriac. Whenever we took a trip, she claimed to feel sick. Tyler played the lap dog, always rushing to her aid."

"You think she was pretending? Just to get attention?"

Susie contorted her face in a manner that was not attractive. "Of course, she was. It happened like clockwork. Colin fell for it at first, but her act was getting old. Tyler, on the other hand, never caught on."

They sat on the beach in silence, breathing the salty air, watching the frolicking sea lions vie for the best position on the rocks and bark at each other when a prod did not prove effective. Giovanna pointed out a passing pod of dolphins, their dark fins undulating with the waves, but Susie kept her head down, drawing stick figures in the sand.

"How did you end up working for Claire anyway?" Giovanna studied Susie. "Do you have a film background?"

"My daddy thought it would be good for me." Susie kept drawing. "He has no idea how they treat me."

What does that mean? "Was there this much discord in your group before Claire died? Forgive me for saying this, but the three of you don't seem to get along very well."

Susie raised her head and stared out to sea. "Claire made us this way. It was time for her to retire." She looked back at her sand sketching and added a few more squiggles. "I had great ideas, but she and Tyler always shut me down, never gave me a chance. I'd make a better documentary star than Claire."

Giovanna opened her mouth to clarify, but Susie had drifted into her own thoughts.

CHAPTER THIRTY-NINE

Leisure Dreams Hotel, Sunday morning

The next morning, Giovanna ate breakfast in the dining room with Michelle and Roberto. Michelle had called Elaine to invite her and Timothy to join them, but they were sleeping in, claiming exhaustion from the journey to North Seymour. Giovanna was grateful not to have to see Timothy.

They were enjoying plates of luscious, fresh papaya when Colin and Susie entered the dining area. Ankle bandaged, walking with an obvious limp, Susie leaned on Colin more than necessary. She'd replaced the high-heeled sandals with flowery flip-flops Giovanna recognized from the hotel gift shop.

Michelle waved, and the couple stopped by the table. "How's the ankle?" She regarded Susie's bandages.

"Better," said Susie. "And again, Giovanna, I'm sorry I made you miss the hike." She gazed adoringly at Colin. "I understand y'all saw lots of blue-footed boobies."

"Boobies, frigatebirds, iguanas . . . wasn't it great?" Colin turned to Michelle and Roberto for confirmation.

"Lots of little chicks," added Michelle. "It's the season." She touched Giovanna's shoulder.

"Victor and I will go there soon." Giovanna smiled, determined not to feel slighted for missing the hike. Except for a brief text exchange about Maria's awakening, she hadn't talked to the detective in over twenty-four hours. Not only did she miss being with him, she wanted to share some observations from her conversation with Susie.

"How's the documentary coming?" asked Roberto. "Your cameraman sure was busy during the outing yesterday."

"We'll meet later today to go through the footage, but Tyler captured the atmosphere from the grand opening," said Susie. "Mr. Roberts will be pleased with the results."

"Aren't you shooting a nature documentary?" Michelle frowned. "Besides the promotional video for the resort?"

"Yes, something about Tío Armando?" Roberto asked.

Colin and Susie looked at each other. Giovanna wondered what secrets they were concealing. And the police might be interested in reviewing the unedited footage from the grand opening, as it could contain clues to Maria's unfortunate accident.

"Tyler got some great stuff on North Seymour yesterday and at the Darwin Research Station on Thursday," said Colin. "Including Tío Armando. Laurel Pardo filled us in on his history. We'll work that into the promo."

"That's it then?" said Giovanna. "I was under the impression Claire had planned a more comprehensive documentary."

Colin cleared his throat. "Obviously, we've had to pivot."

"Mr. Roberts arranged to have Miguel drive us to the El Chato reserve today so we can get more shots of tortoises before we fly back to the States tomorrow." Susie pointed to her ankle. "I want to get home and see my own doctor."

"Miguel's driving you?" Roberto looked puzzled. "I thought he was the groundskeeper."

"He's also quite the tortoise expert, and he knows the people who run the place," said Colin. "Since El Chato is one of the few places in the world where we can see giant Galapagos tortoises in the wild, we couldn't pass it up."

"No visits to other islands?" asked Michelle.

Colin and Susie shook their heads.

"You're flying back tomorrow?" Giovanna quirked her mouth. "Your rooms are booked through the end of the week. Does Detective Zuniga know you're leaving?"

Their silence told her he didn't.

"He might have more questions for you about Claire," Giovanna added.

Colin glanced at Susie, then back at Giovanna. "I don't see how we could help him further. We've already told the detective everything we remember, and he knows how to reach us in the States."

The waitress arrived and set steaming plates of spicy empanadas in front of them.

Colin held up his hand. "Go ahead and eat while your food is hot. We don't want to keep you." With that, the pair walked toward a table in the far corner of the room, Susie's hobbling more pronounced than before.

* * *

After breakfast, Giovanna located Miguel Ruiz, who was watering the flowerbeds in front of the hotel, swaying to the beat from his earmuff-style headphones.

She waved to get his attention, and he pulled off one side of the headphones.

"*Buenos días*, Miguel. Great job keeping all the plants so beautiful. The executives were impressed with how 'on brand' you've made the landscaping."

He let his headphones slide around his neck. "*Gracias, señora.*"

"Roberto enjoyed working with you on Friday," she said. "Thanks again for making him feel useful."

Miguel grinned. "The pleasure was mine. Your father knows a lot about horticulture."

Again, Giovanna allowed Miguel to assume that Roberto was her father. *My grandmother's husband* didn't sound like an adequate description of their relationship, and he didn't fit the grandfather stereotype. If she and Timothy had married, Roberto would have walked her down the aisle. "Gardening has always been a hobby of his, and last year, he took a course from the county to earn his Master Gardener certification. It's made him very critical of other people's pruning techniques, so you should feel honored that he admires yours."

Miguel cracked another polite smile and went back to watering. Giovanna continued to stand beside him until he gave her his attention again. "*Sí, señora?*"

"Maybe you don't know yet, since you'd already left the party when Detective Zuniga started interviewing people, but did you hear what happened to Maria Vasquez?"

The stream of water pouring from the hose wavered. "No, señora. What happened?" He shut the nozzle and moved away to turn the water off at the spigot.

"She fell . . . or maybe someone pushed her." Giovanna watched Miguel as she described finding Maria unconscious on the beach path the night of the grand opening.

His eyelids flickered. "Is she . . . ?"

"She's in the hospital. Detective Zuniga has been to see her."

"Will she be okay?"

"We hope so."

"So, she . . . what did she remember?"

Giovanna shrugged. "I haven't talked to the detective since early Saturday morning. Did you see Maria leave the party with anyone?"

Miguel jutted his lip in thought. "I saw her talking to one of those movie guys."

"From Claire Costello's crew?"

Miguel nodded.

"Which one?"

"I don't know their names. The one taking pictures."

"Were they talking inside or outside?"

"Both."

Giovanna sighed. Miguel could be so oblique sometimes. "Did *you* talk to her at the party?"

"*Sí señora*. We are friends."

"When did you see her last?"

He scrunched his face. "I left the party at about nine. Maria came outside around the same time."

"And, since you're friends, did you speak on the way out?"

Before Miguel could answer, a Puerto Ayora police car drove up. Victor got out and strode toward them.

Giovanna felt the corners of her lips turn upward as he approached.

Victor greeted her with a quick hug and cheek kiss, then turned to Miguel. "Miguel Ruiz, just the person I came to see. Shall we take a little walk?"

Giovanna's eyes followed Victor as he and Miguel headed toward the beach path.

* * *

"Detective, if this is about Maria Vasquez, I know nothing more than what I told señora Rogers," said Miguel.

Victor arched an eyebrow. "Señora Rogers asked you about Maria Vasquez?"

"*Sí, señor*. We were talking about her accident when you drove up. I'm very sorry she fell. I had no idea."

"Maria said she was talking to *you* right before it happened."

Miguel gulped.

Victor waited. When Miguel didn't comment, he pressed, "What were the two of you talking about?"

Miguel lifted his eyes skyward. "She thinks she has a story."

"About?"

"I couldn't help her very much."

"What's her story about?" Victor trained his eyes like lasers on Miguel's face. *Why does he keep dodging my questions?*

Miguel twitched. "My work with the tortoises."

"Why would Maria write a story about your work with tortoises now? You've been a groundskeeper here since the hotel was built."

"Didn't she tell you?"

Victor tried another angle. "Was Claire Costello doing a story about your connection to Tio Armando? How the tortoise mysteriously turned up at

Leisure Dreams after someone moved him from the Beagle Galapaguera on San Cristóbal?"

Miguel shuffled his feet along the ground. "I don't know. I didn't talk to Claire Costello."

"You're sticking to that story?"

"Yes." Miguel's expression had turned cocky. "And what does it matter?"

Victor eyed him, unfazed. "Exactly, señor. There are other ways of finding out what you did."

Miguel's cocksure smile faded.

"How well do you know Pedro Lopez?"

"Who?" The smile was completely gone.

"The Leisure Dreams sous chef. The man who opened the champagne you brought from the cellar for señora Costello."

Miguel scuffed his feet against the path.

"He lives only a few blocks from you. You both have been working at the resort since the beginning."

"I know him, okay. But I wouldn't call him a friend. We're acquaintances. Is that a crime?"

Victor raised his eyebrows. *Why so sensitive?* "That depends on whether you had anything to do with his murder."

"Murder?" Miguel's mouth dropped, but Victor sensed he was exaggerating surprise.

"Surely, word has spread among the staff?" Victor studied Miguel's body language for more signs of deception.

"I heard he committed suicide."

Victor doubted Miguel believed that. Just like Belinda didn't believe Claire had killed herself. "Have you seen Pedro Lopez since Tuesday evening, when you delivered the champagne to the kitchen?"

Miguel's eyes searched Victor's face as if he were wondering what to divulge.

"Let me jog your memory. Maybe in a bar on Wednesday night?"

"Maybe."

"El Pelicano?"

Miguel nodded. "One of my favorites."

"Did you see Pedro Lopez at El Pelicano?"

Miguel sighed. "We had a drink together. But señor, I didn't kill him, if that's where you're going with these questions."

"Did you see Pedro speak with anyone else?"

Miguel shrugged. "I couldn't say."

"Did you leave together?"

"No." Miguel eyed the detective.

Victor could see the wheels turning, calculating the safest response. "No?"

"We may have walked out at the same time, but we didn't 'leave together.' We each went to our separate homes."

"Can anyone verify that?"

"Yes," Miguel began, then bit his lip. "No, señor."

"No?" Victor eyed him. "No company?"

Miguel murmured something unintelligible.

"Sorry, I didn't hear you."

"I didn't see Pedro Lopez after we left El Pelicano."

"Once you got home," Victor asked, "did you stay there the rest of the night?"

"*Sí, señor.*"

"By yourself?"

Miguel looked away.

Victor closed his notebook. "Thank you, señor. So, you were home alone Wednesday night after seeing Pedro Lopez at the bar, but no one can vouch for you."

* * *

Giovanna was poring over the bookings forecast when Victor walked into her office. She looked up from her computer screen and smiled. "Did Miguel give you the answers you needed?"

"Is he always so evasive?"

"He's a man of few words. Sometimes getting information out of him is like trying to catch fish during a rainstorm." A childhood memory of fishing trips with Roberto brought another smile to her lips. "But he does a good job with the grounds."

"Miguel is hiding something."

"You don't think he's a killer, do you?"

Victor shrugged. "I can't rule anyone out yet. And now we have two possible homicides, which may or may not be related. Not to mention Maria's 'accident.'"

"You didn't bargain for all this when you chose this quiet island post, did you?"

His grin exposed the chipped tooth. "It hasn't been boring."

"I was hoping for some peace and quiet, too. One of the reasons I took this job." She sighed. "But it seems like trouble follows me."

"I knew there was a connection: you."

They gazed fondly at each other. "Is there something else I can do for you?" She blushed, breaking the spell. "I mean, professionally. Any more employees or guests you need to interview?"

He nodded. "I know the film crew was anxious to get Claire's notes back, so we've made reviewing them a priority. We're ready to turn them over, but I still have questions. Can you round up the team again for me? And I'd appreciate it if you'd join us; you might be able to answer some of those questions." He fiddled with the spiral of his notebook. "But I should warn you before we start hashing out these notes in front of everyone. Claire wrote several references to Jerome Haddad."

Giovanna shuddered at the thought of her treacherous business partner-turned-attacker. "My day keeps getting better."

Victor's eyes brimmed with compassion.

With a sigh, she picked up the phone. "I'll try to catch them. They're supposed to go to El Chato today with Miguel, and then they've booked a flight back to the States tomorrow."

"Tomorrow?" Victor repeated, eyes widening. "I didn't say they could leave yet."

"Seemed sudden to me too, but Susie sprained her ankle yesterday." Giovanna dialed Susie's room. Listening to the ringing phone, she stole an appreciative glance at Victor, his muscular arms bulging from beneath his short sleeves. "Jim has meetings in the conference room all morning, but we can gather in my suite."

Victor creased his brow. "Weren't they planning to stay for another week?"

Giovanna held up her hand when Susie answered. "Hi, Susie, this is Giovanna Rogers. Detective Zuniga is ready to return Claire's papers, but he has a few questions. Can you and the guys come to Suite 100 at—" She glanced at Victor, and he held up all ten fingers. "Ten o'clock?" There was a pause which she took for agreement. "It won't take long. I'll let Miguel know to wait for you." She could hear Colin talking in the background. "And please pass along the word to the others."

CHAPTER FORTY

Sunday morning, Giovanna's suite

When the film crew arrived at Giovanna's suite, Victor had gone into the bedroom to take a call from headquarters. Colin and Susie settled on the couch, snuggling together even though there was plenty of room to spread out. With a groan, Susie propped her foot on the ottoman.

Tyler claimed one of the armchairs. Leaving the other for Victor, Giovanna brought her desk chair over to the cluster rather than share the couch with the lovebirds.

"Did you let Miguel know we'd be late for the visit to El Chato?" Tyler asked Susie.

"He knows," she snapped.

Tyler shot her a contemptuous look. "Jenny will be joining us."

"The CEO's daughter?" Colin cocked his head. "Why?"

"The kid's into photography, and I promised to give her a few pointers. She's bored hanging around the hotel with no one to play with."

"You'd better watch it around her," warned Colin. "She's a daddy's girl and still jailbait."

Narrowing his eyes at his colleague, Tyler ran his tongue over his front teeth. "Your mind would go there, wouldn't it?"

"Did you clear it with Mr. Roberts?" Giovanna hadn't considered the perceived impropriety until Colin brought it up; in fact, she'd been glad to hear the teenager had found something she wanted to do.

Before Tyler could answer, Victor emerged from the bedroom and seated himself in the vacant armchair. "Let's get started." He held up Claire's notebook. "The other day, you were anxious to get this back."

Susie leaned forward and rubbed her ankle. "Yes, but now our plans have changed. Without Claire, the documentary won't be the same. We couldn't begin to do justice to her vision." Her emphasis on "vision" had a sarcastic ring.

Victor raised an eyebrow. "You're not making the film?"

"The promotional video for Leisure Dreams, yes," replied Colin. "We promised Mr. Roberts. We're almost ready to move into the editing phase, and we can do that from anywhere. The 'true Tio Armando story' has too many holes. Maybe Claire had more information and leads to pursue, but she didn't tell us enough to move forward with it."

"Don't you have a script? A storyboard?" Victor frowned. "I don't know much about making movies, but—"

Colin and Susie looked at each other and laughed. "Storyboard? Script?" Colin snorted. "That's a good one."

"I thought that's why you wanted the notebook," said Giovanna. "Her roadmap for the project."

"Is it even legible?" jeered Colin. "Or is everything written in 'Claire shorthand'?"

Susie giggled and the two exchanged another amused glance as if enjoying an inside joke.

"You told us she kept most of her outline in her head," said Victor. "Is that what you mean by 'Claire shorthand'?" Without waiting for a response, he flipped through several pages. "Here's a location list: *Leisure Dreams*. Check. *Darwin Research Station*. You've been there. *Interview with Felipe Santore*." He looked up.

"Who?" asked Susie.

"Did Claire ever mention him to you?" asked Victor.

"The researcher who supposedly 'discovered' Tio Armando on Floreana." Tyler looked down his nose at Susie. "Which you would have known if you'd done your homework, read the articles Claire sent us. Instead of . . ." He eyed Colin and curled his lip.

Victor continued reading from the notebook. "*Floreana*. Get directions from Santore or Ruiz. Pin down exact spot—might not exist. *Isabela tortoise farm*. Get info from Laurel P. *Beagle Galapaguera* (tortoise reserve on San Cristóbal)." He looked up again. "Sounds like Claire planned to visit at least four islands."

"Get directions from Ruiz." Tyler stroked his chin, tugging on the hairs that were trying to form a goatee. "Miguel Ruiz, the groundskeeper? Was he involved?"

Victor shrugged. "You're planning to spend the day with him. You could act like journalists and conduct an interview." *And good luck getting answers.*

Tyler flinched. "I wanted to continue with the documentary to honor Claire's legacy. But with these two bailing out, I can't manage it alone. We toured North Seymour yesterday, and it was all I could do to get someone to capture the bird sounds and take notes for me."

"It was an accident," whined Susie, wiggling her ankle. The flip-flop fell off her foot, and she bent to retrieve it. "How many times do I have to say I'm sorry?"

"What else does Claire have in that notebook?" asked Colin. "The list you read is pretty sketchy so far. Like I said, 'Claire shorthand.' Ninety percent of her planning stayed in her head."

"There are some detailed rants about you two that you wouldn't want me to read aloud," replied Victor. "Quite explicit."

Colin hung his head. "We never meant to hurt her."

Susie blushed and turned away.

Victor flipped another page. "Here's a list of interviews she planned to schedule. From her phone log," he held up Claire's cellphone, "she might have already connected with some of these sources."

"We knew about Laurel Pardo, and we've met her, but Claire didn't say much about the other contacts," said Susie.

"What did Laurel tell you about how Tio Armando got to Santa Cruz?" asked Victor.

"I started to ask Laurel about the unexpected move, but something interrupted us," said Tyler. "She changed the subject, and we never got back to it."

Victor was not surprised. He'd long suspected Laurel knew more about the incident than she'd ever disclosed.

"What Claire and I couldn't figure out," said Tyler, "and this might be what she planned to uncover in the documentary—was who arranged for Tio Armando to be transported from the Beagle Galapaguera on San Cristóbal to Leisure Dreams on Santa Cruz."

"What was her theory?" asked Victor.

"Jim Roberts?" suggested Susie.

Victor turned to Susie. "Is that what Claire thought?"

Giovanna's first instinct was to defend her boss, but she held her tongue. She'd never learned the whole story. When the resort was first planned, Jim had wanted to exhibit Tio Armando on the property, but he'd tried—unsuccessfully—to accomplish the transfer by legal channels.

"Well," Susie backtracked. "I assumed because of Leisure Dreams."

Tyler gave her a dismissive look. "Claire wanted to interview Felipe Santore. She thought he played a role."

"Did she think he had help?" asked Victor.

"Had to," said Tyler. "But if Claire knew who his accomplice was, she didn't tell me."

The suite's phone rang. Giovanna picked it up. "*Hola.*"

"Señora Rogers." Belinda's voice sounded anxious. "We need you down at reception *ahora*. Please hurry!"

Chapter Forty-One

Sunday morning, Leisure Dreams Lobby

When Giovanna entered the lobby, Belinda was shrinking away from a teen-aged version of Claire Costello, with the same bright auburn hair, hands on her hips in a pose she'd probably learned from her mother. A ruddy-faced, middle-aged man, with thinning salt-and-pepper hair carefully combed to cover a bald patch, paced in front of the reception desk. The pair had enough facial features in common for Giovanna to deduce they were father and daughter.

"Señor, señorita, here is the hotel manager." Belinda's rattled voice smoothed as she pointed to Giovanna. "Señora Rogers."

Jaw clenched, tears of fury in her chartreuse eyes, the teenager whirled toward Giovanna. "I want to see the man who killed my mother. Now."

Giovanna scanned the lobby to determine who'd heard the outburst. "Let's go into my office, and you can tell me who you think did this." She led the new arrivals around the corner and down the hall, out of earshot from the reception area.

"We want answers," said the man as they reached the manager's office.

Giovanna ushered them inside and closed the door. "I'm Giovanna Rogers, manager of Leisure Dreams - Galapagos," she began, even though Belinda had already—sort of—introduced her. "And you are?"

The man extended his hand. "Arthur Costello. And this is my daughter, Lindsey. Claire is . . . was . . . my ex-wife."

Giovanna shook his hand. "Please have a seat." She gestured toward the side chairs facing her desk.

They sat, and Giovanna pulled up another chair close to them. "Sorry to meet you under such sad circumstances. Please accept my condolences."

"What are you doing to catch my mother's killer?" Leaning forward, Lindsey glared with the intensity of a wolf.

"The police are investigating, and they've made this case a priority. Please tell me who you suspect was involved."

"That filthy Colin Ashton, of course," spat the teenager. "Couldn't wait to get my mother out of the way so he could bang that useless Texas tart, Susie Southworth."

"How do you know this?" Giovanna studied Claire's fiery-eyed daughter.

"Lindsey puts a lot of stock in social media." Arthur shook his head. "As you can imagine, the internet is buzzing."

"The police are investigating," Giovanna repeated. "The lead detective has interviewed Colin several times. I can let you—"

"Then why haven't they arrested him?" cried Lindsey. "Susie is in danger— not that she doesn't deserve it. Once he gets tired of her and moves on to some- one else." Lindsey pantomimed a knife slashing her throat.

"Lindsey," warned her father.

"What do you mean by that?" Giovanna asked. "Is there something about Colin the police need to know?"

Lindsey glowered at Giovanna. "If they'd investigated his past, they would have known immediately that he's a murderer."

Giovanna had googled Claire Costello shortly after her death, but the bus- tle of grand opening preparations had interrupted her online search, and she'd never finished researching the rest of the film crew. "Who was Colin accused of killing?"

"Lindsey." Her father pressed his lips together.

"His ex-girlfriend. The actress he was engaged to before he started dating my mother." Lindsey gnashed her teeth.

"That was only speculation." Arthur's long face looked tired. "Hayley Howe's death was ruled a suicide. She died of an overdose of antidepressants, which a psychiatrist had prescribed for her."

Lindsey lambasted her father. "Don't you see the similarities? He got away with it once. Why not do it again? And in a third-world country where there won't be as much scrutiny."

"We're hardly the third world here," Giovanna retorted, offended for Victor and her new country of residence. "Would you like to talk to the police detec- tive in charge of the investigation? It sounds like you have information that could help him."

"Could I?" For the first time, Lindsey lost some of her vengeful edge.

"He's here in the hotel," said Giovanna. "In fact, we were meeting with Colin and the rest of the film crew when you arrived."

She sent a quick text to Victor, then rose to lead Claire's daughter and ex-husband out of the office and upstairs to her suite.

"Lindsey Costello! Is it really you?" Luis Vera, the busboy who'd been crossing the lobby en route to the restaurant, stopped and slapped his palm against his chest. "I've watched all your videos on TikTok."

Lindsey beamed at Luis. Giovanna gave Arthur a questioning look.

"She has one of those teen tips YouTube channels," Arthur explained. "Something about teaching kids how to be cool. She has over a million followers."

Luis already had his phone out of his pocket. "Can we take a selfie?"

Lindsey grinned and leaned toward Luis, posing as if she'd done this countless times before. The camera clicked, and she moved away.

Luis examined the results. "Perfect. Thank you so much." He typed, then looked up and grinned. "Got it on my Insta now. Wow, Lindsey Costello! Here on Santa Cruz!" His face darkened. "You're here because of your mother, aren't you?" Smile gone, he shook his head. "Unbelievable! On behalf of this establishment and my country, I'm so sorry."

"I want to make sure that snake, Colin Ashton, pays for what he's done," Lindsey declared. "I won't let him disappear into the tropics and evade justice."

Luis leaned forward and cupped a hand over his mouth to muffle his stage whisper. "I see him and that Susie Southworth nuzzling in the restaurant all the time. Shameless, if you ask me! Flaunting their affair with no respect for the dead."

"Maybe you could slip some poison into his food," the girl suggested.

Arthur put his hand on his daughter's shoulder. "That's enough, Lindsey."

Luis's eyes darted from the Costellos to a frowning Giovanna, and then he gave a little bow. "I have to get to work now, but it was so nice to meet you."

Giovanna wondered if Luis had been posting pictures of Susie and Colin online, feeding the flames of conspiracy theories and gossip. "Luis, remember our policy about social media," she called after him. She made a mental note to speak with the busboy later, after introducing Claire's family to Victor. And she wondered if Victor had been monitoring Luis's Instagram feed—if not, he should be. "Come on up," she told Lindsey and Arthur. "The detective is waiting for us."

* * *

Victor was alone in Giovanna's suite when she arrived with the Costellos. He still held Claire's notebook and phone.

Lindsey's eyes swept the room. "Where are they?"

Victor stood and shook hands with Arthur. "I'm Detective Victor Zuniga." He turned to Lindsey. "I thought we could chat first."

The teenager moaned and plopped herself into the armchair Tyler had vacated. "Colin Ashton is a murderer. When are you going to arrest him?"

Victor gave the girl a sympathetic look. "We're processing all the evidence, talking to everyone who was around the night your mother died. Why do you think Colin killed her?"

"To get rid of her. So he could be with that slut, Susie Southworth."

Victor shook his head. "They were already seeing each other. And Claire knew. Colin didn't have to kill her to be with Susie."

Lindsey huffed. "Mom would have made it hard for him to cut ties with her. And he stood to gain financially with my mother out of the way."

"Why do you say that? He wasn't a beneficiary in her will. Apart from bequests to a few charities, the bulk of her estate goes to you."

Lindsey swallowed. Her father, standing behind her chair, squeezed her shoulder. "Well, Colin's career would have been ruined," she argued. "If my mother dumped him, he would have been out of a job."

Victor shrugged. "Would it surprise you that the team doesn't plan to continue with the documentary Claire envisioned?"

"They're not?" Arthur raised his brow. "Not even Tyler?"

"They've already booked a flight back to the States."

Lindsey sat up. "That creep Colin must know you're closing in. He wants to leave the country as soon as possible. Don't let him."

"They know we have more questions, and we'll get answers before they can leave." Victor picked up Claire's notebook. "These are Claire's possessions. Her colleagues had asked for them back, but now that they're not making the documentary and her family is here, I'll offer them to you." He opened the notebook. "This is a combination journal and work plan. Your mother made a lot of notes, both personal and professional; many are cryptic. Maybe you can shed light on some of the entries."

Lindsey accepted the notebook and thumbed through the pages. A sad smile emerged, like a sliver of sunshine through a storm cloud. "I love her silly little cartoons." She pointed to the childish doodles in the margins.

"Do they mean anything to you?" asked Victor.

"She wasn't very artistic." Lindsey studied the drawings. "But she said mindless sketching helped her think. This could be a tortoise." She flipped a page. "This drawing is definitely a boat."

Victor pointed to one of the pages. "I thought this was a map; it vaguely resembles the Galapagos archipelago. She may have been planning her route for the documentary, or she may have been speculating about Tio Armando's journey. See, there are little tortoise-shaped markers in several locations."

"Maybe she had a theory about Tio Armando's journey, and the plan for her documentary was to follow his route," suggested Giovanna.

"She didn't tell me." Lindsey gazed at her mother's notes. "We didn't talk much before she left to come here."

Lindsey turned to the pages where Claire had written about Colin and Susie. Looking over the teen's shoulder, Giovanna could see the loopy cursive letters and sentences slanted downward. Adverbs, expletives, and hackneyed descriptions of betrayal found in Country Western songs filled several pages. Lindsey's eyes watered as she read. "How could they do that to her? And they didn't have the courage to face her."

"Love is complicated." The words sounded trite as they left Giovanna's lips, and she wished she could take them back.

Lindsey looked up. "Where is that jerk? When can I talk to him?"

Victor eyed her. "Do you promise no vigilante justice?"

"You didn't show them Claire's phone," Giovanna reminded him. "Want to look at that first? Maybe Arthur or Lindsey will recognize some phone numbers."

Arthur looked at Victor. "Did you think Claire might have—?" He swallowed, eyes watering, unable to finish his sentence.

Victor shook his head as he handed Arthur the phone. "We didn't find anything to indicate suicidal tendencies, or that Claire ever felt threatened."

Arthur scrolled through the call log. He shrugged. "Claire and I have been divorced for a long time, and I'm not involved in her business, even though I'm a silent partner. Not much here I recognize."

Lindsey took the phone from her father and studied the log. She brightened. "Here's a call to me." She shook her head. "Sorry. None of these other numbers are familiar." She passed the phone to Giovanna.

Giovanna glanced at the log. "Laurel's number was her last incoming call. But Laurel said Claire was the one who called her." She held the phone out to Victor. "Here's the outgoing call Laurel told us about, at 8:45 p.m. But Laurel didn't say she called Claire back fifteen minutes later."

CHAPTER FORTY-TWO

Sunday morning, Giovanna's suite

When Giovanna handed him the phone, Victor compared its log with his notes. "Belinda told us Claire received a phone call around nine p.m., while the two were drinking champagne. She overheard an angry voice—she thought male—and the call upset Claire."

"Looks like that call came from Laurel's phone," said Giovanna. "We didn't show any calls to the Tio Armando suite on the hotel line."

"Laurel said she was dining with friends in town that night. Maria Vasquez and Miguel Ruiz were there," said Victor. "I asked her about the call, but Laurel insisted she didn't talk to Claire again. She suggested it was—how do you say it—a 'butt dial.'"

"What if Laurel and Maria got up to go to the ladies' room?" speculated Giovanna. "Maybe Laurel left her phone on the table, and Miguel used it to call Claire."

"Would a woman leave her phone on the table?" Victor frowned.

Giovanna shrugged. "Maybe she didn't mean to."

Arthur, who had so far remained quiet, leaned forward. "Why wouldn't the young man use his own phone? Was he afraid Claire wouldn't take his call?"

"I need another conversation with Miguel." Victor looked at Giovanna. "Do you plan on talking to Laurel today?"

Giovanna smiled. "Want me to ask her about the call?"

"It would save time. See if she tells you the same story." With a glance at his watch, he stood. "I'm going to try to catch Miguel before they leave on that island tour."

"Did you tell the film crew they were free to go?" asked Giovanna.

"They'd answered all my questions. They aren't under arrest, so I couldn't hold them any longer." He headed for the door.

Giovanna turned to the Costellos. "Did Belinda get you a room?"

Arthur brandished a keycard, and they all rose.

As they opened the door to the hallway, Jenny Roberts hurried by. She carried her camera, and a pair of binoculars swung from her neck. She stopped abruptly, binoculars banging against her chest. "Lindsey Costello?"

Lindsey grinned.

"Oh my God," gushed Jenny. "You're here! I love your videos!" She raised her camera and aimed at Lindsey. "May I?"

After Jenny had taken the photo, Giovanna asked, "Are you meeting Miguel and the film crew?"

"Tyler said I could go with them." Jenny glanced at her gold Cartier watch. "They're waiting for me. I better go."

"Does your father know?"

"I left him a note."

Giovanna held up her hand. "They might not be leaving yet. Detective Zuniga needs to talk to Miguel first."

* * *

Victor exited the hotel lobby through the revolving door to find the Leisure Dreams SUV parked outside. Arms crossed, Miguel leaned against the driver's side, tapping his foot on the pavement. Susie and Colin had settled in the back seat, and Tyler stood by the concierge counter, showing Hector his camera equipment.

Miguel groaned as Victor strolled over. "What is it now, Detective?"

"I need to clear up a few discrepancies in your statement, señor." Victor turned to the others. "If you'll excuse us." He put an arm on Miguel's shoulder and led him away.

They strolled down the driveway and around the corner of the building.

"I've answered all your questions, señor," said Miguel.

"But you haven't told me everything," replied Victor.

"What do you mean?" Miguel bent to pull a weed from the flower bed.

"You claimed you didn't talk to Claire Costello the night she died."

"I didn't see her." Miguel straightened. "As I said, I brought the champagne from the cellar to the kitchen and left. Belinda delivered it to her room later."

"Did you speak with Claire by phone?" Victor watched Miguel's eyes scan the ground, no doubt searching for more busy work.

"I said I didn't." Miguel glanced up as a squawking flock of white birds flew overhead. They had black trim on their wings and around their faces. He pointed. "Nazca boobies. We don't see many on Santa Cruz."

Victor gave an appreciative nod and returned to his questioning. "When you left Leisure Dreams Tuesday night, you went to dinner with Laurel Pardo and Maria Vasquez. Is that correct?"

"I told you, yes."

"Did Laurel receive a phone call from Claire while you were at the restaurant?"

Miguel shrugged. "She got a phone call. Maybe it was from Claire."

"She didn't talk about it?"

"No." Miguel looked away.

The birds had passed, and Victor wondered what other distractions Miguel would find. "Did Laurel call Claire back later?"

"Maybe. She's on her phone a lot. I didn't pay attention."

"Did Laurel and Maria get up to go to the ladies' room after dinner?"

Miguel chuckled. "You know women. They always go together."

Victor ignored the stereotypical reference. "While they were gone, did you use Laurel's phone?"

"Why would I do that, señor?"

"To call Claire Costello. Or perhaps to verify the identity of Laurel's last caller."

Miguel swallowed.

"You didn't call Claire Costello from Laurel's phone?" Victor stared at Miguel until he looked away. "But you talked to her before she arrived in the Galapagos, didn't you?"

"I—" Miguel bent to pull another weed. A tiny speckled lava lizard skittered past.

"We have her phone log," said Victor. "Your number appeared several times during the week before she arrived. Some of those calls were long."

"All right, yes." Miguel rose from the flower bed. "We spoke. I already told you I knew her."

"Not exactly, but I appreciate you confirming that now."

"Why does it matter that I talked to her?"

Victor focused on Miguel's face. "What did you and Claire talk about during all those calls?"

"Just catching up." Miguel still wouldn't look Victor in the eye.

"Did she share her plans for the documentary? 'The True Tio Armando Story'?"

Miguel bit his lip. "I don't know what that has to do with me."

Victor closed his notebook, although he hadn't written a word during their conversation. He'd grown weary of the dance. "Come down to the station when you're ready to talk about it."

* * *

On the way downstairs, Lindsey filled Jenny in on her theory about Colin's culpability. Despite protests from Arthur and Giovanna, Jenny was glowering suspiciously at the man by the time they reached the car.

Tyler intercepted Lindsey before she could reach the SUV with his colleagues inside. "Hey, girl." They embraced. Pulling back, he produced a quarter ostensibly from behind her ear. "Well, look what I found."

She giggled and swatted at him. "I know that old trick is fake. You had the coin in your hand already."

"Like this?" He waved an iPhone in a hot pink case in front of her face.

She slapped her hands against her pockets, felt around for the missing device, then stared at Tyler. "How did you do that?"

He grinned. "Wouldn't you like to know?" Sobering quickly, he gave back her phone. "I'm sorry about your mom."

"Oh, Tyler, how could he be so cruel?" Lindsey cried. "Did he have to kill her?"

They both glared toward the SUV where Colin and Susie waited inside.

Jenny stood near Tyler and Lindsey instead of climbing into the vehicle. "Sorry I'm late."

Tyler turned his attention to Jenny. "No worries. Miguel had to step away with the detective." He nodded to acknowledge Claire's former husband. "Hello, Arthur."

Arthur shook Tyler's extended hand. The two stood almost the same height and had similar complexions; Arthur, the older man, had less hair and wore slacks that still held a crease despite hours of travel.

While her father chatted with Tyler, Lindsey approached the SUV, leaned into the open backseat window, and lunged at Colin. "Why did you kill my mother?" Her eyes blazed, and her fists pummeled mostly air as he dodged them. "How dare you!"

From inside the vehicle, Colin shielded his face with his forearms to stave off the teenager's blows. "Hey, cut it out, kid. I didn't kill your mother."

Ignoring his denial, Lindsey turned her fury on Susie, who had slipped a protective arm around Colin. "And you! How could you? My mother gave you a job. And this is how you repay her? You had no experience when she hired you."

Arthur and Tyler pulled Lindsey away from the car. "That's enough, sweetheart," said Arthur. "You promised the detective no vigilante justice."

Hector headed over to mediate, but tempers had cooled.

Giovanna glanced at the security cameras overhead. Victor might want to see a replay of the exchange.

Confident the situation was under control, she headed inside.

Belinda stood behind the front desk, chatting on the phone. Giovanna eyed her assistant manager, wondering how truthful she'd been during the investigation. Belinda was the one who'd served the tainted champagne. Most likely, she'd been the last person to see Claire alive. She'd claimed not to know Claire, but her number had appeared on Claire's phone log.

Victor had not asked to question Belinda again, but surely, it was only a matter of time until he circled back to clear up those discrepancies.

"Anyone checking in today?" Giovanna asked as Belinda hung up her call. "Besides the Costellos?"

"Later this afternoon, we're expecting two families from the mainland," she reported. "The rooms are ready."

"Good," Giovanna replied.

"And they're coming by boat."

Giovanna raised her eyebrows. "Long trip; it must be a good-sized boat. Do we have a slip ready?

"*Sí señora.*"

"Great."

Belinda looked down, but when Giovanna didn't move, she raised her head again.

"Did you tell Detective Zuniga you'd never met Claire Costello before she arrived here?"

"I don't remember." Belinda shuffled some papers. "I don't know what difference it makes. I didn't kill her."

"That wasn't the question." Giovanna gave Belinda the probing stare that had proved effective in her past life as a corporate auditor. "The police have gone through Claire's phone records."

"Ladies," a male voice interrupted.

Giovanna turned to see the four Leisure Dreams corporate team members wheeling their roll-aboard-style suitcases, ready to check out.

Chapter Forty-Three

Sunday morning, Leisure Dreams Lobby

Belinda pasted on her hostess smile, took the keycards from the Leisure Dreams executives, and cleared their room numbers in the reservation system. "How was your stay?"

"Eventful." Steve pursed his lips.

"Certainly not boring," said Andrea.

Olivia turned to Giovanna. "We have a beautiful property here. I'm sure the team will make it a success."

"Thank you," Giovanna replied. *Does "we" and "the team" include me?*

"The unfortunate publicity is a setback," said Kevin. "But it puts us on the map. In a few months, most customers won't remember why."

"Bookings *are* pouring in," chimed in Belinda, looking up from the computer.

"Do you have a ride to the airport?" asked Giovanna.

Jim Roberts strode across the lobby, pounded Steve on the back, and shook hands with the others. "I'll get Miguel to drive them."

"Remember, Miguel's taking the film crew to El Chato today." Giovanna glanced outside through the glass doors where the SUV was still parked in the driveway. "Detective Zuniga is talking to him right now. He has a few more questions."

Jim groaned. "More questions? When is he going to solve the case?"

"That's what he's trying to do, Sir."

"I've already called for a car." Andrea peered outside. "In fact, it just arrived."

Hector came into the lobby. "Señor Blackstone? Your ride is here."

After a round of goodbyes, the corporate team was gone. Giovanna felt waves of tension seep from her body.

She turned to Jim. "Did Jenny tell you she's going to El Chato with the film crew? She said she left you a note."

Jim's blank expression revealed he didn't know about his daughter's plans. As he processed the information, his facial muscles underwent several quick transformations. "I'm glad she took the initiative to get out and do something while she's here."

Giovanna remembered how close-knit the Roberts family had seemed when she first met them on her Galapagos cruise last year. The separation must be hard for Jenny, with her mother and sister left at home. "How is Janice doing?"

"Not great. Taking it one day at a time. Jenny and I video-chatted with her and Jessy last night."

"Please tell Janice I'm thinking about her, and I hope she gets better soon."

He shut his eyes tightly. "I wish I could do more for my wife. But she already has the best specialists."

Giovanna nodded sympathetically, not knowing what else to add. "If you have a moment, can we talk?"

Jim followed Giovanna into her office. "You're not resigning, are you?"

She sat down hard. "Resigning? Why? Do you want me to resign?" Her heartbeat quickened as she recalled the words she'd overheard from Steve Blackstone's mouth, *"She doesn't really fit the brand."*

"Of course not. But I wouldn't blame you after everything that's happened." Jim let out a deep sigh. "And there's the boyfriend from home."

"Timothy?" Giovanna waved her hand across her face in a "no way" gesture. "Please! We were over a long time ago."

Jim eyed her. "Not that it's any of my business, but—"

"I don't know why my grandmother encouraged him to come." Giovanna felt her cheeks reddening. "I didn't invite him, and his presence hasn't changed my mind."

"Good to hear." Jim's face relaxed. "I mean . . . So, what did you want to talk about?"

"Victor has found a lot of references in Claire's notes to Tío Armando." Giovanna straightened some papers on the desk. "And his connection with Leisure Dreams."

Jim gritted his teeth. "Not that again."

"I'm afraid so. When Claire made plans to come here, did she share any information about her documentary?"

"Not much. She heard I was opening a new resort and asked if her crew could use it as a base while they shot the film. I offered a discount on the room rate if she'd produce a promotional video for us while she was here."

"Did she agree?"

"She agreed to think about it, which I knew meant yes. Most documentary makers operate on a shoestring; they always need funders."

Giovanna glanced out the window where several guests from the mainland loitered by the pool, soaking up the sunshine. At least everyone hadn't checked out after all the mayhem. "Do you think Claire was killed over something she planned to expose in her film?"

Jim straightened his collar, although it didn't need straightening. "She wanted an on-camera interview with me, but I assumed it was about the resort. And how we're partnering with the Darwin Research Station to give our guests an enriching and educational experience."

Giovanna stifled an amused smile at how easily the CEO could lapse into brochure talk. "What else?"

"She did mention Tio Armando, and that she planned to meet with Laurel Pardo. I assumed she wanted an update on the breeding program."

"What about Tio Armando's origins? Did she ask about that? And how he ended up on Leisure Dreams property when everyone thought he was still at the Beagle Galapaguera on San Cristóbal?"

Jim swallowed. "I don't—"

"Tyler said Claire was researching that story for the documentary. The news coverage was selective, and the hoopla quickly died down, so maybe she thought she could put a new twist on it."

Jim fanned himself. "It's hot in here. Is the air conditioning working?"

"Seems fine to me." She studied her boss with her "auditor" look. "Did she think you had something to do with moving the tortoise?"

He let out a puff of air. "I was negotiating with the park service and management at the reserve where Tio Armando had been staying. We hadn't come to an agreement yet. You know that."

"I remember when we were on the ship together last year, and we made the excursion to the Beagle Galapaguera. All the cruise passengers were excited about seeing Tio Armando, and they were so disappointed—"

"I swear, I had no idea the tortoise wouldn't be there."

She nodded. "I believe you. The look on your face after you talked to the management . . . I could tell you were stunned."

"They said they'd reached a deal with someone else." He shook his head. "I thought Felipe Santore was partnering with me. I knew he was building his own reserve, but we were going to house the tortoise at Leisure Dreams part-time. He double-crossed me."

"He was working with Jerome Haddad," Giovanna confirmed. "Who, no surprise, double-crossed him."

Jim's face contorted. "That bastard. What he did to Janice!" His face hardened. "What he did to you!"

Giovanna winced, trying to stop the replay of the scene where Jerome Haddad drove up to Leisure Dreams in search of the famous tortoise. The tires from Felipe's black Honda Civic spit gravel across the unfinished driveway. Anger glinted in Jerome's ice-blue eyes as he stabbed Janice Roberts and then turned the knife on her. She could still feel its cold blade against her throat, the stinging nicks every time she tried to squirm away from her captor.

"And then the wire transfer from Haddad's bank didn't even go through," Jim's voice interrupted her traumatic memories. "Those people at the Beagle Galapaguera were sorry they didn't deal with me instead of getting ripped off by Haddad."

"I heard most of that money was never recovered," said Giovanna. "Where do you think it went?"

"You know what a con man Haddad was."

"What if Claire had a theory," said Giovanna, "about how Tio Armando ended up here last year?"

Jim put his hand on his chest as if reciting the Pledge of Allegiance. "I swear, I had nothing to do with it. Yes, I wanted the animal at Leisure Dreams, but only after we were set up to accommodate him and had all the necessary permits."

Giovanna eyed her boss. "You know what people will say. You're the CEO. You should have known what was going on at your resort."

"But I wasn't even here. And as soon as I found out, I cooperated with the authorities. Haddad must have—"

"Jerome Haddad didn't do it. He found out he'd been double-crossed right before his final rampage. That was why he stabbed Felipe Santore and headed here to find the tortoise. Where he didn't expect to deal with Janice and me— two of his former scam victims."

Jim touched his cheek. "You think Claire was planning to make me look guilty? Dramatize the narrative for a larger audience?"

"Like I said, Victor showed us her notes. They were cryptic, but I think she was interested in exposing the missing link: how Tio Armando ended up at Leisure Dreams."

Jim rubbed his eyes. "Did she have a theory?"

Giovanna nodded. "And a suspect. Felipe Santore had an accomplice."

There was a knock on the door. Without waiting to be invited to enter, Belinda poked her head inside. "Señora Rogers, your friend wants to speak to you."

Chapter Forty-Four

Sunday morning, Leisure Dreams Lobby

Timothy and Elaine stood in the lobby, surrounded by suitcases. Elaine sported a new broad-brimmed straw hat like she was ready for a day in the sun.

Giovanna eyed their baggage. "You're leaving already?" She knew Michelle and Roberto planned to stay several more days, and she'd assumed Elaine and Timothy would too.

Elaine nodded. "It's hotter than Texas here, and the food tastes funny." She shook her head. "No offense to your chef. I don't see how Michelle and Roberto travel all the time. A few days away, and I'm homesick for my own bed."

"That's a shame," said Giovanna. "You came all this way, and you've never been to the Galapagos. You should take a cruise or at least some day trips to other islands. Maybe try snorkeling." Although she regretted that the pair had bought expensive airline tickets and then not spent more time exploring the destination, she was secretly glad they were leaving.

Timothy's face resembled a puppy looking through cage bars, like in one of those ASPCA commercials with the sad music playing behind the voiceover. "My reason for coming didn't work out." A hopeful lilt punctuated his sentence as if he wanted her to contradict him.

Giovanna's eyes met his. "I'm sorry."

"The trip wasn't wasted." Elaine grinned. "I saw giant tortoises and iguanas and blue-footed boobies. I got my picture with Tio Armando." She pulled out her phone to show Giovanna.

"Nice." Giovanna nodded politely as she examined Elaine's smiling face next to the ancient tortoise, with Timothy, Laurel, and some unidentified tourists photobombing the background.

Elaine put her hand on Giovanna's shoulder. "We got to stay in your lovely hotel. And watch you in action as a big-shot manager." Again, her use of the word "big shot" dripped with pride rather than derision.

"I'm glad you enjoyed your stay, Elaine," replied Giovanna. "It was nice to see you again, and I'm sorry we didn't have more time to catch up." She turned to Timothy. "You too, Tim."

He brightened. "Really?"

Giovanna elbowed him. "Let's go talk." She addressed Elaine, "Can I have a moment with your son before you leave?"

Elaine winked. "Take all the time you need." She planted herself in one of the lobby's plush easy chairs and turned her attention to her phone.

Giovanna led Timothy out the back door, clear of the waiting SUV containing the film crew, away from the front part of the grounds where Victor and Miguel were still in conference.

Timothy and Giovanna stood beside the pool, admiring the glistening blue water she had yet to dive into. The guests who'd been sunning themselves earlier had left. Water cascaded over the rock feature, and a mockingbird alighted briefly to take a drink. *Leisure Dreams,* she mused. *More like nightmares. I haven't had much leisure since I've been here.*

"I never stopped caring about you." Giovanna touched Timothy's hand.

He reached to embrace her, but she held out her other hand to stop him.

"You're like a brother to me."

His face fell as he pulled back.

She met his watering eyes. "I was an only child, and you befriended me, defended me from bullies, treated me like I mattered."

His lips smiled, but his eyes reflected sorrow. "And I'd do it again. You've always mattered a lot to me."

"But my feelings for you aren't romantic." She touched his shoulder. "Maybe they never were. Maybe I just didn't know what romantic love felt like."

He frowned. "What do you mean? We got engaged."

"Marriage seemed like a logical progression to our relationship. We were compatible; we were comfortable with each other. But that's not the same thing as being in love."

"Of course, we were in love! Don't you remember the first time I told you? We were sitting under that tree on campus—"

"I remember." She smiled. "And I said it back."

"And the first time we made love?" He nudged her. "In your dorm room. The weekend your roommate was gone?"

She continued to smile. "I was more scared than anything else."

"What about that weekend we spent on Pawley's Island? When we rented the beach house."

Despite her efforts to suppress the pleasant memory, Giovanna could still feel the salty breeze against her skin as she and Timothy walked barefoot through the sand, stopping to hug and kiss every few yards, cool waves lapping at their ankles. "It was nice," she agreed.

"A ten out of ten."

"Yes."

"I'm still in love with you."

She narrowed her gaze. "Are you? Or are you clinging to the image of what we hoped we could be?"

"So, now you've discovered romantic love." Clenching his jaw, he gestured toward the hotel. "An exotic boy-toy."

"That's not fair."

"You're from different worlds, different backgrounds. How do you know it's not just the sultry climate and the tropical ambiance?"

"It's much more than that. Victor listens to me. He doesn't try to fix me."

Timothy sighed. "You've always been stubborn. No one can give you advice to keep you from getting hurt."

"That's the way I learn," she agreed. "I make my own mistakes."

"He'll break your heart." Timothy wiped his brow.

"Maybe. But you broke my heart worse than anyone ever has."

A splash showered them with droplets of cool water. Giovanna turned to spy a fat sea lion paddling in the pool. "Get out, Harvey!" she yelled. Stifling a laugh, she turned to Timothy. "That animal thinks our pool is his playground." She rushed toward the pinniped. "Shoo, Harvey, you filthy thing. Back to the beach where you belong."

With a wounded bark, the sea lion hoisted itself onto the pool's edge and galumphed its way back into the brush.

Timothy smiled. "I guess you can't get excitement like this back in Georgia."

She touched his hand again. "Your mother must be wondering what happened to us."

"She won't mind."

"Do you have a ride to the airport?"

He nodded. "I called a cab. It's probably here by now."

They strolled back inside. Most of the luggage was gone, and Elaine, purse strapped over her shoulder, was showing the cab driver her photos. "Don't those iguanas look like mini dinosaurs?" She looked up. "Here they are."

Giovanna gave Timothy a peck on the cheek. "Safe journey."

He drew her into an embrace and started to kiss her, but instead turned his head and held her against him for a moment. "Be happy."

"Thanks," she whispered, easing away. She felt no passion, no regret, nothing but friendship for her childhood sweetheart.

Just as they separated, Victor walked into the lobby.

Giovanna's face lit up when she saw him. "*Momentito, mi amor*," she mouthed. She hugged Elaine, breathing in her freshly applied perfume. "Thanks for coming, and please stay in touch. It's been too long."

"Agreed." Elaine grinned.

"Safe travels." Giovanna stepped away from her ex-almost-mother-in-law.

As he and Elaine climbed into the cab, Timothy stared at Victor.

Victor turned to Giovanna as she watched them leave. "Your friend is going home?"

Giovanna nodded. "It's for the best."

"You're not sad?" Victor studied her.

"More like relieved." She squeezed his arm. Timothy was her past; Victor was her future. "Where's Miguel?"

"I couldn't detain him any longer, so he's off on the island tour. But while we were talking, the group shrank."

Giovanna's eyes scanned the lobby and rested on Jenny huddled in a corner, talking animatedly into Lindsey's cellphone camera. "Looks like Jenny found a new friend."

Victor nodded. "Lindsey asked to interview Jenny for her YouTube channel. Jim will love the publicity his daughter's giving the resort."

"It's just the film crew on the tour then?"

"Not even the whole crew. Susie got upset when Lindsey attacked her, so she stormed off to her room. Colin had no choice but to follow."

Giovanna let out a whistle. "So much drama while I was away! Tyler still wanted to go?"

"He's the only one still interested in making the documentary."

She took Victor's arm, and they walked toward her office. "How did it go with Miguel? Did you learn anything new?"

"He was as evasive as ever. Now he's claiming the phone calls with Claire were of a romantic nature, and they were arranging a date during her stay."

"Whoa . . . where did that come from?"

Victor's lips curled into a half-chuckle. "He never mentioned any romantic involvement before. It sounded more like the first excuse that came to mind. He's hiding something."

"Like his role in moving Tio Armando?" She opened her office door and ushered Victor inside.

Victor sat down in the guest chair. "We don't have any proof that Miguel was involved."

"How do we get proof?"

"Apart from a confession?" Victor shrugged. "Finding witnesses, asking the right questions—probably things Claire planned to do. A charming journalist offering international notoriety might have been able to ferret out facts the park service and the island police couldn't."

"Jim and I talked this morning. I learned a little, but I don't think he knows the whole story."

"We never got much out of him."

Giovanna propped her chin on her hand. "Suppose Miguel was Felipe Santore's accomplice, and he had a role in kidnapping Tio Armando from the Beagle Galapaguera. Hiding him at Leisure Dreams, double-crossing both Jim Roberts and Jerome Haddad. What would be the consequences? Why would it matter so much to hide the truth?"

Victor leaned back in his chair. "We could charge him with wildlife trafficking, but it might not stick, since he didn't take the tortoise out of the country. His reputation would be, how do you say, 'toast'?" He thought for a moment. "And then, it depends on whether he diverted any of the funds from the wire transfer to Beagle Galapaguera. Most of that money was never recovered, even after we seized Haddad's bank account. If Miguel had something to do with it, we could charge him with theft and conspiracy."

"But would Miguel kill someone to keep the secret from coming out?"

Before he could answer, Victor's phone buzzed.

CHAPTER FORTY-FIVE

Sunday afternoon, Giovanna's office

Victor finished his call and looked up at Giovanna, who had been busying herself with emails.

"What's wrong?" she asked. "Is it Maria?"

"No. We got the search warrant." He rose. "I'm sorry, but I have to go."

"Search warrant? For what?"

"Miguel's house." He started for the door.

"Wait. What are you looking for?" She stood.

Victor opened the door. "We'll talk later."

"You're not going to tell me? Miguel is my employee."

"Later." With an enigmatic smile, the detective was gone.

After Victor left, Giovanna remembered her promise to quiz Laurel about the phone call with Claire on the night of the murder. She punched in her friend's number, and Laurel answered on the first ring. "Can you talk?"

"Taking a break so now's a good time. What's up?"

"Did you have fun at the grand opening?" Giovanna twirled a strand of hair around her finger.

"A blast," Laurel replied. "Although I'm sorry about what happened to Maria. It certainly put a damper on the evening. I thought she could take care of herself, but I guess she had too much to drink."

"Have you seen Maria since Friday night?"

"Not yet, but I heard she's awake."

"Victor talked to her, but she didn't remember much about her fall. She was more interested in learning what he'd uncovered concerning Claire's death."

"Yeah, Maria's still on the job. That's a good sign," Laurel said. "You didn't call just to chat."

"No," Giovanna admitted. "I was hoping you could clear something up."

Laurel laughed. "The good detective has you doing his legwork?"

Giovanna felt her face grow warm. "You said Claire called you the night she died."

"Yes, while I was at the restaurant. Surely, Victor has that in his notes. He was doing a lot of writing during our interview. Plus, he recorded it. Very thorough guy, that detective."

Giovanna ignored the mockery in her friend's voice. "Was that phone call from Claire your only conversation with her Tuesday night?"

"I already said it was."

"You didn't call her back later?"

"Giovanna, how many times do I have to tell my story? Does Victor hope I'll slip up and confess something sinister?"

"Did you leave the table during the evening?" Another email popped into her inbox, but Giovanna looked away.

"Maria and I went to the ladies' room after we finished eating. What's the big deal?"

"Did you take your phone with you or leave it on the table?"

Laurel was quiet for a second. "I'm not sure. Why is that important?"

"Because someone called Claire's phone from yours at nine o'clock that evening."

Laurel let out an exasperated sigh. "Miguel."

"Isn't your phone password protected?"

"Yes, but he must have guessed the password."

"What is it, 'Tio Armando'?"

"Too easy? Maybe I should change it."

"Good idea," agreed Giovanna. "Do you think Miguel used your phone to call Claire?"

"He was the only one at the table. Our other friends had already left."

"Why would Miguel call Claire from your phone?" asked Giovanna. "Was he afraid she wouldn't pick up if she knew it was him?"

"Not that I know of. As far as I know, there was no bad blood between them. Maybe it was just easier to use my phone. Although . . ."

Giovanna studied her thumbnail, polish already chipping from Friday's manicure, while she waited for Laurel to finish her sentence. But when her friend didn't elaborate, she asked, "Did you and Miguel talk about Claire that night? Did he know she was planning to interview you?"

"I mentioned it, but he didn't show much interest." Laurel paused for a moment. "Which surprised me."

"Why?"

"I expected Miguel to try to insert himself into the story. Steal the spotlight, prove to Claire that he's the superior tortoise researcher. He'd tell her how he brings Tio Armando his favorite apples every week. And maybe—"

"Apples?"

"Manzanillo apples, from the tree at Leisure Dreams."

Giovanna felt a chill, even though the room was warm. "I thought they were poisonous. *Peligroso.*"

"To humans, not to giant tortoises. In fact, they're a delicacy." Laurel let out a huff. "I bet that's why Miguel called Claire as soon as I turned my back—so he could get in on the glory."

"I thought even the bark and leaves of that tree were toxic," said Giovanna. "How does Miguel harvest the apples without hurting himself?"

"He must wear gloves and a mask," Laurel suggested. "I don't know. I don't watch him gather the apples. You've never seen him do it?"

"I didn't even know the manzanillo was toxic until Claire died. Her camera-man pointed it out to me. As soon as I learned of the danger, I had a fence built around the tree, and a warning sign posted." She paused. "They think Claire was poisoned."

Laurel let out a breath. "Do they think the poison was from the manzanillo?"

"I don't know. They're running tests."

"Or the good detective won't let you tell me . . . or he won't even tell *you*."

Giovanna shifted gears. "Remember when Tio Armando was taken from the Beagle Galapaguera last year? And no one knew where he'd gone until he turned up on the Leisure Dreams property?"

Laurel was silent.

"According to Claire's notes, her film was going to focus on that event," Giovanna continued. "What was your role in it?"

"I didn't—"

"You left our cruise ship the day before our stop in San Cristóbal. We were scheduled to visit the Beagle Galapaguera, where the passengers were looking forward to seeing Tio Armando." Giovanna gave the phone her auditor stare, even though she knew Laurel couldn't see it.

"I had nothing to do with moving him," Laurel declared. "But I knew he'd been moved. That was part of the reason I sneaked off the ship when I did."

"How did you find out?"

"I knew Felipe wanted Tio Armando for the reserve he was building with his American partner—your old buddy, Jerome Haddad."

Giovanna shuddered.

"But Maria and Miguel overheard some Middle Eastern guys making plans to take the tortoise back to Dubai with them," Laurel continued. "They were working with Jerome behind Felipe's back. We couldn't let that happen."

"You told me releasing the story about Tio Armando's relatives—proving he wasn't the last surviving member of his subspecies—would make him less valuable. Was that to dissuade the buyers from taking him? Make them renege on their deal with Jerome?"

"That was all the ammunition we had. Until then, no one had wanted to hear about my findings. Even people who called themselves scientists and wild-life protectors. It was more important to pretend we'd found another Lonesome George."

Giovanna picked at the chipped polish on her thumbnail. "Who moved him? Not the buyers from Dubai. They wouldn't have taken him to Leisure Dreams."

"I don't know," Laurel whispered.

Giovanna wasn't convinced. "You must have some idea."

"I always said Tio Armando should go to the Darwin Research Station," Laurel said. "They have the best breeding program."

"But he didn't go there right away. Who took him to Leisure Dreams?"

Laurel sucked in her breath, then murmured, "Most likely, Felipe and Miguel."

At the time of the incident, Miguel had already been hired as groundskeeper for the resort, Giovanna recalled. And he may have been privy to Jim's desire to house Tio Armando there. "You think Miguel was working with Felipe?"

"In this case, yes."

"But what about Jim? Would he have signed off on parking the tortoise on his property and then relinquishing him to Felipe's reserve after the buyers left empty-handed?"

"Miguel thought Jim was busy entertaining his family on a cruise around the islands. He didn't know the CEO would show up with a group of fellow passengers during a port stop."

Giovanna smiled to herself. "I remember the look on Jim's face when Tio Armando waddled out of the brush that day. If he knew about the move, he certainly concealed it."

"That stunt sure hurt his chances to gain approval for Tio Armando to be housed at Leisure Dreams," said Laurel. "Not that he ever had a prayer of making it happen."

"We flew home a few days later," said Giovanna. "And the news outside was a mere footnote. I'm surprised Maria didn't make it a bigger story. She's like a dog with a bone about Claire's death."

"I suppose I had something to do with it," said Laurel. "I pushed her to cover my discovery about Tio Armando's origins and the exciting news that I'd found his relatives on Isabela Island. The Darwin Research Station immediately got interested in sponsoring a breeding program and hired me to run it."

"But still—"

"Government and tourism officials kept her quiet. Bad publicity for the new hotel and all. No one wanted to piss off the American CEO and potentially lose tourist revenue."

Giovanna pushed a hair from her face. "I wonder why Claire wanted to dig up that story? And who intended to stop her?"

Voices hummed in the background. "*Momentito*," Laurel called to someone before muting herself.

Giovanna listened to silence for a moment.

"Sorry." Unmuted, Laurel had raised her voice an octave. "I have to go. Someone's trying to poison Tio Armando."

CHAPTER FORTY-SIX

Sunday afternoon, home of Miguel Ruiz, Puerto Ayora

Police cars lined Miguel's street; the whole department had shown up. Radios squawked, and flashing lights rotated like warning beacons. Neighbors peered from behind curtains, and a few stepped onto their porches.

Victor rushed up the crumbling walkway to join the forensic team inside.

Uniformed and plainclothes officers filled the small house. Cabinet doors stood open; contents of drawers had been strewn about.

At the dining room table, two officers pored over Miguel's laptop. One looked up as Victor walked in. "As you suspected, Zuniga, the man has extensively researched toxic plants. And how to extract poisons."

"Dosages, effects, antidotes," said the other. "Never deleted his browsing history."

"Look what he saved as a Favorite," said the first cop. "An article about the manzanillo tree. And the active ingredient, physog . . . physo . . ."

"Physostigmine," finished his partner.

The first officer read, "Used as an antidote for some pesticides and nerve gases. Very toxic in its own right."

His colleague nodded. "Toxic indeed."

The first cop continued reading, "An overdose would cause nausea, vomiting, diarrhea, dizziness, sweating, constricted pupils, convulsions. Death occurs rapidly from respiratory or heart failure."

"Interesting," said Victor. "But none of that proves Miguel Ruiz is a killer. He's a scientist of sorts. In his current job as groundskeeper, he works with plants. And chemicals." He peered over his colleague's shoulder. "There's a manzanillo tree on the Leisure Dreams property, which the manager recently learned about. She asked the staff to build a fence around it and put up a plaque warning guests of the plant's dangers."

"Ruiz has done extensive research on poisons," said the first officer. "He even writes a blog about toxic plants. This guy's obsessed. He fits the profile."

"Creepy," agreed Victor. "But research is not a crime."

"Look at all these photographs," said the second officer. "Close-ups of manzanillo trees. The fruit, the bark. He even has recipes."

"The toxin found in Claire Costello's body was consistent with the poison from the manzanillo tree." Victor continued to examine the computer screen. "Physostigmine, you say? Miguel might have been curious and decided to do some research. At any rate, that's what he'll tell me when I question him about this." Victor tried to imagine what tales Miguel might spin.

"These photographs were taken before Claire Costello died," said the second officer. "What will señor Ruiz have to say about that?"

"He'll plead a connection to his work or his research," Victor guessed. "I can hardly wait for that conversation." He looked back at the screens. "Miguel is not a stupid man. If he'd had murder on his mind, wouldn't he have covered his tracks better?"

Another officer, outfitted with a face mask and gloves, emerged from the kitchen. "Zuniga, I heard you were here. You've got to see this."

Victor followed him into the tiny kitchen. The yellow paint on the walls had grown dingy, and the white linoleum floor had not been scrubbed in so long that it appeared gray. The late twentieth-century appliances had seen little use. Ivory cabinet doors hung open, the contents in disarray.

Another officer stood at the cast iron sink. He pointed at a pile of tiny green apples.

"Manzanillo apples," Victor confirmed. "We know Miguel doesn't eat them."

An officer opened the refrigerator door and pointed to a pitcher of dark yellow liquid.

"Apple juice?" Victor guessed.

"We're getting it tested," replied the officer. "And he has a juicer. Cleaned and put away, but it has definitely been used."

"No crime in owning a juicer." Victor played devil's advocate.

The officer opened a drawer. "Syringes. Plastic gloves."

Victor whistled.

"Wouldn't you agree the evidence points to Miguel Ruiz?" asked the officer.

Heavy footsteps marched from the front door into the kitchen. Victor looked up to see his boss, Captain Juan Estevez—stocky, graying hair thin on top. Victor stepped aside so Estevez could look at the findings.

"We have the lab results," said Estevez. "They found traces of physostigmine in the tissue samples from both Claire Costello and Pedro Lopez."

"The toxin found in the manzanillo apple," confirmed one of the officers. "Just as we thought." He showed Estevez the apples in the sink and the juice in the refrigerator.

"We didn't find any toxins in the fruit from the basket, but the champagne in the bottle tested positive for physostigmine," continued Estevez.

Victor said, "I was afraid there wasn't enough left to test after Belinda Chavez spilled it."

"They only need a few milliliters." Estevez smiled.

Another car pulled up outside, followed by footsteps hurrying up the walkway. "What the hell is going on?" shouted Miguel Ruiz. Mouth hanging open, he spun around the room.

Tyler Thompson stood behind him, camera around his neck. His eyes grew wide as he surveyed the scene.

Estevez, Victor, and two other officers met the pair at the door.

"Miguel Ruiz," said Estevez. "You're under arrest for murder."

CHAPTER FORTY-SEVEN

Sunday afternoon, home of Miguel Ruiz, Puerto Ayora

Victor took Tyler outside while his colleagues handcuffed Miguel and informed him of his rights.

"They think Miguel killed Claire?" Tyler's eyes darted around the yard. "I don't understand." He touched the camera dangling from his neck to steady it. "Why would Miguel kill Claire?"

"Why did he bring you here?" Victor searched the cameraman's face.

Tyler swallowed. "I asked him to show me where he lived. I was trying to get a feel for life on the island. What better way than to visit the residence of a local? Do you think he intended to kill me too?" He put his hand on his chest.

Victor frowned; the thought hadn't crossed his mind. "What about El Chato? Weren't you going there to film for your documentary?"

"It got too late," Tyler replied. "We decided we didn't have enough time."

"Did you talk about Miguel's research?"

"You mean about the tortoises? About his connection to Tio Armando?"

Victor held out his hands, palms up. "You tell me."

"It's a sensitive subject. What if it's the reason Claire got killed?"

Victor raised his eyebrows. He found it interesting to watch Tyler go from surprise that Miguel would kill Claire to a theory about motive. "What did you find out? Anything?"

Tyler fiddled with the strap around his neck. "I tell stories with pictures. Claire was the journalist."

"What pictures did you take today?"

"Just some landscape. Video of the town and the residential area." He fidgeted with his camera. "I'd planned to shoot the exterior of Miguel's house, but then we saw the police cars. Miguel figured someone had broken in, and a neighbor had reported it."

"Did Miguel talk to you about his research on the manzanillo tree?"

"Uh . . . no." With a twitch of his face, Tyler looked away.

Victor had spoken to Tyler often enough to read his body language, and the face twitch told him the cameraman might be lying. "Really? You both seem to know a lot about that tree and its properties."

"I'm a nature geek."

"What did Miguel say about Claire Costello?"

"Not much I can remember."

Victor furrowed his brow.

"We mainly talked about what could be salvaged from the documentary." Tyler kept twiddling with his camera strap.

"And what did you conclude?"

"It depends on Colin and Susie, and how committed they are to moving forward. And the other partners, if they think it's even worthwhile to produce a documentary without Claire. She was our star."

Victor gave him a long look, but Tyler averted his eyes. "Looks like you'll need a ride back to the resort."

"Now that you mention it. Unless Miguel left the keys in the SUV."

"Giovanna can send someone to pick it up," said Victor. "I'm headed for the hotel now, so I'll drive you. We can talk more along the way."

* * *

Giovanna was having a late lunch in the Isabela restaurant with Michelle and Roberto when a call from Victor flashed on her phone's screen. Her face blanched as she listened.

"What is it?" Michelle put a hand on her granddaughter's shoulder when she finished talking to the detective. "You look upset."

"Miguel Ruiz has been arrested." Giovanna touched her cheek. "For murder."

"Miguel?" Roberto frowned. "I can't believe it. He seems like such a nice guy. Why would he kill Claire Costello?"

"Something about his past," replied Giovanna. "Claire was planning to expose it."

"And he killed her?" Roberto shook his head. "His history was bad enough to commit murder?"

Giovanna grimaced. "I guess."

"I only worked with him that one day, but Miguel doesn't strike me as someone who would care much about covering up an unsavory past," Roberto insisted. "On the contrary, I think he'd enjoy a little notoriety."

"Depends on the consequences," said Giovanna.

Michelle touched her granddaughter's arm. "I'm so sorry. What can we do?"

"Right now, I need to find someone to pick up our SUV from Miguel's house in town." She pushed her chair away from the table.

Michelle shook her head. "So much drama for a peaceful island resort. I must admit, I've been a little nervous staying here with a killer on the loose."

Giovanna winced. She'd tried not to think about anyone else being in danger.

"How did Miguel do it?" asked Roberto. "And what evidence do the police have?"

"Poisoning," replied Giovanna, settling back in her chair. "The police believe he injected it into the bottle of champagne we delivered to Claire's room as a welcome gift."

Michelle gasped. "That's terrible. What if he'd done it at the grand opening? You could have been—"

"What kind of poison?" Roberto asked before his wife could finish her sentence.

"Physostigmine," replied Giovanna, her tongue tripping over the scientific name. "The active ingredient found in the fruit of the manzanillo tree. We have one on the property, so Miguel had access to the source of the poison. And he was the one who brought the champagne from the cellar to the kitchen. Motive, means, and opportunity."

"I saw the tree," said Roberto. "Anyone could have harvested those apples and produced the toxin."

"But how many people know how to do it?" argued Michelle.

"Victor said they found apples at Miguel's house. And a pitcher of home-made juice in the refrigerator," Giovanna explained. "He certainly wasn't planning to drink it."

Michelle's eyes widened.

Roberto shook his head. "Miguel takes those apples to the giant tortoises at the Darwin Research Station. Apparently, they're not toxic to tortoises."

"I know; Laurel told me," said Giovanna. "But Miguel knows every part of that tree is toxic to humans. Why was he making juice? The tortoises don't drink juice."

"Physostigmine is also used as an antidote to pesticides," said Roberto.

Giovanna straightened in her chair and stared at Roberto as he spoke.

"Miguel said some of the pesticides Corporate asked him to sprinkle around one of the ponds to control the brush were killing birds and fish. He was working on a spray to combat the effects. Extracting physostigmine from the manzanillo tree."

"Miguel never told me about any of that." Giovanna bit her lip. "I wonder if Victor knows."

"I'd hate to see someone arrested for a crime he may not have committed," said Michelle. "Who else had opportunity?"

Giovanna tugged on a strand of hair. "Well, the kitchen staff. They opened the bottle before Belinda took the champagne to Claire."

"They opened it?" Michelle made a sour face. "Why did they do that?"

"Belinda said Claire asked if someone could open it for her. I think Claire meant once they got it to the room."

"Then lots of people had access to the champagne," said Roberto. "And it's easier to slip something into an open bottle than to poke a hole in the cork with a syringe."

"Pedro Lopez opened the bottle and prepared the fruit basket. Now he's dead."

"So sad." Michelle shook her head. "Did they ever find out what happened?"

"Victor said it was physostigmine poisoning too," replied Giovanna. "It's possible Pedro poisoned Claire and then did it to himself, but my gut says no. Chef Gomez thinks his sous chef saw something that night, which might be why he was killed."

Michelle flinched. "So, maybe the same person killed both Claire and Pedro?"

"Miguel was seen with Pedro shortly before he died," said Giovanna. "Victor didn't say, but Miguel will probably be charged with that murder too."

"Was anyone else around when Pedro opened the champagne?" asked Roberto. "Besides the people working in the kitchen and the restaurant?"

"Belinda's the one who took it to Claire's room," replied Giovanna. "I don't think she has a motive, but she had access to the champagne."

"Wouldn't Belinda have noticed if someone tampered with it?" asked Michelle.

Giovanna sighed. "Who even considers the possibility?"

"No reason to," agreed Michelle.

"She had the most opportunity to tamper with it," said Roberto. "Out of sight from the kitchen."

"Belinda pulled some questionable moves," Giovanna said. "First, she accepted Claire's invitation to come in and share a glass of champagne . . . while on duty."

"But nothing happened to Belinda," said Roberto. "If the whole bottle of champagne had been poisoned—"

"She doesn't like champagne and only took a sip to be polite," said Giovanna. "And she felt sick afterward. My guess is, she didn't ingest enough of the poison to kill her. Whereas, Claire downed two glasses."

"Lucky Belinda doesn't like champagne," said Roberto.

"She also found the body," said Giovanna.

Roberto cringed. "The person who finds the body is usually a suspect."

"It gets worse," said Giovanna. "While Victor and I were checking out the scene, Belinda came in and started to clean up the champagne service."

Michelle's mouth opened in a perfect O. "Removing evidence?"

Giovanna nodded. "And then Victor startled her, which made her drop the tray, breaking the glasses and spilling the leftover champagne."

Roberto gave a half chuckle. "If it weren't so sad, it would be comical." He sobered. "Or diabolical."

"It certainly looks bad, but I can't imagine Belinda as a murderer," said Giovanna. "Like I said, she had no motive."

"Are there any others who had access to the champagne?" asked Michelle.

"Claire's colleagues were in the restaurant that evening, but they didn't go into the kitchen." Giovanna thought for a moment. "Wait; that's not entirely true. Tyler saw Colin all cozy with Susie and decided not to stay, so he wandered into the kitchen to place an order to go. And Jim went into the kitchen to talk with Chef Gomez."

"I'd hate to find out Jim's the killer," said Roberto. "Think of the politics."

Giovanna shivered. "Laurel thinks Claire was going to expose something negative about Jim in her documentary. If it's true, and bad enough, he could have a motive."

Michelle shook her head. "Jim would spin the story so the negative publicity would slide off him like Teflon. Murder is not his style."

"And if he wanted Claire dead, why do it at his hotel, right before the grand opening?" agreed Giovanna. "Talk about negative publicity. Jim's main concern right now is making this whole catastrophe go away. But instead, it keeps getting worse."

Michelle and Roberto shook their heads.

Victor entered the dining room and strolled to their table.

"Where's Tyler?" asked Giovanna.

"He asked me to drop him off downtown. He'll take a cab back."

"But you drove out here anyway."

He nodded. "I have a search warrant for that shed where Miguel keeps his garden equipment. Can you come with me and unlock it for the investigators?"

CHAPTER FORTY-EIGHT

Sunday afternoon, Leisure Dreams Hotel

Jim caught up with Giovanna on the way back to her office. "I see there are more police cars out front. What do they want now?"

"Let's talk in here, where it's more private." Surveying the area to gauge whether anyone was listening, she opened her office door and led Jim inside. "The rumor mill will be churning soon enough."

She turned to face her boss. "Miguel Ruiz has been arrested for Claire's murder. They found evidence at his home, and now they're searching the shed where he keeps his garden equipment."

"Miguel?" Jim's eyes bulged. "Surely, you're not serious. Have you spoken with Victor? What are they looking for?"

She seated herself behind the desk, and Jim took the guest chair. He leaned forward. "What evidence did the police find at Miguel's house?"

"Manzanillo juice. It contains physostigmine, the toxin the lab found in tissue samples from both Claire and Pedro."

"Physostigmine?" repeated Jim. "That's a mouthful. I've never heard of it."

"I hadn't either."

"I knew we should have cut down that tree." He wiped his brow. "It's been nothing but trouble."

"There are others on the island. It's not rare." She went on to explain how the search of Miguel's home had turned up manzanillo apples, as well as juice extracted from them, which he could have injected into the champagne Claire drank. "And Miguel was at a bar with Pedro Lopez shortly before he died. Miguel could have slipped something into Pedro's drink. I suspect they'll charge him with that murder as well."

Jim rubbed his forehead. "I can't believe it. Why would Miguel kill Pedro? Miguel gets along with everybody."

"Pedro might have seen him poison the champagne," suggested Giovanna. "Maybe Pedro confronted Miguel after he learned Claire had died, and he put together how it happened."

"But why would Miguel kill Claire?" Jim's face reddened. "He knew she was a VIP guest. We talked about her on the way back from the airport, the video she was making to promote the hotel, and we brainstormed how to make her stay extra special."

"Did you get the idea Miguel and Claire already knew each other?"

"Maybe." Jim adjusted his collar. "She'd been to the Galapagos several times to make documentaries, and most of the 'research crowd' at least knew of her."

"Did you detect any animosity from Miguel? Any anxiety about her coming back here, asking questions about Tio Armando?"

"We didn't discuss Tio Armando." Jim looked away. "We mainly talked about aspects of the resort for her to feature in her film."

Giovanna drummed her fingers on the desk. "Miguel had opportunity and knowledge of how to make the toxin. The police think he has a motive also."

"What was his motive?"

"No charges were ever filed in the Tio Armando debacle, even though laws were broken. Money went missing, and most of it was never recovered. Since all that happened right before Jerome Haddad's deadly rampage, the story got buried, pushed aside by more spectacular news. Mixed in with the misdeeds of Jerome and Felipe. But Claire Costello wanted to dig it up, expose another accomplice."

Jim folded his arms across his chest. "And you think Miguel had a hand in it?"

"Do you?"

His eyes strayed to his lap. "I told Miguel I didn't want to know if he did."

"That excuse wouldn't exonerate you if the authorities decided to file charges," scoffed Giovanna.

Jim waved his hand dismissively. "Do you really think Miguel would commit murder to keep that story from coming out? Even if Miguel *was* involved, he wouldn't get more than a fine, or he'd need to make restitution if they could prove he embezzled any money."

"Roberto thinks the police have rushed to close this case," said Giovanna. "Miguel's motive isn't strong enough to commit murder."

"Roberto's a smart man."

"Roberto also told me Miguel was experimenting with the juice for another reason."

"Well, there you go. Reasonable doubt."

"If Miguel didn't kill Claire and Pedro, who do you think did?" Elbow on the desk, Giovanna rested her chin in her cupped hand. "Who else had motive and opportunity? If the same person killed them both."

"Certainly no one on our staff." Jim set his jaw in determination as if saying so made it true. "It must be one of Claire's employees. Those people know her better; they've had more time to develop motives. And what a great opportunity to pull it off—on a film shoot outside the U.S., at a remote location."

"I hope you're right. I don't like to think we've hired a killer."

"We need to get Miguel a lawyer," Jim declared. "I can't have our employee sitting in jail. Have they set bail yet?"

"They just arrested him, and it's Sunday, so probably not. I have a call in to our local counsel."

Jim looked at his watch. "Will Victor let us know what they find in the shed?"

"I hope so. He tries to keep us updated."

"This case must be putting a strain on your relationship."

She sighed, thinking about everything that had happened since her carefree outing with Victor on Tuesday. "It hasn't been easy. He has a lot on his mind."

They were quiet for a moment, each lost in thought.

Jim broke the silence, "Do you want to join us for dinner tonight? Jenny invited Lindsey and Arthur."

"I had a late lunch with Michelle and Roberto, so no thanks. But maybe I'll stop by your table and say hello. We should listen more closely to Lindsey's theory about Colin and not dismiss it as completely crazy."

Jim smiled. "Those two girls have been traipsing around the property, making TikToks, shooting video for Lindsey's YouTube channel. Jenny's getting all sorts of screen time, plus she's learning how to expand her own platform. What a publicity boon! I never saw that angle for advertising before, but it's been great. Who knows, Leisure Dreams might reach more potential customers that way than through the more traditional promotional video Claire's team is making."

"Isn't Lindsey Costello's audience mostly teenagers?"

"You'd be surprised at how much teenagers can influence their parents." Jim grinned. "And soon they'll grow up, get jobs, spend money. Belinda said she's already seen a spike in bookings today."

"I'm surprised Lindsey's able to focus on her YouTube channel, considering she just lost her mother." Giovanna tried to remember how she'd felt when she lost hers.

"Probably her way of coping." Jim looked wistful, and Giovanna guessed he was thinking about his own family rather than Lindsey. "Sharing her grief and outrage with her fans."

"I hope she's not directing that grief and outrage toward Leisure Dreams. We don't need any more negative publicity." Watching Jim's face crease with worry, she added, "But a spike in bookings is a good sign."

There was a knock at the door. "Come in," Giovanna called.

Victor poked his head inside.

"What did you find in the shed?" she asked.

"Nothing unexpected," Victor replied. "Besides the usual garden tools and supplies, we found personal protective gear, which Miguel probably wears when harvesting fruit from the manzanillo tree."

"He wears a mask and gloves when he's spraying pesticides," said Jim. "What's wrong with that?"

"We also found syringes and a substance that appears to be manzanillo juice."

"But Victor," Giovanna began, intending to relay what Roberto had told her about the pesticides.

Victor's phone buzzed, and he held up his hand. "Excuse me." As he listened, his eyes widened. "I'll be right there."

CHAPTER FORTY-NINE

Sunday evening, Puerto Ayora

Victor approached the reception desk at the hospital. "Thank you for calling me about Maria's visitor. Did he get in to see her?"

The rosy-cheeked, middle-aged receptionist shook her head. "I told him Maria couldn't have visitors at this time."

"Good," Victor replied. "And he left?"

With a conspiratorial smile, she winked. "He shuffled around like he was trying to figure out a way in, but then, yes, he gave up and left."

"What did the guy look like?"

"Tall. *Desaliñado*." Unkempt.

"Local? Or a tourist?"

"Might have been a tourist. He spoke Spanish, but he had an accent."

Victor pulled out his phone and showed the receptionist a picture from Claire's website. "Could it be one of these guys?"

She squinted. "Maybe."

"But you're not sure?"

She shook her head. "Sorry. He wore sunglasses and a baseball cap pulled down over his face. I don't think he wanted to be recognized."

"That's okay. Thank you for calling me." Victor put away his phone. "May I go check on Maria?"

With a nod, she gestured toward the rooms. The door to Maria's was partially ajar, and he knocked gently. "*Hola*," he called.

"*Entre*."

Maria brightened when Victor pushed the door the rest of the way open. Her face had regained some of its bronze color.

"Feeling better?" he asked.

She nodded. "Ready to get out of here."

"Good," he said. "Have you had any visitors?"

Her eyes narrowed. "Besides you?"

He waited.

"Laurel called. She wanted to come by, but I told her I'd be home before she could make it over here."

"She's a good friend."

Maria twisted to get a better look at the detective's face. "So, you've arrested Miguel Ruiz for Claire Costello's murder?"

Victor blinked. *News travels fast.* "Laurel told you?"

Maria nodded.

Did Giovanna tell Laurel already? he wondered. *Or did Miguel call Laurel from jail?*

"Do you really think he did it?" Maria asked.

Victor shrugged. "We have evidence."

"What evidence?"

"Let's just say he had access to physostigmine, the toxin that most likely killed Claire Costello and Pedro Lopez."

"Detective, I understand the manzanillo tree is a source of the toxin, and there's one on the Leisure Dreams property," said Maria. "But everyone had access to that tree, and it's not the only one on the island. It's a native plant."

"Not everyone was aware of the tree's danger, let alone capable of extracting the poison."

She rolled her eyes. "Every part of that plant is toxic, and most islanders know it. The killer wouldn't have to extract the juice to hurt someone."

"But Miguel makes juice. We found it in his home, and there's some in his shed on the resort property."

"I suppose you think Miguel had a motive."

Victor shifted his weight, scraping his foot across the tile floor. "He did have a motive."

"What motive?" Maria slapped her palm to her forehead, then winced at the pain. "You mean Tio Armando?"

Victor nodded. "I'd think, as a reporter, you'd want to expose the story."

"Big deal." She sighed. "Yes, Miguel helped Felipe Santore move Tio Armando from the Beagle Galapaguera to Leisure Dreams. The hotel wasn't open yet, and he thought the resort would make the perfect hiding place." She took a sip of water from the glass on her nightstand. "As the groundskeeper, Miguel could look after the tortoise, even though there wasn't a proper enclosure. Little did he know the CEO was coming to town on a Galapagos cruise and would decide to show off his property to a group of fellow passengers."

"Miguel was definitely Felipe's accomplice?" Victor had always suspected so, but no one had ever confirmed it. Both Jim and Laurel had pled ignorance.

"It wasn't a big secret. And they didn't *steal* the tortoise. They just needed to hide him from Felipe's sleazy American partner, who planned to sell him to a group of investors in Dubai and move him out of the country. Which was totally illegal and outrageous."

"What about the money? Felipe's Tio Armando Foundation supposedly wired money to the Beagle Galapaguera for the transfer, but those funds disappeared."

"Victor." Maria shook her head. "Jerome Haddad was a con man extraordinaire. He made Felipe Santore look like an amateur. The promised money was never sent."

"You don't think Miguel took the money?"

"Does Miguel live like he took the money?"

"That doesn't prove anything." Victor tapped his chipped front tooth with his thumbnail.

"Where's your proof that Miguel took the money?" She lifted her chin.

"I thought you'd be all over this story." Victor shook his head. "Claire Costello thought there was something worth pursuing."

"Claire would have sensationalized it," Maria sneered. "To bring more attention to her documentary."

"And how did Miguel feel about that?"

"I think he liked the attention."

"Didn't he threaten her?" Victor remembered the call Claire received from Laurel's phone; Belinda had heard an angry male voice on the other end.

"Sure, he did. He was baiting her, trying to pique her interest in the story. Make it more than it was."

Victor's eyes bulged.

"You've arrested the wrong man, Detective."

"If so, then who killed Claire Costello? And Pedro Lopez?"

Maria laughed. "You want me to do your job for you?"

A nurse peered into the doorway. "Time for another pill, señora Vasquez." She turned to Victor and announced, "Visiting hours are over."

* * *

Giovanna approached the table where Jim, Jenny, Arthur, and Lindsey chatted over dessert and coffee. "Did you enjoy your meal?" Her eyes swept from face to face.

"The grilled lobster tail was excellent," said Arthur. "Come join us. Have a seat."

Jim stood, pulled a chair from an adjacent table, and positioned it at the side of theirs. He signaled for the server as Giovanna sat down.

Gabriela appeared. "Another espresso, señor?"

Jim and Arthur nodded.

"Herbal tea for me, please," said Giovanna. She noticed Lindsey and Jenny looking at her, then at each other with a giggle. "What?" she asked, when Gabriela had left with their orders.

Jenny nudged Lindsey.

"Miss Giovanna, will you let me interview you for my YouTube channel?" Lindsey grinned.

With a quizzical look, Giovanna eyed the teenagers. "Why do you think your audience would be interested in an interview with me?"

"Oh, go on. Say yes," laughed Jim. "It will be good publicity for the hotel."

With an eye roll, she turned to Lindsey. "Only if you let me approve the recording before you post it."

"Deal." Lindsey picked up her cellphone and aimed it at Giovanna. "Tell me, Ms. Rogers, what made you take this job in the Galapagos?"

Giovanna dragged her index finger across her neck like a director stopping a scene. "Cut! I didn't say we could do it right now."

Lindsey put down her phone. "Tomorrow then?"

"Maybe," said Giovanna. "Can I get the questions in advance?"

"No," Lindsey replied. "I like spontaneity." She tossed a sideways glance at Jenny, and both girls giggled again.

Giovanna appealed to Jim and Arthur. "Are you going to sit there and let a couple of teenagers manipulate me?"

Arthur gave his daughter a stern look. "Lindsey, what did I tell you about being respectful?"

Before Lindsey could respond, her eyes shifted to the restaurant's entrance.

Giovanna followed her gaze. Colin and Susie walked in.

"There's the murderer," muttered Lindsey. "And his slut."

"Lindsey," Arthur admonished.

Colin glanced in their direction and then steered Susie to the far corner of the restaurant.

Giovanna turned to Jim and lowered her voice. "Did you tell Arthur and Lindsey?"

"Tell them what?"

"About Miguel," she whispered.

Jim waved his hand dismissively in front of his face. "Miguel didn't do it."

"Someone has been arrested?" Arthur's eyes roved from Jim to Giovanna. "Who is this Miguel person? Do the police think he killed my wife?"

My wife. Giovanna found it curious that Arthur didn't refer to Claire as *my ex-wife* or *Lindsey's mother.* "Miguel is our groundskeeper. The police found manzanillo apples and juice at his home. The toxin in the champagne Claire drank came from the fruit of the manzanillo tree, a native plant, one of which is growing on our resort property."

"The one by the beach trail with the fence around it, and the plaque?" said Arthur.

Giovanna nodded.

"I've got pictures." Jenny scrolled through her phone.

"Let's do a story about it tomorrow for my YouTube channel," suggested Lindsey.

Did they hear the whole conversation? Giovanna eyed the girls. "Nothing I'm telling you goes on the internet."

Arthur gave his daughter a stern look. "Did you hear that, Lindsey? Promise."

Lindsey and Jenny looked at each other and nodded. "Promise," said Lindsey.

"But Miguel had a good reason for making the manzanillo juice," said Jim.

Clearly, he doesn't want Miguel to be the murderer, thought Giovanna. Miguel was one of his first hires at the new Leisure Dreams property, and Jim had grown fond of him.

"I bet Colin stole some of Miguel's manzanillo juice and used it to poison my mom." Lindsey stared daggers at Colin and Susie laughing together at a table for two across the room.

"Does Colin know anything about poisons? Native plants?" asked Giovanna.

"He must," declared Lindsey. "Duh. He's been working on nature documentaries with my mom for four years."

"He didn't seem to know about the manzanillo tree when I was giving the tour of the grounds," said Giovanna. "But Tyler did."

"Well, of course, Colin would play dumb," Lindsey insisted. "He's a snake."

"Tyler?" Arthur raised his brow. As he did, Giovanna noticed how his receding hairline made his forehead appear larger. "Tyler is quite knowledgeable about the flora and fauna of the islands. He and Claire have made several trips here together."

"But Tyler would never hurt my mom," said Lindsey. "For a long time, he had a crush on her."

Arthur turned to Giovanna. "Lindsey has loved Tyler since she was a little girl. He used to take her rock climbing. And he won her over with his magic tricks."

"Magic tricks?" Giovanna repeated.

"You know, coin behind the ear, sleight-of-hand stuff that kids love."

Giovanna's phone vibrated. She looked down at the screen: Laurel. "Excuse me."

Making her way out to the terrace, Giovanna took Laurel's call. "What happened with Tio Armando? Is he okay?"

"Huh?"

"When we hung up earlier, you said someone tried to poison Tio Armando."

"Oh," said Laurel. "Some bratty kids threw candy into his pen and hopped the fence. They were sitting on him, posing for photos."

Giovanna settled onto a boulder near the pool. "Where were the parents?"

"Laughing, taking pictures, egging them on."

"I guess you put a stop to it."

"I showed more restraint than I felt. Tourists!"

"You need the tourists, though," Giovanna reminded her. "And the opportunity to educate people."

"Yeah, right. But some people are impossible to educate." Laurel paused. "That's not why I called you."

Giovanna waited.

"Did you know Victor arrested Miguel? For murder!"

"They found evidence—"

"Those apples? I told you what he uses them for. Snacks for Tio Armando and the other giant tortoises here."

"What about the juice?"

Laurel was quiet for a moment. "I don't know why Miguel would poison Claire."

"The theory is, she had information about him she planned to use in her documentary," said Giovanna. "Facts he didn't want made public."

"What information?"

"They think it had to do with the unauthorized move of Tio Armando from the Beagle Galapaguera to Leisure Dreams."

Laurel scoffed. "Old news. Miguel would have loved the attention, the notoriety. He pushed Claire to cover that story, and she took the bait. She was all about ratings."

"You're saying there was nothing Claire could dig up that would have caused trouble for Miguel?"

"Trouble, maybe. But nothing worth committing murder."

"Jim doesn't believe Miguel did it, either," said Giovanna. "I've been trying to reach our local attorney so we can bail him out as soon as he's arraigned."

"Don't bother," said Laurel. "I already posted bail. Miguel's home."

Giovanna didn't know whether to be ashamed of the slowness of the corporate machine or nervous that a killer was free.

CHAPTER FIFTY

Sunday evening, Puerto Ayora

After he left the hospital, Victor returned to the police station to question Miguel Ruiz further. Walking toward the one-story stucco building, he replayed his conversation with Maria, which had caused him to doubt some of his assumptions.

He strolled across the cramped lobby framed by bare plaster walls, heading for the holding cell. It was empty. He backed up and addressed the officer on duty, "Where's Ruiz?"

"He made bail," came the reply.

"How?" Victor rubbed his forehead. "Jim Roberts? Someone from Leisure Dreams?"

The officer shook his head. "Laurel Pardo."

Victor shut his eyes tightly. *Nothing that woman does would surprise me.*

Rounding the corner, he strode down a narrow hallway leading to several small offices. He unlocked his, squeezed past two overflowing file cabinets, and sat down behind his metal desk. When he took out his phone to call Giovanna, he saw he'd missed two from her. He pressed the telephone symbol next to her name.

She answered on the first ring.

"You told Laurel about Miguel's arrest?" He hadn't intended to sound so confrontational.

Giovanna laughed. "Is that what you think? Laurel just called to tell *me* she'd bailed him out."

"I thought Jim would have done it." Victor leaned back in his chair.

"We were working on it," Giovanna replied. "But Laurel beat us to it."

Victor shuffled through the papers on his desk.

"Victor?" prompted Giovanna. "Is there a chance you've arrested the wrong person?"

"That's what Maria thinks." He heard Giovanna's breath catch. He sensed she didn't care much for Maria but would never interfere with his friendship with the reporter, their symbiotic working relationship. "I checked on Maria at the hospital this evening." When Giovanna didn't react, he continued, "My job is to follow the evidence."

"About that evidence," she said. "What I started to tell you earlier . . . There might be a legitimate explanation for the manzanillo juice." She related Roberto's conversation with Miguel about how he extracted the physostigmine as an antidote to pesticide poisoning.

Victor tapped his tooth. "Very neat excuse. But who else would know about the juice? And have access to it?"

She was quiet. Victor knew she must be running through her list of employees, not wanting any of them to be a killer.

"Besides Laurel," he said, knowing Giovanna didn't want Laurel to be the killer either.

"You'd like it to be Laurel," Giovanna said. "But she didn't even mention the juice. Only the apples that Miguel feeds to the tortoises. And she has no motive."

"I just want to catch the killer. Whoever that person may be." Victor kneaded his brow.

"If Miguel had the juice in the shed, anyone could have gone in there."

"If they knew about it. And isn't the shed usually locked?"

"Of course." Silence followed; perhaps Giovanna envisioned scenarios when the shed might not be locked. "How's Maria?"

"Better. She'll probably go home tomorrow."

"Glad to hear it." He labeled her tone as ambivalent, noncommittal, like the time he'd suggested taking up S.C.U.B.A. diving. Words that didn't match the attitude.

"I got a call that Maria had a visitor," he explained. "That's why I rushed off."

"You think someone meant to harm her?"

Victor sighed. "Maria's accident was suspicious. Whoever pushed her might have come back to finish the job. Or threaten her in some way. We already lost one journalist, so we're taking precautions."

"Who was the visitor?"

"The nurse at the desk could only give me a description, not a positive ID. She said the man was wearing a baseball cap pulled down over his face and sunglasses."

"Anything else? Body type? Age?"

"Tall and *desaliñado*, 'scruffy.' Spoke Spanish with an American accent."

"Tyler?"

"I don't want to jump to conclusions, but he fits the description more than Colin. And Tyler stayed in town after Miguel's arrest ended their excursion."

Giovanna was silent for a moment. "I can't remember if I told you, but the morning after Claire died, I gave the film crew a tour of the grounds. Maria showed up and started following us. She was so annoying, digging for information about Claire, almost making accusations. When we were down on the dock, we spotted a sea turtle. And while we were all peering over the edge to admire the animal, Maria tumbled into the water. I didn't see how it happened, but I had a feeling Tyler tripped her."

"Maria thought the same thing." Victor ran his finger along the chip in his tooth. "Tyler's not back from town yet?"

"I haven't seen him but haven't been looking for him."

"If you can find out—discreetly, of course—I'd appreciate it. But don't confront him about his visit to the hospital."

"*Seguro, mi corazón.*" The smile in her voice warmed his heart, a welcome contrast to worries about catching a killer.

* * *

The Leisure Dreams van was still parked in front of Miguel's house. Giovanna must not have sent anyone to pick it up yet. Just as well, since Miguel could now drive it back to the hotel.

As Victor strolled up the walkway, his eyes were drawn to a light in the kitchen. He knocked on the weather-beaten front door.

Footsteps creaked the wood floors and rock music played, but no one answered.

Victor knocked again, harder this time.

More footsteps. A curtain parted, then sprung back to cover the window.

"Miguel," called Victor, giving the door another rap. "We need to talk."

After a long pause, Miguel cracked the door and peered out. "I have nothing else to say without a lawyer present."

"I'm not here to arrest you again," said Victor. "May I come in?"

"Are you here to apologize?"

"In a way."

Gripping the door as if he regretted his decision, Miguel pulled it the rest of the way open and stepped aside. The two men made their way into the living room. Victor sat on the couch, and Miguel planted himself in a nearby armchair.

"Tell me about the apples," Victor began as he settled against the cushions.

"Surely Laurel already told you. The giant tortoises like them."

"You know they're toxic to humans?"

"I don't feed them to humans."

"What about the juice?" pressed Victor. "Tortoises don't drink juice, do they?"

"I use the juice."

"What do you use the juice for? Some health concoction?"

The corners of Miguel's mouth twitched up slightly, then went deadpan again. "Very funny, señor."

"Tell me why you make the juice."

"It's an experiment."

"What kind of experiment?"

Miguel sighed. "Leisure Dreams headquarters sends me standard chemicals to spray on the grounds—pesticides, herbicides, fungicides. Some corporate *imbécil* orders the same products for properties everywhere in the world, and not all are appropriate at every location."

"Can't you order what you need?" suggested Victor. "And tell headquarters which products they shouldn't bother sending automatically?"

"They have a system," Miguel explained. "A 'brand' to maintain, they say. They think they know best. And maybe someone in the purchasing department is getting a kickback from the manufacturer."

"So, what about the juice? I doubt they send you that."

Miguel quirked his mouth. "Last month, we had an outbreak of black flies. They were awful; a young whale beached itself and died ashore about half a mile from our property. The park service took away the carcass the next day, but not before hordes of big, black flies swarmed everywhere."

Victor shuddered at the thought of a plague of black flies. "How did you get rid of them?"

"I sprayed the corporate-approved pesticide."

"Did it kill the flies?"

"Not only the flies. Around the lagoon where I sprayed, fish got sick. Some died. And birds were eating those fish."

Victor frowned. "Then that pesticide is not good for the environment."

"Exactly. I started reading about a possible antidote. To *save* the environment, Detective." Miguel gave him a thin-lipped smile.

Okay, Miguel, stop trying to impress me with your concern about the environment. "What did you discover?"

"Physostigmine, the toxin found in the manzanillo, is also used as an antidote for pesticide poisoning."

"So, what did you do?" Victor crossed his legs.

Miguel replied, "It took me a while to adjust the ratios, but I estimate I saved about thirty percent of the affected fish. Not fantastic, but better than nothing."

"Did you tell anyone about your discovery?" Victor watched Miguel's face, waiting for more details that didn't come. "Besides Laurel?"

"Not Laurel. A few other researchers at the Darwin. I posted about my experiment in our online community discussion group, kind of an informal blog."

"A blog? For whom?"

"Just other researchers around the islands," said Miguel. "We're scientists, you know. Scientists appreciate knowledge. We share."

Victor nodded. "I'd like the link to this blog, please."

"Sure, I'll send it to you." He picked up his phone and scrolled. "You'll probably find it boring. Too technical."

Victor ignored the last comment and the condescending tone. "Did Claire Costello or her team have access to this blog?"

Miguel shrugged. "I didn't tell Claire about it, but maybe Laurel did. It's not password-protected; someone could find it on the internet with the right keywords."

"Did anyone at the hotel know about your research? Jim Roberts? Giovanna Rogers?" Saying Giovanna's name made Victor feel closer to her.

"No. Señora Rogers knew about the flies, and she was glad I took care of them. I didn't tell her about the collateral damage or how I dealt with it." Miguel looked at his lap, away from Victor's piercing gaze. "She only recently learned about manzanillo trees, and when she understood the danger, she had a fence built around the one by the beach trail to protect guests."

"I remember. What about the kitchen staff? Or Belinda Chavez?"

"Belinda knew."

Victor noted the way Miguel's face brightened at the mention of Belinda. "What did Belinda know?"

"She came out to my shed one day while I was mixing my antidote, so I explained what I was doing."

"Did Belinda come to the shed a lot?"

Miguel's cheeks and neck had reddened. "Sometimes, to chat."

Victor ran his tongue over his chipped tooth. "Do you two see each other outside of work?" Miguel tried to look away, but Victor could read the answer in his eyes. "Did Belinda ever ask about the poison?"

"I had to tell her the juice was toxic, for her own protection." Miguel fidgeted with his phone.

"How did she react when you told her?"

Miguel shrugged.

Victor continued to stare at him. "Surely, she must have had a comment. You were experimenting with a deadly substance."

Miguel's lip trembled. "Okay, yes, she asked if you could kill someone by putting the juice in a drink. But we were joking. She'd never do that."

Their eyes locked for a moment. *Except someone did it,* Victor thought. "Have you and Belinda talked since Claire died?"

"Not much."

"What about Wednesday night?" Victor raised his eyebrows.

"She didn't do it, Detective."

"I didn't accuse her of anything."

"She admired señora Costello. She was looking forward to having her as a guest at the hotel. No way would Belinda hurt her." Miguel's voice rose.

Victor looked down at his notebook. "What about Pedro Lopez?"

"Belinda had nothing against Pedro Lopez."

Victor looked back at Miguel. "You were one of the last people to see him alive."

"Señor, I told you I had no reason to kill Pedro Lopez."

"When you had a drink together at El Pelicano, what did you talk about?"

"Just *macho* stuff."

Victor waited, but Miguel did not elaborate. "The murder at Leisure Dreams?"

"We didn't know much about the murder then," said Miguel. "Or even that it was homicide."

"No? Belinda found Claire's body early Wednesday morning. By Wednesday night, I'll wager everyone who worked at the resort had heard what happened."

Miguel looked down. "We didn't know poisoned champagne killed her. Most people thought she committed suicide. Overdose or something."

Victor could tell Miguel was lying. He'd questioned him enough to recognize his evasive ticks. The way his eyes shifted away, how his mouth tightened. "You and Pedro were part of the chain of custody for the poisoned champagne. As was Belinda."

"Exactly, Detective. We were afraid we'd be suspects. A good reason to drink." Miguel attempted a smile but quickly retracted it when Victor didn't laugh.

"Did Pedro tell you he saw something suspicious that night?"

Miguel looked down.

"Did he think *you* poisoned the champagne?"

"No." Miguel met his gaze.

Victor eyed him. "Someone else then? Belinda?"

"No. I told you she didn't kill anyone."

"Who, then?"

"Pedro thought Tyler Thompson did."

"Tyler?"

Miguel nodded vigorously. "Tyler came into the kitchen when Pedro was preparing the welcome basket. He asked Pedro where the champagne was going."

"Pedro told Tyler it was for Claire?"

"Yes. And then Chef Gomez called Pedro over to help him garnish the plates for a large order. When he finished, he saw Tyler holding the champagne bottle."

"What happened next?"

"Tyler claimed he was reading the label. Pedro didn't think anything of it until . . . you know."

"Why was Tyler in the kitchen that night? I thought Chef Gomez was territorial."

"Chef did tell Tyler to leave, to place his to-go order with the waitress in the dining room. But she was busy with other customers, someone dropped a tray, Jim Roberts showed up . . . lots of confusion all at once, and Tyler stayed."

Victor reviewed his notes again. "When you and Pedro were at El Pelicano, did you see Tyler?"

Miguel nodded. "He came over to say hello. We expressed our condolences about his colleague."

"How did Tyler react?"

Miguel studied his fingernails. "You know how he is. No emotion."

Chapter Fifty-One

Sunday night, Leisure Dreams

No one answered when Giovanna dialed Tyler's room. Not ready to go to bed yet, she decided to stroll the grounds. It was a clear, warm night, and she wasn't sleepy. Exercise helped her think; being close to nature soothed her spirit.

Hector thumbed through some paperwork at his post by the front door. She stopped. "Señor Sanchez?"

"*Sí, señora?*"

"Have you seen Tyler Thompson this evening?" When his brow wrinkled, she added, "You know, the cameraman with the film crew."

"Not tonight, señora. Is there a problem?"

"No, but if you see him, will you please call me?" She held up her phone.

"Certainly, señora."

"I'm going outside for some fresh air. I won't be gone long."

"Have a nice walk, señora."

The Southern Cross was visible in the unclouded sky; she loved living in a place where night got dark enough to identify the constellations. Moonlight glistened on the bay; the water barely rippled in the light breeze, sending silver-tipped waves toward the shore.

A soft hoot made Giovanna stop to listen. The owl was nearby. More often found on the Prince Phillip's Steps of Genovesa Island, one of these cute, short-eared Galapagos owls had taken up residence on the Leisure Dreams property.

She passed Miguel's shed, a windowless stucco structure tinted the same sandy peach as the hotel. No crime scene tape encircled it, so Victor must have finished with his investigation. *I don't think I've ever been inside this place,* she thought. Was she a good manager? How could she be if employees were experimenting with deadly toxins right under her nose? Her style was to delegate and let them handle their responsibilities as they saw fit; perhaps she should have been more hands-on.

But Miguel was making an antidote to pesticide, she reminded herself, wanting to believe Roberto's theory. *My groundskeeper is a creative, environmentally-conscious scientist; he didn't have murder on his mind. But then, who did?*

She twisted the handle and pushed the door open. Victor had said he locked up after he finished his search, and Belinda was going to check it before she went home. *I should have gone myself.*

As soon as Giovanna entered the shed, she sensed she wasn't alone. A pinprick of light from a phone's flashlight quickly extinguished. She flipped a switch, illuminating a gangly figure bent over Miguel's wooden worktable.

"Tyler?!" she gasped. "What are you doing here?"

He turned to face her, his expression unreadable. Slipping his hand behind his back, he took a step toward her.

"This area is for staff only." With a sweep of her arm toward the door, she strained to keep her voice steady. "Let's go back inside the hotel."

Tyler drew closer.

* * *

Sunday evening, El Pelicano

Victor and another police officer reviewed the security footage from El Pelicano's camera. Black and white images danced across the screen in fast motion as employees bustled behind the bar, serving drinks and removing empty glasses. Customers came and went, back-slapping one another and indulging in animated conversations.

"Stop," Victor waved his hand at the bar manager.

The screen froze on an image of Miguel Ruiz and Pedro Lopez seated at the counter. A lanky figure in rumpled clothing, wearing a baseball cap and sunglasses, was framed in the doorway.

Victor pointed a finger. "That's him."

The bar manager pressed Play; they watched the man walk to the bar and place an order. He cast a surreptitious glance toward Miguel and Pedro.

Nothing unusual happened for several minutes. Customers arrived and departed; the bartender served more drinks. Miguel and Pedro seemed engrossed in serious conversation. The other man sipped a beer in silence.

"Wait," said Victor. "Back up."

They watched the last bit of footage again.

Belinda entered the building and strolled to the counter.

Miguel turned and grinned. Standing, he looped an arm around her waist and gave her a deep kiss. Pedro was laughing at something the bartender must have said. And the other man had stealthily inched closer.

"I don't see anything." Victor's colleague furrowed his brow.

Victor made a looping gesture with his finger. "Play it again. Can we zoom in?"

"These cameras aren't that sophisticated," replied the bar manager. He backed up the recording and replayed the scene.

"Freeze frame." Victor pointed at a figure. "There." He turned to his colleague. "What does that look like to you?"

The officer squinted and moved his face closer to the screen. "¡Ay, caramba!"

Victor studied the static image. "The film is grainy, but that would explain a lot."

The manager restarted the recording. Miguel, arm still around Belinda, appeared to announce his departure. He dropped some bills on the bar, leaving the remainder of his beverage untouched.

Pedro chugged the rest of his and got up to follow Miguel and Belinda. The group stopped for a moment in front of the man with the ballcap, said something, then left. The bartender cleared away Pedro's empty glass and Miguel's unfinished drink.

The man in the baseball cap nursed his beer for another minute, then he too rose and departed.

"We'll need to take that recording as evidence," Victor advised the manager, who handed it over without argument.

As they left the bar, Victor remembered he'd asked Giovanna to check on Tyler's whereabouts. Knowing her, she'd try to question him, go beyond expectations like she always did to get information, which would be a terrible idea this time. He hoped she hadn't found the cameraman yet. Pulse quickening, he punched in her number, but the call went to voicemail.

* * *

Sunday evening, Miguel's shed

Giovanna crossed her arms and inched against the wall. "You're trespassing." She gazed past Tyler to the worktable, where several full syringes lay. Her breath caught.

"What are *you* doing here, Ms. Rogers?" He circled her like a predator stalking its prey.

"Checking to make sure everything is locked up." She moved toward the door. "I'm going—"

He'd maneuvered himself between her and the exit. "Not so fast."

"Mr. Thompson, you're scaring me." He reeked like an athlete who hadn't showered after a marathon. As he loomed over her, she mustered an authoritative tone she no longer felt. "Please, let's go back inside the hotel. There's no reason—"

His eyes bored into hers, and he refused to budge.

She swallowed. "Detective Zuniga is looking for you. He wondered if you'd returned from town after that unfortunate incident with Miguel. We don't mean to strand our guests."

"How considerate."

"Now that I know you made it back safely, I'm going inside to tell the detective. I have a hotel to run." She took another step toward the exit.

The cameraman continued to lean against the door frame, blocking her.

She fumbled in her pocket for her cellphone. Panicked at not feeling its hard case, she plunged her hand into the other pocket.

"Missing this?" Tyler held her phone just out of her grasp.

Her mouth dropped. "Give that back. I'm not in the mood for your magic tricks."

Still keeping the phone away from her, Tyler stared at the screen. "Not much of a signal out here anyway."

"Then give it back." Giovanna reached for it, but he held her at bay. "Fine, don't. But get out of my way."

He folded his arms across his chest, still clutching her phone. "I'm afraid I've given you the wrong idea, and we need to straighten some things out before you run to your cop friend."

"Like what? I just asked what you were doing in a staff-only area."

"You think I killed Claire."

"Did you?" She tried to channel her auditor stare, but her fear diluted its effect.

"You must think I did." He narrowed his gaze.

She averted her eyes. "Miguel Ruiz has been arrested for Claire's murder. Maybe you figured it out as well?" She tried to appeal to his ego. "You recognized the manzanillo tree and its dangers. You must have guessed that a groundskeeper, a scientist like Miguel, would know how to extract the poison."

Tyler nodded. "Miguel has written extensively about his research with physostigmine."

Giovanna found it curious how easily the difficult chemical name rolled off Tyler's tongue. "Where? How—?"

"I read the blog by the Darwin research team. Miguel is a frequent contributor."

"Blog?" *Another thing I didn't know about my employee.* "Why would Miguel hurt Claire?"

Tyler scratched his scraggly beard. "I didn't know for sure or I would have warned her. Of course. I always looked out for Claire."

"You did, didn't you? Nursed her whenever she was sick."

"What are you implying?"

"I'm not implying anything. It's what I've heard."

"She did get sick a lot. Ulcer issues. Probably from stress."

And maybe she had help. Giovanna recalled her conversation with Susie on North Seymour about Claire's frequent, sudden illnesses whenever the crew traveled. And Maria's leading questions during the grounds tour, just before she tumbled into the bay. How many times had Tyler deliberately poisoned Claire, then administered a cure to help her recover, trying to gain her favor? "Why do *you* think Miguel killed her?" Giovanna edged toward the door again, but Tyler still stood in the way.

"He wasn't happy with how she planned to portray him in the documentary."

"But is that a reason to kill someone?" Giovanna scanned the windowless room, searching for another exit. "Miguel might have enjoyed the notoriety."

Tyler's eyes glinted. "You think it was me and not him, don't you?"

Giovanna observed the cameraman. "I don't think you meant to kill Claire."

"No . . ." He looked past her, his face pensive. "I didn't."

He got the dosage wrong. "The poison must have hit her especially hard on an empty stomach full of ulcers."

"She wasn't supposed to die."

"You should tell Detective Zuniga. Let him know it was an accident."

Tyler's eyes met hers. Whatever warmth had once been there was now gone. "I can't do that."

Because you did mean to kill Pedro Lopez. He must have seen you tamper with the champagne, and you had to silence him. Although Giovanna didn't speak the words, she sensed Tyler had read her thoughts.

Gritting his teeth, Tyler grabbed her shoulder and spun her around. With the other hand, he pulled a syringe from his pocket.

Giovanna leaned in and thrust her elbow into his ribs, a move she'd learned in a self-defense course she'd taken in college.

As he clutched his side, she kneed him in the groin.

Groaning, he doubled over.

She squirmed past him, out the door, and into the night.

CHAPTER FIFTY-TWO

Sunday night, Leisure Dreams

"Señora, what's wrong?" cried Hector Sanchez as Giovanna dashed into the lobby, winded, face flushed.

"Call Detective Zuniga," she panted, stopping in front of his post to catch her breath. "I don't have my phone."

"Certainly, señora." Not taking his eyes off Giovanna, Hector grabbed his phone from his pocket. "What happened?"

"If Tyler Thompson comes in . . ." Her breath expelled in uneven pants; her heart still throbbed against her chest.

Hector held up his hand. "Voicemail," he mouthed, then left a message requesting Victor to contact the hotel immediately. "I'm calling the main police station number." He frowned at Giovanna. "Did that Mr. Thompson do something to you?"

Nina Morales, the night receptionist, came out from behind the desk. "Señora, are you okay?" She put an arm around Giovanna and led her to one of the lobby couches. "Let me get you some water."

"Thank you." Giovanna's breathing steadied, but she eyed the front entrance, not feeling safe yet.

Nina filled a glass from the ice water dispenser in the lobby and handed it to her boss. "Can I call someone for you? Your grandmother? Belinda?"

Giovanna shook her head, and her hand trembled as she reached for the glass. She raised her voice to address Nina and Hector, "If Tyler Thompson comes back inside, don't let him leave. Don't—" When Nina let go of the glass, it slipped from Giovanna's hands, soaking her slacks before it tumbled to the floor.

"*Perdón, señora,* I thought you had it." Nina scrambled to clean up the spill. "Let me get you another."

Hector was speaking to the police dispatcher, and from the perplexed expression on his face, Giovanna could tell he didn't understand why he was calling. She caught her name uttered several times in his outpouring of Spanish.

She rose, walked across the room to the concierge counter, and took the phone from Hector. "Hello, this is Giovanna Rogers, manager of the Leisure Dreams hotel." She paused to calm her voice. "Please send Detective Zuniga here as soon as possible. He needs to arrest Tyler Thompson for the murders of Claire Costello and Pedro Lopez."

Mouths dropping as if from broken hinges, Hector and Nina stared at her in disbelief.

* * *

Victor rushed into the lobby, followed by three uniformed officers. The room was deserted except for Giovanna, seated on the couch in the far corner, flanked by two of her employees. Relief washed over him.

She jumped up and ran toward him.

"What happened? Are you okay?" Victor's eyes made a quick assessment: her wet slacks, flushed cheeks, and dilated pupils.

Giovanna gripped Victor's shoulders and pulled him toward her. "Tyler's the killer. He must still be on the grounds somewhere. Last I saw him, he was in Miguel's shed."

"All the vehicles are locked," said Hector. "If he left the property, it would have to be on foot."

"Unless . . ." Giovanna looked at Nina. "Did that group from the mainland check in? The ones coming by boat?"

Nina went back to the reception desk and verified the registry. "Yes," she replied. "They're here."

Giovanna turned to Victor. "Check the dock." She started for the front door.

Victor grabbed her arm. "Don't try to be the hero. Let the police handle this." In hasty Spanish, he instructed the other officers to search the grounds, starting with the shed and then the dock. He turned back to Giovanna. "Let's sit down, and you can tell me about your encounter with Tyler Thompson." As he maneuvered her to the couch, he eyed a welt that had formed on her arm.

* * *

By the time Giovanna finished her statement, the police officers had returned to the lobby empty-handed.

"Was the boat still there?" she asked.

One of the officers nodded. "We searched it, and no one was on board."

"And the shed was empty?" she pressed.

"*Sí, señora.*"

"You didn't happen to find my phone, did you?"

The same officer shook his head.

Victor addressed his colleagues. "Señor Thompson must have it."

Giovanna jumped up. A wave of dizziness hit, but she shook it off. "I can track it. I have that Find My Device app."

Victor followed her into her office. Her hands shook as she logged into her Google account. Nothing came up. "Is the battery dead?" he asked, peering over her shoulder as she typed.

"It was getting low," she said. "Or maybe Tyler turned off the phone." She wiped perspiration from her forehead. "Is it hot in here?"

Victor inspected her arm again. He pointed to a red spot at the hub of the swelling. "This looks like a needle mark. Did Tyler inject you with something?"

Giovanna watched him scrutinize her arm, his dark head blurring against her skin. She wiped her brow again, trying to recall the scuffle. "I don't think so. But maybe . . ." She remembered the syringes on the table, Tyler's hand thrust behind his back when she entered the shed. When he grabbed her . . . She rose, and a wave of nausea hit. "Whoa."

Victor gripped her shoulder to steady her. "Let's call the paramedics and have them check you out."

"I'm going upstairs to put something on this." Her legs wobbled as she started for the door.

"No! Let me go with you."

"I'll be fine. Just need to lie down a minute. You have a criminal to catch."

"Stay here." He waved his phone at her. "I'm calling the paramedics. If he's playing around with toxic substances . . . Wait, Giovanna!" The emergency operator came on the line.

No longer listening, Giovanna exited the office and headed for the elevator.

* * *

In her suite's bathroom, Giovanna downed a Benadryl and slathered triple-antibiotic ointment containing cortisone over her wound. The skin had reddened around the injection site. Had Tyler really stuck her with one of those syringes? But when had it happened?

The air in the room felt heavy, like something pressed against her chest, and the nausea worsened. She walked to the balcony and flung open the French doors. A breeze blew in from the bay, rendering the outdoors cooler than the air-conditioned room, and she stepped out onto the platform to inhale the fresh, salty air.

A rough hand seized her, and she felt herself pressed against a sweaty, smoke-saturated body.

CHAPTER FIFTY-THREE

Sunday night, Giovanna's suite

"Giovanna!" Victor pounded on the door to her suite. He looked around frantically. "Giovanna, open the door." He'd instructed the officers to return to Miguel's shed to search for syringes and other evidence of the toxic substance, and maybe an antidote. The paramedics were on their way. But would they arrive in time? "Giovanna!"

"Detective, can I help you?" Aurora Torres, the night maid, pushed her cart down the hallway.

He stepped aside. "*Por favor, señora.* Let me in."

The maid's face froze, and she ducked her head between her shoulders like a tortoise recoiling into its shell. "Señor, shouldn't we call Señora Rogers first?"

"She doesn't have her phone." He raised his voice. "Open the door; she might be in trouble."

"We can dial the room." Aurora still hesitated. "Señora Rogers doesn't like to be disturbed."

Fuming, Victor flashed his badge. "Señora, let me in. It's a police emergency. A matter of life or death."

Quaking, not meeting his eyes, Aurora produced her master keycard and flung open the door to Giovanna's suite.

Victor rushed inside. His eyes swept the empty living room as he headed for the bedroom.

Giovanna was not in the bed, and its pristine condition told him she had not lain in it yet.

He checked the bathroom, holding his breath, hoping she had not passed out on the tile floor.

The bathroom was empty. A tube of ointment lay on the counter.

He backed out into the living area. After checking the kitchen alcove, he examined the open French doors. Giovanna liked standing on the balcony, contemplating the bay, breathing the salty air. She must be out there.

As Victor walked through the French doors, a muffled whimper resonated from the shadows.

He drew his gun.

* * *

Giovanna writhed against Tyler's chest, trying to free herself from his grasp. She struggled to breathe; his large hand covering her mouth and nose made it almost impossible. "Please," she moaned. "Why?" His face was a blur, like a video call losing its internet connection.

How had he managed to climb up here? The nearest scalesia tree seemed too far away. Could the man scale walls like a ninja? She'd once felt safe on this balcony, but not anymore. A madman had invaded her sanctuary.

The glow emanating from her suite looked far away, a beacon at the end of a tunnel. Fading . . . swirling . . . Why had Tyler come after her? And what did he intend to do?

As his hands increased their pressure, she tried to verbalize the thoughts racing through her head, but her lips strained to form words, emitting only a muffled cry. His body odor had grown stronger from perspiration mixed with adrenalin. Another wave of nausea hit her.

A figure emerged through the French doors, his silhouette illuminated by a halo. *Victor!* Was she hallucinating this dashing action hero, or had the man she loved come to her rescue? Again.

"Let her go," he growled.

* * *

Victor held the gun steady, blinking to adjust his eyes to the darkness on the balcony. "It's over, Señor Thompson. We have the hotel surrounded. Let her go."

Towing Giovanna along, Tyler edged closer to the rail.

"Don't do anything stupid," Victor warned. Giovanna appeared to be conscious, but barely. Her head lolled back; her eyes had lost focus. She was fading, and he needed to free her from this criminal. *The paramedics better get here soon.*

"What are you going to do, Detective?" jeered Tyler. "Shoot me?"

"If I have to," replied Victor. "You can make it easier on everyone by letting her go and turning yourself in."

"Never." Tyler tightened his grip on Giovanna.

"She needs medical care. Let her go so we can save her." Victor strained to keep his voice calm, even, belying the panic swirling inside him.

Tyler glanced at Giovanna and shrugged.

Victor inched closer. "What are you going to do, señor? Try to kill everyone who figures out what you did? Innocent people who never hurt you?"

Like a cornered beast, Tyler's dark eyes flitted from Victor to the balcony rail, to Giovanna.

"It's over, Tyler. Everyone knows what you've done."

The cameraman clutched his hostage tighter.

"You're entitled to a lawyer. You can have a trial." Hands as steady as his voice, Victor kept the gun aimed at Tyler's chest. "Be reasonable."

Tyler made another move toward the rail, dragging Giovanna with him.

"I'm going to count to ten. One, two . . ."

Glaring, Tyler pulled Giovanna closer to him.

"You're on an island," Victor warned. "You can't escape. Three. Let her go. Four."

In one swift movement, Tyler lunged at Victor, kicking at the gun in his hand.

While Victor fumbled to maintain his hold on the weapon, Tyler threw a long leg over the balcony wall and vaulted himself onto the handrail, still clinging to his hostage.

Victor grabbed one of Giovanna's arms, pulling her toward him as Tyler tugged in the other direction.

She groaned.

"Hang on, *mi reinita*," Victor urged, maintaining his hold on Giovanna with one hand and aiming the gun at Tyler with the other. *Is he going to jump? Throw her over the balcony?*

With a surge of energy, Giovanna thrashed against Tyler and shoved an elbow into his side. "Let . . . Go," she cried, wriggling out of his grasp like Houdini escaping from a straightjacket.

The momentum caused Tyler to lose his grip on her, and her thrust sent him tumbling over the edge.

A scream of agony pierced the air like the cry of a wounded seabird. His body landed on the ground below with a thud.

Giovanna peered over the rail at her captor's crumpled limbs and collapsed against Victor.

A distant siren wailed, growing louder by the second.

After holstering his gun, Victor pulled her head to his shoulder and pushed a handful of hair away from her clammy face. "Hold on, Giovanna. The paramedics are coming." He kissed the top of her head.

He scooped her into his arms and carried her out of the room, down the elevator, to the lobby to meet the EMTs. There was no time left to waste.

CHAPTER FIFTY-FOUR

Monday, Puerto Ayora hospital

Giovanna awakened to find Victor standing beside her hospital bed. His thick, black hair was mussed, and dark circles framed his sockets. But when her eyes fluttered open, a smile crept onto his tense face.

Her head pounded as she absorbed the details of the stark off-white room. "Where am I?"

"The Puerto Ayora hospital." He tucked a strand of hair behind her ear. "I'm glad you're awake. I've been so worried. It was touch and go there for a while."

"What happened?" She scanned his face.

"What do you remember?"

"Tyler . . . I pushed him over the balcony." She closed her eyes, straining to recall the scene. "Not the way to treat a guest. Is he—?"

Victor gestured toward the door. "He's down the hall. Broke his pelvis so he won't be going anywhere for a while. Two murders and two attempted murders to answer for."

"Did he admit it?"

"He confessed everything." Victor gave her a grim smile, his eyes tired. New wrinkles lined his face.

Giovanna leaned against the stiff pillow. "What was he thinking? He seemed so . . . together. I didn't suspect him until—"

"He didn't mean to kill Claire. You and Maria figured that out," said Victor. "But he liked to make her a little ill, then nurse her back to health, be the hero. Unfortunately, he miscalculated the dosage of physostigmine, which he'd never used before. Combined with alcohol on an empty stomach, her ulcers, the fact that she was a smoker . . . it was too much."

Giovanna's eyes brimmed with tears.

"He always hoped she'd fall in love with him, but that never happened, and he resented how she kept him in the—how do you call it—friend zone."

"Sick." Giovanna started to shake her head, but it hurt to move it. "Why the others?"

Victor shrugged. "That behavior can be typical of a killer backed into a corner. Murder gets easier the second time, especially if there's a chance it could prevent him from getting caught. It's no longer taking a human life; it's just eliminating an obstacle."

She closed her eyes again, and a tear slid out. "So sad. Does Lindsey know?"

Victor nodded. "She's furious, as you can imagine. Her hero fell off his pedestal."

"What about Colin? Is she letting him off the hook?"

"No way. Even though he didn't kill Claire, he still hurt her deeply. According to Claire's will, Lindsey inherits the majority share of the company. Tyler will have to sell her his portion to pay for legal fees. She's already announced her plans to fire everyone and rebuild the business from the ground up, with her father helping her run it."

"No doubt Claire's daughter will make it a success," said Giovanna. "She already has a track record with that YouTube channel."

"Jim was relieved that none of the Leisure Dreams employees turned out to be the killer," Victor said.

"So am I."

"I guess, with your woman's intuition and all," Victor's dimple set off his cheek mole, "you figured out Belinda and Miguel are an item?"

Giovanna raised her eyebrows.

Victor grinned. "Sometimes an investigation can uncover a secret liaison."

"Not much I can do to stop it." Giovanna let out a small chuckle. "But Belinda can give up her snide innuendos about us."

Victor covered Giovanna's hand with his. Even in her groggy state, its warmth gave her spine tingles.

"You have some visitors waiting to see you: your grandparents, Laurel, and several of your employees. Maria's here too. She wants an exclusive."

"I'll bet," Giovanna scoffed. "Maybe later."

"That's what I told her." He squeezed Giovanna's hand. "Are you ready to see any of the visitors? Your grandmother has been frantic."

"Sure. Send Michelle in first."

They gazed at each other fondly for a few moments, then he bent to kiss her. His lips felt soft and tender. She leaned into his passionate embrace, running her fingers through his hair, longing to be back in his strong arms. As if the clock had been rewound to the day before Claire died.

"I thought I was going to lose you," Victor murmured when he came up for air, his brown eyes watering.

Giovanna smiled. "Not a chance. You promised to take me to North Seymour Island since I missed the hike with the rest of the group. I'm holding you to it."

ABOUT THE AUTHOR

SHARON MARCHISELLO is the author of two other mysteries published by Milford House, the fiction imprint of Sunbury Press: *Going Home* (2014) and *Secrets of the Galapagos* (2019), which is the prequel to *Murder at Leisure Dreams – Galapagos*. She also writes the DeeLo Myer Cat Rescue Mysteries from Level Best Books. Besides novels, Sharon has published short stories in anthologies and online magazines; one was a 2022 Derringer finalist. She has written travel articles, training manuals, screenplays, book reviews, and a nonfiction book (*Live Well, Grow Wealth* - 2018). She earned a Bachelor's degree in French from the University of Houston and a Master's in Professional Writing from the University of Southern California. She is an active member of Sisters in Crime, the Atlanta Writers Club, and the Hometown Novel Writers Association. Retired after 27 years with Delta Air Lines, Sharon now lives in Peachtree City, Georgia. She serves on the boards of the Fayette Humane Society, Hometown Novel Writers Association, and the Friends of the Peachtree City Library.

She loves to travel, including a trip to the Galapagos Islands in 2014.